Called 'the queen of the contemporary Cornish novel' by the *Guardian*, Liz Fenwick is the author of nine books, including the most recent *The River Between Us* which won the Popular Romantic Fiction Award from the Romantic Novelists' Association. She lives with her husband and two mad cats near the Helford River in Cornwall. When not writing Liz is reading, painting, knitting, plot walking, and procrastinating on social media.

You can find her on X @liz_fenwick, Instagram @liz_fenwick, Facebook @liz.fenwick.author and TikTok @lizfenwickauthor.

For more information or to join her mailing list visit lizfenwick.com.

Also by Liz Fenwick

The Cornish House

A Cornish Affair

A Cornish Stranger

Under a Cornish Sky

A Cornish Christmas Carol

The Returning Tide

One Cornish Summer

The Path to the Sea

The River Between Us

The Secret Shore

Liz Fenwick

ONE PLACE. MANY STORIES

HQ
An imprint of HarperCollins*Publishers* Ltd
1 London Bridge Street
London SE1 9GF

www.harpercollins.co.uk

HarperCollins*Publishers*
Macken House, 39/40 Mayor Street Upper,
Dublin 1, D01 C9W8, Ireland

This paperback edition 2024

1
First published in Great Britain by
HQ, an imprint of HarperCollins*Publishers* Ltd 2023

Copyright © Liz Fenwick 2023

Liz Fenwick asserts the moral right to be
identified as the author of this work.
A catalogue record for this book is
available from the British Library.

Paperback ISBN: 978-0-00-853230-7

MIX
Paper | Supporting
responsible forestry
FSC™ C007454

This book contains FSC™ certified paper and other controlled
sources to ensure responsible forest management.

For more information visit: www.harpercollins.co.uk/green

Printed and Bound in the UK using 100% Renewable Electricity at
CPI Group (UK) Ltd, Croydon, CR0 4YY

For the 'Map Girls', the women who worked in all aspects of geography during World War II, and for the men and women of the secret flotillas running from Cornwall and Devon to the coast of Brittany

'The streets of London have their map, but our passions are uncharted.'

—VIRGINIA WOOLF

PART ONE

1

5 May 1942

Today I couldn't be late. Every minute was needed to review the most recent intelligence photographs before the Combined Forces meeting at five this afternoon.

It was ten minutes past six as I pulled the front door shut. I'd been in London seven months and, despite the war, the number 11 bus was pretty prompt. Looking down, I did a quick check. Handbag, gas mask, umbrella, notebook, and a fish paste sandwich for lunch. Something was missing. I turned around, went back inside and grabbed my book from the hallway table. Lunch without Sayers' *Gaudy Night* to relax my mind would be unbearable. With another glance at my watch, I raced down the road towards the bus stop.

Old Mr Lloyd from next door waved as he collected his bottle of milk from his doorstep.

'Love seeing a pretty girl run,' he called out.

I laughed for I was hardly a girl but to his seventy-year-old eyes I could be.

'They'll wait for you.'

'I doubt it,' I replied. He knew everyone and everything about our little street just off the King's Road. This, of course, had its advantages as well as disadvantages.

Despite my sprint, the bus was pulling away from the stop and I chased it, managing to hop on.

'Morning, miss,' the conductor said with a wink. 'Overslept?'

I smiled. 'I wish.'

'Whitehall?' he asked.

I nodded.

'Have a good one, love,' he said, handing me my ticket.

I found a seat and opened my novel to escape from the bomb-damaged streets of London to the dreaming spires of Oxford. London looked like it had been fighting the war by itself, and, as I looked out on the destruction around Victoria Station, the war felt endless.

This morning was bright, yet rain was threatening from the west, which was why I had grabbed my umbrella instead of my book when I'd left the house the first time. Of all Dorothy L. Sayers' Lord Peter Wimsey novels, it was *Gaudy Night* that I'd reread most since my arrival in London. It captured a life that was, for the moment, lost. I hoped it wasn't now set in amber. Forever to be trapped like some poor insect and only to be studied on the pages of academic books and in old photographs.

Lord Peter Wimsey and his detective work had captivated my imagination since I was given a copy of *Whose Body?* for my thirteenth birthday. My fascination with him began then and grew with each book. I adored his clever mind, but I especially loved his appreciation of Harriet Vane. He could let a woman be as clever as he was, and continue to work. The only other man who had been like that was my late Cambridge-educated father. Just thinking about him caused both a smile and a wave of sadness. He had died a year ago on the first of May and I missed him more than I could express.

I'd spoken with Maman a few nights ago. The three-minute telephone call was never enough time to catch up on everything.

She had assured me all was well with the farm in Cornwall and that she was painting again. As the bus stopped, I recalled her unexpected question about my plans going forward after the war. I'd been dumbstruck, then said there was no change. She'd been surprised at my response, saying she'd thought the war had altered everyone. Not me, I'd said.

I opened my book again. The traffic ahead was slow despite the early hour. A few pages lost in the world of Wimsey would pass the time.

'Aren't you meant to be getting off here?' the conductor asked.

I looked up, unaware of where I was.

'Yes, thank you.'

'Head always in a book.' He laughed and I leapt off straight into a naval lieutenant who was walking along the pavement. He was tall. I wasn't short at five eleven but he towered over me as his hands steadied me.

'Sorry,' I said, stepping back.

He tilted his head and studied me. His eyes were the blue of a shallow sea on a sunny day. Something inside me woke up.

'No need to apologise,' he said in an American accent as he bent to pick up my book, which had fallen in the collision. He turned it over. 'Interesting choice.' He handed it to me.

I almost enquired why but stopped. Instead I asked, 'Have you read it?'

'I have but I prefer *Murder Must Advertise*.'

I blinked. 'Were you in advertising?'

He smiled and his eyes creased at the corners. 'No.'

I was suddenly aware of the strong attraction I was feeling to a man who read Sayers. 'Sorry for bumping into you,' I said to cover my thoughts.

'You can do it again any time.' He grinned.

'You never know, I might.' I smiled and turned away as I flushed, not sure why I'd said that. I didn't even care for Americans; they had taken too long to join the war.

Still, he was attractive and definitely my type. At the archway to Horse Guards, I risked a glance over my shoulder but the American was gone. I wasn't sure what I would have done if he'd still been there. Ask him for a drink? I smiled at the thought.

Pushing that aside, I picked up my pace as I headed towards the Citadel, a bombproof subterranean fortress. The entrance, an ugly concrete carbuncle, was tacked onto the end of the Admiralty building. Constructed last year, the Citadel's entrance was disguised from above by a grass-covered roof. In aerial photographs it appeared as nothing more than a lawn next to the Admiralty on Horse Guards and not the beating heart of naval intelligence working around the clock. Appearances could be deceptive; I knew this well.

As I approached the threshold, I prepared to head underground and lose all sense of day or night. I was lucky that I didn't work the rotating shifts that many did. I wasn't nine to five either. It was now six forty-five and I wasn't sure when the day would be finished but I hoped to be done in time to join my housemates at the cinema tonight.

'Morning, miss,' said the sailor who checked my pass at the entrance.

'Morning,' I replied, joining the flow of people descending. On the stairs I met up with one of the typists coming down from the offices above.

'All OK in The Zoo?' I asked.

2

I couldn't afford to make a mistake; people would die if I did.

The dense grove of trees was clear in the image, but the large dark shape near it was not. What concerned me was that the railway was less than half a mile from the smudge, and the strategically significant port at Calais a half mile in the other direction. It could be the ideal location for a munitions factory. Or was it simply a consequence of the photographic development process, a shadow from a cloud, dust on the camera or the negative?

For my whole life, maps had made everything possible. I knew this to my very core, aware that the war would be won or lost based on the quality of maps. I stared at the aerial photograph in my hands. Every missing bridge, new road or altered building was important.

The sound of the teleprinters in the next room interrupted my thoughts. I put the photo down on the battered wooden table in front of me and picked up the map I was trying to update. Aside from the well-recorded build-up around the port and a few artillery installations along the coast there had been no changes observed for some time. But that didn't mean things weren't happening; it simply meant they hadn't been seen.

In the files, I searched for an older photograph for comparison but the last images of this area of Calais were over six months old. So this smudge could be something or it could be nothing. I needed to decide. At least there appeared to be no new armaments unlike the last photograph I'd looked at taken near Brest. I straightened and rolled my shoulders back. For five hours I'd been studying the latest photos and comparing them to the previous ones. Any variations I discovered, I marked in preparation for the Combined Forces meeting. Decisions could be made on even the smallest changes I could observe.

My colleague, Lieutenant Harling, looked up from the map he was working on and held up a pack of cigarettes. His solemn face broke into a smile, making his features almost handsome. But it was his charm that made him exceedingly attractive. Half the women in the building were a bit in love with him. I was not; I had learned early on to avoid that sort of distraction, although I had fallen in love once. Now I kept all my affection for a fictional detective. It ensured there were no complications or distractions that way.

'No, thanks.' I took a deep breath and looked at the slim gold watch on my wrist. 'If I start at noon, what will I use to keep me alert at eight tonight?'

'A gin?' he suggested with a grin.

'Hmm.' I laughed, thinking of the many drinks we had shared since I accepted the secondment here seven months ago from the Inter Services Topographical Department based at Manchester College, Oxford. Our team of two occupied one small room amidst the command and operations centre for the Navy. We coordinated our efforts with the large teams in Oxford and Cambridge where they made geographical handbooks for the services.

Organising the photographs in front of me into a neat pile, I clasped onto the one near Calais that was troubling me and held it out to him. 'What do you make of that large mass in the bottom left, Harling?'

He squinted then turned the picture in every direction. 'Your guess is better than mine.'

'The last aerial photograph of this area we have was taken months ago and it showed nothing.' I circled the blob with my finger.

He rose and we both walked to the large map covering the back wall of our underground room. A trickle of air from the vent in the ceiling moved the loose corner of the chart but did nothing to shift the lingering cigarette smoke that hung in the air.

'Could be nothing. Still . . . ' I tapped the spot. It needed marking despite my uncertainty.

'Miss Tremayne?' a breathless woman called from the door.

I swung around and smiled. It was a typist from the pool.

'You're wanted up in The Zoo.' She drew a breath.

All the typists and the secret ladies as they were known called Room 39 The Zoo. It held the Naval Intelligence team who were an odd assortment of men including an art historian, a writer, a journalist, a barrister and the former head of Thomas Cook's West End office. They all reported to Vice-Admiral Godfrey. Like a modern Noah's Ark, Room 39 contained a collection of some-what exotic creatures for naval intelligence, including my boss.

'And you're to bring your maps for your meeting,' she said.

In haste I marked the unknown object on the map of Calais then rolled it up with the other ones we'd been updating.

'Knock 'em dead,' Harling said, perching on the desk lighting a cigarette.

I made my way down the corridor, stopping in the powder room to check my appearance. With my boss I never quite knew what to expect. I smoothed my hair into place and freshened my red lipstick. Now I was ready to face whatever it was that required my attention. It had to be important to call me away from my preparation for the meeting at five. It wouldn't be an excursion. They were always well planned, and it normally involved soothing ruffled feathers and unpicking the muddles various officers and ministers found themselves in when they looked at a map rather than reading it.

Climbing the stairs, I left behind the artificial daylight lamps and stuffy air conditioning and entered the corridors of the Admiralty. Passing the uniformed guards who knew me well, I walked down the long dull corridor. Only the mosaic tiles on the floors lifted the atmosphere. Their swirling wave patterns were almost whimsical and always struck me as at odds with the solemn activity that took place in the building. I strode on with the sound of my heels echoing in the bleakness on my way to the beating heart of Naval Intelligence.

Reaching a large transept the size of a station ticket booking hall, I noted the chaos of paperwork in transit, boxes, trays, and tea-making equipment. I waved to the women who kept everything working. Without them we didn't have a chance of winning this war and yet here they were almost invisible.

I opened the door to Room 39 and was immediately struck again by the three long west-facing windows. They looked out on Horse Guards and over to the garden of number 10 Downing Street, the Foreign Office, and St James's Park Lake. The parade ground was filled with barrage balloon equipment. The scene was so familiar, I could map it from memory.

The first man to make eye contact was Lieutenant Commander Shawcross, who liaised with me on all things for the topographical handbooks created in Oxford and Cambridge. Lieutenant Commander Montagu nodded a welcome. I was a frequent sight in this hub of activity. The other occupants of The Zoo were too engrossed in their work to acknowledge my presence and the green baize door to Vice-Admiral Godfrey's office was closed.

My boss, Commander Fleming, was the vice-admiral's personal assistant and the department's fixer, knowing everyone who was useful. Currently he was at his desk with a solemn expression on his face. At thirty-three, he was as smooth as they come, with not a hair out of place and a cigarette always in hand. His uniform was immaculately tailored to flatter. He, like Harling, caused the female staff's hearts to flutter.

We had met when Fleming visited Oxford with Harling and they'd sat in on one of my briefings. Two days later I was summoned to London and by the end of the week I was working for the intelligence service. Gone were the hours spent teaching map reading to new officers and making geographical information booklets among the dreaming spires.

Commander Fleming looked up, stood then walked around the desk and pulled out a chair.

'Do sit, Merry,' he said then lit a cigarette. 'The meeting with the Combined Forces has been brought forward.' Fleming tapped on the pile on the desk. 'And new intelligence photographs have come in.'

'Aerial or oblique?' I asked. Each of these provided vital information with the oblique ones identifying natural and man-made defences on the beaches and the aerial providing detailed information on roads, bridges and railways.

'Both.' Fleming perched on the corner of the desk.

'Do I have time to review them before the meeting?' I asked, reaching for the uppermost image.

He glanced at the clock which sat above the huge marble fireplace that dominated one wall.

'No,' he said.

'Do you have any idea what they want?' I was almost certain

he didn't, or that, if he did, he wouldn't say. Everything was on a need-to-know basis and I was becoming accustomed to not being given access to all the information I needed to be fully useful. This frustrated me daily, but I couldn't change the system as much as I might like to.

'Are you ready?' He stubbed his cigarette out and stood.

'Of course.' I clutched the maps I'd brought with me and followed him down the long corridor and up the stairs, suppressing my laughter as he vetted my attire. He struggled to understand my confirmed single status. I was a mystery to most men and the commander was no exception. They couldn't accept that a twenty-seven-year-old woman with a pretty face and a good figure could have a brain and would choose to give marriage a miss.

As a child I had longed for my mother's beauty and elegance but despaired that it would ever come to me. She had regularly reassured me it would happen by saying, 'You are the ugly duck now, ma petite, but you will be the most beautiful swan.' She had been right and the transformation happened at seventeen. Then for a while I'd considered my looks a hindrance, but now I realised they opened doors for me. But I also knew that it was my brain that kept those doors open. This was the combination that was so appealing to Fleming. He had quickly noted that men didn't take me seriously because of my looks, which gave Fleming an advantage. It had taken only one meeting to make Meredith Tremayne his secret weapon.

'Do I pass muster?' I asked, glad that I had taken the detour to the powder room to check my appearance.

'Yes, though I prefer it when you don't look so stern. We have a better chance at everything if you smile.' Fleming held the door open for me. 'Let's do this.'

We entered the wood-panelled meeting room and all heads turned towards us. There were enough officers in here to run the war: two British admirals, two generals, two majors, an air chief marshal, an air commodore, a colonel, and a minister. That wasn't all; the Americans in attendance included three generals and a captain.

'Does your secretary have clearance?' an admiral asked.

'How can she help?' asked the minister.

Fleming smiled slowly, enjoying their discomfort. 'Dr Tremayne is not my secretary, but a geographer, and I'll let her speak for herself.'

The men in the room were clearly surprised by the fact that Meredith Tremayne, BA (Hons), MA, DPhil (Oxon) on the memo was a woman and not some tweeds-wearing member of the Royal Geographical Society. This frequently happened as Meredith was a far more common name for a man. Their faces were pictures of disbelief and I suppressed a smile. Once they had regained their composure, it was time for me to begin the process of reassuring them about my qualifications. It would not be an easy battle to win their confidence.

'Gentlemen, what is possible for us to achieve in this war depends first and foremost on geography. The climatic conditions our soldiers will face, as well as thorough knowledge of the terrain they will need to conquer – this information is vital before any action is taken.' I paused. All eyes were on me as I placed my latest maps on the table with the others already there and unrolled mine. 'Maps are not simply pieces of paper with towns and cities marked on them; they tell us so much more. They inform us about who made them, what was important to them, what they were thinking and how they will be used.'

'We know this,' said one of the generals, clearly irritated by my lecturer tone.

'Then you will know that a map is only as good as the intelligence used in the making of it.' I looked down at the copies of photographs of Calais I'd been working on and moved them alongside a set of holiday photographs sent in by the public taken in 1938 that were also on the table. 'For example here—' I looked up and met the general's gaze. 'If you expected a bridge crossing the canal and it has been blown up you are in trouble if you haven't worked out alternative plans.'

'It is still there.' The general pointed to the aerial photograph.

'But what is the date of the image? A day can make all the difference.'

He huffed. 'So, you are saying this intelligence is useless.'

'Not at all. All these photos provide a way to see the increase of war defences and with them one can make projections on what is to come next and what possible targets will interrupt that progression.'

The general stepped back from the table. 'Hmmm.'

Out of the corner of my eye, I caught sight of Fleming who almost smiled.

'The quality of our intelligence, the questions we ask, and the maps that are made from them will influence the success or failure of every battle and ultimately the war.' Moving away I sat down at one of the chairs lining the wall and waited to be called when my expertise was needed again. I was grateful the spotlight had turned away from me and onto whatever the task was at hand.

After a few moments into the subsequent discussion, I knew that we were looking at invasion. However, each man around the table had a different view on the matter. Fleming and I were not consulted again and the reason for my ongoing presence wasn't clear unless the northern coast of France, particularly Normandy, was the intended invasion site. I turned to Fleming to try and read his thoughts, but his face gave nothing away.

The maps I unrolled were shunted across the table and then one of the admirals took one and tacked it on the wall. My heart sank. It wasn't finished. It shouldn't be here but it was because I'd been in a rush.

'Miss Tremayne. This is your work?' the admiral asked.

'Yes.'

'What am I supposed to make of this?' He pointed to a square object on the map – the smudge that I'd been unable to clearly identify.

I gritted my teeth. That map should never have left the office.

'There's an object or building of some description there—'

'Some description?' he interrupted. 'Buildings come in many shapes, sizes and most importantly purposes.' He paused. 'I can tell it's large by looking at the scale of the map, but there is no indication if this is residential or industrial. What is it?'

I drew a breath. 'I don't know.'

'If it's residential then it would have to be a chateau or extremely large farmhouse, based on its size. We already know there is no chateau here,' he said. 'If I were on the spot being fired upon, what else would this map tell me?'

I opened my mouth, uncertain of what I could say aside from pointing out the obvious – the railway, the port, the canals. I should be asking questions to find out more but I didn't know which ones to ask.

'Excuse my late arrival,' an American admiral announced as he entered the room.

'Ah, Admiral King,' the general said.

The American glanced about the room and his gaze fell on me and Fleming. 'Newcomers?'

'Commander Fleming from Naval Intelligence Division and his . . . geographer Miss . . . err, Dr Tremayne,' said the general.

'Necessary?' he asked.

'Possibly, she is an . . . expert on the northern coast of France.'

'Not needed for today.' He glanced at the many maps on the

table and took one of the North African coast and tacked it over the one of Calais on the wall. 'Unless North Africa is also a speciality.' He looked directly at me.

I met his glance. 'No, sir.'

'Best you leave then,' the admiral said. 'Commander Fleming, please remain.'

I left and returned to the Citadel, to my sandwich and to my book. Hopefully I would find my equilibrium again. I did not like being unable to answer a question or to feel so unprepared. There had to be a way to solve this so I could make better maps that could help us win this awful war. Only when it was won could I return to Oxford and my work.

3

The new photographs shed no further light on the unidentifiable object near Calais, therefore I put in a request for further photographs. Harling and I updated the maps, but I was not confident that I was making correct choices for what was needed to help the men on the ground.

Harling lit a cigarette as he stood. 'Fancy a drink?'

I glanced at my watch. It was already eight and I'd missed out on my evening's plans.

'Tempting but Fleming's asked to see me.'

He laughed. 'See you in the morning then.'

Wondering what the weather was doing, I headed to the door and collected my hat, fixing it at a jaunty angle.

'Are you sure you don't need a drink?' Harling asked and walked to my desk. 'You're forgetting things.' He picked up my book and handed it to me. 'Haven't you finished this yet?'

I took it and shook my head. Harling didn't need to know my obsession with Wimsey and the world that Sayers had created in her books.

'For one so clever you read very slowly,' he said.

'I read thoroughly.' I reread even more thoroughly, I added silently.

'And you don't want a drink either,' he added with a smile.

'Not tonight,' I replied, laughing as I left the office then headed up the stairs into the Admiralty.

In the distance, coming out of Room 39, I spied a broad set of shoulders, blond hair and a confident stride. I could be wrong – this morning's collision off the bus was over twelve hours ago – but that looked like the American. It would be tempting to 'bump' into him again. My evening, or what was left of it after meeting Fleming, was wide open as I'd turned down Harling. It was tempting to think of unwinding over a drink with the American. But it was not going to happen because he disappeared from sight, so I turned into Room 39.

Fleming's desk was empty as were all the others but the door to Vice-Admiral Godfrey's room was slightly ajar and I could hear the faint sound of voices.

Both Godfrey and Fleming walked out of the vice-admiral's office together.

'Good evening, Dr Tremayne,' Godfrey said. 'Time to update the PM, and I'll leave you both to it.' He turned to Fleming. 'If you can have that to me for tomorrow at nine.'

Fleming nodded and watched Godfrey leave. He took a seat at his desk and waved a hand to indicate I should do the same. 'What did you make of today's meeting?'

'Invasion,' I said and silently added *humiliation*.

He laughed drily. 'End goal, of course, but I don't think we have the manpower, ships, or planes yet.' He lit a cigarette and handed it to me.

'True.' I took a drag and exhaled slowly, hoping my frustration would form into proper questions and not mortification as it had been all day. 'I'm not much use to you in a meeting like that.'

He looked up sharply from the note he was perusing on his desk.

'I can put together a good map, and I understand how people use and shape the landscape, but I don't truly understand military needs—' I paused, choosing my words with care '—I floundered under their direct questioning.' This fact had been running through my mind as I listened to the various ministers and military men not only in this meeting but in many others. This incident had solidified it for me.

Fleming continued to stare. 'Is my iron maiden admitting a fault?'

I made a face. 'Iron maiden I am not, but you should take Harling in future. He's actually served on a ship.'

'He has.' Fleming flicked the ash from his cigarette into the metal bin by his desk. 'But I haven't, and I attend the meetings.'

'Our roles are very different,' I replied.

'That is true,' he said.

I chose my next words carefully. 'I could be so much more effective and useful to you if I had field experience.'

Fleming raised an eyebrow. 'You are too valuable to become an agent.'

I frowned. 'I am fluent in French, German and even Breton, although I will accept the latter is a bit rusty.'

'And I imagine with a change of clothing and a different hair style you would look French rather than English. Sadly, you are too beautiful.' The corner of his mouth lifted. 'Beauty is always noted and remembered.'

I crossed my arms, prepared to continue this fight.

'But the real reason you are too important to send into the field is your understanding of the landscape of the northern coast of France,' Fleming finished.

'You have plenty of geographers.'

'None as sharp as you,' he said.

'You have Harling,' I replied.

'He's not a geographer,' Fleming said.

'But he better understands the information the military requires,' I pressed on, needing him to comprehend what I was lacking.

'How so?' He turned, his interest caught.

'I look at, well, "*see*" things differently,' I explained.

'You look at the rock below the surface and basically you delve deeper,' he said.

'I study the rocks below the surface because it impacts people,' I said. 'What will grow or not grow is dependent on the substructure, and this affects the population. The way the sea interacts with the land also affects livelihoods.'

Fleming nodded.

'But this doesn't tell me what is needed by a man under fire,' I continued. 'The general asked me a question and I couldn't answer it as I have never experienced that type of pressure. I have no idea.' My brother's words surfaced to the forefront of my thoughts. 'Oliver spent hours with me to try to explain what he needed as a pilot. It helped somewhat but it would never be the same as flying myself and experiencing first-hand what information was, and, almost as importantly, wasn't required.'

'I can see that,' Fleming said.

'After the battle for Norway,' I continued, remembering Maman's constant worry that Oliver risked his life every flight while Papa had been more circumspect, having survived the Great War. 'Oliver had begged me for better maps because he'd had to use the nineteen twelve Baedeker's map for Norway and Sweden and it wasn't fit for purpose. He explained he needed maps that could be read in low light and with objects and targets clearly and simply marked.' I paused, thinking about the man Oliver was now, and not the scrubby younger brother that had been more like a twin we were so close in age. 'And from that moment on I've been doing my best but it's clear it isn't good enough.'

He stubbed out his cigarette. 'Leave it with me.'

And with that I was dismissed, just as abruptly as I had been from the meeting. I chewed on my frustration as I rose to my feet, preparing to say more before I stilled at the sound of the telephone and watched Fleming pick it up. He turned his back to me. My stomach growled, reminding me it was almost nine and my lunchtime sandwich had been hours ago.

*

I'd missed the number 11 bus. The evening was clear and fresh so I walked back, enjoying the bright greens of the leaves creating contrast to the accumulated dust and dirt. London hadn't been subject to direct bombing in months but the collapse of damaged buildings kept plaster dust in the air and on the ground. Our nearest neighbour Mr Lloyd did his best to keep Bywater Street in good order, especially his house and ours, but it was a continuous struggle. As he pointed out, we were all doing our bit and he was too old for anything worthwhile, yet he'd man the Red Cross relief stations when he could.

A wolf whistle startled me out of my thoughts.

'Hey beautiful. Come have a drink with a lonely soldier.'

'Not this evening,' I called back, giving him a smile and recalling the American in British Naval uniform. Had he been talking to Fleming or the vice-admiral, or both? I wasn't sure if it was his striking good looks or the fact he had read Sayers and liked the books enough to have a favourite that had made the most impact on me. The combination of appearance and intelligence was always intriguing and I found it very compelling.

Reaching Eaton Square, I met Muriel Wright, Fleming's girl-friend, on the lookout for a taxi. She was striking in anything she wore but in the pale-yellow evening gown she took one's breath away. Fleming had met her while skiing years ago, he'd said. It all struck me as very glamorous but I did wonder about her sticking with him. There were many women in his life but Muriel, or Moo as he called her, had been with him the longest as far as I was aware.

'Hello, Merry,' she said.

'You look stunning,' I said, admiring her curls. My own hair was dead straight. 'Out with the commander tonight?'

'No,' she said then raised her hand to a passing taxi. 'We must catch up soon.' She directed the driver to a location in Mayfair and climbed in, waving.

As I walked the short distance to the small house off King's Road, I hoped my housemates had gone to the cinema without me. Since my secondment, I'd been living in Lady Constance Neville's house on Bywater Street with Hester Clifford and eye surgeon Benedict Hartley.

I'd met Constance on my first visit to Oxford for an interview when I was sixteen. Back then I'd been full of questions, unrealistic dreams, and the certainty that there was no other place I should be. Constance had been full of common sense and patience in the face of my endless questions. She lectured in entomology, having specialised in lepidopterology because of her childhood fascination with butterflies. On my arrival at Oxford, Constance had become my mentor, helping me with the choices I needed to make in my early years as a scholar, and now, eleven years later, she was my closest friend.

Currently she was nursing at the eye hospital, returning to the work she had done in the last year of the Great War. It was where she'd met Hester Clifford, her soulmate, who currently drove ambulances. They had been a couple since 1920 but to the outside world they were no more than companions. Benedict Hartley rounded out the house.

No one was home but by the telephone in the front hall was a note.

Merry,
There was a telephone call from Inspector Jenkins of the Helston Constabulary. He is keen to speak to you urgently and has requested that you telephone him in the morning any time after eight.

C

I read the note again. What on earth would they want from me? I picked up the handset and called Maman; she may have some idea. The phone rang and rang but no one answered. It was half past nine. She would be with friends or sorting something on the farm.

In the kitchen I made toast while I boiled the kettle. Before I left for work in the morning I would telephone Maman but I would have to ring the inspector from the office. This was not ideal, but I couldn't wait at home until eight to call him. I had a meeting at nine.

*

There had been no answer again at home when I rang at six in the morning and I wondered if my mother had gone off on one of her painting excursions. She hadn't mentioned it but before my father died she would frequently set off to paint *en plein air* with little notice if the weather was fine. I would probably have a letter today, letting me know her plans.

Just before eight I went to Room 39. Fleming and Commander Drake were chatting. Fleming had a penchant for referring to him as Quacker. The reference to ducks was obvious and I half wondered if he had a nickname for me.

'Excuse me, gentlemen, I need to ring the Helston Police Station on a personal matter,' I said.

Both men stared at me and I waited with my breath held for further questions. They didn't come.

Instead Fleming looked down his long nose and pointed to Godfrey's office. 'Use that telephone; he's in meetings until noon.'

'Thank you,' I said, entering the room and pulling the door to with some trepidation. I couldn't shake the feeling I was being called into the chair's office for a misdemeanour. Not that that had occurred more than twice. So I didn't sit but stood looking out the window while I waited for the operator to connect the call. St James's Park was currently full of vehicles, temporary housing and barrage balloons.

Eventually the line connected and I asked to speak to Inspector Jenkins. I closed my eyes as each second ticked by, trying to figure out what this was about. I hadn't been home to Kestle since Christmas and before that it was for my father's funeral.

'Miss Tremayne?' a man asked.

I opened my eyes and focused on the scenery below for I was certain he knew I was Dr Tremayne but chose to address me as miss. 'Yes, I'm Meredith Tremayne.'

'Thank you for coming back to me. I've tried to contact your brother but Flight Lieutenant Tremayne has been unavailable.'

I frowned. Why were they trying to reach us? 'How can I help you, inspector?'

'Mrs Nance, your mother's housekeeper, reported Elise Tremayne missing yesterday morning.'

'Excuse me?'

'Yes, your mother was last seen on the morning of the first of May by the vicar. She was putting flowers on your father's grave.'

Of course she had. It was the anniversary of his death.

'Your father, Colonel Tremayne, died in a riding accident?'

I drew a deep breath. 'Yes.'

'We have made some enquiries but thus far have nothing to report other than there is some concern that your mother . . . is French.'

'Why is that a concern?' I knew what he was implying but I wasn't having it.

'It appears there is some concern she might be a spy.'

'Balderdash,' I said.

'We cannot dismiss this as there is a war going on.'

'I am very aware of that. I am involved in war work and my brother is risking his life with each sortie he flies.'

'Of course, I understand your feelings,' he said.

'Inspector Jenkins, my mother, I assure you, would do nothing to put her son's life in further danger.'

'There is talk in the village about her odd behaviour.'

Becoming angry with a man trying to do his job was not going to help so I pushed it aside.

'My mother is a painter and she would stand out anywhere let alone running a farm by the Helford River,' I said. 'She is not a spy.'

'I take your point,' he said.

'Thank you.' I perched on the desk. This was the last thing I had expected from this telephone call.

'Do you have any information that could help us?' he asked. 'When did you last speak to her?'

'On the evening of the thirtieth of April.' The gaze from the eyes of the portrait of an admiral fixed me to the spot.

'Did she mention a trip?' he asked.

'No,' I said. 'But she frequently goes painting.'

'Mrs Nance mentioned this but also said that she hadn't taken anything with her.'

'Nothing?' I sank into the vice-admiral's chair.

'Her bicycle and painting box are missing, which fits with what the vicar told us, but Mrs Nance told us she usually takes other things on her painting excursions.'

'Possibly Mrs Nance is mistaken.'

'Hmm,' he said with a sceptical note in his voice. 'Thank you for your time. You will let me know if you hear from her.'

'I will, inspector.'

I put the phone down and found Fleming standing in the doorway with his hands in his jacket pockets. How long had he been there? Learning point, never turn your back to a door as people could be listening.

'Interesting conversation.'

I sent him a look. What did I expect? He was in intelligence. It would have been so much better to have had this telephone call at Constance's.

'Your mother is missing and someone thinks she's spying for the enemy?'

I nodded, anger filling me again. 'My mother is many things but not a spy.'

He raised an eyebrow. 'You are certain?'

'Yes,' I said without hesitation. 'My father's death brought about huge changes in my mother's life. Not just being a widow but the farm.' I sighed. 'Kestle went to my brother on my father's death but he is serving so she took it on for him. This is not her natural habitat as an artist and had it not been for my father she wouldn't have been there at all.'

'Where would she be?'

'Painting society portraits for a living, seascapes for passion and wherever else her heart led her.'

'I see.' He offered me a cigarette and I accepted it. 'Where do you think she is?'

I took a deep drag on the cigarette. 'She is probably painting or maybe she went to friends. Crop yields, animal welfare and keeping the nation fed are not things to hold Maman's interest for long. It must have reached the point where she needed a break.'

'Is she not liked locally?'

'Maman will always be suspect in local eyes. Her father had been a Breton fisherman and her mother a renegade Parisian socialite – not at all the sort of people who might produce a suitable wife for a respectable Cornish farmer and retired army colonel.'

He nodded. 'Do you think this is something you need to investigate?'

Today was Tuesday the fifth. Mrs Nance would only have noticed her absence yesterday morning because she worked Monday through Friday. She might have tried to reach me and no one had been home.

'Not at present,' I said, thinking logically. 'I believe the inspector is jumping to premature conclusions about my mother.'

'You are not concerned?' he asked.

I weighed his words before saying, 'If my mother wasn't an artist who loved nothing more than venturing into the landscape to paint for days on end, I might be.' In my childhood, she had done this frequently and always returned. My father never took any notice. He said, after I questioned him once, that this was something she needed to do for her art and her soul.

'It is early days, of course,' he said. 'And, as you mention, it could be a simple case of lack of communication. However, I wouldn't want these rumours about your mother to tarnish you.'

I nodded, understanding fully what he meant. I knew my mother was not a spy, but I had no proof to the contrary and my role here was vital.

Fleming led the way out of the office and stopped by his desk, handing me a stack of photographs.

'Best figure out what that object or building is.'

'Yes, of course,' I said, taking them. 'The meeting?' I asked, glancing at the clock.

'Postponed,' he said. 'I'll let you know when it's rescheduled.'

I nodded and left, grateful I had some time to think through things, even if it was only on the way back to my desk. I assured myself that my mother would be home when I rang this evening, and this was simply a storm in a teacup of village gossip. The best course of action was to focus on my work for the remaining hours of the day.

4

On his return from lunch, Fleming had caught me finishing my sandwich in the afternoon sunshine and suggested I come to Room 39 with him. He explained en route, 'Merry, I want you to ring home. Your mother may be there.'

Once at Fleming's desk, I picked up the telephone and gave the number to the operator, grateful, not for the first time, that my father had had a telephone installed in the house as soon as it had been possible.

'Kestle,' Mrs Nance said.

'It's Merry.'

'Oh, my dear, your mother isn't here and I'm beside myself. I did try and ring you and Master Oliver too but wasn't able to reach either of you so I did what I thought right and called the police. Have you spoken to them? Have you heard from her?' The words rushed out in a fast flow, not allowing me to speak. 'This is a terrible thing, as people are beginning to talk. It's been several days.'

'I spoke to the inspector yesterday and, no, I haven't heard from her. I'm sure she's painting.'

I heard Mrs Nance draw a breath through her teeth. She was a good woman but she didn't entirely approve of my mother or me for that matter. But she'd been devoted to my father's family and she was a great help to my mother with the house and the farm.

'I thought the same but the things she usually takes are here like her small tent. All that's missing are her bicycle and her paintbox.'

I let these facts sink in. She could still be painting. 'Have you rung her friends?'

'Not as yet. I wanted to speak to you or Master Oliver first.'

'Please start as soon as we end this call. She could easily be with friends.'

'She normally leaves a note, and well, she's . . . '

I cut her off. 'Let me know anything you discover?'

'I will. Are you coming home?' she asked.

'My work . . . ' I began.

'You and your work,' she huffed. 'I know, I know all the war work and everything but . . . '

I didn't need her warming to her subject, which she would, with no encouragement at all, so I interrupted, 'Keep me informed, please, Mrs Nance. I'll ring if I haven't heard from you tomorrow.'

'Yes, fine,' she said, and the line went dead.

'She speaks loudly enough that I have the gist of it,' Fleming said. 'Your interpretation?'

'It remains the same. She has her paintbox. She is off painting.' She might have a portrait commission and be staying with the sitter. There was nothing further I could do right now so work was the answer. I straightened my shoulders, ready to make my exit.

'I suggest you try and reach your brother now.' Fleming took a seat at his desk.

I studied him.

'He may well have spoken to or heard from her and be able to clear things up.'

'True.'

'To be blunt, I can't have your mother's disappearance and questions about her loyalty affecting your work.'

I nodded, picked up the handset again and spoke with the operator. Fleming reviewed some paperwork on his desk. The line connected and I asked for Flight Lieutenant Tremayne. Another few moments passed where I could hear good natured banter in the background.

'Tremayne here.'

'Oli, have you heard from Maman?' I held my breath.

'I spoke with her last week. Thursday, I think,' he said. 'What's this about, Merry?'

'She's not home,' I said. 'And Mrs Nance has called in the police since she hasn't been seen since Friday morning.'

'Nothing unusual there. Painting, I suspect.'

'That's what I think too but thought it best to check with you to see if she'd mentioned going away.'

'No, she hadn't. We had other things to talk about.'

'Like what?' I asked.

'Can't tell you now as I'm being called,' he said. 'Maman will be back when the weather turns wet again.'

'True. I'm sure she'll be surprised at the fuss,' I said, keeping my voice deliberately light.

'Right, must go. Love you,' he said.

My heart tightened as I heard the noise of plane engines in the background. For each sortie Oliver flew, there was an all too probable chance that he wouldn't return.

'Love you too,' I said, and I prayed that he would remain lucky. I couldn't bear thinking of the alternative.

'Well, that resolves that.' Fleming stood and handed me a pile of papers. 'Please review this and update accordingly.'

I'd caught up with all the new intelligence that had come in during the day. The newly annotated map in front of me was up to date and it was eight o'clock. I rubbed the back of my neck.

'Thought you'd still be here,' Fleming said, coming into the room. 'Let me take you for a drink.'

I frowned at him.

'I have a proposition for you.'

'Now, Commander . . . '

'Not that type of proposition,' he interrupted, 'but one I think might interest you. Meet me at the main doors in five minutes.'

My curiosity piqued, I listened to the sound of his footsteps retreat as I dug into my bag to find my face powder to freshen my appearance. The last thing I wanted this evening was to be out but many of our most interesting and important conversations were held over a meal or a drink.

'The Savoy?' Fleming asked when I appeared.

I nodded and we strolled along the pavement in silence. From experience, I knew that Fleming wasn't going to enlighten me any further until we were seated with a drink in our hands.

Once inside he swiftly manoeuvred us into the American Bar and secured a table well away from others.

'Whisky?' he asked. 'Or something else?'

'Dubonnet.' I leaned back in the chair and closed my eyes for a moment while he ordered the drinks. When I opened them, I found he was focused on me.

'Your mother must be weighing on your mind.' He played with his cigarette case. 'But as always you are a professional.'

'Thank you.' There was no rushing him to his point.

'And I have been thinking about what you mentioned yesterday, and it happens I have need of some information and you could be exactly the person to acquire it,' he said.

I waited, not sure where this was heading.

'On the Helford River, which you know well, there is a small band of men,' he began. 'A cartography unit.'

It was clear that it was not a cartography unit at all. Whatever these men were doing it was not ordinary mapmaking – it was classified.

'They could use the assistance of a geographer,' Fleming explained.

'Which is what I am.' I leaned back in my chair as our drinks were delivered. 'Exactly what are you after?'

Fleming smiled and sipped his whisky. 'There are several operations happening along the coast of Devon and Cornwall, controlled by different sections . . . all officially unofficial.'

It was a short distance from there to the north coast of Brittany so I could imagine the movement of people and supplies taking place.

'The two operations are not being as effective as they could be.'

'How so?' I asked.

He waved a hand. 'That's the thing. I have an idea but I can't pin it down and I'd like to know what you make of it. You see things clearly and won't be biased towards one branch or the other.' He lit a cigarette.

Fleming was brilliant at seeing something, a problem or a potential solution to one and then letting others sort it. I had watched and experienced it on many occasions.

'And, if you join them, it will give you the opportunity to investigate your mother's disappearance.'

'That would be useful,' I said. My concern was growing because his was.

'Like I'm sure you have, I have questions about it.' He took a drag of his cigarette. 'Because, in the current situation, you don't cast these aspersions without some reason.'

I pressed my lips together. He didn't know village life. 'It's simply because she's French,' I said, pausing to look at him closely. 'Or do you know something?'

'I do not.' He placed a hand on his chest.

I nodded and took a sip of my drink, letting my thoughts settle.

'On the Helford, you will see how an operational unit works,' Fleming said. 'They are in training mode now, and it will give you the time to see what these men are facing and what they need from their maps.'

I had no idea what this might entail, no matter how hard I tried.

'We can't spare you forever as you are too crucial to intelligence here, but it would work for a short while.' He stubbed out his cigarette and lit another. 'Questions?'

'Of course,' I said. 'Where exactly is it based and when do I join them?'

'On the north side of the river where the officers are headquartered in a house called Ridifarne.'

'The Bickford-Smiths' house?'

'I believe so. The team is led by an acquaintance of mine: Holdsworth.'

'Timing?' I asked.

'I suggest you head off tomorrow after you clear your desk.'

'That soon?' That would take some doing.

'I think you need to spend a few days trying to get to the bottom of your mother's . . . disappearance, and then join the team at Ridifarne on Monday morning.'

I sipped my drink. This was not what I had expected at all

but working with an operational team based on the Helford was ideal in many ways. I knew the area and would not have to waste time trying to learn the location but would be able to focus on acquiring experience.

'Have dinner with me?'

It was never a good idea to turn down dinner at The Savoy, so long as it didn't then lead to a night of dancing. With Fleming, however, it was impossible to predict how the evening would end.

5

7 May 1942

Last night, Fleming, Muriel and I had ended up at the 400 Club after dinner and I'd returned home an hour ago at five. Despite feeling woefully under-dressed all evening, I'd had a lovely time. Fleming and Muriel were good company and, for a moment, I put my concerns aside to laugh and dance. It had done me good, but the lack of rest hadn't.

My suitcase lay open on the bed. With a sleep-deprived mind, I tried to pack for an indeterminate amount of time in Cornwall, doing God knows what. I began with an off-white evening gown, just in case, and followed it with the overalls I kept for emergencies.

Constance walked into my room, carrying two steaming cups of tea. She was a tall handsome woman who of late appeared creased with tiredness. Her dark hair, pulled severely back as she always wore it when nursing, added ten years to her forty-one. Yet, despite having been on her feet all night, her eyes were still full of concern and even mischief.

'How was the shift?' I asked, taking a cup from her.

'Fine. Where on earth are you going?' She peered into my suitcase and noted the two distinct articles of clothing.

'Cornwall.'

She arched an eyebrow. 'Is it about the phone call?'

I tilted my hand back and forth. 'The call was regarding Maman. She hasn't been home since Friday morning.'

'Taken a lover?' Constance sent me a sideways glance. 'She is French, after all.'

I laughed. 'Not an impossibility but definitely one I hadn't considered nor had the inspector. I wonder if I should mention it?'

'It could make his day,' she suggested. 'Why else are you going? Not that your mother isn't reason enough, but she has been heading off on trips for as long as I've known you.'

'True. Also a project for work.' I folded a slip and placed it in the suitcase then added some stockings followed by three pairs of trousers and some shorts. These would be essential for doing anything on boats.

She peered again into the suitcase. 'That is an odd selection of clothes but may I suggest you also add in the blue evening gown as it brings out your eyes?'

I pulled it out of the closet and held it up, glancing in the mirror. It did set off my eyes. They were blue-green like my father's. My brother had deep dark-brown ones like Maman. I swallowed and tried to fold the dress in such a way that it would crease less but it wasn't working

Hester joined us. 'Thought I heard voices.' She glanced at the suitcase. 'Leaving?'

I nodded.

She took the dress from my hands then expertly folded it and placed it in the suitcase. 'Interesting clothing choices. Don't forget dancing shoes, sturdy boots and plimsolls to go with what you've packed.'

Both Constance and I laughed. Hester wasn't an academic and was very good at keeping our feet on the ground, no matter how engrossed we became in our work.

'Who were you out with last night and do tell if you were kissed?' Hester asked.

'I was out with Fleming and Muriel, and I wasn't kissed but I did dance until dawn with a handsome captain. He was charming and a bit wicked.'

Constance yawned.

'Bed,' Hester said, pointing to the stairs.

Constance obediently rose to her feet, gave me a hug then kissed Hester tenderly. They were very discreet about their relationship everywhere but at home. Despite being twelve years Constance's senior, Hester appeared younger with her delicate features and clear blue eyes. Her beauty had not faded.

'Safe travels,' Constance said. 'And keep us informed.' She went to her bedroom on the floor below. She was working nights this week.

Hester went to the kitchen in the basement while I completed my packing, collected my notebook and a selection of books, including my favourites of Sayers.

I placed my suitcase by the door and made my way downstairs where I found Hester.

'Time for breakfast before you set out?' Hester asked, walking past me. She was dressed for travel, too, in a high-waisted pair of trousers and floral blouse.

'Would love breakfast,' I said, filling the kettle. 'Where are you off to?'

'Mother.' She huffed. 'Summoned. She's not well. I'm having to move back there with her until she recovers or dies.'

'Hester,' I said, trying not to be horrified.

'I know it's a terrible thing to say about my mother, but she doesn't care that there is a war on and that I have a role. She claims she needs me and has had me transferred to the Red Cross in Bristol,' she said, crossing her arms. 'And she did so without asking.'

'But Constance . . . ' I'd never known them to be apart for more than a few days. In their devotion to each other, they reminded me of my parents, balanced and loving.

'I know but I have no choice,' Hester said, her voice tinged with bitterness. 'She couldn't ask my sister because she has a husband to look after . . . and, of course, I couldn't argue.'

Benedict Hartley arrived in the kitchen, ready for a day at the hospital. His family had moved to the countryside during the Blitz after their house was bombed. He'd taken up Constance's kind offer of a room when finding lodging had proved difficult.

'Morning, ladies. Someone leaving?' He glanced down the hallway to the suitcase.

'Yes,' we answered in unison.

'Losing both of you at once.' He poured himself a cup of tea.

''Fraid so,' Hester said. 'Mother calls.'

'And I'm off to Cornwall,' I said.

'I know enough not to ask more,' he said to me as he began laying the table while I sliced more bread. Hester used up her ration allowance and fried some eggs and bacon. We were all hands in at Bywater Street, and that was one of the things that I loved about my life here. All of us contributed to the war effort and each job was vital in very different ways therefore household chores were spread equally. Constance had made that clear at the start of Benedict's residence, and he took it with good grace. Whether Benedict held up his side in his own home was up for speculation.

The hallway clock chimed the quarter hour, reminding me I had so much to do before taking a train later. Eating quickly, I cleared my plate for I couldn't linger. The telephone rang as I was gathering my things by the front door. Distracted, I picked up the receiver.

'Morning,' I said.

'Merry?' Oliver's voice rose in surprise. 'So glad I caught you. I'm in London. Any chance I can see you?'

'Yes,' I said, wondering how I could make it work. 'But I'm off to Cornwall this evening.'

'You've heard from Maman?' His voice rose.

'Sadly, no,' I said. 'I'm taking the nine fifty. Can you meet me at Paddington Station Hotel tonight?'

'I can meet you for a drink at eight thirty,' he said. 'I need to catch a lift at ten from Marble Arch.'

'See you then,' I said.

I put the phone down, thrilled to have this unexpected chance to see my little brother, and at the same time curious about what was bringing him to London.

*

There was no sign of Harling as I cleared my desk. This was not unusual, but it would be good to know who would be here manning the office while I was away. Leaving everything up to date, I headed upstairs to Room 39 to see if Commander Fleming had anything further to say.

Fleming was alone and he looked up from his desk. 'You're off.' He glanced at his watch. It was ten to seven.

'Who will be working on the maps while I'm gone?' I asked.

'I've called in another bluestocking,' Fleming said with a smile.

I raised an eyebrow.

'You've been such a success I thought I should find someone like you.' He pulled out his cigarette case and held it out to me, but I shook my head. 'She's a don from Cambridge.'

'Good. She'll make sure that things will not slip.' I picked up my suitcase. 'I'll be in touch.'

'Remember, Merry, no one must suspect your true purpose is to find out the reason for the disputes between the two operations,' Fleming warned.

'Of course.'

'You'll be on home ground and the locals will think they know you and your business,' he continued. 'In their eyes you are a bookish spinster who has chosen to follow a career. The community will all have drawn their own conclusions about you.'

'As you once did,' I replied.

'Ah, yes, but I'm a fast learner.' He lit his cigarette. 'You'll be in good hands working with Holdsworth. He's first rate and runs an ace team of men.'

'Thank you for this opportunity.'

'It will be tough at times, both working with an operational unit and digging around the Helford regarding your mother. As they say, there is normally no smoke without fire.' He tapped the spine of *Gaudy Night* bulging out of my handbag along with my notebook. 'You can go and be Harriet Vane but God knows who will be your Wimsey.' He laughed. 'Only a woman could write a man like that; they just don't exist.'

I smiled, for I knew Wimsey or men like him were rare. I'd learned this by experience, but it was a good thing such men didn't. I needed nothing to distract me from my work. Reaching this point had required total focus.

'Speaking of Wimsey types, I met your ex-fiancé at lunch. Garfield was quite dismissive of you but I don't need to tell you that you did well to ditch him. He's not good enough for you.'

I didn't react because I would not reveal how I felt about my personal past being brought to the present. I was grateful I had not encountered George even though he was in London on some general's staff. Falling for Lord George Garfield had been the mistake of an eighteen-year-old me who had been won over by his looks, charm and wit. He seemed to be everything I could have wanted, and he thought I was exactly what he needed. But, as it turned out, he wanted a clever wife, not a clever wife with a career who intended to continue her education to the highest levels. Achieving my DPhil had been hard won, and I'd had to convince my dons I was serious, serious enough to commit to the life of a spinster at a young age.

'Is there anything else?' I asked, wanting to move past this discussion.

'Not at the moment. Safe travels and keep me posted.' He walked to the door with me, but I proceeded down the corridor alone, contemplating the challenges of being a spy at home under Mrs Nance's watchful eyes. But I didn't linger too long on that thought as I searched for a taxi.

It took ages to find one and I'd walked half the journey before that happened. It made slower progress to Paddington than I had on foot, and it was a few minutes past eight thirty when I walked into the hotel lobby to meet my brother. My heart stopped for a moment when I saw Oliver. I remained still until I had composed myself. As the elder, I needed to be the stronger of the two of us. He was the softer, more loving one. Maman said that he was more like Papa, gruff on the surface, but soft like a crab under its shell. Standing there in uniform, he was so like Papa – tall and strong with his heart so open and believing.

'Merry,' he said, waving. He took big strides before he wrapped me in an enormous bear hug, lifting me and my case off the ground. 'God, you are a sight for sore eyes.'

After putting me down, he collected my case, led me into the bar where we found a table and ordered. Only then did he take my hand in his. 'Do you think we should be concerned?' he asked, searching my face for answers. He'd always looked to me to sort things out. If it required brute force, he was your man, but he left the heavy thinking to me.

'To be honest, I don't know.' I looked at my bitten fingernails in his large capable hands. 'This isn't something I can solve with one of my maps.'

He laughed sadly. 'Have you tried?'

'Not yet,' I said. 'I don't have enough information.'

The waiter brought our drinks.

'Is there anything we can do?' He pulled some sunglasses out of his pocket and played with them. The tutor who'd taught us both at home from the age of nine had eventually given up on stopping Oliver fidgeting. It wasn't possible or practical. 'She's been gone six days.'

'I honestly don't know.' For once I couldn't be the clever one and have all the answers, which felt wrong. Although not as physically strong, I was the more resilient of the two of us. He had tried not to show how much our father's passing had affected him but to anyone who knew him at all, his world had been destroyed. I'd been devastated too but I reminded myself he died doing something he loved, riding the land. He hadn't suffered. The coroner said it would have been instantaneous. Poor Maman, though. She had been bereft. He was with her at breakfast and gone by lunch. Those first few months I had worried about her but she threw herself with greater gusto into helping the evacuees from Belgium and France who had begun landing on Cornwall's shores since the start of the war.

'Do you think . . . ' His voice faded away.

'Maman is dead?' I shook my head. 'I don't, but I can't explain why.' This feeling bothered me for it was not grounded in evidence.

'Well, if it helps, I don't think so either,' he said.

'I'm pleased we are agreed.'

He chuckled. 'That doesn't often happen. I swear you always took the opposing side just for the challenge of the debate.'

I shrugged and grinned.

'Why are you heading to Cornwall?'

'Work.' I kept the explanation brief.

'Enough said.' Oliver had drawn his own conclusions about my war work, for he knew it was all about maps.

'What brings you to London?' I asked then took a sip of my beer.

'Love.' He grinned. 'The one good thing to come out of this this wretched war.'

'I could argue against that one,' I said thinking of the opportunities that women had been given during this war, but now wasn't the time.

'Just because of one bad apple doesn't mean all men are like George,' he said, rolling his eyes. 'I never liked him anyway.'

'I wasn't thinking about George,' I said but clearly everyone else was.

'Good. You should try again.' He twisted the near empty glass in his hand.

'Falling in love is incompatible with my career,' I said. 'Or I should clarify, marriage is.'

'So you have said,' Oliver observed, 'repeatedly, and of course you are a proponent of free love.'

I gently pushed his foot under the table. I was not going to discuss that with him here. I pulled the sunglasses from his hands and tried them on.

'Changing the subject?' He laughed. 'They suit you.'

'Do they?' I angled my head to appear innocent.

He nodded. 'I'll try and source another pair. These came from an American in an Eagle Squadron.'

Taking the glasses off, I placed them on the table. I didn't want to spend my short time with my brother discussing sunglasses or Americans. 'Tell me all about your new love.'

'Caroline Moore.' His expression softened. 'She's a nurse and I've asked her to marry me.'

'What?' I exclaimed. This was sudden. 'When? I haven't given my approval yet!'

'She's making me wait.' He picked up his cup. 'At the moment I've got a conditional acceptance. Says if we make it through the war then she will make it official.'

'Wise woman.' I liked the sound of Caroline. Her head and heart were in the right place.

'God, I love her so much it hurts.' Oliver sighed.

I chuckled. 'When did you ask her?'

'Today,' he said. 'When I spoke with Maman last week, she told me not to wait a minute longer. In fact, she posted me her ring.'

'That sounds like Maman,' I said, reaching out to him. 'Wait . . . when did she post it? What was the post mark?'

'God, I don't know. I didn't look.' He shook his head. 'I came back from a sortie on Saturday and it was there. God, I should have paid attention.'

'Why should you have?' I smiled at him.

'I don't know,' he said. 'I didn't spend my spare hours reading detective stories like you.'

'No, you were out climbing, building things and helping Papa,' I said.

The waiter checked on us and we both glanced at the clock on the wall. Our time was running out too fast. Oliver squeezed my hands in a silent gesture. 'What was it Maman would never let us do?'

'Go to bed angry and without telling each other I love you.'

'God, my friends at Harrow thought I was such a mama's boy when they heard me on the telephone.'

'Well, that was true but they wouldn't understand. Maman said it took ages to bring Papa around. So did you have to convince Caroline to love you or was it immediate?'

'Immediate.'

I raised a mocking eyebrow then smiled. 'Tell me more about Caroline?'

His face lit up at the mention of his fiancée. 'She's wonderful.'

'Details?' I laughed. 'How am I to build a picture of her from such a vague term?'

Oliver leaned back in his chair. 'Trust you to want precise details.'

'Always.'

'She's twenty-two, the youngest of five, her father is a doctor, and they live in Cambridge,' he said.

'I wasn't asking about her family, although they sound wonderful.' I picked up the sunglasses again and turned them in my hands, catching first a reflection of myself and then of Oliver.

'What do you want to know?' he asked.

'What made you fall in love with her?' Love could happen in an instant, I knew. Sadly, it could end as quickly – especially in a time of war.

'Her laugh,' he said.

'That I wasn't expecting,' I said. Oliver's joy was infectious. My spirits lifted with his. My little brother was twenty-five, nearly twenty-six, and in love.

'Glad to know I can surprise you,' he said. 'I can't wait for you and Maman to meet her.'

'Soon.' I glanced at my wrist. Our meeting had been wonderful, but it was time for us to go if I wanted to catch my train and he his lift.

'Keep me up to date, please.' Oliver stood. 'And Merry – be careful.'

I laughed. 'I work with maps and other data while you hurtle about the sky, and you tell me to be careful.'

Oliver kissed my cheek in farewell. 'I mean it.'

'I know.' I hugged him a bit tighter than normal then disappeared to catch my train.

6

8 May 1942

The guard woke me at Redruth where I changed trains. At Gwinear Road I almost fell asleep standing while waiting for the branch line train to Helston but the noise from the schoolboys and a few women kept me alert. Once seated on the train, I nodded off to sleep and was woken again at Praze-an-Beeble when the station master called out 'Praze, Praze, Praze.' I dozed again until we reached Helston and the volume of noise from the schoolboys had reached fevered pitch.

The morning was cool and bright as I stepped onto the platform, hoping that Matthew Skewes, Kestle's farm manager, would be here to collect me. After a night sitting on a crowded train, I was far from refreshed.

A busy hive of people and produce filled Helston Station and I couldn't see Matthew in the crowd until he waved his cap. A big grin spread across his weathered face.

'Oh, Miss Merry, it's good to see you,' he said, taking my bag from my hands.

'I'm glad to be here.' I breathed in deeply, wondering what I would discover at Kestle.

'It's a good thing too.' He walked towards my father's old car.

'My mother's not back?' I asked, hoping that this part of my trip would be nothing more than a few days with her.

He shook his head slowly. 'People been talking.'

I translated that to mean Mrs Nance had been talking and people had been drawing the wrong conclusions. 'What are they saying?'

''Tisn't good and it be wrong.' He tilted his head. ''Tis all because she's French.'

'They are at war with the Germans, too.' I climbed into the passenger seat.

He sucked in a breath. 'Not right. But your mother has been acting a bit different of late.'

I frowned. 'How so?'

'Been using your cottage to paint.' He started the engine and we set off.

That was odd. The light was all wrong for a start, and she had a far more suitable studio for her use.

'Anything else?' I asked.

He glanced at me but remained silent. There was no point in pushing him although I wanted to. Matthew Skewes was a man of few words and a good heart. He would speak when he felt like it.

To pass the time, I glanced out the window at familiar scenery. The fields were still full of cauliflower and swede, which surprised me.

'Are you still harvesting the winter crop, Matthew?'

'Yes, the turnips and the brocola are just about done.' He cleared his throat. 'Early potatoes go in next week.'

I smiled at his use of the Cornish names for the vegetables. I remembered all too clearly visiting cousins in Oxfordshire and arguing over what a cauliflower and a swede were called.

'Began planting the barley and the wheat on the fields near the creek this last week,' he said as we passed the double lodges at Trelowarren. It was all a blur as the weariness of the overly long journey settled in. I yawned. It was eight thirty in the morning, and I longed for my mother's welcome and a cup of her strong coffee while we laughed at the gossip that had sprouted up like weeds in the wake of her impulsiveness. Then we could walk down to the creek and enjoy the peace to be found there.

It would be a perfect bonus day with her, like when I was a child, and she would pull me from my lessons at home, leaving Oliver with the tutor. We would take a picnic and her Peter Pan gramophone then set off in my father's car to some remote beach, hill or valley. Together, just us girls. She would paint. I would sketch, mapping everything I would see while in the background was the sound of opera. My mother adored the Italian soprano Maria Lucia, particularly her *Tosca*. My mother would sing, badly, along to 'Vissi d'arte'. All the while I'd complain and wrinkle my nose, saying I preferred *Carmen*. She would ruffle my hair and comment I was so like my father. Those were perfect days, our girls' days out.

As the lanes twisted and became narrower, the old excitement of homecoming filled me. Ahead, the large Methodist chapel loomed. Matthew turned at the crossroads, heading down the narrow lane to turn again into an even smaller one, when something hit the bonnet and rolled to the windscreen.

I squinted at the dirt-covered bulb sitting against the wiper. 'Is that a daffodil bulb?'

''Tis a shame but nothing for it.' Matthew sighed. 'They all had to come out for more vegetables, but the girls keep finding them. They just toss them out of their way. 'Tis such a waste but makes a drive a jolly event in early spring as so many have settled on the tops of the hedges.'

'I can imagine. Poor Mr Williams,' I said, thinking of the local man famous for his early daffodils that were sold in London.

'Big loss but . . . ' Matthew shrugged.

'War,' I said, stating the obvious.

The lane narrowed further as we approached the small cluster of dwellings at Kestle. Looking at it now, it was hard to imagine that Kestle, meaning castle or settlement, could once have been a bustling place. But it had been, back in the misty past when travel by road was rare in this part of the world. Our home sat on a plateau perfectly placed for its residents to slip down to the secretive Frenchman's Creek to the west or into the village of Helford to the east.

The first sight of the house lifted my flagging spirits, until I saw Mrs Nance standing in the door. The difference between my mother and the housekeeper was marked not in age, as they were of similar years, but style. Mrs Nance's fair hair was greyer and she was of solid proportions with a dour expression even on bright days, but her hazel eyes held warmth in them.

Kestle, since my father's death a little over a year ago, was officially Oliver's. I'd been given Pill Cottage, tucked in the woods at the top of Frenchman's Creek, a short walk from the family home. My father had said he wanted me to have it so I had a place of my own. That precise bequest made me laugh and cry. '*One foot on the land and one in the sea and happy I will be*,' I used to sing as a child as I raced along Frenchman's Creek with him. Papa always said I was a funny mix of him and Maman, loving the land like he did and the sea as she did. He was right. Even my course at Oxford, focusing on coastal geography, had been shaped by these equal passions.

On this golden May morning, everything was as it should be with bluebells and Lily of the Valley in the borders and the air sweet with scent. Everything, of course, except that my mother wasn't here.

Mrs Nance greeted me with a nod, and she looked me up and down with her usual critical eye. Only then did she open her arms and hug me.

'I'm so pleased you're here,' she murmured in approving tones into my neck. The last embrace like this one was when my father had died. That had rocked her. Her uncle had been a farm manager for my grandfather and she'd known my father all her life.

'It's good to be here,' I said as she dropped her arms and we walked into the hall. It was good in the way that coming home always felt and yet it wasn't that same wraparound hug feeling of the past. I spun about, noting everything from the tall clock to the table by the stairs. It was clear that Mrs Nance had arranged the flowers because they didn't have Maman's flair. But it wasn't that. Something else wasn't right. And it wasn't that the hall and the stairs were submerged in permanent gloom. The arched window on the landing had been covered with old potato sacks in September thirty-nine. My bearings were off but my normal markers were in place. I couldn't pinpoint what it was and that must be because of two nights with little sleep. Or it could be that Maman wasn't here.

'Tell me everything,' I said, turning to Mrs Nance.

'You need breakfast and tea. You've lost weight.' She tutted as she headed into the kitchen and I followed. I did need tea, and breakfast wouldn't go amiss.

I paused on the threshold and absorbed the atmosphere. Dried herbs hung from the gnarled wooden beams. The large range dominated one end and pumped heat into the room so that, even on the coldest days, this room was warm despite its size.

'Have you brought your ration card?' she asked while removing the cosy from the teapot.

'I have but I'm only staying at Kestle until Monday morning.'

She placed the cup and saucer on the table.

'Not staying longer?' She shook her head. 'I thought when I heard you were coming that you'd returned to look after things here until . . . ' her voice trailed away.

'I won't be far, just on the north side of the river,' I explained, hoping this would stop her conjecturing.

Mrs Nance frowned as only she could. The north side of the Helford was another country to her.

'Just what will you be doing there?'

'Working, but I will be able to keep an eye on things until my mother returns.'

'It's most odd.' She shook her head as she cut thick slices of bread and placed them under the grill to toast. 'She hasn't taken her ration card.'

'You know how impulsive Maman is,' I said, watching Mrs Nance purse her mouth. I shouldn't wind her up but it was hard not to. Oli and I had gently riled her for years. 'I'm certain she made a decision to head off once she was already out and about.'

Mrs Nance continued to shake her head as she added some bacon fat to a frying pan then cracked an egg into it. My mouth watered. I'd missed her cooking.

'You mentioned her bicycle and paintbox were gone. So she must have set out painting and met another friend or artist.'

'I know what you're saying but it's been a week since the land girls and vicar saw her.'

This worried me too, but once she had gone for three weeks without a word.

The phone in my father's study rang and I raced towards it, hoping it was Maman.

'Manaccan two-five-three.'

'Is that Merry?' a woman asked.

'It is,' I said.

'It's Genevieve Dreyer.'

She was my mother's closest friend. 'Mrs Dreyer, I'm so pleased you rang.'

'Yes, most peculiar as your Mrs Nance left a message with

Michael to ring and I've been away in the Highlands with Jenny and the kids. It was about Elise being missing.'

'Yes, she's been gone a week,' I said.

'And you're worried?' she asked.

I laughed. 'Not really, but because Mrs Nance hadn't been able to reach Oli and me she called the police.'

'Really?' Disapproval dripped from Mrs Dreyer's voice.

'Yes, I think she'll be back soon, wondering what all the fuss was about.'

'Exactly.' Mrs Dreyer chuckled. 'Now, tell me, Merry, how are things? Have you met any delicious men yet? Any marriageable ones?'

I rolled my eyes. 'Many delicious ones but I'm not the marrying kind.'

'You are a wicked thing trying to buck the system. My Fergus is still single,' she suggested.

I was complimented that she felt me good enough for her precious son but that was Fergus's problem and always had been: he was precious. 'He wouldn't have me and you know it.'

'True, true, but you would have beautiful children.'

I laughed.

'Look, dear, let me know when she returns.'

'I will. Send my love to all the family.' I put the handset down, grateful someone else aside from Oli and me were untroubled by her disappearance. Fleming's interest concerned me. I of course understood the implication but it was simply a storm that would pass with her return.

The smell of toast and bacon called me to the kitchen but I stayed in the comfort of my father's study for a moment. Running my hand over the top of my father's desk, I looked around. Framed on the wall was the first map I had ever made when I was eight. It was simple and showed all of Kestle's childhood wonders, from the woods, to the creek, to the fields. I'd tried to capture each detail in miniature: the badger set; the paddock where I'd learned to ride my pony Jezebel; the climbing oak, as we called the ancient tree by the hay barn; and the secret den in the woods. There was a heart where the house stood. Maman always said home was where the heart was. As I became older my heart shifted to Oxford, with my books and research, and I came to understand that my parents' home was with each other – no matter where they were.

I heard Mrs Nance and Matthew chatting in the kitchen when I left the study. Matthew nodded to me but went out the kitchen door.

'Sit down. You look exhausted.'

I did as I was told.

'I'm so sorry it's not more.' Mrs Nance put a plate filled with a fried egg, bread and potatoes in front of me. It was a good reminder that some foods were much more available here.

'It looks wonderful,' I said and Mrs Nance poured a cup of tea for herself then sat opposite, squinting at me. Her disapproval of my life choices had never been hidden. Mrs Nance believed education was wasted on a woman. A woman only needed to know how to read, write, add and subtract to keep a family. A degree from Oxford? A job in London? None of these were what well-bred Cornish girls did. But this plate of food and the concern in her eyes told a different story.

'My worry grew with Mrs Tremayne being gone since at least nine in the morning on Friday.' She took a sip of her tea. 'I had no concerns as I left Friday at five but when I returned on Monday morning, well, it did worry me so I spoke with Matthew and the girls.'

I nodded, my mouth full. This was a tactic of hers to speak when you couldn't reply.

'So by four o'clock on Monday I tried to reach you and Master Oliver but had no luck.' She took a sip of her tea. 'That was when I called them in Helston and let them know.' She glanced down at her hands.

'But Maman has gone off before.'

'I know she did, but it was the arrival of Mrs Tonkin on the pretext of seeing if we had any spare veg that worried me.' She looked at me. 'You see, they were already talking about it in the village, saying what a selfish thing to flit about the countryside like there wasn't a war on.'

'How did they know she wasn't here?' I asked. Maman didn't really go to either Manaccan or Helford often.

Mrs Nance looked down then up. 'I may have asked if she'd been seen when I went to Helford to the shop.'

I nodded. It was all becoming perfectly clear. Mrs Nance, by her concern, had stirred the ready-to-boil pot of gossip and rumour that abounded in the best of days and bubbled over frequently during these tense times.

'I'm so pleased you're here, even if you have to go to the other side.'

I smiled. This was a big concession.

'So she was fine when you left on Thursday,' I said.

'Oh yes. Mrs Tremayne was on the telephone with Master Oli. Her voice was all jolly like and sounding more . . . ' Mrs Nance paused ' . . . French, like she did when she was excited.'

'I suppose she did.' My mother was enthusiastic about many things and when she liked something she didn't hide it. This, my father said, had been a real challenge in the early days of their marriage. He would keep things to himself, and she wouldn't have it. She hated secrets, probably because she was so bad at them. Even Christmas and birthday presents couldn't be kept hidden if she knew about them. And she always revealed what she'd bought or made for you. My father had had to take over shopping for our gifts for this very reason.

Maman was a force of nature until my father's death. It had taken half a year for her to pick up her paint brushes again but once she had I knew her grief was easing.

'On Friday morning?' I prompted Mrs Nance, keen to discover the full story as quickly as possible.

'The house was empty but, as you know, that's not unusual.'

I nodded. Maman would frequently disappear before dawn to be on location to paint with the rising sun.

'I left a prepared plate of food for her in the larder and didn't give it another thought until Monday when it was still there.' Mrs Nance leaned forward. 'At that point I consulted with Matthew Skewes.'

'And?'

'I asked him to check your cottage.' She pursed her lips with disapproval. 'I once found her there with a foreigner, you know.'

'Painting his portrait?' I suggested. 'Or one of the refugees she helped?'

'No.' She clasped her hands together. 'I don't take with these foreign types. Can't trust them.'

'You mean anyone not from here.' I smiled to soften the statement of fact. 'Matthew mentioned that my mother had been using the cottage to paint.'

'Your mother had even taken to sleeping down there, which made no sense when she had a perfectly good and comfortable bed here.' Mrs Nance stood and picked up the teapot. 'Matthew reported that her paintbox was gone as was her bike but not her little tent or any of the other things she always took on extended trips.'

I stood to clear my plate. 'Did her friends know anything and what of her diary?'

'It was empty.' She sucked her teeth. 'It was the first place I looked, but there weren't any appointments for sittings there.'

'And her friends?'

'I spoke with Mrs Petherick, but she hadn't heard from your mother in ten days or so.'

'Anyone else?'

Mrs Nance hesitated, then pushed on, her cheeks pink. 'All of them as you asked.'

'And none of them had heard from her?'

She slowly shook her head. 'I don't like the feel of this.'

I placed a hand on her shoulder. 'It will be fine.'

I left the kitchen and headed back into my father's study to think.

The room held so many memories from the books that lined the shelves to the photographs on the mantle. Maman had not altered a single item in here in the last year. My father's tobacco for his pipe still sat beside the inkwell, along with a photograph of her.

'Maman, what on earth are you up to?' I whispered, placing my finger on its frame.

I needed to find the answers and not jump to conclusions like the rest of the village; I had to consider everything. Beginning with the only fact I had: she was not here. Nothing was right. There were daffodils in the hedges, rather than the fields and my mother was painting in Pill Cottage. War had altered everything.

7

9 May 1942

Soft light streamed through the gaps in the curtains and I woke, for a moment forgetting the reality of now. I was simply the beloved daughter of Andrew and Elise Tremayne, older sister to Oliver. My world had been here at Kestle and on our yacht *Mirabelle*, which took us off to the Isles of Scilly and then on to Brittany and my grandfather each June. I would chart our course eagerly, waiting for the day when we would set sail. But those days were long gone.

Outside, the world was noisy with robins and blackbirds, and I was on my feet before the thrushes chimed in. By the time I was out of the bath, the three W's – wrens, warblers and wood pigeons – had joined the cacophony. The farmyard rooster wouldn't make a sound until near noon, the lazy beast.

The flagstones of the kitchen floor were icy under my bare feet as I added fuel to the range and placed the kettle on top. Outside the kitchen door, the low light caught the dew on the tall grasses and the gentle sound of the cows in the nearby field added a base point to the birds. While waiting for the water to boil, I dashed upstairs and completed dressing in an old navy dress I'd found in my cupboard. It was a bit dated but showed off my waist nicely. Looking in the mirror, I was no longer the ugly duckling of my past. There was very little of that me left and I saw a striking woman in the mirror. At the time I never thought it would happen. I was certain I was destined to have piano legs and hairs on my chin like my father's mother. The latter may yet happen but the last traces of the old me were gone, never to return except in my dreams when I was worried, like now.

In the mirror, my pale skin looked unhealthy. I added only a dash of red lipstick as it was hard to come by but just because I was in the country didn't mean I couldn't highlight my best features. However, I wouldn't fuss with my hair. A few brush strokes and it was sleek as I pulled it back into a low chignon. Nothing I could do would give it a fashionable curl. I could roll it in the current style but sometimes the ease of pulling it back off my face was sufficient.

Yesterday I had gone through all my mother's correspondence, looking for anything at all that would shed any light on her absence. There was only one thing that struck me as odd: although her diary had the key farm dates in it and birthdays, there were no others. No lunches or dinners with friends; no sittings for portraits. It was empty as if her life stopped on the first of May and she didn't exist anymore. But on the third flip through, I had found things that had been pencilled in later in the year but erased. We all do that but, because of the emptiness of the next few months when she would normally be busy, it had stayed with me.

There had also been a file of newspaper clippings about the French and Belgian refugees from their arrival. Maman had spearheaded the local effort to source clothes and furnishing for them, and it was clear from the cuttings that she had continued to follow their plight.

Slipping outside through the kitchen door, the air was fresh, the grass wet, the scent of the lilacs glorious. It wasn't until I was here that I realised how much I missed it. If I allowed myself to see beyond the war, I could imagine my summers and holidays here. Hopefully Oliver and Caroline would have a large family to fill the house behind me. And I would be the doting eccentric aunt who was a professor of geography at Oxford, and there to teach them about the land and the sea.

I laughed. It was all so clear in my head but the chances of that future were slim, even if we did win the war. Only two women were full professors at Oxford. Other universities were better at including women in their faculties. I knew I should consider them but Oxford was the home of my heart because it was where I became fully me. Yet looking around as I crossed the lane, that wasn't entirely true. Cornwall had made me the person I'd grown into. All my foundations were here and I was grateful for my father's foresight to give me the cottage.

As I looked across to the hills making up neighbouring farms, it would be easy to forget we were so close to the water. Like my mother, I was more at home on a boat than on the land. Our yacht, *Mirabelle*, was sitting on her cradle at Gweek, waiting for days when it was safe to sail, but my old canoe should be tucked into the undergrowth by the cottage. A quick paddle along the creek might clear my thoughts later.

Coming up the path was one of the land girls and I waved.

'Morning,' she said with a smile. Her basket was filled with wild garlic leaves. She noted my interest and explained. 'Your mother taught me how to make a lovely potato and wild garlic soup.'

It was my turn to smile. I knew the soup well and my mouth watered at the thought of it.

'Could you tell me about when you last saw my mother?' I asked.

'Oh, I am so sorry but of course.' She adjusted her headscarf and continued. 'You look so much like her I had thought for a moment she had returned.'

'Sadly no.'

'On Friday morning, it must have been around five thirty or six,' she said. 'Mrs Tremayne was collecting flowers, Lily of the Valley I think.'

'Did you speak to her?' I asked.

'Yes,' she said. 'But not much more than a good morning.'

'Did you notice anything unusual?' I asked.

'No, she was in painting clothes; you know, the trousers and the fisherman's smock.'

I nodded. During my childhood Maman was either in painting clothes or evening dress. I loved the contrast she presented to the world.

'So I assumed she was off to paint for a few hours at St Anthony. The tides would have been right for her there, although, with all the defences on the beach, it isn't as lovely as it was before the war.'

'You knew St Anthony before the war?' I asked, stunned because she didn't sound local.

'Oh, yes. My grandmother was from Helston and she used to bring us there on Good Fridays to go trigging.' Her face lit up. 'It was a grand day out and the whelks weren't too bad to eat either.'

I remembered the trigging. The shores around Treath and Helford were a great source of the whelks too. Oliver and I would join in, and Maman would add the whelks to her fish stew for supper that evening.

The noises of cows on the move appeared before we saw Matthew Skewes herding them down the lane to the milking shed.

'I best be off,' she said.

'If you think of anything else, please let me know.' I glanced down at the basket full of garlic leaves, longing for the past when everything was certain and love came in the form of a steaming bowl of soup.

'I will,' she said, dashing off.

Continuing on my way down to Pill Cottage, I hoped it would reveal something to help. Maman's use of it was the most obvious deviation from her normal routine. Questions about her circled in my mind, and, instead of enjoying the delights of spring, I searched for clues that my mother had passed this way recently.

Foxgloves reached up from the hedges, soon to open. The grass in the field was long with daisy heads peering through. Leaving the open space behind, the track twisted into the woods with trees closely lining both sides. The old smugglers' path ran parallel, but it was overgrown and well-hidden. The tales of their boats hiding in the creek must have inspired Du Maurier's book *Frenchman's Creek*. The novel had come out last year. We had met her when she was on honeymoon and mooring in the creek nearly ten years ago.

Once, people and things had moved almost unseen to and from the creek. But it was different now. Residents were alert to any unusual activity and a boom across the mouth of the river made any entrance and exit difficult without permission.

The rutted path began its steep descent to Frenchman's Creek. When I was little, I thought it was named for my mother. Her background had sounded like something out of a novel. I'd asked Papa if he had named the creek after her. He'd laughed and said then it would be Frenchwoman's Creek. He rustled my hair and said he didn't know why it had that name. When he was growing up it had been referred to as Frenchman's, Treveder or Pill Creek. Pill was the French word for creek and there is also a field on the western bank called Frenchman's Close. So there was some history of the French here long before Maman.

The shaded air was damp in the tunnel created by the towering trees and it smelled of earth, wild garlic and the hint of blue-bells. The dried mud held footprints of varying sizes – more than I would expect but then maybe more people were fishing to supplement their rations. The woods showed evidence of someone, or something, having been through them as there were broken branches and flattened foliage. The ancient wood was filled with oak, ash, elder, hazel, hawthorn and lately beech. This route had been worn down by regular, steady rains racing down to the creek.

Along the path, the emerging fiddle heads danced with the opened fronds in the breeze. Except for the signs of heavier use, nothing struck me as out of place. As I neared the creek, the calls of wading birds greeted me. The shanks, plovers, oystercatchers, and, most haunting of all, the curlew. The tide must be out. Once I would have known exactly where the tide was and it saddened me that I now didn't. Living in London, it bore no relevance to my life whether the Thames was in full flow or not.

Reaching the bottom, the path split. To the right it followed the creek to the old quay and another small cottage at the mouth, and to the left to my own Pill Cottage. The path was clear. It had taken more than one set of feet to carve it out of the bulging mounds of wild garlic. Could Mrs Nance be correct, and my mother had been meeting a foreign gentleman here? If so, who was he and where was he? Was Constance's cheeky question spot on? Heading off with a lover on an impromptu tryst, could so easily explain her disappearance. It was war time and people were acting in ways that they would never contemplate otherwise.

The mellow lime-wash on the walls of the cottage glowed in the sunlight. It was picture-perfect as I opened the gate in the stone wall. Once, it had been used by farm workers, but since the Great War it had been a playhouse for Oliver and me.

My mother's recent use of the cottage made no sense. My

father had created a studio for Maman out of one of the barns near the house, which had been the place where her artistic magic had happened when I was a child. There, pigments and canvas were brought together to create beauty and drama. Stories were told and lives were revealed, all through my mother's skilled hands.

Maman hadn't given up her promising career because of marriage, which was most unusual, but then my mother had never been conventional. Her talent had brought her first from Brittany to Paris and then at eighteen to study at the Slade in London. At the outbreak of the Great War in 1914, Maman had trained as a nurse and that was how she'd met my father. He'd claimed she'd saved his life in more ways than one.

I was born just three months after their marriage, which had stopped her nursing but not painting nor loving. My brother had arrived after me, according to my paternal grandmother, with indecent haste. At the end of the war, Maman had convinced Papa to follow his heart to the land and he'd bought Kestle. His brother had inherited a vast estate in north Cornwall but Papa had always loved the gentle land near the Helford where his mother had come from. My grandmother had thoroughly approved of him leaving the army as she had lost her two other sons to the war.

As I expected, the door to the cottage was unlocked. The scent of turpentine, glue and stuffy warm air greeted me when I entered. Scanning the room, I noted a half-finished portrait on the easel. The background was soft washes of blues and greens, with the torso outlined in charcoal. The hair was laid down in what my mother had taught me was dead colouring, thin layers of diluted oil paints, as were the contours of the cheeks. The full mouth was hinted at as was the long neck. But these were shadows. The only finished part of the painting were the eyes, rich black coffee-coloured, and watching me as if she was holding a secret.

The eyes were my mother's.

This was a self-portrait.

All through my childhood, my mother had covered canvas after canvas, documenting mine and Oli's growth along with Cornish seascapes and a continual stream of commissioned portraits. When my father died, Maman had downed her brushes for a while. She'd pushed her grief into work with the refugees as her file had shown me yesterday.

At Christmas, I was happy to see she had gained some weight and there was an energy about her again. During those precious few days of leave, we spoke of the farm, the importance of food production, and things that had altered locally because of the war. She was fully engaged in everything. The painting was further evidence of this positive change. I scoured the table, the floor, and the walls for preliminary sketches that might tell me how long she had been working on it. But there were none.

I stepped away and turned to look at where my mother's gaze fell. In the past, we'd had treasure hunts and my mother had left clues for me to follow, like following the sitter's gaze or connecting the teapot in the background to the teapot on her shelf of painting props. But this wasn't a treasure hunt, and the unfinished portrait was not a clue.

Still, my mother's eyes challenged me from the canvas.

I checked the small parlour. All was neat with the fireplace stocked with wood. I flipped through the paperwork on the table. There was no note, merely sketches of limbs and noses. Up the steep pitched stairs, I found both bedrooms prepared as if guests would be arriving shortly. In the main bedroom I stopped. There on the wall was another self-portrait of my mother. She held one-year-old me on her hip. On the canvas I stared at her with adoration while she looked at me in the mirror. This painting had once hung in the library at Kestle. It was odd that she had moved it here.

There were no answers at Pill Cottage as to her whereabouts, only more questions. Closing the door, I locked it and, out of habit, put the key in its place under the flowerpot.

I headed straight to the place where I had hidden the canoe at the start of the war, but the canoe wasn't there. Maybe Maman or even Matthew had used it to fish. I retraced my steps and looked in the undergrowth near where I used to launch it.

It was there and it had been used, the earth around it recently disturbed. I turned it over and pulled it to the bank and into the light. The paddles were held in place with leather ties. The tide had come in swiftly while I'd checked the cottage. I removed my shoes and tossed them into the boat then pushed it into the water. I was not best dressed for a paddle but the call of being on the water was too intense to resist.

Reaching the middle of the channel, a feeling of peace descended, which was odd in war. But here it felt far away on this creek surrounded by ancient woods and I would enjoy the moment. My father had loved every acre of this land and had taught Oli and me everything he knew about it. That passion, more than the tutor who made sure we had the necessary Greek and Latin, had brought me to Oxford and geography.

I paddled against the tide towards the river. The trees hung high above the waterline for the moment but soon when the tide was full they would dangle their branches in the creek like fingers trailing over the side of a boat.

My father and Oliver, with the help of the shipwright in Helford, had made me this canoe. I was a tomboy then, trying to match Oliver in everything. For a while it had worked. We were just over a year apart in age, and soon his size and strength had made physical comparisons useless, although I'd pushed for as long as I could.

There had been no competition while on the water. This old canoe had provided us endless trips on the Helford and around its creeks, while we'd pretended that we were travelling on the Amazon, or the Nile, or the Yangtze. The bending oaks and hollies had become far more exotic and dangerous.

Now the water was flat, belying the strong current I paddled against. A white egret perched on a dead oak tree caught my eye. It was like a beacon with nothing to distract from it. Years ago at Oxford, I realised the only way for my worth to be seen was to stand by myself like that egret.

When I reached the mouth of the creek, the north-west wind carried a chill and I felt alone as I hadn't ever before. No doubt this was because I was missing the company of Fleming, Harling, Constance, Hester and Benedict. I was here, my mother was not, and I had no idea what the group of men I would be meeting with on Monday would be like. The only thing I did know is that we were all working towards winning the war. A common goal had helped many a disparate group come together.

The cabin hidden by the pines at the mouth of the creek was untenanted and had been for a while. The quay opposite was empty too as I pulled up to it. The fishermen were still working but clearly not using this quay.

Tying on, I scrambled onto it and into the ruins of the old hut that had once stood here. As children, Oliver and I had haunted this place, pretending it was a fort, and we'd needed to protect the land from attack. Branches carefully selected had been used as our weapons . . . rifle or sword depending on the era we'd chosen.

My foot caught as I walked the remains of the old fish cellar and glanced out of what once had been a window. Looking down, there was a pile of rags and old fishing nets. I untangled my foot and found two rifles, loaded. I stilled, listening. This was no longer a child's game. Examining the rifles closely, I could see they were a French make: MAS. I placed them back under cover then changed my mind. Gathering them, I returned to my canoe, wondering whom it was best to report and hand them over to. These rifles wouldn't change the course of this war, but they had unsettled me. Unlike my earlier feeling, the war wasn't far from here at all; it was an illusion. I paddled swiftly away, looking over my shoulder, but I was alone with the rooks flying overhead, shouting at me to go away.

My pace slowed as the creek became narrower. I picked out the trails that lined both sides. I knew them both intimately. Oliver and I were forever racing along them night and day when not in the school room.

Back at the small landing, I stored the canoe out of sight and checked the rifles. I emptied the rounds in the cartridges, placed them in my pocket and began the journey back to Kestle. I stopped when I smelled smoke. It rose from the chimney of my cottage. My heart lifted. She was back. I dropped the rifles into the mounds of wild garlic and raced down the path, grateful for her return. I had a million questions to ask but in this moment they were unimportant. She was home and we would soon be able to laugh at the fuss and I could wrap her in my arms.

Nearing the cottage, I called out, 'Maman?'

My steps quickened and I ran through the door. 'Maman?'

I sniffed the air . . . smoke, cigarettes, but no perfume. My skin prickled, I slowed my breathing, listened. But nothing. I pushed the door open to the parlour.

'Hello?'

Silence.

A trail of smoke rose from the log in the open fire. My mother's work was still in place. The old kettle was warm. I picked up a fire iron and searched the bedrooms. They were empty too.

Back downstairs, I stood, looking around, wondering who was using my cottage. If it was my mother, she wouldn't hide from me. Whoever it was must have heard me and fled. I returned the poker to the dying fire and closed the door behind me before looking for the key under the flowerpot. It was there, and I locked the door and took the key with me. Something was happening at the cottage.

8

Mrs Nance was in the hall when I returned to Kestle, carrying the rifles. Her glance fixed on them as I put them down on the hall table.

She looked at me, while wringing her hands on a tea towel. 'I was about to send Matthew to find you.'

'Oh.' I blinked, letting my eyes adjust to the darkness in the house after the bright spring day outside.

'Yes, the police.' Mrs Nance paused. 'They rang.'

'And?' I asked.

'I told them you were here, and they asked to send you immediately,' she said, with her glance darting this way and that. 'They found something.'

'What did they find?' Everything in me was on high alert.

'They didn't tell me.' She sighed.

'Until I discover what they have found,' I said, 'I won't draw any conclusions.'

She grabbed my hand and gave it a squeeze, saying nothing. That didn't help me at all. I wanted reassurance but I wasn't going to receive more than what Mrs Nance had given already. Her face was glum but I wouldn't take that train of thought.

I glanced at the tall clock and it was ten thirty. 'If you could ask

Matthew to bring the car around, I will go freshen up.' Walking to the stairs I refused to believe what they'd found was anything important at all. I would remain positive.

*

With my hands folded and my ankles crossed, I waited at the police station. I'd speculated on what they might have discovered on my journey. In the end, I'd concluded it was best not to think about it, but thinking was what I did and did very well.

'Miss Tremayne?' a slight man asked.

I rose to my feet. Now was not the time to correct him. 'Inspector Jenkins?' I asked.

He nodded and said, 'Follow me, please.'

The inspector led me past the front desk and down a corridor. He paused in front of a room with his hand on the door handle, waiting for me to catch up. I held my breath as he opened it and we entered.

No body.

I breathed again. This was not the morgue and I knew that. I focused on what *was* lying on the table instead: the scarf I had hand-painted for my mother for her birthday fifteen years ago. It was unexpected. She had shown me the technique and I had made it for her while she was in London for an exhibition. The colours clashed but she had declared that she loved it more for its uniqueness. She hadn't worn it in years.

'Is this your mother's?' he asked, closing the door.

The bold splashes of blue, red and mustard I'd painted when I was twelve were as recognisable as the shoreline of the Lizard.

'Yes,' I said, my throat tight, 'this is my mother's scarf.'

'Are you certain, Miss Tremayne?' Inspector Jenkins asked.

I nodded. 'Where did you find it?'

'A sergeant in the Home Guard found it near Kynance Cove and reported it when we put out a call on a missing woman.'

I glanced up. 'On the cliffs?'

'About halfway down the path.' He picked up a file and opened it. 'Mrs Nance informed us Mrs Tremayne is French? From l'Aber Wrac'h?' His voice was laced with suspicion.

'She is,' I said.

'She is fluent in German, according to Mrs Nance, and of course her native tongue,' Inspector Jenkins said, noting something in his file.

Silently I added Italian. I would not give them more evidence to make a case against her.

'Was there anything else found with the scarf?' I asked, hoping to move the conversation in a different direction.

'Nothing.' Inspector Jenkins closed the file in his hands. 'We did a thorough search at Kynance.'

'And no one saw her there?'

'She was seen the afternoon of the first, painting on the beach and the cliffs,' the inspector said. 'From interviews, we know that she picked Lily of the Valley, and the vicar informed us she placed flowers on your father's grave at St Anthony. When they exchanged a few words, he noted the paintbox strapped to the back of her bike and another small bag in the basket. We haven't been able to locate these.'

'What happens now?' I asked, ignoring the lump in my throat.

'Mrs Nance has searched her things for a note or any other clues.' Inspector Jenkins smiled kindly. 'I understand you are staying in Kestle.'

'Until Monday then I'll be on the north side of the Helford.'

'Miss Tremayne, if you find anything that would help, please let us know immediately.' He paused then said, 'There is a war on, and we are short of manpower.'

I stood with my hands clenched at my sides, not sure what to say.

'Your mother, according to the housekeeper, has been behaving strangely.' Inspector Jenkins lit a cigarette. 'We have to acknowledge that there is a strong possibility of accidental death or . . . that she is working for the enemy.'

'And do you have cause to believe the latter?' I asked.

'Personally, I think it's more likely, as she is a fifty-year-old-woman, that she was overcome by grief,' he said.

I didn't respond.

'By all accounts your parents were devoted to each other, and she was devastated at your father's death. She was still laying flowers on the grave.'

'They were devoted, and the first of May was the first anniversary of his death,' I said, not liking his current thinking. My mother hadn't been behaving like she was wrapped in unbearable grief at Christmas nor was she down when we spoke. 'But how does that change things?'

'In cases like this, we have to consider her taking her own life.'

'Surely accidental death or even abduction or murder are more likely?' His logic was flawed and it was beginning to rile me. We were discussing my mother, not some grief-stricken soul who hadn't done anything in the past year.

'The latter two not likely here; maybe up London way but not here.' He looked me in the eyes, and said, 'There is no body so the case will remain open. And you are correct; it's possible it was an accidental death.'

'How so?' I asked.

'According to Mrs Nance, your mother left behind her handbag with ID card and ration book, which suggests she had not planned to go away.' He coughed and sent me a sympathetic glance. 'Perhaps she drowned, caught in a riptide and with all the boating activity . . . ' His voice trailed away.

The inspector had no way of knowing that my mother was half mermaid and swam in all weathers. She wouldn't have drowned. She had taught me how to read the water on a beach, an essential skill living near the sea as we did.

'Thank you, Inspector.' His words had been kindly meant but they didn't inspire hope – quite the opposite. I felt numb. I needed time to think and to sketch out a map of my ideas as well as my mother's movements. 'Is there anything more you need from me?'

'Not at this time, Miss Tremayne.' He walked to the door and opened it.

In silence we retraced our steps back to the reception area. Minutes ago, I'd half expected to hear my mother was dead, perhaps hit by a vehicle in the dark on her way home. But with no evidence except a scarf, and no body, I again believed she was off painting, blissfully unaware of the chaos she was causing.

He bowed his head when we had reached the front desk, saying, 'Take care, Miss Tremayne.'

'My mother's scarf?' I asked, not wanting it here as strange evidence of something as yet undefined.

'Ah, yes, there is no point in us holding on to it. The clerk will arrange it.' He turned and spoke to the man while I sank on the empty bench. My legs no longer wanted to support me, nor did my brain want to work. It rejected the thoughts that came crashing down. Instead, I focused on my breathing as my father had taught me when too many details vied for my attention while sketching observations in the field. Once my mind stilled, the order of things would naturally appear. The seemingly logical conclusion that the inspector had drawn – that she had taken her own life – I could not accept.

'Miss Tremayne?' The clerk stood in front of me as I opened my eyes. 'If you could sign for it, please.'

I nodded and scratched my name on the paper then collected

the scarf and walked slowly outside into the afternoon sunshine. Nothing made sense. Where was Maman and who was using Pill Cottage?

I drove back to Kestle while my thoughts stopped and started like a scratched record where the needle kept jumping back to the same notes. Where were her paints and bicycle? Where was she?

*

When things didn't add up, I turned to maps. From the age of eight, I'd been mapping my life day by day since my father had first taught me how to draw one. With his innate surveyor's skill, and with the battlefield cartography training he had, he encouraged me to plot my world. Doing this allowed me to see things with perspective, distance and authority.

Thankfully, Mrs Nance was nowhere to be seen when I returned and I had the kitchen to myself. On Saturdays and Sundays Maman had created magic in here with food and laughter. Pulling down her favourite porcelain teapot, I made tea then opened to a clear page in my notebook. I drew a box in the left-hand corner for the legend of the map. In it I wrote Elise Marie Tremayne née Botrel and the rough scale. With quick strokes, the clear shape of the Lizard appeared on the page. I marked the boundary of the Helford and the Channel then the location of Kestle, depicting it in almost childish imagery of a house. Then I added in St Anthony on the shores of Gillan Creek, and Kynance Cove. Quickly I added in my cottage and I refused to allow my thoughts to linger on the still smouldering fire earlier.

With the main reference points laid down, I let my thoughts cycle backwards through what I knew. On the evening of the thirtieth of April my mother and I had spoken at about ten. As I looked out on the kitchen door to the garden, one thing struck me: love had been on my mother's mind. But then it frequently was where it was almost never on mine. Of course she had spoken to Oliver earlier and that conversation had been all about love.

My parents had loved each other with an astounding passion that hadn't smothered their individuality or careers. My mother's painting had gained depth and insight from my father's belief in her and her work. I knew from my experience with George that such a generous love wasn't on offer often. Most love asks too much.

My ex-fiancé George hadn't cared for Cornwall and that was a warning that I'd ignored from the very start. He was also not good on the water; he couldn't swim well and hated that I rowed for Somerville College. He'd even point-blank refused to punt on the Isis and this had led to many a picnic with me staring longingly at the river while eating sandwiches. It was funny how hindsight provided such a clear image, but it had been muddied by hormones at the time. Hormones, according to Miss Price, were the downfall of many a promising scholar.

I had been in the thrall of hormones that May, stealing off to be together whenever there was a chance. He had not been my first lover. That had happened the summer before when we'd gone to Brittany. I had flirted outrageously with a local boy and he'd proved a good distraction for the month Maman and I had spent there. She'd known what was happening but had only cautioned me to take care and not lose sight of what I truly wanted.

I'd thought I'd found that in George. In my mind he had become my Wimsey except we were sleeping together. But with hindsight he wasn't as clever. I was not sure why he was on my mind now. It had ended years ago. Smiling ruefully, I looked at the date. That was why he was on my mind. Nine years ago today he had proposed. I was eighteen and he was twenty-one.

Banishing thoughts of George, I added Maman's date and place of birth to the map's legend, her marriage to my father and noted the first of May a year ago when my father had died. Maman had thrown a bouquet of Lily of the Valley into my father's grave, followed by a fist of earth.

In the top right-hand corner, I sketched a sprig of her favourite flower. Traditionally in Helston, on the eighth of May, men wore Lily of the Valley in their buttonhole and ladies on their gowns as they danced through the streets celebrating Flora Day. Until my father's accident, my parents had taken part in the noonday dance. And each year Maman kept the French tradition and would give us a sprig of the heavenly scented white bells for the Fête du Muguet to provide good luck for the year.

I pushed these older memories aside and began to trace Maman's last known steps. Her journey from St Anthony to Kynance was almost due south and would have taken at least two hours, longer if she'd met an acquaintance along the route. Knowing her penchant for early morning light, she would have reached Kynance as early in the day as possible. She wouldn't paint when the sun was high, and the colours flat. I loved the mid-day light for sketching as everything was sharper, but she loved the shadows.

My pencil hovered over the page. I longed to mark the spot where she could be found, but something deep down told me it wasn't yet on this map. I could only hope that one day it would be.

She was the legend on Oli's and my map, the key to our lives. I didn't want to think about navigating my life without her but, as each day passed, that thought kept growing.

PART TWO

Associated Press
May 1, 1940

Neutral

The United States is neutral, we are told. What does neutral mean? Is there really such a thing? On my car's gearbox it means nothing is engaged. My car will idle going nowhere. Very rarely are we in a position of not leaning one way or another on any given subject. This is for many reasons . . . most of which we never think about on the surface. For the past six years, I have covered the length and breadth of Europe, providing general sweeping pictures of these countries where so many of our ancestors come from, and other times I dived down into the detail to provide a balanced view. I did this when addressing the situation in Ireland. I went into the topic neutral. My father's family sits on both sides of the issue, with his mother a Catholic from Kerry and his father a Protestant from Belfast. They emigrated first to Nova Scotia and then on to Maine so that they could be together. I wrote my reports using that internal pull, but did that make me or my report neutral or simply more invested?

Just weeks ago, I was in Norway when it fell to the Germans. I lost all pretence of neutrality then. My mother is a Norwegian immigrant to the

United States. My first name is Jakob, the Norwegian for James. I held my grandmother's hand as she bid me farewell, not knowing if I would see her again or what hardships lay in front of her, my aunts, and my cousins, along with the rest of the population.

For this reason, almost immediately after my return to the United States, I crossed the border into Canada and joined the Canadian RAF, lost my US citizenship, became a Canadian and now I find myself sitting in a part of Britain I had never visited before, North Yorkshire. It is a beautiful county filled with hills, dales and a sparkling coastline. The beer is warm and the welcome from the locals even warmer. I hadn't expected that.

My stints in London had shown me a different side to the United Kingdom and it was vastly different.

I always thought the Navy would suit me best with my love and knowledge of the sea, but now I have taken a side along with a ragtag collection of fellow Americans flying fighters across the channel. There's Fred from Boston who, like me, crossed the border. He was born in Liverpool but came to the United States at two years of age and couldn't stand by any longer. Then there's Eric, the farmer, from Minnesota, whose family come from Sweden. We are a few of the men who make up what they call the Eagle Squadrons and we have chosen our side.

This is my last article for the *Associated Press*.

Signing out.
Jake Russell
England

9

11 May 1942

After a fitful night's sleep listening to the owls cry, I rose before the birds, dressed with care, and went into the garden to watch the rest of the world wake up.

My mother loved this time of day as the sun was rising. She explained how she saw it in shades of purple until the light began to turn on the more vibrant colours. I wandered through the fields until I reached one with a view to the mouth of the river. An inversion cloud covered the water with pale-blue sky above it. The rising sun glowed, tinting the edges of the clouds with gold. I turned as if my mother was beside me to ask her how she would paint the scene, but she wasn't there. Since my arrival, I'd felt both her presence and her absence with every step.

Standing high on the plateau above the Helford, I watched the world change from the indistinct shapes of dawn to the defined ones of the day, and I recalled my mother's search for what she described as *impossible light*. It was the moment when the beauty was so sharp, so clear, it hurt and broke into your mind and your soul giving everything new meaning. The only thing she had been able to compare it to was when she'd fallen in love with my father. In that moment of understanding, her perception of everything changed.

The clouds hovering above the mouth of the river dispersed while the sound of the birds, from the caw of the rooks to the sweeter notes of the sparrow, filled the air. Bending to the ground, I ran the soil through my fingers. There hadn't been rain in days, but the earth still retained some of the dew. A mackerel sky – cirrocumulus clouds as my father had taught me – foretold that the weather would change in the next few days, bringing much needed rain to the crops.

Walking back to the house via the lane, I saw Matthew heading off to tend the cows. He nodded at me, and doffed his cap. I dashed towards him.

'Who is the head of the local Home Guard?' I asked.

'Oh, not sure, but Reggie Cannicott would know.' He narrowed his glance. 'Why are you asking?'

'I found two fully loaded French rifles in the old fishing quay on the creek, and in the news about the discovery of my mother's scarf, I neglected to inform the police.'

'I see.'

'Do you know anything about the rifles?' I studied him and he didn't look at ease but I couldn't say why.

'I don't, Miss Merry.' He paused. 'Cannicott's your man.'

'I'm leaving to go to the north side of the river this morning. Can you contact him for me and tell him I have locked them in my father's gun store.'

He nodded.

'Also, have people other than my mother been staying in the cottage?' I asked him. 'There's someone using it. The fire was lit.'

'No, don't think so.' Matthew cleared his throat. 'Don't go down there unless asked, Miss Merry. Must be off to move the cows.' He set off across the fields towards the one near the chapel without another word.

Something about Matthew's reply and the way he refused to

meet my glance suggested he knew more than he was saying. What was the secret? Why had my mother been sleeping at the cottage?

Back inside the house, my bag was packed. Inside was a slip of paper where I'd noted all the changes in the house I'd observed in the hopes that they would tell me something when I had a chance to study them. There was one more place for me to go and I'd been postponing it. With the time remaining, I went up the stairs and straight into my mother's room, wondering if staying alone in the bed she had once shared with my father had become too hard?

Inside, my mother's scent still hung in the air – lemon, lavender and sandalwood. My father's favourite book, *And Then There Were None*, still remained on the nightstand.

On the wall by my father's side of the bed was the old map of the Lizard that he loved. The coast was lined with the rocky cliffs defending the land from the easterly winds and crashing seas. Coves, some beautiful and others functional, appeared at the base of these cliffs. It wasn't a gentle landscape except for the Helford.

Her dressing table appeared as if she would breeze through the door at any moment. Her nightgown was laid out ready for wear. A flash of red then a prism of rainbow colours played off the wall. My mother's diamond and ruby crucifix hung from the dressing table mirror on its intricate gold chain. She never took it off.

I sank onto the stool and lifted it from the mirror. It felt heavier in the hand than it looked. In the centre was a ruby in the shape of a heart. The cross was made of diamonds, with large rubies marking each end. As a child, I had been fascinated with it. Each time she held me, I would pick it up and hold it to the light, watching the stones glow and almost fire. She would say, 'Ah, ma petite, ma maman gave it to me to remind me of her love and of God's love.' She would kiss my hair and hold me closer. 'Some day it shall be yours and it will remind you of God's love and mine.'

Slipping the chain over my head, the cold metal settled above my heart. With a last glance in her dressing room, I walked downstairs and noticed Maman's painting of our sailing yacht *Mirabelle* was missing and in its place was one of the coast of Plage des Anges, near L'Aber Wrac'h. It didn't quite fit the space of the previous and the ghost outline remained on the wall.

I hadn't seen this picture in years, although I remembered her painting it. It was the summer I was fifteen and we were visiting her father. Then, I was less interested in the beach and more intrigued by the boys. It had been a golden month. A few years later, I'd gone back again to do field work for my degree, but by then my grandfather had passed away.

After noting the change in the painting on my inventory, I collected my bag and my boots. It was still early and Mrs Nance would be in later so I left a note on how she could reach me.

The farmyard was deserted when I walked past the barns, my mother's studio and through the gate. I followed the path along the edge of the field that sloped down to the bottom land, which, over time, had become woodland.

Approaching the stile in the hedge, I paused. Each stone told a story, and I had learned about them at my father's side as we'd walked the land. He'd taught me about the development of civilisation here on this remote peninsula, so like the one across the channel that had produced my mother's family in Brittany.

Once over the stile, I headed into the cover of the towering beech trees. Unlike the native sessile oaks, which kept low to the ground, the beech trees reached to the sky, creating a cathedral in this space. The stream rushed down the valley centre towards the creek at Helford. I hopped my way across the stepping stones and onto a path that was forever muddy. Like I had as a child, I climbed onto the old wall to avoid the worst of it.

This sacred space around me felt primeval but the fresh scar of a bomb crater proved that the war was here as it was everywhere else. No place was safe, not even here in these magical woods.

My pace quickened as I came to the first houses of the village. Children were heading towards me on their way to school in Manaccan. They raced and darted about, calling to each other. I remembered those days. My brother and I had attended Manaccan school until a tutor had arrived; then we had both been educated together at home until he'd gone off to Harrow.

With Oliver gone, I'd missed the little schoolhouse and the other children more than ever. My loneliness had been filled with books and study. But, looking back, I think my parents had sensed that I needed more than could be offered in a small school. The old tutor continued to work with me after Oliver had left as he had seen that I was the scholar and not Oliver. In the end, Oliver had followed his heart and attended agricultural college, and I had followed mine to study geography. Both of us had a love of the land in our hearts but had found very different paths to it.

The tide was full. Sunlight fell on the women washing their front steps and the fishermen readying the nets. Helford couldn't look more beautiful on this May day.

'Morning, Miss Merry,' the postmistress called from the shop door as I turned on to the old footbridge.

I waved then walked on past the pub. With so many witnesses, the news that I was carrying a case and heading north across the river would be around the whole area of the Meneage by noon at the latest.

Raising the flag to signal for the ferry, I waited, enjoying the cool breeze and the promise of the heat to come. As I watched the ferry make its way across the river, I reminded myself I had a job to do for Commander Fleming. I may not be quite sure what the exact details were, but, as I had learned, this would become clear if I listened and watched.

'Thought that was you, Merry,' said Jock from the small boat that was serving as the ferry currently. He had filled out since I'd last seen him when he was a gangly youth. Jock and I had been at Manaccan school together. As a child he'd lost an eye and at school he'd worn a patch that had made him look like a pirate, and it still did.

'Hello.' I handed him my bag and boots before I climbed into the boat, grateful I had chosen to wear trousers.

'Good to see you back.' He grinned.

'It's good to be here.'

'Any news on your mother?' he asked. As usual, everyone in the village knew everyone else's business and made no attempt to hide the fact. It was so different to life in intelligence in London.

'None,' I said, and settled on the bench at the stern.

'Mighty odd just disappearing, don't you think?' Jock pushed off with the oar and began to row.

I stared at him.

'Sorry, but 'tis mighty strange,' he said, holding my glance.

Turning from him, I studied the river. It was empty except for an odd collection of vessels consisting of a motorboat launch painted in military grey, and what looked like a French tunny fishing boat. My grandfather had one like it. Out towards the bay, I could just make out the boom that protected the mouth of the river.

'So, with you being a ge . . . og . . . raph . . . er,' he said, breaking the word up slowly like it bothered him, 'will you be heading to that funny lot at Ridifarne?'

'Why funny?' I asked. Two could play the game of gathering intelligence.

'Well, they don't do much.' He sent me a glance with his good eye. 'But I suppose they are all about maps and that don't take too much hard work, as you know.'

I smothered a sharp retort. 'Making good maps takes a great deal of information. Can you imagine if a map didn't show you exactly where the Manacles were?'

'But we know where they are.' Jock rolled a shoulder towards the bay.

'*We* do,' I replied, 'but many don't and it's important our Navy knows these things, too.'

Jock shrugged and hopped out of the boat as it hit the sand on the beach in front of the Ferry Boat Inn. He pulled it well up so I wouldn't have to walk through the water. Standing on the beach was a tall broad-shouldered man. He carried himself in such a way I gathered he must be Commander Holdsworth although he wore no uniform. The man grabbed my bag from Jock.

'Are you Dr Meredith Tremayne?' The man looked me up and down. 'Oxford scholar and map wizard?'

Fleming had clearly played his favourite joke.

'Yes, I'm Dr Tremayne,' I replied. 'You must be Commander Holdsworth.'

'I am,' he said.

Clearly Holdsworth considered this sufficient introduction in front of Jock, for he strode in the direction of Ridifarne past the row of cottages and then down on to the beach. Only then did he turn to me, saying, 'Most of the officers left before first light for training and won't be back until this evening.' He stopped in front of the steep steps that led up to Ridifarne's gardens. 'I know from Fleming you are born and bred here. Have you been to Ridifarne before?'

'I've been to drinks with the Bickford-Smiths many times,' I said. 'Although the Helford divides the area, the communities are small.' I paused on one of the garden's many terraces to admire the striking water feature in the shape of a Celtic cross. It nodded to the history of the area, both Celtic and Christian. 'How many men do you have here?' I asked.

'We have six officers staying here at the house along with my wife Mary and myself,' Holdsworth said. 'There are a further sixteen crew who live on the boats.'

A petite elegant woman appeared on the upper terrace.

'Allow me to introduce you both,' Holdsworth said. 'Mary, this is Dr Meredith Tremayne.'

'This is a most unexpected, but delightful, surprise.' Mary smiled, then glanced at her husband. 'I'll have Mrs Newton make up the small room. If you'll excuse me a moment.'

'Yes, we can't have you bunking in with the men as we planned,' the commander said.

I laughed.

'Glad to see you have a sense of humour,' Holdsworth murmured.

'I work with Commander Fleming. If I didn't have a sense of humour, I would go mad,' I said, lowering my voice to a confidential whisper.

He assessed me again.

'While Mary is sorting your accommodation, I can show you the map room, aka the dining room,' Holdsworth said, leading the way.

We entered the house through the French windows to the sitting room. It was exactly as I remembered it from previous visits, with the unusual fireplace flanked by an alcove either side. The beamed ceiling was high and painted white while the furnishings were comfortable but covered in charts at present. The hallway was bright and spotless, but as we turned into the small dining room, the chaos was overwhelming. Every surface was covered in maps, with more still on the walls.

From a quick glance at them, I could see where these men had been on the northern coast of Brittany. From those yearly trips to visit my grandfather in L'Aber Wrac'h, I knew that a yacht could make the journey to that part of France in twenty-five straight hours with favourable winds. This team might make the journey during the hours of darkness in the right boat. But unless the launches were very fast, the short summer nights to come would soon prove a problem.

'How often do you make the crossing to Brittany?' I asked Holdsworth.

'That didn't take you long.' He placed his hands on the table. 'Not often enough is the simple answer.'

'You need to wait for the right tides,' I mused, studying the nearest map. 'Enough darkness too. How long does the crossing take?'

'Depends on the boat. But when we have an MGB,' he said then clarified, 'a motor gun boat, provided the conditions are right, we can do a journey in three and a quarter hours.'

'Travelling at—' I paused to do the maths '—roughly thirty knots.'

'No wonder Fleming recommended you,' Holdsworth said.

'Commander Fleming's reasons are clear only to himself,' I said. 'Am I right in thinking that, having seen the boats in the river – none of which are able to do that speed – you are not making any crossings presently?'

'You would be correct.' He sighed. 'We have become a training unit because the MGB sits in Dartmouth with the team from SIS and is not given to us.'

'Isn't that a bit wasteful?' I asked. From the commander's

statement it was clear this team was not part of the Special Intelligence Service, therefore they must be a part of the Secret Operations Executive formed in forty.

'Well, I've just met you, but I can tell you'd be wasted on making maps alone.' He walked to the door. 'I'm off to join the training. Take the day to settle in and this evening you can meet the team. We have dinner planned at the Ferry Boat Inn.'

'Lovely. I haven't been in years.' I looked at the chaos and then at the commander. 'May I sort these out?'

'Please do and make yourself at home. Ask Mary for anything you may need. She runs things.' He left and I turned to the task at hand.

While sorting the mess, I took my time examining the maps. Like the Cornish coast, the shoreline of Brittany was riddled with reefs, reaching out into the sea, ready to grab an unwary mariner. Crossing and landing at night would be treacherous. I found some buoys marked on one chart, but not on another which covered the same area. They weren't dated so there was no way to tell which was more accurate. Both the Allies and the Axis had been making all navigation harder with lights shut off or dimmed. Some lighthouses were repainted in camouflage so that enemy pilots couldn't use them on their flight paths. Trinity House, who looked after all of the United Kingdom's lighthouses, had pilots who worked hard through the nights to bring our ships safely into ports. Holdsworth's men had no such assistance. It was no wonder they hadn't been as successful as they wanted to be. In fact, it was a miracle they had succeeded at all.

All they had were these charts. Maps were as much about what one saw on them as read onto them. But in this chaos around me, the information could be lost. With so many buoys missing or their light removed, the navigator would have to be precise. My grandfather had spoken often of reading the water. There were few masters who could navigate from sound and smell alone but then he had fished the waters of Brittany all his life. I preferred working with equations and charts. Dead reckoning rather than instinct for me every time. I was much more comfortable with the calculations required to determine where my boat was using a set position incorporating estimates of speed, direction and course over time.

There was a knock and the door opened.

'I'm sorry to disturb you while you are working—' Mary stood in the doorway '—but I thought you might like some lunch.'

I'd been so involved in getting acquainted with the work being done from Ridifarne that I'd lost track of time and surroundings. I stood and flexed my shoulders. 'Yes, thank you.'

'As it's such a beautiful day, I've brought it outside,' she said, gesturing towards the garden.

I held my hand over my eyes and stepped out onto the sun-drenched terrace. As always, it struck me how different the river appeared when standing on the north side. The view was stunning. Opposite Ridifarne was Helford Point, with the Shipwrights Arms beyond it and the village to the left. Further along the bank of the river was the cluster of houses at Treath with its quay followed by the buildings of Golden Gear and onto the grandeur of Pengarrock, which was only visible by its tower from this angle.

'When did you arrive here, Mrs Holdsworth?' I asked as she passed me a plate of sandwiches.

'Mary, please, and may I call you Meredith?'

'Merry, please,' I replied.

'How lovely. Is your family Welsh?' she asked.

'No, Cornish and Breton,' I explained. 'I was named after a Breton saint, Meriadek or Merasek in Cornish, but my father opted for an Anglicised spelling to keep it easier for everyone involved.'

'How fascinating,' Mary said. 'As for your question, we arrived last summer. Mrs Bickford-Smith was so kind to simply hand the house over and it's perfect with its own beach front and enough land around it not to be overlooked.'

That statement confirmed the commander's earlier remark that Mary ran things and was more than aware of all the activity the commander's team were involved in. That would make things easier between us as I wouldn't have to dance around possibly confidential topics.

'You'll enjoy the men. They are a good lot. There are a few characters among them, of course, but Gerry wouldn't be without a single one.' She poured the tea. 'I bet Gerry's face was a picture when he realised that Dr Tremayne was a woman.'

'It was but I'm used to it,' I said wryly.

'Frightful, isn't it?' She shook her head. 'Have you had to struggle . . . I mean sacrifice a great deal to become so accomplished?'

'To achieve anything there are always things that drop by the wayside,' I admitted, taking another sandwich filled with thickly cut ham, a luxury I hadn't had in a while. The rations must be greater for an operational team. 'But there are more opportunities in the current environment than in past times when women were given few chances outside of the home.'

A woman approached us, and Mary rose to her feet.

'This is Mrs Newton,' said Mary, making introductions. 'She helps with things here. This is the commander's new geographer, Nellie, Dr Tremayne.'

I stood and held out a hand. 'Hello.'

The woman shook it firmly. 'Nice to meet you, Dr Tremayne.'

'Nellie's husband, Bonnie, was working on a merchant ship in Scotland when Gerry recruited him,' Mary said. 'Mrs Newton and her boys were there too, although originally from Guernsey.

In fact, it was Commander Fleming that suggested to Gerry that Bonnie Newton join the team.'

I was not the first to be implanted here at Ridifarne. I filed this piece of information away.

'I won't keep you but wanted to say I'm off now and to enjoy this evening.' Mrs Newton smiled at both of us and headed down the path through the garden.

'Shall I show you to your room now?' Mary asked.

'If it's fine with you I'd like to get a bit more done with the maps,' I said, hoping to leave the room in a state of order so I could start afresh tomorrow morning.

I helped to gather the lunch plates before I headed back to the work at hand, wondering whether the rest of the team were as likeable and competent as the Holdsworths and Nellie Newton.

10

Mary had apologised several times about the quality of the room, but the space was more than adequate even though I looked out on the rising hillside that faced the lane and not the river. This room would have been used by the Bickford-Smiths' maid, but it was fit for purpose with a single bed, a chest of drawers, a nightstand, a sink, a small desk and a spindle back chair. Either Mary or Mrs Newton had unpacked my bag and heavens knows what they made of the strange mixture of clothing they found within it.

It was a good thing I'd included two evening gowns because it was clear that standards were kept despite the war. After washing my face, I lay on the bed for a few minutes, preparing myself to meet the officers. Voices calling to each other heralded their return. The plumbing groaned and the atmosphere of the house changed. It was no longer a sleepy quiet place but one full of testosterone and reminiscent of the atmosphere in the Oxford boathouses.

I'd been lost in maps until late afternoon when Mary dragged me from the dining room to walk in the garden and to show me the quirks of the house. Drinking water came from the stream that ran under the house and was filtered in the pantry through a nifty contraption. The second bathroom had a comfortable tub and the views from the windows in the three south-facing bedrooms were breath-taking. They offered up such a different perspective on the land and river I knew so well.

The house appeared imposing from the roadside where the tall door of carved granite made for a grand entrance into what was essentially a blissfully comfortable cottage with quirky fireplaces and all the hallmarks of the Arts and Crafts design. I'd mapped the layout from the kitchen with its larder and pantry to the five bedrooms and two bathrooms upstairs. I even knew the names of the men in each room, thanks to Mary's tour:

Lieutenant Commander Francis Brooks Richards
Lieutenant Jake Russell
Lieutenant John Baker
Sub-Lieutenant Edward Smith
Sub-Lieutenant Thomas Johnson
Warrant Officer Michael Stubbs

The clock in the hall chimed the quarter hour. I rose and slipped on my evening gown. It was blue that suited my dark hair which I'd rolled and pinned. With a touch of lipstick and powder, I was as ready as I'd ever be to face this.

After one last glance in the small mirror above the washbasin to check I had no lipstick on my teeth, I picked up my evening bag and went downstairs. I paused on the bottom step, preparing myself. Walking into a sitting room filled with strange men was no worse than walking into a lecture hall for the first time. Each new meeting I attended for Commander Fleming was the same. But this group would know that I was a woman by now and that would immediately change the atmosphere. My evening gown accentuated my femininity rather than my mind. But this could be useful too, I had learned – and they would have no qualms about my intelligence once we started working together.

The sitting room door opened, and a tall man stood on the threshold. He stared. Finally, he found his voice.

'Welcome . . . Dr Tremayne,' he said.

Commander Holdsworth had withheld the key information regarding my sex after all. The clock struck the hour.

'Pink gins at six,' he said, once the tolling had stopped.

A little Dutch courage would not go amiss. 'How lovely.'

'You are indeed.' He opened the door wide so that I could enter. I cast him a sideways glance, wary of his charm.

Four men in evening dress all turned as I entered the room. Commander Holdsworth's steady gaze helped me to brace myself for their scrutiny. Their expressions clearly stated, 'she can't be clever because she's too pretty', but instead of focusing on their disbelief, I let the glimpse of the river through the open doors calm my nerves. Of course, these men would have been more comfortable working with me if I was a man, but as there was a war on, they would have to manage to work with a woman instead.

The lonely cry of a herring gull broke the stunned silence in the room.

'Gentlemen, this is our new expert from the halls of Oxford via the Admiralty and Commander Fleming,' Holdsworth said. 'Dr Meredith Tremayne.'

'Trust Fleming to find the only beautiful Millie the Mapper in England,' one of the men muttered to his companions in a distinctive American accent.

'Merry the mapper,' I corrected and looked directly at the American for his voice, although whispered, had been clear. Then my breath caught as his glance met mine. He was the American in the British uniform. The glint in his eye told me he remembered too. Oh God, how awkward that I would be working with a man I'd flirted with. I'd have to be careful.

'Excellent, I can see we're off to a good start,' Holdsworth said. 'Dr Tremayne, this is our irreverent resident Yank, Nipper.'

'Jake Russell, hailing from Maine,' the American said, staring openly at me.

'Nipper?' I raised an eyebrow and accepted a pink gin from the man who opened the door to me. 'Looks more like a Great Dane.'

'Agreed.' The commander laughed. 'But a Yank nonetheless.'

'Nipper was so keen he crossed the border and joined the Canadian RAF in forty. You can trust a Jack Russell, or in this case a Jake Russell, to hunt down his prey,' said the commander.

'You're a pilot?' I asked, immediately thinking of Oli.

'He is, and a damned fine sailor too. But Nipper tends to let it go to his head, and we make sure he keeps returning to solid ground,' the commander said. 'Fleming sent him our way just like you.'

I took a sip of my gin, digesting this information. That was why he was in Room 39. But why had Fleming sent me here if the American and Newton were already feeding back information to him?

'Nipper's been with us awhile,' the commander continued.

Yet America had only entered the war in December. Why was he so eager to join the fray? English surname. Scandinavian appearance.

The American stepped forward holding out his hand. 'Hello, Dr Tremayne.'

'Lieutenant,' I said, noting the blond sun-washed hair and the smattering of freckles across his nose and cheeks; very wholesome. His build was the same as every rower I had ever met on the banks of the Isis. Tall, very tall, lean but muscular, especially the thighs. I would put money on the fact that this American had rowed competitively.

'This is Francis Brooks Richards, my second in command, and rounding out our international team is Irishman John Baker,' Commander Holdsworth said. 'It's a small gathering this evening, but the others will be joining us later.' He took a sip of his gin then continued, 'And to further put you all in the picture, gentlemen, Dr Tremayne brings with her degrees in geography, ace sailing skills, a keen knowledge of both the Cornish and Breton coasts as well as fluency in French, German and Breton.'

'A paragon,' said Baker, raising his glass. He was immaculately dressed and reminded me of a smart City banker. His blue eyes danced with mischief.

'I wouldn't go so far,' I said wryly, as we all stepped out onto the terrace into the evening sunshine. I could see the banter here would be similar to the boathouse and I was fine with that.

Brooks Richards came to stand beside me.

'There's *Mutin*,' he said, pointing to the sizeable sailing ketch by Helford Point that reminded me of my grandfather's boat. 'She's our operations headquarters and the ratings live on her.'

'Is it a tunny boat?' I asked, admiring her lines.

'Well spotted,' Brooks Richards said. '*Mutin* is very similar but it was built by the French Navy in nineteen twenty-six as a training vessel for pilots to learn how to steer through coastal waters.'

From the bay, a stream of fishing boats made their way towards Helford with a cover of gulls announcing their arrival. It was such a peaceful sight. Yet the boom across the river was being raised into place, a reminder of the war and why we were all gathered here.

'The men are off to the Shipwrights Arms, I suspect.' He pointed to a small rowing tender leaving *Mutin*'s side. 'It's all training currently as the nights are so short.' Brooks Richards took a sip of his gin before asking, 'You've sailed from here to Brittany?'

'Many times,' I said. 'My mother is Breton.'

'Does she live in Cornwall?' the American asked as he came to stand with us.

I swallowed. This was the first time I needed to speak about Maman to people who had no knowledge of her. What could I say? The truth was the only way forward on this one.

'Currently I don't know where she is. She hasn't been seen since the first of May.' Saying it made it real in a way even dealing with the police hadn't. Maman was gone ten days.

'Disappeared?' Russell asked, sending a look to Brooks Richards.

'Yes,' I said, my mouth drying.

Again he looked to Brooks Richards.

'It's very worrying,' I continued. 'And frustrating as there is little if anything I can do.'

'I'm sorry.' The American's voice softened. 'It must be very hard not knowing.'

I turned to him, looking up. His insight surprised me.

'My mother hasn't had any news from her parents in Oslo since Norway fell to the Nazis,' he said.

I had been right about his Scandinavian ancestry.

'She says that's what bothers her the most,' he said. 'Her thoughts track to the worst while praying for the best.'

'I'm sorry for your mother and her family.'

'Thank you.' He looked at me directly and attraction coursed through me.

'I want to apologise for what I said earlier,' he said.

'For calling me Millie the mapper?' I asked.

'Yes, it was dismissive and wrong.' He smiled ruefully.

The apology was unexpected. But he was proving to be just that in every way.

I laughed. 'I've been called far worse. Besides I love nothing more than making a map and telling people where to go.'

'Somehow that doesn't surprise me.' He took a sip of his drink but continued to watch me while doing so. It was as if I didn't add up for him in some way. He didn't add up for me either.

Mary came to my side while the American was pulled into conversation with Baker.

'Thank you for becoming part of the team,' she said.

It seemed a strange comment and I wasn't sure where she was heading with it. Nothing was quite what I'd expected. But then that was why I was here.

'They're risking their lives on every mission, and the more information they have on coastlines, towns and villages, the better,' she continued.

Looking at the fishing boats safely at anchor, I imagined that never knowing when the men were coming back from enemy-occupied territory must be unbearable for Mary. It was clear the Holdsworths were a couple very much in love. But it was war, and women all over the country faced this fear every day. Mary, at least, played an active role.

We finished our drinks and set off down through the garden and onto the footpath that led to the river. The sight of men in evening dress walking along the beach reminded me of summers past. Both Oliver and I brought friends home during the holidays. Sunburns, sailing, and evening wear every night all felt very distant and yet this evening echoed it. Those days were filled with careless abandon while tonight, despite the smiles and pink gins, there was a solemn feel.

From the beach we continued on to the small lane lined with whitewashed cottages. Children played with a ball and fishing nets were laid out to dry over the walls. It was a timeless Cornish scene with cumulus clouds just stealing some colour from the setting sun.

Lieutenant Baker strolled by my side with a cigarette in hand. 'How long will you be with us, Dr Tremayne?' he asked.

'As long as I'm helpful,' I said. 'Or until I'm needed elsewhere.'

'Suitably vague,' he said. 'I'm impressed.'

Two more men joined us as we walked and I assumed they must be Johnson and Stubbs.

'It is . . . an interesting group,' I said.

He laughed. 'Diplomatically put. We are a ragtag bunch of misfits with the posh, the American, the northerners, and me. But somehow we have pulled together as a team.' He took a drag of his cigarette. 'Funny how war unites a group that would never be together otherwise.'

Commander Holdsworth entered the inn first and led us towards a large table, past many faces I recognised including Lady Seaton. By tomorrow people on both sides of the Helford would know of my return and with whom I had been seen. In fact, the great lady rose to her feet and called out to the commander in a voice loud enough for the whole restaurant to hear.

'I'm so pleased you've listened to my advice, Commander, and contacted Meredith.' Lady Seaton beamed at me. 'We all thought her foolish to have gone to university, but I understand she is very good at drawing maps, which should be of some use to you.'

'She will fit in with the team very well.' Commander Holdsworth glanced first at me then at his second in command, Brooks Richards, his lips pressed tight to disguise his amusement.

Lady Seaton reached out for my hand as I neared. 'Good to see you, Meredith; you must be so worried about your mother.'

'She's on a painting trip,' I said, not wanting this conversation at all. Lady Seaton was well-meaning but interfering. Maman's disappearance must be the main topic of conversation around dinner tables. Scandal is a good topic at any time but it would offer a great form of distraction during a war.

One of the skills I had tried to learn from Maman was to have an exit strategy in every situation. If I didn't find one now, Lady Seaton would demand more of my time, inconveniencing those waiting for me.

For years I'd watched my mother in similar circumstances and had finally asked her about it.

'Very well, ma petite, you are old enough to understand.' She had looked to the far side of the room. 'You must always have an exit, an emergency one from a room or a situation. And exits sometimes require more than doors. They can require windows but more often words of . . . excuse or invention.'

This room offered many doors and windows but they were not helpful. The team were all standing and waiting for me to join them. The last thing I wanted to do was to hold them back from anything, even their dinner.

'If you'll excuse me,' I said, dropping my voice to almost a whisper, debating whether to use an excuse or be truthful. Looking at her face, I tried to assess which would cause the least discomfort to Lady Seaton, an indomitable woman of title who expected priority. She would accept the urges of nature, I guessed, over my need to join my party at the table. No doubt Maman would have found something much more creative and possibly wicked.

'I need to powder my nose,' I said.

'But of course.' Lady Seaton stepped aside, holding my hand for a second. She was well-meaning for the most part and concerned about my mother.

Standing in the ladies' room for long enough to have the trip appear realistic, I peered in the mirror, silently apologising to Maman for the total lack of imagination on my exit. It was neither clever nor gracious but it had worked and that was all that mattered. I checked my hair. Taking a deep breath, I adjusted my mother's crucifix around my neck and wished I could ask her what to do about the American. I smiled, thinking her answer might surprise some but not me.

I turned from the mirror and wicked thoughts. Tonight, I had to demonstrate my worth as a part of what I had already seen was a closely bonded team. Once that was achieved, I would dig deeper to find the difficulties between the teams operating covertly to the coast of France.

11

12 May 1942

The smell of bacon rose from the galley and mixed with the aroma of coffee and diesel. The engines rumbled below, and *Mutin*'s anchor was lifted. At the end of dinner last night, the commander decided that I would join them for their training exercises today. The time of departure was 0400 and the location was a beach. No further details were provided.

The waters of the Helford were untroubled by the southerly wind, unlike my hair, which was whipping my face as I stood on the deck. Dawn was an hour away and I felt the excitement of a childhood Christmas morning pulsing through me. I wanted to see, hear, and experience everything today, witnessing a team in action. Hopefully this would begin to fill the gaps in my knowledge.

With no set duration for my placement here, there was no time to relax. Each moment must be used to seek out information for Fleming, to gain key insight to what was needed on maps to aid our forces, and either find my mother, or to come to some peace about her disappearance.

Water bounced off the hull as we slipped through the narrows, reminding me of countless journeys through this restriction of the estuary. On a morning like this in June thirty-eight, my parents, Oli and I began six weeks together sailing the coast of Brittany. The trip provided so much fun and laughter as well as the opportunity for some fieldwork on the coastline. On that trip, I'd refined our charts. They could be useful for this team. Tomorrow I would collect my canoe, head to the boatyard at Gweek to check on our yacht and recover them.

The moody sky lightened as we neared the mouth of the river. The boom across it had been lowered for the fishing boats. They would have set off an hour earlier as had half the team who were travelling by road to Praa Sands. The freshening breeze tickled the surface of the water, and I enjoyed the feel of the vessel making its way into the bay away from the protection of the headlands.

We passed the sensuous curves of Nare Point. Various decoy structures had been built on and around it to make it look like Falmouth docks in the darkness, in hopes it might fool an enemy pilot on a cloudy night. But from the sea it remained unmistakable. As I searched the horizon for the buoy that marked the treacherous Manacle rocks, the sound of feet reminded me that I was not on the boat to enjoy the view, but to be a part of the crew.

Pierre Guillet, a solid man of the sea with dark hair and brown eyes, was a tunny fisherman from Brittany I'd been told last night. He was teaching a new seaman and I smiled at his use of the English language. Tapping into memories of time with my grandfather, I moved to one of the ropes and tidied it.

Pierre spoke while my mind translated what he said, 'You know your way around a tunny boat.'

'I did once,' I replied in his native language.

'You speak Breton,' he said, surprised.

'A bit but I'm out of practice these days. It was my mother who taught me.'

'They told me you were an English girl,' Pierre said.

'Not everything is always as it seems.' I glanced across the boat to where the American was speaking to the Irishman Baker, wondering why Fleming had placed Jake Russell here.

'True,' Pierre said.

We were a little too close to the Manacles for my liking and I was about to say so when Pierre spoke abruptly to the seaman on the helm. The boat turned sharply, and Pierre muttered that the man in question had had too much beer last night.

'That's not good,' I replied.

'Today it is not so important,' he said. 'We go to Praa beach, but it will matter more a different time.'

The commander called to me and I ventured below. On the table were charts that I hadn't seen yesterday.

'Do you think you could take the information and update them for us?' he asked.

'Yes,' I said. 'Shall I do them now?'

'Today is about training. On board we have a newly designed dinghy to test because the surf creates one of our biggest challenges.' He walked to the door.

'With the Atlantic at your back it would be.' I glanced down at the charts and asked, 'Commander, when was the last operation?'

'We haven't done any for a month,' he replied, not meeting my glance but pushing a chart aside. 'Why do you ask?'

'I was wondering how current this is?' I pointed to the map of L'Aber Wrac'h.

'Very, although there might be a more up-to-date one on the SIS's MGB in Dartmouth. We last used it a month ago.' He sighed.

His frustration was tangible.

'Do you share crews as well?' I asked.

'Sometimes it feels that's all we are . . . crew or a training unit.' His hands clenched. 'Our skills and manpower are wasted. I mentioned as much to Fleming the last time I saw him.'

'Do you see any solutions?' I asked.

'None that I'm allowed,' he said and went on deck.

Looking at the disarray on the table in front of me, I was determined to make obtaining the charts on *Mirabelle* a priority tomorrow. But I wasn't here solely to update maps and I would guess it wouldn't be long before the commander realised that, if he hadn't already.

Back on deck, I studied the small array of boats looking for the one the commander mentioned. Out of the corner of my eye, I saw Lieutenant Russell with Pierre. They were speaking French. Russell's grasp wasn't perfect, but it was reasonably fluent. He turned and met my glance. It wasn't a welcoming look unlike a few days ago. But who was I trying to fool? I was a woman among men. It was a case of tolerating my presence because they were told to. My worth had yet to be proven and I wasn't here to do that but to gather information.

The relationship between the crew members was jovial, with them ribbing each other regarding things I knew nothing about. So, I listened and learned. Despite the defined roles of skippers and coxswains and so on, they all chipped in, including Commander Holdsworth.

As we rounded Lizard Point, dolphins surfaced, and joy filled me as it always did upon sighting them. The pod swam along with us and the sky changed from a faint blue to vibrant orange. The sea state rose with waves dashing against the Man of War rocks. The spray brought the taste of salt to my tongue. A sense of well-being filled me which I shouldn't have now. Too much was wrong in the world but in this moment I was whole. It was something to hold onto in the midst of it all.

'A penny for them?' the American asked, interrupting my thoughts.

'They are not worth that,' I said.

'A moment ago, you were smiling and the sun shone, then the clouds rolled in,' he said.

His eyes were kind and I bit back the sharp retort that would have been so easy to make.

'I could say my happiness was due to looking at the oldest rocks in Cornwall.' I pointed to the Man of War outcrop as a wave crashed against them.

'And the unhappiness?' he asked.

'Nothing,' I lied.

'Your mother?' he asked.

I half smiled. 'She is never far from my thoughts at the moment.'

'Understandable.' He paused. 'What's her name?'

'Elise.'

'Are you like her?' he asked, holding onto one of the halyards as the boat rode the swell.

I opened my eyes wide. Was he making small talk or was this an inquisition? For the moment I would assume the former.

'In appearance yes,' I said, picturing her on the deck of *Mirabelle* with her hair blowing in the wind and a smile on her face. 'In disposition no.' I turned from him and watched the sea. Artistic, impulsive and loving. Those words described her as well as wicked. Her sense of fun was infectious and ever so naughty. I'd put those characteristics aside during my studies. It was hard enough to be taken seriously as a woman in an academic world. This saddened me but sacrifices had to be made to succeed. If I didn't it would be harder for the women following me. I had seen what my tutors had given up and I understood the same would be required of me. However, since working with Fleming, some of my old self had reappeared. It had helped keep my sanity when information on my desk was bleak.

'Did you sail often? It's obvious that you know one end of a boat from another.'

I shook my head to clear it.

'It's in the genes,' I said. 'My grandfather was a fisherman.'

'So Pierre mentioned.' Russell looked to the Breton who was instructing the youngest member of the crew, a fellow Frenchman. 'Nothing's a secret here – not among a crew this tight. Our lives depend on trust.' His glance met and held mine for a moment.

I was here to relay information back and I had to assume the same was true of him. Did he know this about me or simply suspect it? How did that fit in with trust? Or were truth and trust entirely different things?

In an uncomfortable silence, we watched the passing coastline displaying steep cliffs with their feet in pristine coves, caves with seals popping their heads out, and lone defensive lookout posts peering into the distance. He didn't have to stand here with me. It was beginning to feel like this was his assigned role but not from Fleming. I was certain Fleming hadn't warned him of my arrival. His surprise had been genuine. Or had that simply been the reaction to the fact I was a woman, the one with whom he had flirted early one morning a week ago?

I glanced over my shoulder to see what the others were doing. All were busy with tasks except the tall American. Surely there was something he could do. We were under full sail with strong south-easterly winds, achieving, I imagined, close to ten knots.

'How often do you train?' I asked.

'Most days, whether it's rowing for strength and endurance or firearms both night and day,' Russell said, his voice as smooth as his Hollywood-like appearance. I couldn't help thinking that he was too good to be true, and therefore not to be relied on. But by doing that I was reacting the same way people responded to me. I must keep an open mind.

'That's a rigorous regime,' I said, tucking a strand of hair back. His glance followed the movement of my fingers and I wished

I'd taken more time with my appearance this morning, which was the last thing I should be thinking today. I would need to be careful around this man. Turning away from his direct stare, I spied Mullion Island ahead. Despite the choppy sea, we were making good progress.

'The physical strain of some missions would defeat many,' he said. 'We can be on an operation for days with no rest if a storm blows in or a drop is missed.'

'How long have you been with Commander Holdsworth?' I asked.

'Fleming pinched me just before the US joined the war in December,' Russell said.

'And why Nipper?' I asked, still trying to gather information. 'Did this crew give you the nickname?'

He laughed. 'No, I'm afraid it's been with me since my under-graduate years at Bowdoin. My love of music and the Jack Russell logo on RCA records were obvious to my friends.' He pointed. 'What can you tell me about that?'

'Loe Bar is one of the most treacherous shorelines on the Cornish coast, with its steep shingle beach, dangerous currents and powerful waves.' It looked deceptively welcoming in the glori-ous morning light. 'Behind it is Loe Pool, the largest freshwater lake in Cornwall.' I squinted into the distance. 'It's a beautiful if eerie place.'

'Eerie?' he asked.

'Well, apart from the riptides on the beach, the lake itself can be treacherous,' I explained. 'I wouldn't swim there.'

He fixed his intense blue eyes on me. 'No?'

'Too many have drowned there,' I said. 'The lake is filled with weed, and many have been caught in that. Legend has it that Excalibur was thrown into the pool.'

'King Arthur's sword?' He studied the coastline more carefully.

'The very one,' I said. 'Tintagel Castle on the north coast is . . .'

'Where Arthur was conceived,' he finished. 'I studied various versions of the legend from Mallory's *Morte d'Arthur* to Tennyson's *Idylls of the King* in my freshman year.'

So Lieutenant Russell was a romantic.

'You studied English literature?' I asked. This might explain his reading Sayers.

'Don't sound so surprised.' The corner of his mouth lifted into a half smile.

The boat pitched steeply, and I reached out and grabbed a halyard.

'Steady,' Russell said, his hand at my elbow where it remained for a second longer than necessary. I shook my arm free and returned my attention to the landmarks in the distance.

'And Porthleven is coming up,' I said.

'You really do know these waters.'

'Like the back of my hand.' I scanned the sea. 'Each cove tells a story.'

'Of shipwreck, lost treasure?' He grinned. 'I like the idea that they tell stories.'

'Some do,' I said. 'But mostly they speak about the people who have lived and died there. The shore is both the beginning and the end.' I turned to him, unable to make him out. 'How did you become a sailor?'

'My father was a fisherman,' he said quietly. 'He died at sea twenty years ago. As you mentioned, the sea isn't always kind.'

'I'm sorry for your loss,' I said. 'You were very young to lose a father.'

'I didn't think so at the time.' His voice was tinged with regret. 'I was fifteen and full of myself.'

Jake Russell aka Nipper was full of surprises and like no one I'd ever met.

12

The long wide sweep of Praa Sands appeared. Waves rolled in, racing up to the cement defences scattered along the beach like a child had spilt their box of blocks. After securing anchors fore and aft, the men began lowering the varied boats I'd seen stowed on the deck. The one with a bow at both ends meant it wouldn't need turning around, which could save time and lives. There were several canoes that required assembly as well as long white boards reminding me of belly boards but far longer.

'What are they?' I asked Brooks Richards.

'A surfboard I am told. An idea gleaned from an Australian chap,' he said. 'They can be good fun but I'm not finding them fit for purpose.' He walked over to a group assembling a collapsible canoe.

'We are going to do some practice landings,' the commander said as he passed. 'I don't suppose you'd volunteer to be a passenger?'

'Of course,' I said and scrambled over the side of the boat and into a dinghy, riding roughly over the charging surf. Boxes of cargo, a coxswain and three seamen on the oars joined me. The elbow of the young rating next to me bashed into my side.

'Pardon, Mademoiselle,' he said.

'Row, Piron, and don't kill the passenger,' said the coxswain. 'Or flirt with her.'

Piron blushed. He looked impossibly young, and I was intrigued that they had at least two Frenchmen in the crew.

The boat crested a wave and came crashing down the other side. The load felt unbalanced, and we would be lucky not to be swamped, overturned or both as the waves rushed onto the beach. Conditions could be worse, like those these men worked in, under the cover of darkness and heading onto treacherous beaches that might be mined. My thoughts raced to find what I could do to help in the moment but also what I could add to a map.

The boat climbed to the peak of each wave and came down hard into the trough, filling the dinghy with water. After three waves I was soaked top to bottom. The men on the oars pulled hard to fight the tide forcing us out to sea while the wind worked with us. The cox was doing a fine job of steering us towards the beach, but he wasn't helping the men to work in unison. Progress was slow and I longed to take an oar, or, failing that, begin calling orders. As it was, it was difficult to keep my seat in the boat. If I had an oar, I would have had something to hold onto.

On the beach, several men walked down to the shore. They had binoculars, clipboards and one held a cine camera. Another boat overtook us and I noted that the American lieutenant was acting as the cox.

Russell called out to his oarsmen to pull together, and they did. The men around me responded in kind. I watched the interplay between the men under his command and his confidence.

'Pull!' he shouted. His American accent drifted across the rough sea to our boat. 'You can't control the conditions when rowing, but you can control your response to them.'

'We're not the bloody Harvard crew,' the man behind me shouted.

The American laughed. 'You'd never make the cut.'

'And you would?' the coxswain of our boat shouted.

'Did. The captain, I'll have you know,' he said, but it was his winning smile that stayed with me. The man oozed competence and it was hard not to find it attractive.

By the time we'd reached the beach, the other boat was halfway back out to *Mutin*. Lieutenant Russell stood on the water's edge, chatting with the men who had been observing us.

'Enjoy the ride?' Russell asked as he walked towards me.

'I've had better,' I replied.

He took a second look at me before asking, 'Do you want to have a go?'

'Love to.' I smiled. There had to be a way to manage these conditions better and, to figure it out, I needed to feel the sea.

A man lying flat on a surfboard with a gun mounted on the front rode onto the beach. It certainly coped better with the sea state, but I couldn't see the purpose unless you were delivering one man then destroying the board. It would take as much effort to paddle back out to *Mutin* as rowing the boats.

The American's crew arrived back to the beach and Baker walked up to us.

'They are getting better but it's shi . . . let me rephrase . . . difficult and soaking work.' He reached into his pocket and pulled out a small object and unwrapped it. From it, he extracted his lighter and cigarettes. 'Cigarette?'

I shook my head.

'Nipper?' Baker asked.

'Later; time to reload the boat. Dr Tremayne is taking an oar,' Russell said.

'Is there no end to your talents, Dr Tremayne?' Baker's smile softened his words.

'No,' I said with a grin. I could play this confidence game too.

Experience had taught me, in the world of men, not to show weakness. This team were no different. I followed Russell to the small dinghy, climbed aboard the small craft and sat on the two-man seat with more confidence than I felt. The man beside me nodded and focused on sorting the rowlock.

Lieutenant Russell pushed the boat out into the surf before he hauled himself onboard, taking the rudder. He called out instructions and we pulled into action.

It was hard to break through the incoming surf, but with full concentration we left the beach behind. Before long the rowing eased despite the swell. The first few strokes were awkward but then my muscles remembered their task. The joy of working as a team took over, even if it was under the watchful eye of Jake Russell.

We looped about *Mutin* then went back to the beach, landed and unloaded in silence before returning again to *Mutin*. The wind had dropped, and the sun baked us all. The men shed their canvas smocks and changed their trousers to shorts while I was still in my overalls, sweltering. My envy knew no bounds but my blouse underneath would be transparent and the men didn't need that distraction nor I the attention.

After another three return trips, I watched from the deck of *Mutin* with the commander beside me. Every so often he'd raise his binoculars and I longed to know what was going through his mind.

'Impressive boat skills, Dr Tremayne,' Holdsworth said. 'You've handled oars before?'

'Yes, growing up here, it was simply part of life.'

He nodded slowly. 'And at Oxford.'

'Yes, but this reminds me a bit more of pilot gigs.' In the past, gigs had raced to be the first out to an incoming ship so that their pilot would be paid to guide the ship safely in. But this boat was not long and thin, simply double-headed. 'Pilot gig meets coracle.'

He kept his binoculars pointed on the beach. 'Yes, the new surf boats are effective.'

'Who are the men?' I asked.

'Three of Slocum's men from Dartmouth.' He peered into the distance.

'What does Commander Slocum have to do with you?' I asked. I had met him. His team called him Dep standing for Damned Elusive Pimpernel. Slocum was the Deputy Director of Operations Division.

'He holds the ropes so to speak for the boats. We can't have access without his approval,' the commander said and waved to one of the boats. 'Lunch has arrived on the beach.'

He climbed into one of the boats and waved to me to join him. I shook my head and remained, watching the men on the shore. Who were they and what was their purpose here?

One of the surf boats began to make its way back to *Mutin*. The rest of the team walked off down the beach and up the steep bank in the direction of the village. Only the cook, Lieutenant Baker and I remained until the boat pulled up and Lieutenant Russell climbed on deck. A box was handed up and the smell of pasties quickly followed.

'Hungry?' Lieutenant Russell held out a pasty to me.

I breathed in. 'It smells good.'

'Tastes better, and, according to our resident Cornishman, Rendle, it tastes da . . . good.' He stopped but continued to hold one out to me.

'You don't have to censor yourself in front of me. I am accustomed to men swearing.' I took the pasty.

He frowned. 'You may be accustomed as you move easily in the company of men, but it is not how I was raised.'

'Fair enough.' I bit into the end of the pasty, savouring the peppery mix of onion, swede, potato and a healthy chunk of meat.

'Your verdict?' he asked.

'Full marks, Lieutenant.'

'Call me Jake or Nipper.' He bit into his own and I tried to focus on the delicious flaky pasty and not his bare chest. It was very distracting but so was the pasty.

'I think I'll stick with Lieutenant for now.' I took another bite of the pasty.

'Suit yourself.' He shrugged. 'The men have gone to the pub for a pint.'

'Not you?' I asked.

He shook his head.

'You were chatting with the men on the beach.' I glanced to the shore. They were still there. 'Who are they?'

'SIS from Dartmouth.' He pointed to the man with the clipboard. 'Warington Smyth's a good man and he designed the double-ended surf boat we were in. The one with the cine camera is a new navigator and the other one is Davis.' He frowned.

'And you don't like him.' I watched the expressions play across his face.

He laughed drily. 'Not *don't like* exactly. He's a bit cocky.'

I waited, hoping for more information.

'I was on a run with them at the beginning of the month,' he said. 'Pierre was supposed to come. Davis had no time for Pierre or his knowledge of the coast. He refused to take him because he was too scruffy. We missed the pickup because we missed the beach.'

I squinted, trying to bring the men on the beach into focus. They looked very formal compared to this crew who were all naked to the waist except the commander. 'Do you crew for them often?'

'If they are short of men, many times we are called to help.' He dusted the crumbs of pasty off his chest and his hands. I tried not to watch but failed. He met my glance when I looked up and he smiled. I flushed, forgetting what I wanted to ask him, then said, 'This team is part of the SOE?'

He snorted. 'Fleming didn't provide you with that piece of information.'

'No,' I said. It was clear that Fleming expected me to work that out so I wouldn't be prejudiced.

'So you work with Fleming,' he said.

'And he placed you here,' I countered.

'He did indeed. He felt it would suit my skills.'

'And does it?' I asked. Just what set of skills did the American possess that Fleming wanted here? Rowing? Spying? Or something I hadn't worked out yet?

'For the moment.' He gazed into the distance, watching one of the boats return. He called out to the young rating Piron. 'Arms and shoulders last.'

'Before the war, what did you do?'

'Reporter. And you?' He turned back to me.

'Lecturer in geography at Oxford.'

'Impressive.' He smiled, then went to the men returning for their afternoon session of training.

The wind had come round to a strong south-westerly, which should make quick work of the journey home. But it had increased the wave size we had to tackle here on the beach. What could I add to charts that would make their operations easier? Thus far, today had showed me nothing other than what a well-bonded hard-working group of men they were. There was nothing I'd learned this morning that I could add to a map.

13

13 May 1942

The dawn chorus was in full voice and I lay staring at the ceiling. My body ached from the type of exertions I hadn't done in years. However, after a day on the water, I had slept like the dead, but now my mind wouldn't still. I was thinking about an impudent American with piercing blue eyes. I was an educated woman; not a silly young thing swayed by a smile. Yet that wasn't entirely true. There had been the visiting Italian Classics scholar. That had been a gloriously fun affair while he was in Oxford, which had left us both satisfied. We'd known from the start it would finish and that was perfect.

I should be using this time of clear fresh thinking to figure out how to help Commander Holdsworth and his team improve their operations, to move their activities further south now that the Germans had increased their defences on the north coast of Brittany. Instead, the bare torso of the American when he climbed out of the sea at the end of the day filled my head. The sound of his voice ran through my mind. This shouldn't be happening, but it was. I was not that woman, but it appears I was wrong. His smile, his laugh, his competence and his sharp mind were all tugging at forgotten parts of me.

This was so inconvenient. I turned over.

The attraction would pass. It always did. I was here for a short time. War was never a good time for love, or even lust. But right now, part of me ached, ached for something I'd forgotten it wanted. It was raw, primeval and all-consuming.

There was nothing for it but to dress and go for a walk to expel him from my mind. Lying here and thinking was making everything more intense. With that thought, I rose, washed my face in cold water, tamed my hair and dressed with care. After a day on the water, a few freckles had appeared on my cheeks and my skin had acquired a golden tint. No make-up would be required today to lift my complexion. I went downstairs and out the kitchen door into the cool misty morning. Reaching the small strip of beach, I removed my plimsoles and carried them. The tide was on the turn, and I strolled towards the Pedn Billy boathouse.

Feeling the sand between my toes, I thought of the forces of nature that had created the Helford ria, a drowned valley forming a river open to the sea. Cornwall contained a number, including the Camel, the Hayle, the Fowey and, nearby, the Fal. These estuaries were routes to trade for centuries. Helford had been a hub of commercial activity yet, looking on it now, it was a sleepy forgotten place. The fishing boats were at anchor as were the ones used by this team. If I had my canoe, a quiet trip upriver would be ideal. Instead I made do with paddling along the beach and skimming stones. Finding the perfect one had been a continual battle between Oliver and me. Somehow, he always won. But as I counted the skips, I was pleased with the ten jumps.

'Impressive skill,' Lieutenant Russell said, standing a few feet away.

I turned to him, wondering if I had wished him here with me somehow.

'Yours is clearly sneaking up on people.'

He shrugged. 'Part of the job.'

I couldn't argue with that. 'What are you doing up at this hour?'

'Could ask you the same.' He bent to pick up a stone then stood rubbing his thumb across the surface.

I looked away.

'Woke early.' And left my room because I was thinking about you, I added silently.

'Thought I might row a bit.'

'Didn't you do enough yesterday?' I asked, rolling my stiff shoulders back.

'Helps me to think,' he said.

'Big concerns?' I asked.

'I have a few things on my mind, a few things to weigh up,' he replied.

'The rhythm of the repeated action helps to make connections in the brain,' I said. What was he trying to link or make work?

'Exactly.' He smiled, his eyes crinkling delightfully in the process. He was too appealing.

'I don't suppose you could take me into Frenchman's Creek, Lieutenant Russell?'

'Is that a proposition?' he asked with a straight face.

I blinked, half wishing it was, then I laughed. 'Absolutely not. It's simply that my canoe is there, and I'd rather like to have it.'

'Your canoe?' He threw the stone in his hand. It skipped five times before sinking.

'It's by my cottage,' I said.

'The small one at the end or the one at the mouth?' he asked.

'The one at the mouth is called Bosworgy and hasn't been used in a long time,' I clarified.

'Bosworgy?' He made a face.

I laughed. 'Cornish for house above the water. My family own the farm that covers the east bank of the creek and around parts of Manaccan.'

'This really is home for you.' He headed towards the dinghy by the boathouse.

'It is.' I joined him, put my plimsoles in the boat and took the bow, bringing it down the beach. I climbed in assuming that he was willing to take me although he'd never said as much.

'It has to be hard for you then with your mother missing.' He studied me. 'Being here that is.'

'It is . . . and it isn't. If that makes sense.' I inhaled. 'At least by being here I'm closer in some way. However, another day has passed with no further news and my sense of helplessness grows,' I admitted. Around me was the river she had captured in its every mood. Being on it brought her closer somehow.

'Tell me about her.'

'She's an artist,' I said, puzzled by his interest.

'What type? You mentioned she's Breton,' he said.

I studied him but he turned his head away to the direction we were travelling. 'She's known for her portraits, but I think she truly excels at seascapes or painting those she loves.'

'Do you have any thoughts on what could have happened or where she could be?' he asked.

I shook my head. 'Despite logic now pointing to her being dead, I don't think or even feel she's dead, which I can't explain. When my father died, there had been a finality about it. The funeral drew a line under it. "Missing" is such an open term. All I truly know is she's not here. That is a fact and everything else was speculation.'

He turned from me to check his direction then took three strokes with his left hand. The bow pointed towards the mouth of the creek and he didn't look back to me. The strangest thought that he might know something came to me. He couldn't yet the thought wouldn't leave.

'You're very interested in my mother?'

He looked up and didn't reply immediately like he was considering his words carefully. 'I'm interested because I sense your concern.'

'I see,' I said, not seeing at all.

He gave a rueful laugh. 'Or it could be the journalist in me always digging.'

That was a fair point, yet his words and concern didn't ring true and an uncomfortable silence fell between us as we passed the old folly of a summerhouse perched above the river. I refused to be drawn into watching him row and studied the water instead.

Once we entered the creek, the pull of the outgoing tide was less fierce, and he turned to me. 'It's beautiful. I love the way the trees reach down to the water.'

'Magical, isn't it?' I said. 'It's typical of the estuary creeks here in the south of Cornwall with bosky banks coming down to the water.'

'Bosky?' he asked.

'It means covered by trees,' I explained.

'It's like entering a different world,' he said.

'My favourite world filled with ancient trees.'

'I would have thought the dreaming spires were your place.' He paused from rowing and looked at me more closely.

'I do love Oxford but here is special.' I trailed my hand in the water.

'I can see why.' He looked over his shoulder. 'Where is this canoe of yours?'

'Hidden from sight.' I pointed further down the creek past Withan Quay to where the trees almost merge.

'Wise,' he said.

'Always,' I replied.

'Always?' He stopped rowing.

'Yes. I follow my head and not my heart, so always wise,' I clarified.

He stared at me as if I was an alien species, and, in a way, I was, a rarefied type who lived in academic or religious communities.

'You never consult your heart?' He leaned back and assessed me again.

I laughed. 'Maybe when I buy presents for people.'

'Phew.' He mockingly wiped his brow. 'For a moment I was worried that your heart was so tucked away.'

I cast him a glance. He shouldn't be worried about my heart.

'My heart is safe,' I said, pulling on my plimsoles.

He studied me. 'Yes, I can see that.'

'Drop me here, please,' I said as we reached the quay and I climbed ashore. He threw me the painter line and I caught it. 'You don't need to stay.'

'Call me curious,' he said.

'Nosy might be more apt,' I said.

'As I mentioned before, it's the reporter in me.' He climbed ashore, and took the line from me, securing it before following me along the narrow path that led back to my cottage.

'Someone's been using this path a fair bit,' he said, echoing my own thoughts. Would the intruder be back? Was he or she the reason the path was so well trodden and what of the rifles I had found?

We crossed the stone bridge over the stream at the head of the creek. Russell paused, looking up the steep bank. 'Your cottage sans white picket fence.'

I frowned. 'White picket fence?'

'An American dream home has a white picket fence.' He stood beside me, studying the cottage.

'Is the fence essential or does it symbolise something culturally that I'm missing?' I stood still, waiting for his response.

'It represents the idealised vision of your own place.'

I nodded, not quite understanding. 'Here in Cornwall, it's hedges that define fields and separate the house from the productive land.'

'I've noticed these hedges. Solid things.' He tapped the stone of the remainder of one that surrounded the cottage.

'Have you lived through a winter here when the wild winds blow?' I asked. With the carpet of bluebells covering the ground, the reality of winter was far away.

'I have and I can see their use for keeping the soil in the fields.'

'And animals protected from the weather too. I presume your white picket fence doesn't do that.'

'Absolutely not.' He raised his hands in defeat.

'Nor, I imagine, does it harbour the nests of blackbirds and thrushes and wildflowers like primroses and violets or as now, bluebells. Many of the hedges date from Bronze Age settlements but some are even more ancient,' I added.

He held out a hand to help me up the bank because the steps had been eroded in the winter rains.

'You know a lot about hedges,' he said.

I took my hand from his because I was enjoying the feel of it too much. 'I do, and field systems too. Part of my study of geography but mostly from my father's love of the land.' I smiled realising I was slipping into lecture mode and the last thing I wanted to do with him was teach.

We reached the path and I turned away from the cottage. The door was closed and Maman was not sitting on the bench by the door with her coffee. That was a foolish hope.

'Are you not going to show me inside?' he asked.

I glanced over my shoulder. 'Not today.'

'Is that an invitation for another time?' he asked.

I laughed. 'Only you would assume that.'

'Why only me?' He stood, waiting.

'I was being polite,' I said.

'By not saying, mind your own business, I don't want to show you the cottage.' His head tilted to the side, making him appear younger than his thirty-five years.

'Exactly,' I said.

'The British really are a special people who make an art of being polite by not saying what they mean.' He shook his head.

'I'd never thought of it that way,' I said. 'But you may have a point.'

'One for the Americans,' he said with a smile in his eyes that was very appealing. 'Now where is your canoe?'

'This way.' I led him along the path to where it was hidden in the undergrowth.

I pulled the canoe out and he grabbed the other end.

'I didn't expect an actual proper canoe,' he said. 'You're full of surprises, Dr Tremayne.'

I stopped and turned to him. Dr Tremayne suddenly sounded far too formal with echoes of the schoolteacher I'd been sounding like a few minutes ago.

'You may call me Merry.' I met his glance as I spoke.

'But are you . . . merry?' he asked. 'She who thinks with head alone.'

'I can be merry—' I paused and gave him the full power of my stare '—when it suits me.'

He laughed. 'That tells me. May I borrow your canoe some time?'

I frowned. He had access to a string of boats and spent most of his time on the water.

'I'd love to explore the many creeks more thoroughly and the canoe can travel more easily, and you paddle forward instead of looking behind.'

'You could reverse row,' I suggested. 'Work a different muscle group.'

He shrugged.

I climbed in and kneeled at the front. 'You may, of course, borrow it.' I paused, about to say, Lieutenant, but I had just given him permission to call me Merry and that would be odd. I couldn't call him Nipper – it sounded ridiculous – but Jake would work.

'There are nine tributaries to explore. The largest being Gillan Creek but with the boom in place that's off limits,' I said. 'They're beautiful and peaceful for the most part, and, on a few, you will see the remains of past industry.'

He pushed the canoe further into the creek and joined me kneeling in the stern.

'You can drop me off on your way past.' He grabbed the second paddle and we fell into a rhythm and made our way to the quay where he collected his own boat.

By the time we reached the mouth of the creek the sun had risen, the mist had cleared, and the day promised to be as lovely as yesterday. But it was not the start I had anticipated. Instead of freeing my mind of thoughts of Jake Russell, I had collected more images and impressions to review. Those would have to wait until after I had studied the aerial photographs which had been received from the airbase at St Eval. I promised myself I would put the lieutenant firmly out of my thoughts.

14

After yesterday's training and its failure to provide me with new insights, it was a relief to return to photographs which I knew were useful. The intelligence images spread across the table showed new and enlarged fortifications on the north coast of Brittany. The team's last operation, Hermitage, in April, had been fraught, but the package had been delivered, and vital intelligence retrieved and sent to London.

Now Commander Holdsworth's team were seeking a way to continue their operations. Further west and south was the obvious answer, but it meant longer transit times. It would be impossible to complete a crossing under the cover of darkness even in midwinter. There had to be a way. Scanning the photographs again, the answer was obvious. The fishing fleet was visible, and I knew from my sailing days their primary catch.

'I don't suppose you have access to a sardine boat?' I asked the four assembled officers and pointed to a shot taken near the Île de Groix.

The commander looked up. 'There might be one in Newlyn or Mousehole.'

'Pierre might know,' Jake said, studying the photo.

'We could head to Newlyn,' the commander said. 'I can also check with Falmouth to see what they have.'

'The shipwright in Helford is excellent and, with Pierre's knowledge, I'm sure you could adapt one.' I paused. 'But can you have the engines converted?'

The commander rolled his eyes. 'I'll run it past Slocum. But it may be a battle.'

'But why?' I asked. 'Surely you are all on the same side.'

He laughed bitterly. 'You would think so, but as I've said we have been stymied the whole way.'

'Do you know why?' I tucked my pencil behind my ear.

'Jealousy,' said Jake.

'Surely not,' I said.

'No, of course not, but at times it feels that way.' Jake turned and looked out of the window.

The commander sighed. 'They are trying to build networks and we are trying to disrupt the enemy which they feel threatens their networks.' He paused. 'And they have a point.'

'I see.' With the two incompatible objectives, there could be no resolution. 'Hence your comment yesterday about only being crew and being used for training.'

'Yes.' He studied the photographs again.

'But you have delivered agents and brought airmen back?' I looked at all four men. Dejection was writ large on their faces.

'We have,' said Baker, lighting his cigarette. He never seemed to be without one.

'Sounds to me like successful operations then.' I crossed my arms, facing them all. They needed to acknowledge what they had achieved.

Jake laughed. 'One way to see it.'

'A very good way and I think that is the way forward for the moment.' The commander stood. 'We still need to land provisions and agents as well as obtaining mail so let's find the right boat and make a case.' He left the room and picked up the telephone in the hallway. Lieutenant Commander Brooks Richards headed to the garage while Baker announced he would collect Pierre.

Jake remained and leaned against the door frame with his arms loosely crossed. 'Good insight.'

'Thinking with the head and not the heart.' I gathered the photographs. Looking up, I added, 'Works every time.'

He laughed. 'One day, Merry, you will find it doesn't always work.'

'The head processes things clearly, logically, using the information provided. The heart makes wild guesses and acts based on intuition.' I paused. 'It's like setting out on an expedition to an unknown location without a map, a compass, or even sufficient supplies or footwear.' I looked directly at him. 'I know which I would rely on every time.' But in the back of my mind, I heard my mother's voice saying, 'Ma petite, trust your heart; it will show you the true way. The head only gives you part of anything. The heart always gives its all whether it's love or hate.'

'Have it your way,' he said and left the room.

And I would. If they could find the right vessel, this could work.

Brooks Richards returned. 'Dr Tremayne, would you like to join us in Newlyn?'

I glanced at the table and the charts then looked up and said, 'Yes.' The charts could wait a few hours.

*

The harbour at Newlyn was different to my last visit ten years ago with my mother. She loved to paint here because as she said there was a special energy. French and Belgian fishing vessels were moored up together with the local ones even then. These men of the sea knew each other well for they all had faced the same risks on the water. The five of us strolled up to the military check-point. As always, I was the subject of scrutiny, but nothing was said. The guard vetted the permits and allowed us to access the harbour to examine the many boats alongside. I knew from Maman that the Belgians were the first refugees to arrive at the start of the war, and the Bretons followed soon after de Gaulle's radio address in June 1940.

That was two years ago, and we were still at war with no sign of an end. These people had come for what they had hoped was a short time but had now settled in, from the looks of things. The close links between Cornwall and Brittany were always so clear to me as a child growing up. Both proud Celtic people with a distinct language and customs. The Cornish and Bretons were closer to each other in these two things than they were to the English or the French.

Pierre engaged in fast conversation with a fisherman, and I followed as best I could. It had been too long since I had spoken Breton in any great length.

Pierre looked up and smiled.

'I think we have a boat.' He waved his hand towards the side of the quay. The familiar sounds and smells of the quayside surrounded me as we walked towards it. Diesel, fish and seaweed interlaced with cigarette smoke. I spied the vessel and quelled the horror in me. This sardine boat had seen better days.

'Yes, Pierre. She'll need a lot of work, but she is just the ticket.' The commander climbed on board asking, 'Do you know where the owner is?'

Pierre frowned. 'He is dead but his widow lives in one of the cottages in um . . . *trou de souris*.'

'Where?' the commander asked.

'As you say, the place where the rodent comes in.'

I chuckled. 'Mousehole.' The evacuees had been placed into the abandoned fisherman's cottages along the front. These dwellings were very basic, with no running water or facilities. Before the war, these cottages had been emptied and the residents had been encouraged to move to new houses further up in the village. The old buildings would be better than what the refugees might be facing at home, but hard to imagine how they were surviving.

'I'll go and have a word with the harbour master about arrangements. Nipper, can you take Pierre and Dr Tremayne to the widow.'

'Brooks Richards will help me here and you can collect us on your return.'

We set off along the quay and I couldn't help noticing how much attention we attracted. It could be the over-tall American or the muscular Breton, or more likely the odd combination that we made.

My step was lighter as we walked to re-join the commander and Brooks Richards. The widow had been delighted to sell the boat and it meant that she could better look after her three children. For once the wheels of the war machine brought some relief to a widow. Both Pierre and the American were smiling too. The lieutenant had played ball with the youngest boy while Pierre and I spoke to her. Her smile was still with me.

'There you are,' the commander said, his face solemn as we approached. 'Dr Tremayne, a message from the Helston police has been forwarded to us.'

I tensed.

'They have found a bicycle and a paintbox and wish you to come to the station at your earliest convenience,' the commander said.

I nodded, unable to speak.

'Nipper, please take Dr Tremayne to the station and we will complete our business here and arrange a lift back.'

Lieutenant Russell agreed then placed his hand lightly on my back, directing me to the car.

'Are you ready?' he asked as he started the engine.

No, was my first thought, but I nodded. With everything that was in me, I didn't want this bicycle and paintbox to be hers. I stared out of the window and thankfully the lieutenant sensed my reluctance to talk and didn't try to make conversation. He drove in silence until he needed to ask for directions as we came into Helston.

We arrived and he dashed round the automobile to open my door and followed me to the station entrance.

'You don't have to come in with me,' I said.

'I know but I'd like to if you don't mind.' He opened the station door.

'Fine.' I didn't need help, but his quiet presence was surprisingly reassuring. We entered the building, and, after speaking to the man behind the desk, I sat on the same bench I had before. Everything was the same except now something else had been discovered. To stop my circling thoughts, I focused on the dust motes highlighted in the sunshine streaming through the window, but it didn't work. If these were my mother's, what did it mean?

'Miss Tremayne.' Inspector Jenkins stood in front of me.

I rose to my feet and so did Jake.

'I'm Lieutenant Russell.' Jake held out his hand.

'American?' the inspector asked.

Jake nodded and I sighed. None of this was important.

'This won't take long,' said the inspector, opening a door off the entrance hall into what looked like a storage room and waved a hand. My mother's bike was propped against the wall and on the table was her paintbox.

'Do these belong to your mother?' he asked.

My mouth dried but I managed a yes.

'Are you certain?' he pressed.

'Without a doubt.' I moved around the bike and traced the bold splashes of colour I had painted on the outside of the paintbox as a child. 'Where did you find them?'

'This is the strange thing.' Inspector Jenkins looked from me to Jake. 'We didn't find them near Kynance Cove where she was last seen, but in Porthoustock.'

'Porthoustock?' I asked.

'Yes. Did she paint there often?' He looked from me to the man towering behind me.

'Not ever that I'm aware of,' I said.

He nodded. 'These things were reported yesterday. The bicycle with the paintbox strapped to the back was propped against the cliff face above the high-water mark under some dead foliage. A child playing on the beach discovered them.'

I pictured the large shingle cove sandwiched between the quarry on one side and the large stone mill on the other. From the beach you could look out to the Manacles buoy. On a low tide, the rocks rose above the surface of the water like teeth ready to catch anyone foolish enough to come too close. Many had.

'This might indicate she went swimming,' said Inspector Jenkins.

'How so? Were pieces of clothing found or her shoes? Did someone see her?' I asked, trying to make sense of this.

'No,' Jenkins said.

I closed my eyes. That didn't work. Why would she choose to swim on Porthoustock beach with large vessels regularly coming in and out for the quarry when she could swim in the calm of the river or the creek?

'No body has been found,' I said.

There was pity in his glance. 'There is so much activity in the area . . . '

I wanted to shout no but instead I wrapped my arms about myself.

'Please feel free to take these items now, Miss Tremayne.' He handed me the box and wheeled the bicycle into the foyer.

Jake took the bicycle. 'Dr Tremayne, you mean,' he said, looking directly at the inspector. He turned to me. 'I'll try and fit this into the car.'

'The clerk will sort the paperwork . . . Dr Tremayne. It shouldn't be long,' the inspector said.

I sat on the bench and I opened the paintbox. The mixed scent of turpentine and glue hit me. A piece of heavy watercolour paper covered the paints and brushes. I lifted it while I waited for the paperwork. The blues of the sky and sea were familiar. My mother's sure brush strokes were like a signature.

'Miss Tremayne,' the clerk called, interrupting my thoughts.

Placing the watercolour back, I closed the box and stood. Signing the paperwork made it feel so final. But it wasn't. There was no body and, no matter what the inspector thought, I knew that she wouldn't have been swimming off that beach.

True to his word, Jake had fit the bicycle into the car by removing the front wheel and using rope to hold the boot halfway closed. I sank into the passenger seat with the paintbox on my lap, numb. My brain refused to process the items recovered.

Halfway back to Ridifarne, Jake picked up my hand. I looked at his sun-tanned fingers holding mine and the reality of my mother never holding my hand again hit me. I gulped and pulled my hand from his.

He sent me a glance.

I forced myself to breathe slowly.

'Finding these items doesn't mean you should give up hope,' he said.

My eyes were full of unshed tears. Hope. 'What do I have to hold onto now? That she's a spy as the village gossip implies?'

The car jerked sharply.

'Sorry, rock on the road,' he said.

I hadn't seen it but my eyes were not clear.

'But my mother would never betray France or her adopted country.' I sighed. 'There is no body and because of that I don't think she is dead. She is simply missing.'

'True,' he said.

His profile was set against the bright-blue sky and I turned away. I needed to speak with Oli. He would help me work this through. Until then there was no point in talking about it anymore. I closed my eyes and created maps in my head but they were useless as there was no reason to make them.

Back at Ridifarne, I telephoned my brother and left a message to ring me urgently. My next call was to Fleming.

'What do you make of this news?' he asked, after I had updated him.

'The inspector assumes she drowned,' I replied.

'But you clearly don't,' said Fleming.

'I don't or maybe I don't want to.'

'Hmm,' he said.

'How are things in the office?' I asked.

'The bluestocking, Margaret Priestly, is settling in well and Harling is back,' he said. 'But I want you to carry on where you are.'

'I will,' I said as the call ended. But carrying on was the last thing I felt like doing. Walking upstairs to my room, I ran through the facts that I had but I couldn't force them to make sense.

Her paintbox sat on my bed. I released the catch but then closed it again. I knew what was in there. Paints, brushes, palette knives, rags and small bottles of water, turpentine and her last painting. This wouldn't help anything. Instead, I took my notebook and opened it to the map. St Anthony made sense as did Kynance but not Porthoustock. That was the outlier. The village was small and not as scenic, but I marked it for it was a known fact. It was remote and sparsely populated, but between the fishermen, those working the quarry and those working the land, there were people present all around the area. My mother cut a striking figure being tall and beautiful. She was someone people would have noticed, especially on that cove.

The rocks of the Manacles were as clear in my mind as the buoy that marked them. That buoy had always been the fix for our navigation to Brittany. Maman would laugh at me as I worked the calculations, saying, 'Trust yourself, ma petite, you have made the journey often. Your instincts will be right.' But I would never leave navigating to my experience. Safe travel was down to careful planning and calculations beginning with the fix point.

15

14 May 1942

I'd spent the day immersed in charts so I wouldn't be able to dwell on my mother, my brother, or even my attraction to Jake, and now dinner had finished. The tide had an hour to go until it was full and the desire to retrieve the charts from *Mirabelle* had had to wait until now.

'Mary, if you'll excuse me, I'm off for a paddle in my canoe.'

'All OK?' she asked, studying me with concern.

'Yes, fine. I need a bit of alone time,' I said, instead of the truth. I left the others muttering about heading to the pub for a drink. They had been training again today but I hadn't joined them, instead I added the latest intelligence to the charts.

I set off upstream towards Gweek and the boatyard at the head of the Helford. The tide was with me and before long I passed Merthen Wood with its coppiced trees and the old quay where the colliers used to bring their coal. I then passed Bishop's Quay, which housed the pilchard boats and finally reached the old boat yard at Gweek. All was quiet as expected and *Mirabelle* was laid up in her cradle. It was the time of year when she should be on the water ready for day trips or longer; instead she was covered and dusty.

Not a soul was around in the boatyard with only the swallows above diving for their evening meal. I wobbled my way up an old ladder, lifted the canvas cover and I ventured into the main cabin. Although dark, the layout was so familiar that I soon retrieved the hidden key for the secured locker under the galley bench. Moving the cushion aside, I turned the key in the lock and opened the lid, feeling around for the charts. It was empty. I tried the space under the bench on the opposite side. It contained ropes and various spare parts. Undaunted I checked both again but no joy. There was no sign of damage. The lock had not been forced and the wood was smooth, but the charts were gone.

I went to the fore cabin and looked in the only other space they could be, and that too was empty. When war broke out, I'd helped my mother ready the boat for coming out of the water. I recalled we had locked the charts away, hoping that we would soon be using them again. That was almost three years ago.

Questions circled. Those charts had been moved or taken and there was only one person who knew they were there: Maman; and she wasn't here to guide me. Despite the bicycle and the paintbox, I refused to believe she was dead. That was unacceptable even more than her being a spy. It was clear she must have moved them for safety as the war wore on. They must be in Kestle somewhere.

The sky was still light at nine thirty when I climbed down the ladder and made my way to the canoe. Shapes were beginning to loom as the shadows grew into darkness. There was no one about yet I was uneasy. Missing charts were bad enough but ones of the coastline of France in the midst of a war was criminal. Glancing over my shoulder, I tried to dismiss the sense of being watched. It was clear the boatyard was deserted behind me, and that my feelings were running away based on nothing but a few looming shadows.

Once paddling away from Gweek and able to see all around

me in the low light, I tried to dismiss the feeling, to think with my head and not my fear. It didn't work and I remained alert. I was grateful the tide had turned to help speed my progress towards Ridifarne.

I secured my boat on the beach and walked along to the Ferry Boat, assuming Mary and the men would still be there. The evening was warm, and I didn't want to be alone with my thoughts. The uncomfortable feeling of being watched lingered and the missing charts from *Mirabelle* played on my mind.

There were reports of enemy planes flying low over the river, gathering intelligence. Not long before the outbreak of war, Von Ribbentrop, then the ambassador to the court of St James, had been staying at Glendurgan with the Foxes. My parents had been invited to join them one evening but had declined. However, they had bumped into the party at the Ferry Boat Inn on one occasion. Vile, was my father's comment, but he had gathered how much the man had liked Cornwall. His host reported on their guest unfavourably afterwards and this surprised no one.

In the distance I saw the team perched on the wall by the beach and Mary waved.

'Dr Tremayne,' the commander said, rising to his feet. 'What can I get you to drink?'

'A beer would be lovely,' I said, sitting beside Baker on the wall.

'Anyone else in need of a refill?' the commander asked. He and Brooks Richards went inside with everyone's order. After a head count, I noted that Jake wasn't there.

'How did the training go today?' I asked Baker.

'Well, we didn't kill each other so I count that as a win.' He smiled.

I laughed. 'That's a good day?'

'Just enough to keep us on our toes.' He offered me a cigarette. 'It's not what I was trained to do, not what I was told we'd be doing and most of the time we seem to be kicking our heels.'

'What should you be doing?' I asked, leaning forward for a light.

'It was all supposed to be blowing up bridges and sabotage.' He laughed bitterly. 'But in reality, it's a ferry or mail service.'

'Important, though,' I said.

'Absolutely, but we are underutilised,' he said. 'What about you? Surely a woman as clever as you is wasted helping us?'

I took a long deep drag of the cigarette, letting the hit of nicotine fill me. 'I'm here to gain knowledge.'

'So you're a spy.'

My heart stopped for a moment as that was a little too close to the truth.

'I'm seeking the type of information that is really required on a map,' I explained.

The commander and his second emerged from inside to hand out the drinks. I sipped my half pint and watched the men. They communicated in short phrases that only made sense to themselves. Their natural pecking order was apparent without the ranks attached to them. I'd overheard that Baker was the best shot and Jake was the best rower. Brooks Richards quietly worked things out. They listened to every word the commander said. Respect poured out of all of them.

Jake walked towards us. Where had he been? Despite wanting to, I couldn't take my eyes off him. It was the confidence in his stride.

'Handsome git,' said Baker.

I flushed. It was not often I was caught admiring someone, because it was not often that I did.

'He's not bad,' I said. 'For an American.'

I turned to Baker. He looked at Jake with the same sort of hunger I felt, and I realised he wanted Jake too.

'Perfect timing, Nipper, it's your round.' Baker raised his empty glass.

'God, I've been blessed with great timing, haven't I?' He scanned the group. 'Same again everyone?'

It was clear there was a set of unspoken rules. They trusted each other implicitly. They had to on missions. One slip-up could not only cost their lives but jeopardise far more.

Baker's glance followed Jake. I knew from Constance how difficult life could be if you didn't fit in with what society expected.

'Does he know of your . . . interest?' I whispered.

Baker looked at me then drew on his cigarette. 'I imagine so, but sadly it isn't returned.' He laughed drily. 'Not a bad thing either. It would also complicate life here a bit too much.'

I nodded. 'Affairs of the heart always do.'

He shook his head but said no more. Across the water in Helford, men's voices carried.

'The Shipwrights must have run out of beer,' said Baker, finishing his pint.

It was interesting that they hadn't joined the officers here. When we trained in the surf boats there was no distinction, and I imagine on a mission there wouldn't be either. But there was a defined one here and I doubted it was that the Shipwrights' beer was less watered down. Society was a funny old place divided up in the strangest of ways. I would enjoy this moment of belonging or appearing to because aside from Oxford I fit nowhere.

The commander walked over to me.

'Tomorrow we are practising in the woods of Pengarrock, and I thought you might like to come along,' he said.

'I'd love to,' I said.

'Are you sure she'll be OK?' Jake asked, handing out beers.

Right that moment I was determined to be fine, no matter what the training was.

The commander laughed. 'I have no doubt.'

I didn't glare at Jake, but I wanted to as he handed me another half. I took the glass and said, 'Thanks,' but then placed it on the wall as I hadn't finished my first. They were all thirsty after their exertions today, but tomorrow could be rigorous so I would be careful this evening. I did not need to slip up.

There was something about Nipper, as they called him. Something didn't ring true. I couldn't place it. Suspicion hovered over every one of our interactions and it wasn't one-sided, that was for sure. Was it the cultural differences or something more? Even now he was watching me watching them. The rest were unwinding, and they weren't excluding me nor were they including me. I would need to earn that. It always worked this way. I had earned my position in the geography department at Oxford, then with Inter Services Topographical Department and finally with Fleming in London. The same would be required here. Even though I was on home territory, I was the outsider.

16

15 May 1942

Today was an unknown but being sensibly attired would help. Therefore I pulled on my overalls. Looking in the mirror, I wound a navy scarf around my upswept hair. Whatever the training was ahead, I would not intentionally slow them down. My face was pale and large eyes stared back at me. I looked younger than I was and a bit frightened. This wouldn't do. I picked up my lipstick then put it down again. It might help my appearance but would not be necessary for today, I was certain.

Downstairs in the kitchen, I grabbed a piece of bread and a bowl of porridge. It was five and the house was strangely quiet, although I heard the creaks of the plumbing indicating someone was about. Mrs Newton had put the oats on last night and now they were a perfect soft and warm consistency. I had finished a bowl before the kettle had boiled. Making a large pot of tea, I glanced out towards the river. Unlike yesterday's bright skies, a sea fret had rolled in, subduing everything except my mood. Fear mixed with excitement. Maybe today would provide the insights I was looking for or simply the thrill of the unexpected.

Light footsteps spoke of Mary or Mrs Newton but the latter didn't normally arrive until after her sons had left for school.

'Morning,' I said.

'Goodness, you're ahead of the crowd.' Mary smiled and filled two cups with the tea. Handing one to me she said, 'But as women we have to be.'

'Yes, we do.' I was about to continue when Jake walked through the door, looking fresh with his hair still damp.

'Morning,' he said. He served himself a large bowl of porridge and sat at the small table beside me. I finished my tea quickly then washed my things before I slipped out the door, not wanting to make conversation or fill my head with more images of Jake.

Cool air bathed my face and restored my equilibrium. I scanned the sky. Despite the thickening fog, it was bright, and I squinted as I made my way to the beach. After checking my canoe was still secured, I went to the water's edge. My robust boots made deep imprints in the damp sand. A smooth flat stone caught my eye and I picked it up, weighing it in my palm. It was ideal for skimming. Testing it without throwing, I swung it back and forth a few times before I released it, watching it bounce seven times before it sank.

'This is a favourite pastime of yours,' Jake said.

I jumped. I'd been too focused on the stone and the fog muffled the sound.

'What's your record?' he asked.

'Twelve.'

He strolled to my side, wearing sunglasses in the fog. 'I'm not sure I believe you.'

'You don't have to.' With the glasses on, I couldn't read his expression, but I couldn't glance away.

'Ah, but you're one of our team at the moment and complete trust is essential.'

I swallowed. Did he suspect my true purpose? 'It's useful in all relationships.'

'True, but war plays hell with trust,' he said. 'And relationships.'

'You speak from experience?' Had he left someone at home or was there someone here? It bothered me that I couldn't read him. I understood English and French men well but Jake was a new breed to me.

Before he could answer, Brooks Richards arrived on the beach. 'Tom Long is heading this way now with the dinghy.' He glanced around and said, 'Don't suppose we could use your canoe, Dr Tremayne?'

'Of course, but I'm assuming it's because of curiosity rather than need.' They had their own collapsible ones, which had been used to good effect on Praa Sands. My traditionally made one would be of no use to them.

'And you'd be correct.' He smiled and walked with me up the beach to untie the canoe and carry it down to the water. Jake watched us.

'Trust the Nipper to stand and watch a lady do the heavy work,' said Brooks Richards, as he put his end in the river.

Jake laughed. 'I rather think this lady can look after herself.'

In that moment I knew he had heard my conversation with Mary.

'No, you're a lazy git, I'd say,' Brooks Richards said.

I climbed in and Brooks Richards joined me.

'See you on the beach, Nipper,' he said.

With two paddling, we cut through the water with ease.

'What do you make of us so far?' Brooks Richards asked.

I tried not to look on the question with suspicion. 'A well-organised operation.'

He laughed. 'When we are allowed to operate, this is true.'

'The commander mentioned your last journey was in early April.'

'True for us as a whole but, as he mentioned yesterday, we supply crew. Nipper, Edwards, Long, Pierre and Cable were on an operation the first few days in May.' He sighed. 'There had been an almighty cockup – sorry, mess up – when Davis wouldn't have Pierre on his boat so they had to make the journey three times before they could land.' He sighed. 'Bloody arrogance and such a waste of time and resources.'

Behind us, the sound of the rowlocks of the dinghy creaked loudly on the morning air even though muffled. A canoe could be more stealth-like, but it wasn't ideal for all conditions, as I had discovered when I was a child. I'd headed off towards the bay in a foul mood and the huge swell brought up by an easterly had nearly swamped my canoe and drowned me.

We moved our paddles with precision, cutting the surface of the water with little noise or splash until we reached the narrows. More effort was required as the tide forced its way through the smaller space, but, before long, the boathouse on Pengarrock's beach appeared through the fog.

Landing the canoe, we pulled it above the high-water mark before Brooks Richards said, 'That was a joy.'

'It was and I can hear the others,' I said, scanning the river but I couldn't see them.

He walked towards me. 'It's a good thing they are not trying to approach stealthily.' He laughed as two dinghies appeared through the mist.

After the boats had been secured, they brought a large chest up the beach. I envied their shoes, lightweight with enough grip on the soles, almost like boxer's boots. Mine were practical but heavy.

The commander handed each man a colt revolver with a silencer attached, then he walked towards me, asking, 'Have you used one before?'

'I haven't used a silencer before,' I said.

A local member of the crew, Howard Rendle, watched me with a smile on his face. He was from Porth Navas, and we'd been on many a shoot together. After all, I was a farmer's daughter and being able to fire a shotgun was a standard of country life. I hadn't fired a revolver in a while but was confident I could hold my own. It was more a case of adjusting to the extra weight of the silencer. My father's Browning was of similar weight to the Colt, and he had taught both Oli and me how to use it. Maman had been half horrified. Papa had said she should have expected this, marrying an army man. She wasn't a bad shot herself.

The gun was fully loaded, and I checked the safety. The men began heading into the woods above the beach. At first, they stuck to the path then turned into a field where targets were lined up. Five men took places, and I noted their accuracy.

When their round was finished, I stepped up to a space and took a deep breath. Readying myself for the kickback, I widened my stance and focused on the target and the target alone, even though I felt everyone's scrutiny, especially Jake's. Only when I concentrated on my breathing and shut out the distractions, did I fire. The first one was to the side of the mark. Moving my feet further apart I fired again, and this time hit dead centre. I repeated the process until the cartridge was spent. Lowering the gun, I heard clapping.

'The lady can shoot,' said Brooks Richards.

Rendle laughed. 'Could have told you that, had you asked.'

I smiled at him and Wilfred Skinner, the gamekeeper for Pengarrock who had arrived while I was shooting.

'Always the best gun on a shoot, but never seen her with a Colt before,' Skinner said. 'I've checked the woods along the river and it's all clear.' Skinner looked up at the sky. 'Mind you, it's going to chuck it down before noon.' Then he set off towards the house after telling us there was no one in residence at Pengarrock at the moment.

'Next target practice is in the woods where you'll find iron men throughout.'

'Dr Tremayne, do you wish to join?' asked Brooks Richards.

I nodded.

'Work as a team with Nipper and after lunch I wondered if you could give the team a lesson on map-reading?' The commander smiled encouragingly.

'Of course.' This I could do in my sleep. But why on earth would they need it?

'Don't look so puzzled. Commander Fleming said it would be foolish not to take advantage of your teaching skills while we had you here.'

I smiled. Fleming must have something up his sleeve.

While we waited for the other teams to head off at timed intervals, Jake offered me a cigarette and I accepted. Searching for and shooting at human-like structures was not something I had contemplated, and I didn't like the idea. But it was war, and these men could encounter the enemy at any point on a mission. Things seemed simple when looking at photographs and maps sitting in an office, but the reality was setting in as rain had begun to fall in earnest. I finished my cigarette and crushed it under my foot.

'Ready?' he asked.

I wasn't but I nodded and followed behind him, focusing on keeping my steps light and all my senses alert. This was harder than I'd expected, with rain streaming down my face. Even Jake had abandoned the sunglasses he'd worn earlier. We continued in silence, and he waved me to the front as we followed an old path up the hillside. In the distance, I heard a metallic ping sound. Turning to Jake, he nodded, and we crept on and suddenly I spied the shape of a man. I froze. Even though I could see it was a flat cut-out I couldn't raise my weapon. Jake fired and hit the metal figure in the chest with a huge metallic crash. He looked to me. It should be easy. It wasn't real and I knew that but everything in me fought it. I could shoot a target or game bird, but I was frozen in place.

'Try.' It was quietly spoken. Not a command nor a plea, just a word of encouragement. I took a deep breath and raised the gun. One shot and I had taken out the knee. The resulting sound echoed.

'Well, he couldn't run after you, but he could still kill you,' he said.

'True,' I admitted. I needed to look at things differently. This would require a bigger leap than I'd anticipated.

'But a damn fine shot for your first in such foul weather.' He waved me onward. There were other targets to find before a return to Ridifarne and back to what I could do with my eyes closed.

*

Rain had soaked me through, and I squelched with each step I took up to the house. Mary and Mrs Newton took one look at me and sent me straight to the bathroom. Before long, I was immersed in blissfully hot water, trying not to think about the morning. Jake and I had found all ten targets and after that first one I hadn't hesitated. It was the head or the chest each time. It was difficult to shut off the thinking side of my brain. Instinct wasn't my strength, and I didn't trust it, but with the foul weather I'd had no choice. Continually, I reminded myself it was a case of them or me.

There had been little conversation with Jake. At the end I could tell I'd passed some test but nothing like anything else I had ever encountered. It would be a relief after lunch to return to familiar territory. I understood maps. They are assertions of naming, orientation and scale. They were clear, direct, but I realised after this morning's training only part of the whole. As much information as I could place on a map, there was nothing I could do to provide experience. A map was a guide, but you needed all your senses to complete the story.

After the bath, I dressed with care in a neat pair of trousers and a crisp blouse. The focus needed to be on what I said and not on how I appeared. It would be different teaching men I had trained with and had begun to know on a comrade level. In the past it was always students or, since the start of the war, a group of raw officers who thought they knew everything. Today I saw these men knew much more than I did and willingly risked their lives transporting people and information. For them, maps needed to facilitate their work; nothing more.

Downstairs, I headed to the kitchen where the scent of chicken soup filled the air. Ideal for the mid-May day that was more like September.

'Will you be joining us on the night training?' Brooks Richards asked as he handed me a bowl.

I looked up and said, 'If I won't hold you back.'

He smiled. 'Of course you won't.'

I laughed. 'You're very polite.'

'Don't be fooled. Brooks Richards is only polite when it suits him,' the commander said. 'Once the men are finished lunch, they will all come here, and we'll set up in the sitting room.'

'Thanks.' I sat down at the kitchen table beside Mary, half listening as weariness set in. The conversation flowed around but I wasn't fully listening until Jake spoke.

Lieutenant Russell could be bluff when barking rowing instructions, but he was, as I'd witnessed, a brilliant shot, and it wasn't only his American accent that made his voice so arresting, it was its depth. That was why I'd heard his whispered comment on my arrival. It had a quiet authority until he laughed, like now. I hadn't heard what Brooks Richards had said but the laughter was deep, rich and loud. It was not a discreet laugh but one that filled the room. He turned and his eyes met mine. I held his gaze for a moment before looking into my soup bowl. I did not want to feel this way.

'How did you come to mapping?' asked Baker, sitting opposite me.

'By way of my father who learned cartography in the army,' I said. 'Then formally during my study of geography.'

'Hope you don't mind me saying but it seems an odd choice for a woman.' He dipped a piece of bread into the soup.

I put my spoon down and considered my words carefully. 'Do you mean that geography is too scientific for a woman's mind?'

'Watch how you go, Baker; this one's mind is too sharp to fall into your trap.' The commander took a seat.

The youngest officer Edwards said, 'You *are* rather beautiful and—'

'It's a waste in your view.' I grinned at him as he flushed. 'I rather think it would be more of a waste if I didn't use the mind that God gave me.'

'And by all accounts we should be grateful she is using it.' The commander lifted his glass of water.

'But don't you want love and marriage?' asked Baker, his glance narrowing.

'No.' I debated saying more but chose not to.

'I mean no offence but I'm curious,' Baker said. 'You are a beautiful woman, as Edwards said, and of a certain age.'

'You mean a twenty-seven-year-old spinster,' I said the words that he hadn't.

'So no marriage in your future?' Baker pushed on where most men would have the sense to stop.

'No.' I smiled.

'Just no,' said Jake, clearing the finished soup bowls.

'Rarely are things ever simply no. Women have a choice . . . career or marriage. Unlike men, both are not possible.'

'I take your point, but don't you feel you are missing out?' Edwards asked.

I raised an eyebrow. 'Missing out on cooking, cleaning and doing laundry rather than exploring, mapping and being acknowledged for my brain?'

Mary smiled at me.

'When you say it like that,' said Baker, 'I can see your point.'

An uncomfortable silence filled the room and only a loud slurp broke it. With the easy conversation gone, I rose, washed my bowl, and said, 'See you in half an hour.'

*

The sound of their chatter and the occasional loud burst of laughter came from the sitting room. I hesitated before entering. It should be easy as I have walked into hundreds of classrooms, but this was different. During the past few days, I'd seen the personalities of each man, his strengths as well as his weaknesses and I had learned so much from them. They had opened my eyes and I was uncertain what I could teach them. Taking a deep breath, I entered into the room.

'Hey, teach,' said Jake from the back.

I forced a frown. 'I'll take no sass from the back row, or it will be detention.'

'Is that a promise?' He grinned.

I ignored him and pointed to the Manacles on the map. 'As you all know, this is a chart of the waters of Falmouth Bay to Lizard Point. It shows the coast, the rocks and the known currents.'

Heads nodded.

'You don't simply read from maps, you read onto them.' I paused letting that sink in. 'You take the knowledge you have and use that to interpret or even translate the map as you look at it from the scale to the legend. You apply what, if anything, you know of the climate.' I scanned the intent faces, but it was Jake's that nearly threw me off track. He was so focused on me. 'Therefore . . . what would you have me as . . . ' I paused, glancing at Jake, 'The mapmaker to add to this chart? What would you include that isn't there?'

'I don't see the Manacle buoy,' said Rendle.

I peered at the chart, and it wasn't marked. With a pencil I added it. 'Anything else?'

Silence.

'This one of the northern coast of Brittany, what would you want to see on there that you don't see?' I pointed to the other chart.

'The enemy,' said Tom Long.

I smiled. 'Tricky to map a moving object.'

'Where's the best beer to be had?' asked Baker.

I laughed.

'Seriously, it's the rocks and the tides and the mined beaches,' Brooks Richards said from the back row.

'Do you receive this information from the local agents?' I asked and watched their faces.

'Sometimes, and other times, we discover it ourselves by finding cart tracks on the beach.' Tom Long leaned forward as he spoke.

'Anything else?' I prompted.

'Houses where the Germans are living.' My back was to the room so I couldn't see who spoke and I didn't recognise the voice.

'Good point. Anything else?' I pressed further. Many times it was only after pushing through the initial thoughts that the key ones would arise.

'Why are you asking us?' asked one of the ratings.

'Because you have more information than I do. The last time I sailed the coast of Brittany was in nineteen thirty-eight. Munitions factories have been built. Towns have been bombed but I don't think the sweep of the tides has changed.'

Briggs laughed. 'No, ask Jones about it. Early on, he tied up to a quay and disappeared into a bar. Returned in the dark and fell ten feet onto the deck of the boat.'

Jones rubbed his head. 'Hey, I'm not a sea dog like you.'

'The tides here on the Helford are extreme enough during the springs but along the coast of Brittany the swing is sharper, and your counterparts will have to work with them to reach you at the designated spots.'

'We know this,' said the young Piron.

'I know you do but others who may follow you may not, so what would you add to the charts?' I asked, and noted each of the suggestions, of which there were many, once they understood the process.

'Anything else?' I asked yet again as I scanned the room putting the pencil down.

'What did you study?' asked Tom Long.

'Basically, physical geography.'

'In layman's terms, please.' Long smiled.

'I look at the natural development of land, plants and animals plus climate, but I specialised in coastal geography, how the ocean and land affect each other and the people living there.

Based on your activities, and others, it's proved a good thing to have studied.'

'Couldn't agree more,' said the commander, rising to his feet. 'The coast is such a fascinating place.'

'The beginning and the end,' I added.

'And as we'll be beginning again at eleven this evening,' said the commander, 'I suggest everyone get some rest.'

17

16 May 1942

We stood on the beach below Ridifarne. It had gone midnight and a light rain was falling. I wasn't sure what was going to happen on this training exercise let alone what part, if any, I would have. My nerves were on high alert, even though this was practice. I hoped to learn something about how they operated and possibly this could be the source of the difficulties with the other teams operating the same routes to France.

'We will work in pairs tonight. Use the B grouping; and Nipper, you will go with Dr Tremayne.' The men broke up into their pairs.

'You're stuck with me again,' I said, wishing it had been anyone else. My attraction to him was an annoyance and a distraction that I didn't need.

Jake shrugged and half smiled. I looked away. His smile was not going to help things.

'Right, each pair must recover one item. You must accomplish this while being undetected. Brooks Richards, Baker, Stubbs, Johnson and I will be on patrol.'

The commander handed me a slip of paper. 'Don't open until we have dispersed.'

I tucked it into a pocket and saw Jake had done the same with his. Were we given different pieces of information? Could

I trust him? In most things I suspected not but when it came to war games I could. This was my gut saying it and not my head, and I pushed that realisation aside, for with it came the mocking voice of the American saying I told you so.

We set off in my canoe towards the middle of the river. The tide pulled us out, and once we had reached the steps at Golden Gear, Jake turned to me.

'If we make for the rocks just past here, we can check our messages,' he said.

'It's a bit late,' I noted. 'You may have pointed us in the wrong direction.'

'True but hidden among the rocks our light won't be seen and we can make a plan.'

This was why he had been paired with me and was not on patrol as the other officers were. Once behind the rocks, I pulled the paper from my pocket. The ink was smudged with the rain and the light from the torch barely illuminated it. His was the same. I didn't know the rules of this game therefore I watched closely, looking for a reaction of some kind. But he wore a poker face. For all I knew his piece of paper said I was a spy, and he should lead me to my death.

Mine read:

A mailbag was dropped at the wrong point because the agent was followed. It was supposed to be hidden by the mill at Carne. Instead, he left it safe where the buzzard's nest and nuts crunch but no one can hear.
Trust no one.

Marvellous. Did that include my companion? There was no way I could do this on my own. No, that wasn't true. It was clear to me immediately where the mailbag was to be found. But I couldn't go straight there if I was to trust no one. How was I going to lose Jake? But what was the discussion we had had that you must trust your team? Head or heart?

'What happens now?' I asked.

He frowned. 'Buzzards?'

'You had the same message.'

'It would appear so.' He nodded. My eyes were adjusting to the darkness and, as the boat moved, the phosphorescence in the water glowed like stars had come down from the sky.

'My first thought would be the big Monterey pines by Pengarrock but that seems too obvious.'

'Agreed.' I made my decision. 'It would have to be around the church at St Anthony.'

'Thought that too.' He pulled out a map.

I put my hand on it. 'Normally I'm all for maps but, in this case, I don't need one.'

He laughed. 'Fair point.'

'We can't go round by sea as the boom will be up.'

'If we continue along the coast to Pengarrock beach we can land the canoe there and cut across the headland.'

He nodded and we left the protection of the rocks and let the pull of the tide move us silently down the shore. Looming shadows marked the coastline and I listened. Waves gently washed the rocks. If we hit them, it wouldn't cause damage in this craft. From Pengarrock there were old trails that were still navigable. Not easy in the dark but more hidden than seeking the way via the lanes.

We reached Pengarrock Beach and secured the canoe then set off silently up the path through the dense woods. Progress was slow, with me tripping all the time and forever catching on brambles and twigs. Eventually we reached the path along the side of the fields.

Everything was still except my heartbeat. It raced even though

I understood we were safe. I knew this land; the biggest threat was the bull two fields over and yet this felt real. There would also be local men watching the night sky and we must be alert for them. I didn't want to come face to face with a man holding a gun who had worked all day and was exhausted to the core. Reluctantly I headed into the field. The woods offered some protection, but we had to break cover to reach the churchyard. It was not yet one in the morning. An open field and the path past the vicarage were all that was left to navigate before we reached the churchyard.

Jake tapped my arm. In the darkness, with a cap covering his fair hair, he was no more than a vague shadow in front of me. We kept close to the hedges for as long as we could. The rain returned and the mud beneath our feet squelched with each step. I was soaked, and rain ran down my face. I couldn't recall ever being this wet when not swimming.

Reaching the fence, he climbed over it then held out a hand for me to take. I scrambled over and bumped into him. He steadied me then we took small steps, past the vicarage and onto the lane where he headed for the gate into the churchyard. But I beckoned him up the lane a bit and over the back hedge. I didn't know if each team had the same task, but only a local would be aware of this way into the graveyard.

Up the rough steps in the hedge, I paused, listening to the cry of an owl who appeared to be the only other animal about on this foul night. I jumped down and my father's grave was three headstones in front of us. Beyond that, below the big beach tree, there was the old grave with the buzzard and the ship on it. Behind it the land dropped to a field. It would be easy to hide a bag in the mass of foliage that marked the boundary.

Jake stopped me and put his finger to my lips. I stilled but my heart did not. It pounded in my ears, and I couldn't hear what he had to say. We stood so close together that I could feel the heat of his body. An animal scurried over my foot in the tall grass, and I bit my lip so as not to call out. I was not afraid of mice or even rats but everything in me was wound tight. It was merely an exercise. Nothing was at stake, I repeated to myself five times silently, and my breathing slowed. I bent down and began to feel around the gravestone and into the long grass. Jake joined me and together we covered the area. The scent of leaf mould and wet earth filled the air, but we found nothing. Stuffing aside the disappointment, I sat back on my heels because I'd been so certain it would be here. I rose and began to walk away when I tripped, falling flat on my front with a thump. Jake was at my side in a second.

'Don't move,' he whispered.

I wasn't sure I could at first, but I began with my toes and then my fingers.

'Anything hurt?' he asked.

I laughed as quietly as I could then rotated my ankles. All good there. Slowly I sat up and stayed still until things steadied. I pressed my hands into the ground beside me when a slate by the grave moved. That was what I had caught my foot on and feeling around I found an upside-down flowerpot. Lifting it, I discovered a small, waxed cotton bag. I handed it to Jake without a word then stood. Everything on the front of me hurt from my knees to the palms of my hands.

'Well done,' he whispered. 'Are you OK to head back?' He held out a hand to me.

'I'd better be because I don't fancy a night in the churchyard even if my father is here.' I took his hand until my walking improved, and the tightness eased. It would be a long journey back to the beach at this pace but then I recalled a path that cut down past Condurrow and came out closer to Pengarrock beach. I pointed up the lane and we crept along in silence.

When we finally reached the canoe, I could have cried.

'Just sit and don't try and paddle,' he said.

'Don't be foolish. The tide is still on its way out. It will be quicker if I paddle as well,' I said.

'Suit yourself, ma'am.' He shrugged and held the boat still while I climbed in awkwardly. Once out in the current, I regretted my words as each stroke hurt but I wouldn't be defeated. I was beyond pain by the time we dragged the canoe up the beach in front of Ridifarne. The other teams were still out and Mary was waiting up. On seeing my condition, she poured me a stiff whisky then ran me a bath.

I took a sip then pulled my sodden headscarf off.

Jake laughed. 'You look like something the cat has had.'

'Thanks. You sure know how to compliment a woman.' I sighed, pushing damp hair from my face.

'Oh, I do, I assure you, but I'm honest too.' He poured himself a whisky. 'You are one hell of a lady, that is for sure.' He raised his glass.

'I'm not sure how to take that.'

'It's a compliment,' he said. 'I'm clearly losing my touch.'

Mary walked back into the sitting room. She looked from me to Jake and back again. 'Merry, your bath is ready.'

'Thank you,' I said, placing my empty glass down.

'And straight to bed after that,' she said. 'The others won't be back for hours, I imagine.'

Nodding I cast a quick glance at Jake who I knew would wait for their return. Mary would too but despite the desire to be a part of the team, it would be best to bathe and sleep and be of some use tomorrow.

I lay on my bed but every time I closed my eyes images of Jake's smile came to mind, and not the rest I needed. There was one way to sort this problem: map it. Sitting, I pulled out my notebook and made a sketch of Jake. I had none of my mother's skill and it showed. On the side of the paper, I listed what I knew. He was from Maine, had done his undergraduate degree in English Literature at Bowdoin College and his masters at Harvard where he was captain of rowing. He was a pilot and an American of Norwegian and Irish descent. He liked Sayers' books.

What I couldn't write down was why I found him so fascinating. He was arrogant and yet at times thoughtful. None of what I'd written could I plot on a map even if I drew a map of the north-east coast of the United States and added in his crossing the border to Canada to join the RAF. But then there was his work here.

There was something about Jake that I couldn't trust. I couldn't put my finger on it without a map. I was missing something obvious. Were those pesky hormones, as my tutor had called them, clouding my judgement?

I ripped the page out of the book, crushed it into a ball and threw it in the bin. In the time of rationing, that exercise had been a complete waste of paper and of my time. I retrieved it and unfolded it. On the back I remembered a map from my early studies of the head and the heart, emotions and logic. I drew one of each. It would be easy to plot what assets of Lieutenant Russell fit on the head map and which fit on the heart one. I tore the paper to shreds. Thinking like this was no help at all.

Placing my head in my hands, I longed to chat to Constance. She would help me to see things correctly. Jake had become like an itch that I needed to scratch. I laughed. Of course, that was exactly it. Years ago, standing by the field where a ram had been put with the ewes was when my mother had decided to expand my knowledge of the facts of life. I was thirteen.

'Ma petite, it's time I spoke to you about . . . how shall I say the bees and the flowers.'

'Maman, I know how babies are made!' I crossed my arms in front of my chest.

'This is true,' she said as we watched the ram mount a ewe. 'But there are key things you don't know yet.' She tugged my plait gently. 'There we see nature doing as it should. It is a call and an urge we all feel.'

I wrinkled my nose.

'It is like an itch that absolutely must be scratched.'

I stepped back.

'The more you think about it the more you need to scratch it,' she said.

'Then why don't you?' I asked.

She laughed. 'Well, you do, sometimes. In its simplest sense you scratch the itch . . . by yourself or another does it for you.'

I looked out onto the field because I didn't want my mother to know what I was thinking.

'We are all animals, and we are all itchy,' she said with a roll of her graceful hands.

'But . . . ' I said.

'No, ma petite, we are all itchy, but some people are better at not scratching.'

'So that is all . . . ' I struggled to say the word and a smile hovered around Maman's mouth. 'That sex is.'

'No, not at all. We humans love and it is love that makes the act of scratching different,' she clarified.

'How?' I asked.

'When you add love, it is no longer scratching but . . . how do you say, a communication, a knowing, a giving and receiving and, aside from making babies, it is a gift,' she said.

The ram mounted another ewe.

'You see they are doing as nature intended them to do and it does not matter too much who does it as long as they are healthy.' She smiled.

We stood in silence for a while, watching the ram make his way through the field.

'How do you know it's love and not just scratching?' I asked.

Maman threw her head back and laughed. 'Oh, ma petite, your heart will tell you.' She kissed my head then took my hand and we walked back to the house.

As my body reacted to thoughts of Jake Russell, I knew I had to avoid him if possible, otherwise he was an itch that might require some scratching. But once scratched I could forget him, as I had forgotten other lovers.

18

We had just finished dinner. It had been a lively affair taken in the garden making the most of the glorious weather and the light evening. Again, we were all suited and booted for the meal. It almost felt like pre-war life. But the drone of aircraft above was a reminder this was far from normal. I sensed these days of dressing so formally for dinner were disappearing and a small part of me was sad. This war was altering life as we knew it. I had seen so much progress in women's rights since the start with the greatest strides being achieved through women's war work. This should eliminate the many barriers placed in front of us going forward.

Mrs Newton raced out to us, saying, 'Dr Tremayne, your brother's on the telephone.'

All decorum lost, I ran to the telephone.

'Oli,' I said, a bit breathless.

'She is actually gone.' His voice was flat.

'No, no, I don't believe it,' I said.

'I hadn't either,' he said. 'But I've given it a lot of thought. There's no other alternative, Merry. She's not off painting.'

I drew a deep breath, wanting to stop him.

'I don't think she's dead,' I said, knowing I had nothing to ground that statement on.

'She is, as much as it kills me to say it.' His voice trailed away.

'I don't accept it,' I said, wanting to shout at him not to give up hope but his voice told me he had.

'I know how hard it is, God,' Oliver said. 'I can barely believe it but there's no other explanation.'

'Oli . . . ' I began.

'No, Merry, she's dead,' he said. 'Just accept the facts as I have.'

I pressed my lips together. I wasn't going to argue with him; I would prove him wrong.

'I love you,' I said.

'That tells me you are not going to accept it and there's nothing I can do.' He laughed bitterly. 'I love you too, Merry.'

The line cut off. I placed the handset down and sank onto the bottom step with the weight of Oli's certainty holding me down.

Brooks Richards came through to the hallway.

'We are heading to the Ferry Boat for a bit of dancing,' he said.

'I'll join you in a few minutes.' I rose to my feet, forcing a smile.

'Of course.' He left me and I walked up to my room and stood in front of the mirror. Did I look like a fool? Was Oli right? Clear eyes stared back at me. Despite what he said, I believed she was alive. People don't just disappear. If my mother was dead, I could and would accept it. Yes, I would be devastated but she had always taught me that death was part of life.

The voices outside faded away. Picking up my powder, I applied a bit more, seeing not myself at the mirror but my mother as her cross around my neck glimmered in the light. Once this would have been fun, even conspiratorial, but now it highlighted her absence. Sixteen days since she was last seen. Oli was certain she was dead, and I was more and more positive she was not. But I couldn't explain why, for I had no evidence other than that her body had not been found.

I sighed. Did I even want to go dancing? No, but there was

nothing I could do right this minute. She of all people would not want me sitting alone. Maman thrived on being with people and she would push me out of the door if she was here. 'Go and live,' her voice said in my head. After a last glance in the mirror, I walked downstairs and found Jake Russell. He was not the distraction I needed.

'You didn't need to wait for me,' I said.

'I couldn't let a lady walk on her own.' He held out his arm.

'I'm more than capable of walking to the inn alone.' I stopped on the bottom step.

'I won't argue with that,' he said. 'But I enjoy your company.'

I studied his face looking for insincerity but saw none as I took his arm and he smiled. We went out into the garden. My thoughts oscillated between my conversation with Oli and why Fleming had placed Jake here in the first place? Nothing was clear but there was one thing I could do . . . focus on my task of gaining information for Fleming.

'Can you tell me what it's like to work with the SIS team from Dartmouth?' I asked.

'Why do you ask?'

'Curiosity,' I said with a smile, tossing his own words back at him. 'Brooks Richards mentioned you and a few of the men had a tricky mission at the start of the month.'

'Did he?' He raised an eyebrow.

'According to him it took you three attempts to land on the right beach.'

'That's true,' he said, allowing me to walk in front of him down the steps to the beach where the tide was almost in.

'Davis wouldn't allow Pierre on the boat.' He shook his head. 'Maps are wonderful but they require the skill of the navigator. Pierre knows the waters like the back of his hand.'

'What was the purpose of the trip?' I asked, lifting the hem of my gown above the sand.

'It was their operation,' he said, not meeting my glance.

'And those differ from yours?'

Above the sky had turned that velvet blue of my favourite evening gown, rich and full of depth. I took a deep breath of the evening air, fragranced with pine, seaweed and salt.

'Yes.'

'What was the purpose then?' I asked.

He stared at me. 'Just why do you need to know?'

I paused and considered how best to answer. 'So that I understand what I should be including on maps.'

He sent me a look. He didn't trust me.

'On this operation we were moving one person and supplies,' he said.

'A person? An agent, you mean.'

'The SIS work differently to us. As crew we know nothing more than is needed. A woman boarded the boat and we were not allowed to speak to her nor did I know what supplies we landed.' He paused. 'Is that enough information?'

'It's a start. Thank you,' I said, thinking about a lone woman being landed and how brave she must be.

He stopped and pointed up. The stars were just appearing and a shooting one cut across the heavens. 'Well, that's the bit of good luck that we need.'

'You think it's luck we need?' I turned to him.

'Yes, it always helps even if you are on the side of right,' he said.

'True.' We needed everything: luck, intelligence, cunning and, possibly being here in Cornwall, a touch of fairy dust.

'What do you do when you are not out helping teams like us?' he asked, as we strolled along the waterline.

I glanced at him. There were few people who had any idea of what I did, and that was how it would stay. 'Well, I'm a geographer, and every war needs them by the bucket load.'

We stopped walking and he turned and stared directly into my eyes. I swallowed. He was far too attractive.

'I sense you still haven't forgiven me regarding that comment when you arrived,' he said.

'Hmm.' I considered his words then set off. This might be the best way to stall the attraction between us.

Catching up to me, he said, 'You are hard.'

'Am I? I do my job and I do it well. Does that make me hard?' I asked.

'That's not what I meant.' He drew a breath. 'I meant that you don't give a guy a break.'

I turned to him.

'Maybe you are right, I don't; but every day I face prejudice because, instead of being a man with a white beard, they find me. I think that has given me some sharp edges,' I said. 'But I would hope that I'm not hard in my dealings with people . . . maybe a bit stern sometimes.'

'Isn't that the case with all teachers?' He laughed.

I frowned, puzzled by the comment.

'My mother is a teacher,' he said with a smile. Behind him the river flowed out to sea, leaving more sand exposed as the moon rose.

'So, I'm like her?' I asked.

'In a way.' He studied me. 'She'd like you.'

'Did your mother work when you were little?' I asked, trying to figure him out but I didn't have the knowledge of life in the United States to understand him as I could with British people.

'Money was tight, and the woman next door used to watch over us, but it wasn't long before I could look after my sisters. I'm six years older,' he said. 'Education was, and is, everything to my mother. My father had a good love of poetry and could recite it at the drop of a hat, or a drop of whisky, but his mathematics was terrible, and my mother used to teach him at night when we'd gone to bed.'

I tried to picture his world, but there was more than the Atlantic Ocean between us. Growing up here on the farm with two loving parents and a private tutor, Oliver and I wanted for nothing. Jake's childhood was very different, having lost his father when he was fifteen.

We passed the cottages, and I missed the warm light that used to spill from their windows. The need to keep everything dark was isolating and yet there was a tall American right beside me. I was far from alone.

Music greeted us as we arrived at the Ferry Boat. Tables had been pushed back against the walls and a three-piece band played in the corner. Lady Seaton was foxtrotting in the arms of a Polish airman. Her granddaughter – Amelia, I think, and not the other twin Adele – was rather too close to a lieutenant. There were more familiar faces in the crowd and the famous actor, Godfrey Tearle, was tucked in the corner, watching the shenanigans.

The music changed to 'When Smoke Gets in Your Eyes' and Jake turned to me. 'Well, Merry, do you dance?' He held out a hand. 'Or maybe that should be, will you dance? Or are you merry enough to?'

'I do and I am,' I said.

I took his hand, and a little shiver ran up my arm as his fingers closed over mine. We wove our way through the others and passed Brooks Richards with a Wren. They looked like they could only see each other. Jealousy held me for a moment. Not that I was interested in Brooks Richards, but they displayed a sense of completeness. The same aura had surrounded my parents. Before I could consider it fully, Jake's arms were about me and we moved slowly at first, finding each other's rhythm.

Jake Russell could dance. His nickname made a bit more sense.

It was clear he loved music as he held me close. It flowed through him and me. Instinct and the beat of the music took over. Right in this moment I wasn't Meredith Tremayne, BA (Hons), MA, DPhil (Oxon) but Merry, the woman. She didn't come out to play very often. Last seen at a May Ball in the arms of George. But this was different. I wasn't eighteen but twenty-seven and I understood my body's reaction to being in the arms of a handsome man. It hadn't forgotten. The song ended and the band struck up Glenn Miller's 'String of Pearls'. Jake seamlessly changed tempo and twirled me around.

Coming back into his arms, I asked, 'Where did you learn to dance?'

'In the kitchen,' he said.

I blinked. 'That's the last answer I expected.'

'Because of my father, we mixed with the Irish community, and, after eating, the kitchen table would be pushed aside, and the accordion and the fiddle would appear,' he said.

I tried to picture this, but it didn't fit with the man in front of me, dressed in a dinner jacket and holding me in his arms.

'You danced like this in the kitchen?' I asked.

'No, not like this but I learned to hear the music and move to it.' He spun me around. 'This sort of dancing came from Bowdoin and Harvard.'

He twirled me again. 'I've surprised you.'

'You have.' So many things did and the biggest being the way I felt in his arms as the dance came to an end. I didn't want to leave his embrace and I didn't want to end the conversation. These situations were to be avoided. I glanced up at Jake, knowing I didn't want to avoid him at all.

'What can I get you?' he asked as he led me to the bar.

You would do nicely, I thought, but said, 'A Dubonnet, thank you.'

I turned from him and scanned the room. Where was my exit? My mother's voice in my head asked me why I was trying to exit from the company of a charming man. I replied silently: I don't have time to waste with him. I could hear her laughter at that, and I frowned.

He handed me the drink.

'Is something wrong?' he asked.

'No, purely a thought about something I might have missed on the photographs today,' I lied.

He placed his beer down. 'Shall I walk you back?'

Dear God, that's all I need, more time alone with him under the starlight, I told myself.

'No, it's fine. I'll fix it later,' I said as we walked towards the door. Amelia dashed up to us.

'I thought it was you, Merry,' she said, with her glance darting from me to Jake.

'How lovely to see you,' I said, squinting, trying to be sure before I said her name.

'It's Amelia.' She laughed. 'Adele didn't feel like dancing tonight.'

'Is she still looking at going to university?' I'd spent many hours answering Adele's questions about an academic life. She had the capability, but I wasn't sure she truly wanted it. Time would tell.

'Hard to look at anything but the war,' said Amelia.

'True. What are you doing?' I asked.

'Waiting for my eighteenth birthday so I can join up without father's permission.' She looked towards the Wren talking to Brooks Richards then she smiled at Jake.

'Sorry,' I said, remembering my manners. 'Amelia Seaton, this is Lieutenant Jake Russell.'

He held out his hand and shook hers, saying, 'A pleasure to meet you.'

'Oh, an American, how lovely. My grandmother can't stand you lot, said you took too long to come to fight.' Her glance narrowed.

'I agree with your grandmother and I have written so many times,' he said.

Amelia batted her lashes. 'You aren't *the* Jake Russell who wrote those dispatches, are you?'

'One and the same,' he said.

'I loved reading your view of us and how well we were coping.' She smiled at him. 'I don't suppose you'd ask me to dance.'

'But of course,' he said. 'If you'll excuse me, Merry.'

I nodded and he led Amelia out onto the dance floor. I looked away as something like jealousy twisted inside me. That was an emotion that had no place in my life.

Baker walked to my side as I headed outdoors with one quick glance over my shoulder.

'I see our resident ladies' man has made another conquest,' Baker said.

'Ladies' man?' I asked.

'The Nipper has a girl in almost every port, I'm led to believe.' He looked at me and lit another cigarette. His glance moved onto Jake then back to me. 'Are you about to be the next, I wonder?'

'I'm safe from his charms,' I said, and added silently, *if not totally immune to them*, and Baker wasn't either. It couldn't be easy being a homosexual in the services.

'Where in Ireland are you from?' I asked as we left the noise and music behind for the clear air outside.

'I'm from Fermoy, County Cork, but I've lived in London since nineteen thirty-one,' he said.

'And what did you do in London?' I asked.

'Before this,' he said, waving a hand towards the river. 'Banking.'

I nodded. That fit his dapper appearance.

'Why aren't you two dancing?' the commander asked as he joined us.

Baker laughed. 'I'd need another drink for that.' He raised the now empty glass in his hand. 'Can I get either of you anything?'

'I'm fine, thank you.' I glanced at my own glass, which I hadn't touched.

'Me too.' The commander smiled.

'Fair enough.' He bowed his head and set off into the building.

'Baker's a good man for an Irishman and . . . ' His voice trailed away.

I turned to him. 'You know?'

'Hard not to when we work so closely, and he only has eyes for Nipper.' He laughed. 'He's damned good at what he does and has one of the sharpest brains I've ever worked with.' He paused to take a sip of his beer. 'I wouldn't be without him, no matter what his sexual preferences. He's our best marksman and I'd choose him over a more . . . conventional type any day.'

I smiled, liking the commander more and more. He offered me a cigarette.

'No thanks,' I said, looking out to the rising moon.

He took a drag of his cigarette then exhaled. 'Thank you for your help.'

'I feel your frustration . . . ' I paused, trying to find the right words.

He laughed. 'I'm a man of action.' The sound of a dog barking across the river carried on the night air. 'Those damn dogs.'

'Don't like them?'

'Love dogs but they alert everyone to your movements. Those are the gamekeeper's dogs at Pengarrock. Any time we leave or arrive under the cover of darkness, they hear us and sound the alarm. Even Tom Long who is courting the gamekeeper's daughter can't keep the damn things quiet.' He shook his head. 'It's bad enough here but when landing in France it's positively dangerous.'

I listened to the barking with a new understanding. I spent so much of my time looking for physical obstacles and ways forward that I hadn't thought of what they actually faced. It wasn't just big tides and dangerous rocks. Nor was it simply where the munition plants were or the train stations. It was the human and animal threats that mattered as much. 'I can only imagine.'

'With your language skills I'm surprised they haven't moved you to France to gather the on-the-ground intelligence.'

'Sadly, not on the cards.'

He studied me. 'I bet you'd be excellent in the field. Level-headed and, having watched you these past days, quick and creative in your thinking.'

I sighed. 'I've been told I'm too important elsewhere.'

'So, my instinct was right: you would like nothing better than to be working in France.'

I nodded.

'For what it's worth, having seen you with the team I'd take you along with us.'

'Thank you,' I said.

Inside the music changed.

'That's Mary's favourite so I best go and ask her for a dance,' he said. 'If you will excuse me?'

'Of course.' I stared back across the river, just making out the outline of the hills in the moonlight. I would love to go on a mission, but I knew that it wouldn't happen. I was lucky to be allowed to join them training.

19

17 May 1942

I'd woken at dawn with my mother on my mind. My short conversation with Oli was at the forefront of my thoughts as I took a quick bath. In the past I had done some of my best thinking while soaking in hot water but not today. No new insights arrived from my subconscious. No reason why I felt my mother was still alive.

On this Sunday morning, I stood dressed and ready for the day in front of the mirror. 'Maman is dead,' I whispered. Unbelieving eyes looked back at me. 'Maman is alive and is . . . somewhere.' That's what I believed yet Oli was probably correct.

With a frustrated sigh I collected my notebook and crept to the kitchen through the silent house. I made a pot of tea and, while it brewed, I flipped to my map. Home, St Anthony, Kynance, my cottage and Porthoustock.

'Morning.' Jake's deep voice was tinged with sleep. His damp hair looked like he'd run his fingers and not a comb through it.

'I didn't expect you, or anyone, up for hours,' I said, helping myself to a bowl of porridge.

He grabbed another cup and saucer and set it beside mine. 'Could say the same of you.'

'I was in bed by midnight.' I put my pencil down.

'I wasn't far behind you.' He poured the tea, making a face.

'What's wrong?' I asked.

'Tea is for the afternoon. Coffee is for the morning,' he said, handing me a cup then sitting down.

'I see.' I sipped my tea and hid my smile behind the cup.

He peered at me. 'Do you?'

'You're grumpy in the morning.' I placed my cup down.

'True. My mother has always given me a hard time about it.' He glanced at the notebook between us. 'Working?'

I shook my head. 'Looking at the last known locations of my mother.'

'May I?' he asked.

I turned the book to face him and slid it across the table.

His fingers traced the marks.

'My brother thinks she's dead.' I cradled the teacup in my hand. Would saying she was dead often enough make it become a fact or help me to accept it?

He looked up at me. 'And you don't.'

'No, but as each new day arrives that's more likely.' The haunting image of the unfinished self-portrait in the cottage came to mind.

'And you miss her,' he said.

'Yes.' I picked up my tea. 'She preferred coffee first thing.'

'Wise woman. I like her already.'

I studied him, seeing him through my mother's eyes. It would be the angles, the lines and the shadows that she would see, whereas my glance fell on his full mouth. 'She would like you too, I think.'

'Good.' He pushed the book back to me. 'Does mapping help?'

'Normally, yes, but this makes no sense. The only thing that fits is her putting the flowers on my father's grave.' I tapped on St Anthony.

'Have you traced her steps in person, not just on the page?'

'No. There hasn't been time.'

'It might help.' He stood and helped himself to a bowl of porridge.

'How so?' I asked.

'It could jog a memory or if nothing else make you feel you have done something.' He returned to the table and sat down.

'The latter would help.'

'Well, it's Sunday and we're not scheduled to do anything today. I could come with you.' He took a spoonful of porridge.

'That's kind,' I said, not sure whether I should be grateful or suspicious.

'Ulterior motive.' He grinned. 'You could show me some of the local sites.'

'Problem,' I said. 'No transport.'

'I have access to a motorcycle. Have you been on one?'

'Yes, my brother has one.' I shivered, remembering the hair-raising rides with Oli going far too fast down winding lanes. We both thought we were invincible then. Oli still thought he was and I hoped that was true.

'Well, then, what do you say?' He looked out the window at the clear sky.

'Why not.' I stood and cleared my cup to the sink.

He stood. 'Shall we leave in a half hour?'

'It's a plan,' I said and headed back upstairs, debating what I'd let myself in for. Had I said yes solely because I was attracted to him or did his idea have merit?

*

Mary sent me a look as she watched me climb on the back of the bike, wrapping my arms around Jake.

'Do be careful with her, Nipper. You nearly broke her the other night,' she said.

'She did that all by herself.' He laughed and it reverberated through me. I hadn't considered the practicalities of being on a motorcycle with him or my bruises and scrapes from the night training. If I had, I might have said no. But it was too late to turn back now as we set off up the drive at a sedate pace. I hadn't been this close to a man since the Italian scholar and this was the same and yet entirely different. Matteo had been quietly cultivated and nothing about this man felt cultivated or quiet. But he wasn't loud either. Jake Russell was a mystery to me.

We turned sharply at the end of the lane, and I held on tightly as we leaned into it.

'Where to, Merry?'

'Head towards Porth Navas,' I directed.

Things passed in a blur as the cool air rushed across my face. It was hard to think of anything but the man in front of me and that was not what this journey was about. The lanes wove up and down following the landscape along the river, passing through small clusters of houses so typical of Cornish habitation. Finally, we reached Gweek, and Jake stopped.

'Seems strange to see this from the land side.' He glanced over his shoulder.

'When have you been to Gweek?' I recalled my last visit to the boatyard and the sense of unease. Had Jake followed me? He'd arrived at the inn after me. But why would he have? I saw no reason, yet he always seemed to be near.

'I've rowed my way up and down most of the river,' he said, looking away from me. 'Where to from here?'

I pointed up the hill because I hadn't considered which location we would go to first. This excursion had been his idea and it had merit. Before long we were on an unfamiliar lane. With the road signs gone, I only knew we were speeding south from the sun and the shadows. Jake slowed the motorbike. I didn't think it was possible for me to be lost on the Lizard but I was.

Finally I found my bearings. To our right the land rose and flattened to Goonhilly Downs. There was a small pool in the distance reflecting the deep blue of the May sky. To our left, the fields were smaller, divided by hedges currently woolly with grasses, bluebells and the spikes of foxgloves. The land sloped down, no doubt to a stream. The grass in them was green whereas the moorland was soft shades of gold and brown.

Jake pulled up and didn't speak for a moment then said, 'The dramatic change always astounds me.'

'The fields become less fertile with the substrata of serpentine,' I said without thinking. He didn't need explanations of geography and as I thought that I also questioned when he'd been here before.

'It's so striking.'

'My mother painted the downs often while I had explored and mapped the moor. I was fascinated with the standing stone, or the Dry Tree as it is called locally.'

Jake put the motorbike into gear and we proceeded at a gentler pace until the sound of a plane engine disturbed the peace. Jake took us to the cover of a tree as the plane swooped low. I held onto him a little tighter as my heart skipped a beat until I recognised it as one of ours. It must be landing at the new airfield at Predannack, built after France fell.

We pressed onwards towards the last known siting of my mother. The distance across the moor to the cliffs above Kynance took no time and we didn't encounter another soul. Despite the heavy rain of two days ago, the ground was firm and dry, and it was easy to bring the bike right to the cliff edge. Below, the tide was obscuring the sand. Rollers built up momentum and barrelled towards the cliffs but the air around us was still. Somewhere there was a storm creating the swell.

'Stunning,' Jake said, scanning the horizon.

'When the tide is out, the beach is perfect.' I pointed to the stacks below being pounded by the surf.

'Your mother was painting here?' he asked.

'That's what they said, and it was one of her favourite places too.' I looked down to the waves crashing below. 'She normally worked from beach level.'

'Was that a crow?' Jake pointed to a large black bird with red legs and beak.

'A chough, the bird of Cornwall, but sadly there aren't many left,' I said.

'Why?' He turned from the view towards me.

'Poaching, collecting the eggs, trophies for display cases,' I explained.

'I can see why an artist would love it here.'

I walked down the cliff road towards the beach, searching for anything of hers that might have gone unnoticed.

'What are the rocks?' Jake asked as he caught up to me.

'Serpentine, an ancient rock that's been intruded and heavily altered in the process. It somewhat resembles snake's skin, hence the name.' I paused, taking in the beauty of the site. 'Of course, there is also granite, gneiss and basalt around here.'

'Are you sure you didn't study geology?' he asked.

I stopped and turned to him. 'You need to know what underlies what you see, especially in coastal areas.'

He held up his hand. 'I was joking.'

'Sorry,' I said. 'I'm passionate about my subject and forget that it's not that interesting to others.'

'Being passionate about something is always good.' He smiled and for a moment I forgot why I was here.

Below, the sound of the sea brought my thoughts back to my mother. I hadn't properly looked in her paintbox, which was foolish. From her painting I could have seen where she had been standing. I had no idea what had caught her eye that day as we'd passed Thomas's private hotel, which appeared closed, as was the café. With the tide still high but on its way out, there was not much beach. I stopped when we reached the mass of boulders that led to the sandy cove still hidden by the outgoing tide.

'There's nothing here but memories.' My shoulders slumped.

'This is hard for you,' he said.

I nodded. 'Shall we head off?'

'Sure,' he said.

As we turned to leave, a stone caught my eye. I bent and picked up a heart-shaped piece of red serpentine. The surface had been tumbled smooth as if someone had shaped it. I held it out to Jake.

'Beautiful,' he said, taking it from me and rolling it on his palm. Handing it back, he said, 'Your heart.'

I laughed and slipped it into my pocket rather than throw it back onto the beach. Taking one last look at the sea, we began the long climb up to his motorbike.

Both of us were breathless when we reached the top. A man from the Home Guard was standing by the bike.

'What are you doing here? Can I see your IDs?' he said.

'I'm Dr Tremayne and this is Lieutenant Russell, and we're here trying to trace my mother's footsteps. She's missing.' I handed over my identity card and Jake did the same.

'Who be she?' he asked, scanning the documents and returning them.

'Elise Tremayne of Kestle,' I said.

'Oh, yes.' He nodded. 'Did you find anything?'

'No. Did you see her?' I asked.

'She was painting here for a while, and we had a chat about the weather.'

'The weather?' I had hoped for more.

'It was due to change, I recall,' he said, glancing up at the blue sky above us.

'Do you remember when it was you spoke to her?' I asked.

'About two, I think,' he said.

'Thank you.' I smiled then turned to Jake who threw a long leg over the motorbike and waited for me. I took one last look down to the beach before climbing on behind him.

'Ready?' he asked.

I slipped my arms around his waist. 'Yes.'

He revved the engine and we set off down the track and onto the main road towards Lizard Point. The sky became bluer, and my heart broke further the more I considered this whole exercise. But consider it I did as I gave directions. My mother had been on her bicycle. It would have taken her two hours to reach Kynance from St Anthony. If she painted for a few hours, it could have been as late as four or five by the time she left.

Again, depending on which route she took, it would have been another hour and a half or even two hours to reach Porthoustock. That would make it around seven or later. Still light but not for painting on a cove facing east. The sun would have set at roughly eight thirty and then a few hours of twilight, which was past the magical hour that my mother loved. But all of this was assumption.

Our speed reduced and Jake came to a stop, and I was pressed into him, making me acutely aware of our proximity. He pointed to a gap in the hedge where I could see a small stone building surrounded by blackthorn, hazel and elder trees covered in bits of fabric. I smiled. It's not that I didn't notice these things, but they were normal. For an American it would be very odd.

'In the States we have many things, but not that,' he said.

'There's a holy well enclosed in the building and people bring their wishes and troubles here. They dip the fabric into the water, rub the part of the body they are worried about and tie it to the tree,' I explained. 'As the cloth disintegrates the illness goes, they say. But people also use them as prayer trees.'

'Superstition,' he said, switching off the engine.

'In a way, or another form of prayer, one that is more tangible,' I replied.

He twisted around to look at me directly. 'How does the scientist in you view this practice?'

I laughed. 'Anything that makes people feel better is fine by me, especially at present. Do you want to see it?'

'What do you think?' He grinned.

I slipped off the seat and straightened, pushing a loose strand of hair from my face. 'There are hundreds of sacred wells in Cornwall, and as many, if not more, clootie trees.'

'The Cornish are a pagan people?' he asked, peering at the bits of fabric.

I shook my head. 'Not pagan, if you mean without religion; quite the opposite. The Cornish are a people of deeply held beliefs which they've fought and died for . . . and maybe that is why they cling to the old ways, the ways that don't require words or rituals but actions and belief,' I said, digging into my pocket and finding my handkerchief. Clutching it, I climbed over the hedge and pushed through the brambles to the old well. Normally the area around was kept tidy but people had other things to do.

'Does it have a name?' he asked, bending low, looking through the door.

'Either St Ruan or St Grada. The local parish church is St Grada. But I agree with my mother that it is St Rumon, also known as St Ruan, who was Irish and is venerated in Brittany as well. In fact, it is almost his feast day in Brittany.' I took a deep breath and bent to the water, dipping my hankie in it. When I stood, Jake was studying me.

'You are one interesting woman.' He folded his arms across his chest.

I laughed. 'Interesting, good or bad?'

'Good, passionate about your subject, yet you are an academic and here you are following an ancient tradition.' The corner of his mouth lifted and I had to look away as my stomach tightened.

Moving past him, I bowed my head and said the Our Father, silently revisiting the many times my mother had brought Oli and me here on the first of June.

The hedges were covered in white with the hawthorn trees in bloom. The blossom was joyous against the clear sky. Carefully I pulled an undecorated branch towards me and tied my hand-kerchief on it, praying for my mother – not her soul but for her life. The tree would bring her love and protection, and, in my bones, I knew that was what she needed.

Jake stood a few feet from me, studying the various bits of cloth. 'There is a story with each one, isn't there?'

I walked to him. 'Absolutely.'

He lifted his hand and selected a bare branch and there he tied on his handkerchief. I raised an eyebrow. He smiled and said, 'I copied you, for I find it's best never to dismiss a local custom.'

'Wise.'

He laughed and I was about to ask who or what he was pray-ing, wishing, or hoping for, when I spotted my mother's crimson hankie. I didn't need to touch it to know it was hers. Her initials were clear in wobbly white stitches sewed by me. EMT. Elise Marie Tremayne. Everything in me wanted to untie it and hold it close to my heart but I couldn't break the magic. The fabric was faded from years of use. Seventeen years ago I'd given it to her for Christmas. Years of washing and pressing had made the cotton softer than silk. It had wiped mine and my brother's tears as well as her own as we'd laid my father to his final rest.

'Something wrong?' Jake's tall frame cast a shadow over the ground and up to the nearby trees.

'This is my mother's.' I pointed to the hankie.

'Certain?' he asked.

'No doubt.' I traced the letters.

'Then she was here possibly on the day she went missing.' He glanced around at the nearby trees. 'She chose the hawthorn as you did. Is there a reason?'

'In Celtic lore it is for love and protection.'

'What about the holly and . . . ' he squinted '. . . elder?'

'Elder is good health and prosperity and the holly peace and good will.'

'So, do you think she made a deliberate choice?'

I looked around. My mother lived by her instinct, but she always made each stroke on a canvas deliberately. She was Celtic to the core and religious and loving. 'Yes. She would have carefully selected the branch and the tree it was on.' My own choice, aside from selecting the hawthorn, had not been so well thought out. It was nearer the well but facing north. My mother had chosen a tree and a branch facing the south.

'Are you going to take it?' he asked.

I shook my head. 'She had a reason to stop here. I don't know what it was, but it was important.'

'Important?' he asked.

'My mother did things with her heart and with care. She would choose the flowers for my room on my return not simply for their beauty but for what they symbolised. Nothing was done without thought but, for her, thought came from the heart and not the head.' I began walking back to the road.

'And you only do things from the head.' He caught up with me.

I stuck my hands into my pockets. 'It has to make sense logically. I see no point otherwise.'

'And yet you are here.' He waved his hand back towards the well.

I smiled for I couldn't argue because what I had just done had no rational explanation.

'It wasn't your head that brought your feet to the well but your heart,' he said.

'Touché.' I looked around and my heart was full. 'Memory had . . . which is both heart and head.'

He laughed. 'Have it your way. But these trees and wells are fascinating.'

'Each is unique and Cornwall is filled with them.' I smiled. 'There is one near Liskeard. Whoever drinks first from its waters will determine who will wear the trousers in a marriage.'

'I have no doubt that, with or without drinking the water, you will wear the trousers in your marriage.' He glanced down at my legs.

'It will never be an issue as I will never marry.'

He frowned.

'Oxford will not entertain the idea of a married woman teaching.'

'And Oxford means everything to you.'

I nodded but hearing him say it sounded feeble.

'Are all English universities this foolish?' he asked.

'I hadn't thought of it as foolish, more that it's a vocation and marriage would be a distraction.' I paused. 'Is it not the same in the US?'

'Once, but things are changing.'

'I'll be in my dotage by the time Oxford reforms its ways.' I went over the stile.

'Now to Porthoustock.' He climbed on the motorbike and started the engine.

I was still contemplating his words as I took my position behind him. It was hard for men to understand the sacrifices women had to make in academia because it wasn't asked of them. It was intriguing that things were changing in America.

The village appeared below through the dust cloud from the latest blast in the quarry. Fishing boats sat on the vast shingle beach and a ship was tied to the quay loading. In the village, I spied nets laid out to dry and the fishermen mending other ones. I waved a greeting, knowing Jake looked like a stranger, and I was a woman in trousers. We would be spoken about.

After I climbed off the motorbike, I waited for Jake to join me, before I moved towards the wall where the men sat.

'Good morning,' I said, using my most winning smile, the one I used with hostile ministers.

The nearest man nodded but his glance narrowed as he looked at Jake.

'I'm Merry Tremayne,' I said. 'Colonel Tremayne's daughter from Kestle.'

Again, he nodded.

'I was told that my mother's bicycle and paintbox were discovered here recently.'

'Yes,' he said and returned his attention to the net.

'Do you know who found them?' I had a thousand questions, but I must be patient.

'My lad.' He didn't look at me as he spoke.

'Is he at home? May I speak to him?' I asked.

He pointed to the nearest cottage.

'Thank you,' I said and walked there. The door was open. I knocked on the frame and called out, 'Hello.'

A second later a woman appeared holding the hand of a small child.

I smiled at her and the little boy. 'I'm Merry Tremayne and I believe your son discovered my mother's bicycle and paintbox.'

'He did,' she said. 'I wondered if you'd come but I'd heard from the police that you work up there in London.'

'I do but I wanted to find out about . . . '

'Your ma.' She nodded. 'Tough thing it is, missing your ma.'

'It is.' I swallowed a lump in my throat.

'You don't know what to do,' she said.

I studied her. This was not what I'd expected.

'Me ma went off when I were sixteen.' She looked me straight in the eyes, chin raised. 'She came back, though.'

She didn't smile and I was at a loss on how to react. 'That's wonderful.'

The woman shook her head. 'No, she wasn't the same. She were me ma, but she weren't.'

'Oh, I'm sorry.' I wanted to ask how she was different, but I couldn't.

'So I know how odd you feel.' She dropped her son's hand. 'The police found anything more?'

'No,' I said. 'Where did he find her things?'

She pointed to the left and I saw a low-growing mess of shrub oak, bracken and grasses at the base of the cliff. 'The bicycle and box weren't there when the police said they was on that Friday.' She ruffled her son's hair. 'He's made a den there and I have to haul him out of there most days.'

'And it wasn't there before?' I frowned.

'No,' she said. 'They weren't there until after Monday.'

'Thank you. Is there anything else?' I asked.

'Maybe she don't want to be found,' she said. ''Tis funny old times.' She looked beyond me to the beach.

Her little boy went into the house, and I turned to see what she was watching. Jake.

'Not from round here,' she said.

I nodded and she had turned back into the house. There was nothing more I could ask and yet all I had were more questions. The woman's words stayed with me . . . maybe she didn't want to be found.

20

It was late afternoon by the time we returned to Ridifarne, and Jake was immediately pulled into a meeting. I mentioned to Mary that I was going to Kestle and would spend the night there. There were answers to be found if I had space to see them and to look at things another way, as my father had taught me so long ago.

Mary studied me closely but said nothing.

'I'll be back tomorrow when the tide's in. If I'm needed urgently, you can ring Kestle on Manaccan two-five-three.'

'If you're sure.' She sent me a worried glance.

'I am.' I dashed up to my room to pack my bag. My mother's paintbox might as well come with me as it served no purpose here except to remind me of her absence.

On my way out of the house, Mary thrust a parcel of sand-wiches and a thermos of tea into my hands.

I took them and smiled. 'They do have food on the south side of the river you know.' There had always been a divide between the north and south of the Helford. Living in Ridifarne, I was more aware of it than ever.

'I know but I think you have other plans in mind and Jake mentioned a remote cottage.'

I huffed then said, 'Nothing passes him by.'

'True.' Mary put a hand on my arm. 'Take care.'

I placed my other hand over hers for a moment, grateful for her kindness then waved farewell as I set off to the beach. The late afternoon was warm, and the tide would be high in two hours. It would be a quick journey to the cottage.

Once I set out, it wasn't long before I could let the current do the work and I allowed my mind to wander from the tall pines to the fresh warm southerly wind. A buzzard overhead rode the thermals. What a view he must have, being able to see the plateau and deep ria of the estuary.

Past the entrance to Porth Navas creek, I began to paddle towards the south-west. I spied the small chapel built in memory of Dr Leo O'Neill by his sisters. As a child, I loved to visit it. The carved statue of St Francis with the animals always appealed to me. My father and I would visit on foot and sometimes via the water. A sharp stab of grief for my father wrapped itself around me.

A little egret sat on the bleached trunk of a fallen tree. Mullet darted around the seaweed. Rooks chattered and the rest of the world didn't exist. I was sixteen again and I believed everything was possible . . . an education, a career, and love. Love above all else because that was what I had known. To have two such parents that loved each other, helped each other and believed in each other was how life was supposed to be. It made everything possible, even the impossible.

My golden view of life changed once at Oxford. My tutor had made it very clear that, bright though I was, I was a risk for I was too beautiful. Beauty was a problem as were hormones. Both took away a woman's choices in life. I had assured her then that I didn't want love and marriage. But I'd lied. I wanted what my parents had. However, in the world of Oxford colleges, that wasn't a possibility. Therefore, it became a question of what I wanted more. The harder I worked, the more focused I'd become; I pushed aside all else to attain my DPhil, working to a professorship at Oxford. Few women attained this despite their qualifications.

At Withan Quay, I secured the canoe. There wasn't enough water to navigate further for another hour. Taking my bag and supplies, I was on the lookout. Despite the moment of peace I'd experienced on the creek, I knew it was an illusion. A plane swooped low over the river, and I stilled in the cover of the trees. Nothing was certain, nothing guaranteed especially the outcome of this war. I had control of so little, simply the quality of my maps. The better they were, the better our chances.

When the sound of the plane engine was distant, I picked my way along the path where the spring growth bushed out, obscuring the track. It hadn't been used in a few days. The woods were filled with spring delights like the bright pop of deep pink from a few campions. Coming here was the right thing to do and I would be able to search for the charts from *Mirabelle*.

I paused on the stone bridge with the cottage in full view. There was no smoke from the chimney and the front door was closed. It all appeared serene. Climbing the bank, I saw Matthew come round from the back of the cottage.

'Miss Merry, good to see you. Any news on your mother?' Matthew asked, coming to my side.

'Yes, I collected her paintbox and bicycle from the police,' I said, holding the box up to show him. 'Oddly, they were found in Porthoustock. What do you make of that?'

He went quiet.

'Matthew, if you know something please tell me,' I said.

''Tisn't what Mrs Nance thinks . . . these foreign men,' he said.

'What is it then?' I asked.

His glance darted to the left and the right. 'She asked me for help with the refugees. They were landing all over the coast. So we put a few here until we found them other housing, knowing you wouldn't mind.' He looked at me and I nodded.

'Then it became just the odd one or two and she didn't want Mrs Nance or anyone to know about it,' he said. 'She began spending more time down here and less people came through.'

'Did this worry you?' I asked, trying to put a picture together of what was happening.

'No, it was your mother, and she was . . . I mean *is* the best of people. She was helping those that had no homes, nothing left because of that Mr Hitler.'

'Thank you, Matthew,' I said.

He patted my arm then off he went. I watched him go, wondering if my mother could be working with the Free French. I unlocked the door and once inside I opened the windows then I went to the standpipe for water before gathering wildflowers. It was the seventeenth of May and the countryside was at its most glorious. Back inside I arranged the campion, the bluebells and some forget-me-nots. Instantly the atmosphere of the cottage softened as did my mood.

That done, I opened my notebook and marked St Ruan's well on the map. Nothing was added to a map unless it mattered, regardless of what type of map it was . . . be it political, topographical or climatic. I would be hard-pressed to make a proper legend for this map. The balance was missing. No equilibrium existed on it. It was merely marks. Discovering that my mother had stopped at the holy well and her things had not been at Porthoustock the day she went missing confused matters rather than clarified them.

I stepped away but distance didn't help. Looking at this map, I recalled my frustration trying to draw Prisk Cove and my father's gentle patience. It had seemed an impossible task at the time and a bit like this.

Tears had run down my cheeks and onto the page when Papa had found me. 'What's wrong?' he'd asked as he'd settled beside me on the boat.

'This.' My grubby lead-covered finger had pointed then I'd thrust the map at him.

In silence he'd studied it. 'You've plotted the points well.' He'd handed me his handkerchief then picked up my pencil while holding the paper at arm's length, closing first one eye then the other.

'I can't do it,' I said.

He placed an arm around my shoulders and handed me the map. 'Maps are not made in one attempt. They require patience.'

'It's impossible,' I said.

'Making maps is possible but it takes many a redrawing to make it accurate.' He smiled. 'Remember, some things come in an instant and others require great study, care and time, especially those things worth doing.'

'But Papa,' I protested.

He ruffled my hair. 'Look at the shoreline again but this time with your eyes half closed.'

'How will I see it clearly then?' I crossed my arms against my chest.

'You will see it differently and you will feel it.'

'That makes no sense.' I pouted.

'Try it and you will find it does. Map-making takes patience, diligence and application, but rewards you with insight.' He held the map and pencil out to me.

I took them back from him. 'But I want it done in one drawing.'

'Anything worth doing or having is worth the time to redraft, revisit and enjoy with each attempt.'

I sighed and closed my eyes halfway as he had instructed. The shapes changed and became easier. Opening my eyes fully again, I saw the rocks differently, but they were still impossible to map.

'Persevere, Merry. You have chosen the coast, which is always changing. Think about why you are making the map. Who is it for? Someone on the land or someone on the sea?'

I leaned back now, missing his quiet wisdom. The map in front of me didn't tell me a story, it begged more questions. Like Papa, my mother would stay with a painting until she found the way. 'Look at it differently, try a different light, a different brush but never give up, Merry, never give up.'

Sinking into the chair, I pulled my mother's paintbox to me. I couldn't grieve for her. The unknowing held everything in check, even the ache in my heart. Lifting the lid, the light aroma of turpentine wafted out. Time and environment disappeared. I closed my eyes, and my mother was here. Opening them again, I glanced at the unfinished self-portrait and readied myself to see her last work again. I pictured the cliffs, the beach, the stacks all so fresh in my mind since this morning.

I turned over the heavy paper. Beautiful bright colours and soft washes captured the vivid blue sky fading as it met the horizon. The sea was turquoise by the sandy beach, turning deeper and darker to where a yacht anchored near a large rock. My fingers reached out to the boat. It was *Mirabelle*, of that I was certain, but this was not Kynance Cove. It was not Cornwall. I traced the rock. It was Côte Sauvage. Maman always dated her work. This must be an older one painted on our last sailing holiday in Brittany. I'd swum to that beach in the hot July sun. Yet on the back, in clear strong pencil marks, was *1 May 1942*. Why would my mother go to Kynance to paint a view from a beach in Brittany when beauty abounded in front of her? I flipped it and studied the painting again, noting each detail, trying to read it like a map.

Propping the painting on the bookcase, it felt like a message somehow, but I didn't have the cipher to decode it. Perhaps it wasn't meant for me, but who else would ever see it except me, possibly Oliver and the police? I glanced from the painting to the map.

A shadow blocked the light and I swung around. Jake stood in the doorway. I hadn't heard him which worried me until I looked at his feet; they were bare. But he held his shoes in his hand.

'What on earth are you doing here?' I asked.

He stepped inside. 'That's a fine greeting for someone who crossed a river for you.'

He was silhouetted in the light from the doorway, so his expression was lost in the darkness of the room.

'But it could be you had an emotional morning and Mary is worried—'

I held up my hand to stop him.

'I'm fine.'

He walked to my side. 'What's this?' He pointed to the painting.

I picked it up again, hoping something I hadn't noticed earlier would explain why my mother who painted landscapes *en plein air* had created one from memory, from such a specific memory.

'She's very talented.' His glance remained glued to the watercolour.

'Yes.' This was true but it wasn't her skill I wanted to discuss but answers.

'Stunning. But that's not where we were today.' He turned to me.

'No, it's in Brittany,' I said.

'Thought it might be.' He glanced from me to the painting. 'And this is a problem.'

'Yes, she never painted like this.' I paced the small space.

'From memory, you mean?'

I nodded.

He picked up the watercolour and turned it over before placing it back on the bookcase. 'Was this place special to you?'

'No more so than any beach we visited in Brittany.' Like reading a map, I broke it down to each element. Water, sky, sand, rock, boat. It was morning from the shadows cast.

'So, it does have meaning,' he said.

'Possibly. When we were there, we'd come ashore, gathered some driftwood for a fire. My father and brother had fished off the rocks while my mother and I had made coffee and spoken about my future.'

'Your future?'

'It seems strange now when the future is so uncertain, but back then I was full of plans for travel, writing and teaching. My undergraduate degree was behind me, and I was ready to carve out my career.' I closed my eyes, hearing my mother's voice.

'Good for you if it is what you want, what you truly want.'

I had studied her, looking for insincerity but there was none. I thanked her for not doubting me and she had chuckled before saying, 'Ma petite, from day one you have known your own mind.' She'd taken my hand in hers and continued, 'Just promise me to keep your eyes open. Plans can change in the most delightful ways.' Her glance had strayed to my father. 'He was not in mine nor were you and your brother.'

'Do you regret this?' I asked.

'No, my love, I wouldn't change a thing. Because of all of you I became a far better painter and an even better human.' She kissed my hand and rose to her feet.

'I don't know what you are thinking but it must be good.' Jake's words broke into my thoughts, and I opened my eyes with the last image of my father and brother walking towards us, carrying fish.

'It was good.' I looked at the painting again; it was beautiful but not her best. The more I studied it, the more unfinished it appeared. Immediately my attention turned to the bottom of the painting and indeed it was not finished because she had not signed it. That was always her last task. She'd added her name, her maiden name, to the bottom corner when she was satisfied.

'I've lost you,' he said.

'In a way, yes . . . in memories and in details. My mother didn't sign the picture therefore she hadn't finished it.'

'That is important?' he asked.

'I wish I knew. I'm seeing things or perhaps trying to where possibly none were intended.' I tapped my fingers on the table. Something was just out of reach.

'Anything to fix the unknowing.' He leaned against the railing on the staircase at ease but he appeared a bit too large for the small space.

'Exactly that,' I said. 'I simply can't find my way around her not being . . . here or anywhere.'

'No map for it,' he said.

'Nothing is as it should be.' I glanced around. 'My mother was using this cottage to paint, and the light isn't right here but she would wait hours for the right light, an almost impossible light.'

'Impossible light?' he asked.

'Have you ever watched the sunrise and seen it change things from indistinct shapes to defined features as the rising sun picks them out?'

He nodded.

'My mother searched for that light always.' I smiled, thinking of her. 'She compared it to how love changes you.'

'Well, it sounds like it's worth waiting for.'

I shrugged. 'I think it must only come to those who would understand it . . . both the love and the light.'

'Not you?' he said, with his mouth lifting into a half smile.

'Definitely not me.' I laughed. 'I wouldn't see it either.'

'But you just beautifully described the landscape as the sun rises.'

'Using my mother's words,' I said. 'She saw beauty in everything.'

'Her use of the cottage to paint was wrong because of the light,' he said.

'Follow me.' I walked up the steep stairs. 'Mind your head,' I said but I was too late as I heard Jake's muttered curse.

In the main bedroom I stared at the painting. Each time I saw something different but unlike in the past when I felt the strength of her love, this time my heart broke.

'You've brought me to your bedroom?' He raised an eyebrow.

'Only to see this painting.' I pointed to it.

'Amazing.' He walked closer and studied it. 'The resemblance is striking.'

'She was a few years younger than I am now,' I said.

He looked from me to the painting. 'Both beautiful.'

'Flattery,' I said, 'will get you nowhere.'

'True; you invited me in here without it.' He grinned.

'I did indeed.' I paused. 'This painting should be hanging in the library at Kestle, not here.'

'She was living here?' He glanced from the bed to me.

'According to the housekeeper, she would spend many nights here and the farm manager just mentioned that she housed refugees here.'

He came around the bed to stand beside me. The thought of him in the bed disconcerted me and I exited the room and went downstairs without a word. As much as having an affair with Jake appealed, more than appealed, we were part of a team, a finely balanced one.

When he reached the bottom step, he said, 'Thank you for showing me the portrait. I can now see what you mean regarding this painting.'

'Not her best.' I turned to the unfinished portrait . . . those eyes.

'More of a study,' he suggested.

'Yes, that's it exactly.' Picking the watercolour up, I scanned it again. That's why it wasn't signed. It was a note. I peered at the right-hand corner and, like her letters to me, there was an X, nothing more. My mother was in France, it said. But where? I didn't know how she travelled but as I looked up at Jake I suspected.

'When you went on the last operation with the team based in Dartmouth.' I paused and he watched me warily. 'This lone woman . . . '

He took a step back. 'You know we aren't supposed to discuss operations.'

'I do.' All the misplaced items, such as the charts from *Mirabelle*, suddenly were pointing me to Brittany, including the painting in her paintbox. That was her note and now it was as clear as if she had said, Merry, I'm off in Brittany for a while. 'My mother disappeared on the first of May and you made a journey to Brittany shortly afterwards.'

He continued to look at me but not say a word. Of course, he couldn't. He had signed the Official Secrets Act too.

'I think my mother was on that boat with you,' I said.

He leaned against the wall and crossed his arms.

'I know you can't say anything but you said trust was important when you worked as a team.'

'It is.' His face was solemn.

'But all this time I've been working with you and you've known where my mother is.'

He didn't move.

'We look alike; you would have known immediately.' I stared at the unfinished portrait. Taking several deep breaths, I tried to calm myself. Emotions vied inside me. My mother was alive and he'd withheld this information from me.

'How could you not tell me?' I swung around. 'How could the others have kept it from me?' I walked out the front door. I knew he couldn't have told me but that didn't take away my anger.

'I'm sorry,' Jake said as he reached my side. 'I wanted . . . but couldn't but I hoped . . . '

'I'd figure it out.' I gritted my teeth. 'That's what today was about.' All this anguish and half the team knew. They probably planted the bike and the paintbox on a cove of her choosing. Talk about keeping secrets. I wrapped my arms around myself. But Maman, being true to herself, had left me clues that I hadn't seen. I snapped a twig lying on the low wall.

My mother hadn't drowned or been kidnapped. She was fighting for France. And as those words sank in, my mouth dried. It was the right thing. I was proud of her, but she was risking everything. I closed my eyes for a moment and prayed to St Garda and St Ruan to keep her safe.

Leaving Jake outside, I entered the cottage and looked at my mother's painting again. Had I bothered to study it earlier, I might have worked it out sooner. I sighed, glancing at her self-portrait. My mother's eyes looked at me, full of love. She might forgive me for my incompetence at figuring it out but I couldn't.

Jake came into the cottage and I turned to him, softening my expression. It wasn't his fault she had followed her heart.

'Why are you here?' I asked, when I truly longed to ask more questions about Maman but it wouldn't be fair. He couldn't say. A restless energy filled me and I couldn't wait to call Oli and tell him that she was in France. That she had followed her heart yet again; not thinking, simply doing. He would protest but as I looked at the painting again, it was clear.

'Fleming telephoned.'

Thoughts of my mother stopped, and I stood straight. 'And you are the messenger.'

'Yes, Mercury, quick-footed,' he said.

'And witted?' I raised an eyebrow.

He grinned. 'Always. The message was to ring him at his office.'

'Office?' It was Sunday evening. It must be important. I picked up my bag and headed out the door. When I looked over my shoulder, I saw Jake following behind.

'Where are you going?' he asked.

'Up to Kestle to make the call,' I said. I was so grateful that Maman was alive and that I could now focus fully on my part in Fleming's task. The only way to help Maman and Oli was to win the war. That required better maps. My path was clear.

'May I join you?'

I studied him. Did he have nothing better to do? 'Yes.'

I would need to ring Oli after I spoke with Fleming. He needed to know but it was a matter of how to tell him. It would have to be coded in some way.

'Tell me more about these hedges,' he said, looking around.

I blinked. 'Hedges?'

'Yes, you said they were special.'

'In Cornwall they have been less interfered with than in most other parts of the country,' I said. 'Most of those around us are post medieval but when you see them rounded or smaller, they are older. The best examples of the Bronze Age ones are in the far west of Cornwall.'

'You mentioned the Bronze Age before.'

'This land has been cultivated for a long time and then Christianity arrived; monasteries were built, and communities developed around them.'

He nodded, looking at various farm buildings and the cottages.

With the house in view, my thoughts went to Fleming and what on earth would be so urgent that on a Sunday he would ring. He must need me back in London.

'How old is the house?' he asked, running his hand along the cob wall enclosing the kitchen garden.

'Old.' I looked at him.

'I can see that, but do you have any idea of its origins?' he asked.

'It's ancient. People have been living and working the land here for thousands of years. At one point this was a much grander house.' I stopped, studying it with new eyes. Its shape and windows were so familiar to me that it was almost invisible. But to a newcomer it would appear worn, old and a bit sad.

'Have your family been here long?' His face was full of wonder as he looked at the roof line with its many chimneys and dipping eves.

'My paternal grandmother was from the area and my father bought the farm in the mid-twenties,' I said. 'The house is classic Cornish domestic architecture and the hamlet represents the development of small clusters of houses rather than villages pre-Christianity . . . ' I paused. 'This area flourished because it was well suited to early travel when roads were difficult and the sea was the best option.' I stopped in front of the door. 'In Falmouth you can see this legacy with the name Carrick Roads.'

'I had wondered about the name.' He smiled.

I opened the door and Maman's absence had lifted in a strange way. Light flooded in through the west-facing windows. She could not tell me directly what she had done. Secrecy was necessary. I understood that but it stung. Thinking back to our last conversation, she was saying goodbye as she had with Oli.

Showing Jake into the sitting room, I said, 'I'll ring Fleming now. Feel free to look around if you wish.'

The conversation with Fleming could be about the operations on the Helford, therefore I wanted to make sure that Jake wasn't in the room with me when I rang. I closed the door to my father's study behind me, lifted the handset and dialled the operator then asked to be put through to the Admiralty and then to Fleming.

I heard the line connect.

'Commander Fleming,' I said.

'Merry. I'd hoped they'd find you.'

That wasn't a normal Fleming response. I tensed.

'They sent the American as the messenger. I was in my cottage,' I said.

'It's good you're not alone,' Fleming said. 'Merry, it's Oliver.'

'No.' My legs went and the hard surface of the oak chair caught me.

'Shot down. No parachute seen. Not good.'

I swallowed.

'Merry, are you still there?' he asked.

'Yes.' It came out more of a croak than a word.

'I'm so bloody sorry,' he said.

'Thank you.' It was all I could think to say.

'I'll ring you tomorrow,' he said. 'Will you be at Kestle?'

'Yes.' I looked around and there was a picture of Oliver beside his plane, taken in 1940. A big smile on his face. 'Thank you for telling me.'

'Christ, Merry, I'm so sorry,' he said. 'I'll talk to you tomorrow.'

I put the phone down, wanting to pick it up and call Oli. Maman is alive . . . but he is not. My fun-loving, earnest brother gone.

I lifted the photograph and looked at him. Dear God, I hoped it was quick. I pulled it to my chest and closed my eyes. Breathing was hard. Thinking impossible. It couldn't be true. It mustn't be.

21

I registered the knock, but my mouth was too dry to speak. The door opened and Jake peered around it. God knows what he saw. He moved so fast and pulled me into his arms, holding me still clutching Oliver's picture to my chest. Then the tears came. Human contact and I sobbed. He stroked my back, and the simple act of comfort broke me.

Everything was different now. It wasn't that I relied on my brother, but all throughout childhood we were inseparable. My parents were a pair, and Oli and I were too. We conspired, we laughed, we embraced our differences. Without him I was less and would never be more again.

When my sobs eased, Jake brushed the tears from my cheeks and pushed my hair from my face. Kindness. Taking the photograph from me, he laid it on the desk with reverence then he took my hand, led me to the sitting room and settled me on the sofa. He returned moments later with two glasses of whisky. I sipped it but I didn't taste it.

Jake sat beside me, and I felt his warmth but I was cold through. My hands were white, and my face must be the same. The alcohol hit me, and I began to shake. He moved closer and placed an arm around me. I rested my head on his shoulder and focused on my breathing, or his. I wasn't sure which.

I must have dozed for when I opened my eyes it was dark and Jake was still holding me. 'I'm sorry.'

'This is an aspect of the English I will never understand,' he said. 'Apologising for something you had no control over.'

I laughed a little.

'That's better. Shall I make us something to eat?' he asked.

'I'm not hungry,' I said.

'I know that, but you need to eat something.' He stood, and he held out a hand. I took it, feeling its strength and the callouses from rowing. I walked through the house to the kitchen, seeing ghosts of past happiness in every corner and feeling an emptiness inside so deep I could drown in it. But Jake's hand kept me afloat.

In the kitchen, he pulled out a chair for me and looked at what food was available. Finding cheese, two eggs, an onion, a few potatoes and some day-old bread, he moved confidently about the kitchen as if this was something he had done frequently. After rolling his sleeves up, he scrubbed the potatoes before setting them on the range in salted water. Next, he chopped the onion and found some bacon fat and softened them in that.

He turned from his tasks and said, 'I think I had better ring them at Ridifarne. Would there be a spare room I could sleep in?'

I blinked and looked at the clock on the wall. It was nine thirty. The tide would have turned, and the creek would be drying out. 'Of course.'

He smiled. 'Thank you. I'll be back in a moment.'

The last time I'd been at this table with Oli was the night before we'd buried my father. My mother had cooked a simple Breton fish stew and Oli had found a bottle of good wine in the cellar. We'd sat at the table together and celebrated my father. It had felt right then but could I do that for Oli? He was twenty-five with everything in front of him. Oh God, there was his girlfriend. I'm sure his friends would have told her. Maybe it hadn't been his plane. I would give anything for them to be wrong and for my mother to be here.

Rising to my feet, the need to drink wine until I could forget was the only thought I had. In the distance I heard the deep sound of Jake's voice, but I didn't register what he was saying. With the light on, I ventured down into the cellar. Memories and cobwebs surrounded me. Watered wine with dinners, bottles of table wine in French cafés, and laughter. Who was I going to laugh with, or would I ever laugh again? Who would stop me from taking myself too seriously?

I pulled a bottle off the rack and wiped down the label, a Bordeaux, 1934 Latour. That would do, more than do. It was my father's favourite wine. I grabbed the railing as my head wasn't moving at the same pace as the rest of my body. Shock. Of all the things I'd expected Fleming to say, it wasn't Oli. Oli had been the lucky one. I sagged against the door frame when I reached the top. Jake was walking through the hall.

'You look like you've encountered a ghost.' He pulled a long thread of spider's web from my hair.

'Maybe I have; they lurk in wine cellars, don't they?'

'Didn't have any wine cellars growing up but I wouldn't mind lurking in one.' He took the bottle from me. 'What have you chosen?'

'A favourite, I hope it hasn't gone bad.'

'What are the odds?' he asked.

'Fifty-fifty,' I said.

'I'll take them.' He waited for me to go into the kitchen first. The smell of the onions was wonderful.

'Do you have any herbs?' he asked.

I nodded and walked out of the kitchen door and into the

darkness. My mother always had them growing in the greenhouse during the winter and about now she would have moved them out. Once my eyes adjusted, I ventured to my mother's herb patch and I rubbed the leaves between my fingers. The scents made my heart ache. I cut some parsley, oregano and rosemary then thought of the abundant wild garlic and wandered further to gather some.

When I returned to the kitchen, Jake had opened the bottle of wine, laid the table and was quietly humming a song I didn't recognise. I rinsed the herbs, dried them and asked, 'Do you want them chopped?'

'Yes, please.'

I located my mother's favourite knife and began dicing the herbs. Jake put the wild garlic in with the onions then the cooked potatoes. He grated cheese, sprinkled the rosemary and the oregano before mixing in the eggs to bind it all together. He served it with the fresh parsley on top. It smelled divine and it looked wonderful. I was impressed.

'Do you often cook?'

'Not these days but I was the oldest and I would cook if my mother was late coming home. She taught me because she felt it was a skill that everyone should possess.'

I nodded. Despite my mother's best efforts to teach me, I wasn't very good. I tried a bit and it melted in my mouth. The varying array of flavours worked. 'It's delicious.'

'Thank you.' He raised his glass of wine.

I lifted mine. 'To my brother.'

'To your brother and all who have made the ultimate sacrifice,' he said.

I met Jake's glance before I drank. The wine blended beautifully with the food and part of me relaxed. My companion wasn't asking anything of me, and I was grateful.

'Tell me about yourself, please.'

'Nothing interesting.'

'You can cook,' I said. 'Which is more than almost every man I know.'

He laughed. 'OK, I won't argue that point, but my mother was different to many other mothers. My father cooked too, which he used to complain about bitterly, but he had a way of preparing fish that was wonderful.' He took a sip of wine.

'Tell me about him?' I tried to imagine my father cooking anything but I couldn't.

'His parents emigrated so they could be together.'

'Couldn't they be at home?' I asked.

'No, he was Protestant, and she was Catholic.'

I wrinkled my nose. My father had served in Ireland and had lost his youngest brother there. 'My father was Anglican and my mother is Catholic.'

'The reverse of mine.' He took a sip of wine.

We were so different in so many ways. 'Tell me more about you besides rowing for Harvard?'

'I finished rowing for Harvard years ago. I travelled Europe, became a hack and sometimes teacher of journalism.'

'For whom did you write and where did you teach?' I asked.

'*Associated Press* and I taught at Wellesley.'

I lifted my glass but stopped mid-way. 'A women's college?'

'Yes,' he said.

I smiled.

'What on earth are you thinking?' he asked.

'That your classes must be well attended,' I said.

He bowed his head for a moment and said, 'They were.' He topped up my wine and cleared the plates to the sink. 'Now, what about you? Did I see a map of yours framed in the study?'

'You did,' I said. 'Clearly my finest.'

'It was obvious in the use of the purple ink,' he said with a smile.

I found a tea towel and began to dry the dishes.

'What was that song you were humming earlier?' I asked.

He paused for a moment. 'Oh, it was "An Angel's Whisper", an Irish lullaby that my father used to sing. Do you know it?'

'No.'

He began to softly hum.

'Thank you,' I said, putting the cutlery away.

He looked at me intently. 'For what?'

'For being here,' I said.

'I'm glad I was.' He put a dish down. 'I had no idea I was the messenger bearing bad news.'

'No one wants to be that, but you've been kind,' I said.

He smiled. 'We all need that sometimes, no matter how strong we are.'

'True.' I tried to smile in return but it didn't work. It fled in the face of my grief.

He took my hand in his. 'You're very strong but this would break anyone.'

I nodded and took my hand from his and picked up another plate to dry. 'You didn't have to stay . . . '

He raised his hand, stopping me mid-sentence. 'I did. It is right and I wanted to.'

I swallowed.

'Mary's worried about you.'

I looked up from the plate.

'You may not have been with us long,' he said. 'But you are part of the team.'

I nodded, feeling a fraud but I wanted to be a part of the team more than I could admit. Before I could say anything, I heard the telephone ring. Glancing at the clock above the range, I saw it was late, and I dashed to the study to answer it.

PART THREE

July 4, 1940

Happy Fourth of July

It's an odd thing to be celebrating Independence Day in the country it was gained from. There are no hot dogs or three-legged races or screen doors for that matter (they are called fly screens here when you find the rare one). On this celebration day, I find myself in the Savoy's American Bar, alone. The last time I was here with an English pilot also on leave, I bumped into an old acquaintance from my foreign correspondence days. This debonair chap is now serving in the navy, and he spent the whole evening trying to encourage me to do what I'm doing now. Write. He wants me to tell you about Britain, what it's truly like and how I feel about it.

So, no neutrality, just my thoughts. No balance. My personal view. This is all very different from the Jake Russell reports of the past. I'm tempted. You see, once a writer, always a writer, and writers long to be read.

Today, I came down to London from the ancient heathland of Suffolk. The trains were packed and slow, but everyone was jolly about it. One dear woman offered me one of her sandwiches, saying, 'I'm so grateful you're here.' I took her sandwich, which was nothing like ours at home. Rationing has hit hard and this offering of thin bread with something called fish paste would fill a gap but nothing more. However, I know how little food there is about and this was her way of saying thanks, and even if the sandwich was less, it was more.

On my arrival, London bustled despite the damage from the bombing the night before. Smoke, not just from fires but from the rubble of fallen buildings filled the air. Craters appear without warning, but people smile and get on with living. I can't help but admire them for it.

I came to London to meet a woman of the Royal Navy. She's a telegraphist and I met her on a previous leave. But she hasn't arrived. Now I don't think I was deliberately stood up. Transport is unreliable. Bombs hit train tracks or trains are full to bursting and there is no room. So, I walked into the bar and pulled out my notebook like the old friend that it is. In a few moments my impressions have filled pages and I hope to give you glimpses of life here in Britain in between my sorties. Each day I grow more and more impressed with the people and their indomitable spirit. Despite everything that has been thrown at them, they will not, as they say, let Mr Hitler win. I am glad to be doing my small part.

There is one thing I'll never understand: why the British don't like ice in their whisky, or Scotch, as we call it. But straight whisky beats warm beer any day, especially on the first Fourth of July when I'm longing for home but grateful I'm here.

Jake Russell
London

22

29 May 1942

It was with mixed feelings that I left Cornwall this morning to meet Fleming and apprise him of the situation on the Helford. I didn't think I'd be returning, therefore I'd packed all my things ready to be sent on to me. The train had arrived in London at five. Fleming had said to go straight to the American Bar at the Savoy, but I'd protested and gone via Constance's where I'd changed my travel clothes and freshened up. Something inside me wouldn't allow me to show the world how I truly felt. That was letting the enemy win, and, while I had it in me, I would do everything in my power to make sure it didn't happen. My role wasn't any more important than anyone else's, it would take all of us and I wouldn't let the side down.

I arrived first and was seated at a table in the corner. The volume of conversation around me rang in my ears. The audio assault had begun at Paddington and hadn't stopped. Although the effects of the war were much in evidence in Cornwall, the noise, bar the planes overhead, was not. Except of course for the evenings at the Ferry Boat, but even then the volume seemed less frantic than here.

Fleming appeared and spotted me.

'It's good to see you,' he said as he reached the table and studied me. I looked away. 'You can't hide from me.'

'No doubt you've had reports on me,' I said.

He sat opposite. 'I was concerned.'

'I'm fine.' I drew a deep breath and smiled. 'How do you know Lieutenant Russell?'

He raised an eyebrow. 'Don't tell me an American, of all men, has turned your head.'

'No.' I held his gaze.

He signalled to the waiter.

'From my reporting days,' Fleming said. 'A Dubonnet?'

I shook my head. 'A pink gin, please.'

He sent me a look, but I didn't respond. Cornwall and my time there suddenly felt private but, of course, ultimately I'd been there on Fleming's behalf.

'He said he was a hack,' I said.

Fleming laughed. 'Not like an American not to blow his own horn.' He glanced about the room. 'He won the Pulitzer for his work on the Irish Problem a few years ago.'

I raised an eyebrow.

'Clearly he hasn't impressed you with his brilliance,' he said. 'He's a good sort and a damned fine reporter.'

I digested this information as the waiter returned with our drinks.

Once he departed, Fleming said, 'Despite being as beautiful as always, you are dimmed, which does not surprise me.'

I shrugged.

'Merry—' he took my hand in his '—your brother knew the risks.'

'I know, and I couldn't have stopped him, but . . . ' I looked away from him. 'That doesn't ease the loss.'

'Of course it doesn't,' he said.

I leaned back in the chair, and he released my hands.

'It also does not affect my work,' I said.

'That goes without saying.' He pulled out his cigarette case and offered me one.

I accepted and he leaned forward to light it for me. I was smoking more. It had crept up on me. In the past I hadn't needed them but now it was a different story.

'So they are fighting each other rather than the enemy,' Fleming said, jumping to the reason for our meeting.

'In a nutshell, yes,' I said. 'Different objectives, it seems.'

He took a sip of his gin. 'And Holdsworth is stymied.'

'Wasted.' I lifted my glass and breathed in the aroma of the bitters. Instantly I was back in the sitting room of Ridifarne, listening to the good-natured banter covering the underlying frustration that they weren't doing more. 'They were trained to blow things up and not act as a postal service,' I said, thinking of my conversations with Baker and the commander.

'That's what I needed confirmed,' he said.

'From what I gathered, it's been a good training operation and some spectacularly successful missions, but they have been hampered by lack of . . . equipment that fits the requirements of the tasks.'

'Boats.' He turned the glass in his hands. 'Not bloody fast enough.'

'For summer at least,' I added. 'It's clear in the short time I've been there that the two operations are working against each other, wasting necessary energy needed to fight the war. But aside from the exercise on Praa Sands, I haven't encountered the team from SIS. Therefore, my views are one-sided.'

'That confirms what information I'd received.' He rubbed his temple.

'From Russell or Newton or Holdsworth or all of them?'

He laughed but didn't reply. I picked up my glass. He wasn't going to give me any more information regarding them.

'What's your plan?' I asked.

'For you or for the team?' He put his cigarette down in the ashtray.

'Both,' I said.

'I will suggest that Holdsworth be moved to where he will be of better use.'

'Oh,' I said. 'I hadn't expected that.'

'It's not like you to not have worked things out.' He peered at me. 'But as you say, Holdsworth is a man of action; he needs to act.'

'How soon?' I asked, thinking of Mary and Mrs Newton.

'That, I don't know. Things can take time,' he said. 'And as for you . . . '

Turning the glass in my hand, I tried to figure out what was next but couldn't read him. 'You have your answers and I have mine.'

He looked me in the eyes. 'You've learned what more is required on your maps?'

'No, not sufficiently yet.' I took a sip then said, 'Regarding my mother . . . she is in France.'

He flicked the ash off his cigarette. 'Makes sense.'

It did. All hands were needed to effectively fight this war and my own desire to have her safely back in Cornwall didn't matter. 'You didn't know?' I studied him, looking for signs of evasion. He was the best-informed person, but I hadn't figured out how. Yes, he was networked but it was also the way he uniquely viewed things.

'I didn't, which means it might have been on behalf of the Free French,' he said.

'Her involvement with the refugees might have led to it,' I said, thinking of Matthew's information. Housing refugees could have easily slipped into housing agents, and could explain the rifles I'd found.

'Possibly.' He waved to the waiter and ordered more drinks. Mine was still half full. I needed to pace myself.

'You haven't mentioned what your plans for me are?' I cradled my glass.

'Although you're missed, I'd like you to stay in Cornwall for a few more weeks.'

'Really?' I raised an eyebrow, suspicious.

'Well, you admitted you haven't learned all you needed,' he said.

I smiled. 'That could take a lifetime.'

'You can't have that, but there will be something coming up soon that you will be needed for, but until then I think you will be more effective helping the team and . . . gaining knowledge.'

'Thank you.' It would be good to see more of what they do. There had been talk of having use of the motor gun boat for what they called lardering soon, and that might give me the opportunity to see more first-hand.

Across the room a couple caught my eye. He was in the RAF, and she was in the Women's Auxiliary Air Force. Had Oliver brought Caroline here? While I was in London I planned to try and contact her. I know how much I was lost without him, but they had planned a future together. How was she feeling now? I couldn't begin to imagine.

'Where have you gone, Merry?' he asked.

'Oli's girlfriend,' I replied.

He tapped another cigarette on the case. 'Ah, difficult.'

'Yes. Love complicates life.'

He sent me an odd look and said, 'In the best possible ways, I hear.'

'You would say that.' I sent him a rueful smile.

'You don't want the complications as you have made clear.' He raised his glass.

'Correct but that doesn't mean I don't understand them,' I said.

'I think you do very well but for your own reasons you choose not to take part, and I respect that. Although life would be more interesting if you dallied in the messy pursuits like the rest of us mere humans.' He lit yet another cigarette as our drinks arrived. 'Now, I need you to come into the office from Monday until Wednesday and then you may return to Ridifarne.'

'What's happening?' I leaned forward.

'I'd like you to meet a few people,' he said.

'Fine.' I leaned back in my seat. 'It will give me the weekend to catch up on things here and hopefully find out how to contact Oli's girlfriend.'

'I have those details for you.' He slipped a hand into his inside pocket. 'I thought you would want them.'

'Thank you.'

He nodded. 'How does dinner sound?'

I laughed.

'That's better. You could use a bang-up meal,' he said.

'I'd be delighted to join you but that does not mean dancing afterwards.' I placed my hands flat on the table.

'We'll see, shall we?' He stood, waiting for me to join him. His charm was almost irresistible, but I was made of stronger stuff.

23

30 May 1942

Early morning sunlight and the scent of the jasmine climbing the back wall filled the air as I opened the kitchen door. After putting the kettle on, I looked in the near-empty larder and pulled out a loaf of bread. A pathetic bit of butter sat in a dish on the side. It would be plain toast, which was fine, as the meal with Fleming last night had been good. I'd even managed to dodge the dancing as Muriel had arrived as we'd left the Savoy. I'd gladly waved them off and caught a bus back to Constance's.

The front door opened and closed, and footsteps echoed in the hall. Constance stopped in the entrance to the kitchen.

'Merry, my goodness. How wonderful to see you.' She wrapped me in a hug then held me at arm's length, no doubt noting the dark circles under my eyes. I glanced away from her scrutiny.

'Tea and a chat before you fall into bed,' I suggested, then I swallowed down the wave of grief that hit me. There was so much love and compassion in her glance.

'Yes,' she said.

'Where's Benedict?' I asked.

'In the country with the family as his youngest became very ill but she is thankfully on the mend.' She sank into the nearest chair, yawning. 'When did you arrive?'

'Yesterday at five, changed, met Fleming, and the rest is history as they say.' I poured the tea.

'Is he still trying to get into your knickers?' She looked over her shoulder at me.

I laughed. 'Stopped that ages ago.'

'Good.' She placed a hand on my shoulder. 'I've been worried about you.'

I shrugged. 'I'm not the only one who has lost—'

'No, but that doesn't make your loss less,' she said. 'And your mother's disappearance.'

I glanced down into my cup. The milk had formed a greasy surface on the top and it reflected the sunlight coming into the kitchen. I couldn't tell her where Maman was and I didn't want to dwell on Oli.

'OK, changing the subject,' she said. 'How long do I have the pleasure of your company?'

'Until Thursday morning.' I longed to be back in Cornwall, but I wasn't sure if it was the Helford I was missing or something else.

'You can't hide from your grief.' She paused, putting her cup down and fixing me with a direct stare. 'The one thing I know is that it is better to face it otherwise it will come back and knock you off your feet later when you least need it.' She drew a breath. 'People won't understand then.'

'People have been kind,' I said.

'Anyone in particular?' She watched me carefully.

'Why do you ask?' I looked out the window at the morning sunshine and felt its warmth. Jake Russell came to mind.

'That smile,' she said.

I looked down at my hands. 'The whole team have been wonderful to work with.'

'I'm pleased to hear that.' Constance stifled a yawn.

'And have you been taking care of yourself without Hester here to remind you to?' I asked, rising to my feet.

Constance laughed. 'Caught.'

'She'll be furious with you,' I said with a touch of jealousy running through me. Their relationship was special but came with the caveat that it must remain hidden.

Constance pursed her lips before saying, 'Yes, but I'll worry about that when she comes back.'

'Do you have a return date?' I asked, bringing the toast to the table along with the jar of marmalade and the fragment of butter.

Constance raised her hands. 'I wish I knew.' She stood and smoothed down her skirt. 'We are no different than any other couple that are separated by this war.'

'True, I hadn't thought of it that way,' I said.

'You wouldn't be alone in that. But it's better that people are unaware and those who are don't focus on it.'

'I hear Hester telling us to eat.' I pushed the plate of toast across the table.

'She would be, and she'd be asking all about who you were working with,' she added.

I wrinkled my nose.

'I know you can't say but give me some useless details to satisfy her when she calls,' she said.

'Fair enough.' I took a sip of tea. 'They are a fine lot of mismatched men plus one woman.'

'A woman?' Constance sat back in her chair.

'Yes, the wife of the com . . . head of the team,' I said.

Constance raised an eyebrow.

'Mary knows all and keeps everything going,' I explained. 'And there's an Irishman, who is queer and fancies the American.'

'American?' she asked.

'Well, not anymore,' I said. 'He's Canadian. He crossed the border into Canada to join the fight.'

'Determined,' she said.

Jake's smile came to mind. 'Yes.'

'Does he return the Irishman's interest?' she asked then took a sip of tea.

'A ladies' man, by all accounts.' Amelia Seaton had been drawn to him like a magnet.

'Your whole face lights up therefore he must be. Tell me more?'

I laughed.

'Come on. He's caught your eye?' She leaned closer to the table. 'Is he one of those toothy handsome creatures?'

'Exactly that,' I said.

'How on earth is he in Cornwall?' She rose and poured more hot water into the teapot.

'Fleming,' I said.

She rolled her eyes. 'That man has his hand in everything.'

I couldn't argue with that, so I sipped my tea and nibbled on the toast.

'What's this American god's name?' Constance spread a little butter on her toast.

'Jake Russell,' I answered.

'Russell? English or Scots?' she asked.

'Irish and Norwegian.'

'Sounds complicated. So he's Viking.'

I nodded. 'That sort of fits him, six foot five, lean, tanned . . .'

'Blond? Blue eyes?' She spread a thin layer of marmalade across the barely buttered toast.

'Yes, to both,' I said, picturing him rowing.

'Brain?' she asked.

'Don't we all have one.' I took a sip of tea.

'In varying degrees.' She laughed, rising to grab another jar off the shelf. 'This is the last of the marmalade. Then it's on to my cousin Alice's bramble jam from Cornwall, which doesn't last long with less sugar, but it does taste divine.' She opened the jar. 'You were telling me of this golden god that makes you smile.'

'Hardly a god but he has been kind.' I picked up my cup. My wary view of him had changed a bit and was altering still with the information gleaned from Fleming last night.

'Kind?' she asked.

I nodded. 'He was with me when I heard about Oli.'

'I thought the name sounded familiar. And you like him?' she asked.

I swallowed. 'Of course I like him. He's part of the team.'

'That doesn't necessarily go hand in hand.' Constance rested her head on her hands, her glance not leaving me.

'True, but these men and Mary all have their heart in the right place.' I thought of them gathered for their pink gin before dinner.

'Good. I'd hate you to be working with bastards.'

I opened my eyes wide.

'Don't looked shocked; the world is full of them.' She rubbed the back of her neck.

I couldn't argue with that. 'Enough about me.'

'Trying to divert me from this man?' she asked.

'I could never do that.' I tried to keep a straight face but failed.

'You are smitten with him, and I haven't seen you this interested since the visiting Classics scholar.'

I rolled my eyes. She knew me too well. 'Fine, he does intrigue me.'

'Ha, I knew I was correct.' She grinned.

'Only because I can't figure him out.' I opened my hands as if I had my notebook. 'I tried to map him.'

'Now this,' she said, 'sounds interesting.'

'It didn't work.'

Constance grinned. 'I love this, the un-mappable man.'

I pressed my lips together.

'Oh, he has beguiled you.'

I sighed, giving up. 'Yes, he has.'

'Good,' she said. 'We are in the middle of a war, and we have no guarantees of anything . . . anything at all.' She looked me in the eyes. 'Grab what happiness and joy you can find.'

I frowned. 'Really?'

'Yes, really. No one knows what's ahead of us so if you find a few moments of love . . . '

'Ha, love, no.'

'Lust then,' she said.

I nodded. 'Fine. I will remain open to . . . lust, for now.' I sipped my tea. 'Now, tell me how Hester is?'

'Bored of her mother but that is not new.' She cradled her tea in her hands. 'I miss her.'

I reached across the table. 'I'm so sorry she's not here.'

'Me too but I'm lucky to have Benedict here. He's good company.'

'Remind me how you met him?'

'In nineteen seventeen, I left Alice in Penhale and came to London. I quickly found work as an aid in the eye hospital looking after injured officers. Benedict was a junior doctor. He and Hester saved me from having my heart broken by one of them by informing me of the man's fiancée.'

I opened my eyes wide. 'Oh, do tell me more.'

'Nothing to tell. I had fallen for Thomas, who I had known as a child, and I thought because he couldn't see me it would be a good match.'

'Couldn't see you . . . good match?' I studied my friend, not understanding.

'Unlike you I wasn't blessed with a fine appearance and especially not at the age of seventeen.'

I made a face. Constance was handsome with clear blue eyes and thick brown hair. Anyone would be lucky to have her love.

'Enough of me,' she said. 'What are your plans?'

I pulled the sheet of paper out of my handbag. 'I hope to contact Oli's girlfriend, Caroline Moore.'

'She's a delight,' she said.

'You've met her?' I couldn't keep the surprise from my voice.

'Once. They stopped by here before a night out,' she said. 'They were adorable.'

'He was so in love, he said.' It was still so hard to believe him gone. No grave, no funeral, no ritual to help me accept the unacceptable.

'He was, and she will be devastated. Will you write?' she asked.

'I suppose.' I looked down at the newspaper. 'I want to meet her. I long to be with someone who loved him.'

'Understandable,' she said. 'But she may not be ready.'

'If I write now, the letter could make the morning post.' I stood. 'Thank you.'

'No need.' She rose to her feet and hugged me. 'Good luck finding the words.'

I nodded and went to the sitting room to the desk where I knew there was stationery.

Dear Miss Moore,

I'm Merry Tremayne, Oliver's sister, and I want to express my condolences. Oli told me how much he loved you and how wonderful you are. I am sure that, like me, you are lost and coping with a heart that is aching.

If you feel it would be appropriate, I would love to meet

with you. I am working in London until Wednesday and can be reached on the number above. Or you can also reach me from Thursday at Ridifarne, Helford Passage, Mawnan Smith, Cornwall.

Yours sincerely,
Merry Tremayne

It didn't say what I wanted to say, but hopefully the meaning would be felt.

I addressed the envelope and went in search of a postage stamp. Constance was still in the kitchen, reading the newspaper.

'Some days,' she said, 'I struggle to accept that we are in another war and that so many young lives are being lost.' She put the newspaper down and reached into a cup on the dresser and handed me a stamp.

I glanced at the paper and saw the article.

'I know we can't let Hitler win and his vile actions must be stopped but—' she paused and placed a hand on her chest '—oh, my heart aches.'

'The news coming out of Europe is terrible,' I said.

'It is.' She sighed. 'If you're quick you'll catch the first collection.'

I nodded and dashed out the front door and down the street. London was awake and it would be a beautiful day. Not beautiful like on the Helford but glorious nonetheless.

24

1 June 1942

Harling leapt from his chair as I appeared in the doorway to our office. My glance darted about the small room and I noted an additional desk and different maps lining the walls.

'Merry, my God, it's good to see you.' He kissed my cheek. 'I'm sorry about your brother.'

'Thank you,' I said, looking over his shoulder. A petite woman rose to her feet with a smile softening her stern features. This must be my replacement and I approved. Her hair was touched with grey at the temples, but her face didn't indicate that she was much more than ten years my senior.

'This is the wonderful Margaret Priestly.' Harling stepped back and I walked towards her with my hand outstretched.

'I've heard wonderful things of your work with maps,' Margaret said.

Glancing at the organised state of the room, I saw that she was a good influence on Harling. Certainly better than I had been.

'Thank you. Commander Fleming mentioned you're from Cambridge,' I said.

She nodded. 'History.'

'Perspective,' I said, and a slow smile spread across her face.

'Margaret does a bang-up job of keeping, not only me, but our commander in line.'

'Excellent.' I was relieved but also a bit jealous that someone else had slipped into my space with such ease and success.

'Our great leader is expecting you upstairs,' Harling said, glancing at the clock on the wall. 'Shall we grab dinner and a drink tonight?'

'Maybe,' I said with a smile to soften my words. 'Let me see how things stand at the end of the day.'

He sent me a look and Margaret laughed.

'I want to hear all about your time in the field,' he said. 'Compare notes.'

I opened my eyes wide. In no way did I feel as if I'd been in the field. I'd done training but had been far from any danger at any point.

'I know I prefer the field,' he said. 'Do you?'

Thinking of my experiences training with the Helford crew, I wasn't too sure I had it in me. I shrugged. 'See you tomorrow,' I said.

'Later,' he corrected.

The corridors were bustling as I made my way up above ground. Fleming met me outside his office door and led me to a meeting room where several men were standing.

'Colonel Brown, I'd like to introduce you to Dr Tremayne,' Fleming said.

The surprise registered on the colonel's face, and I hid my smile. The men with him struck me as academics, but not of the British variety, and there was an American general which provided me with a clue.

'Commander Fleming says you are a secret weapon,' a man said. His accent puzzled me. It was an American one but not like Jake's.

'Hardly that,' I said, studying them all.

'I read your paper of the coastal geography of northern France. Excellent.' The man held out his hand. 'Allow me to introduce myself, I'm Professor Fox of Harvard and this is my colleague Dr Cabot and Major General Simpson.'

'Gentlemen.' I nodded.

'I referenced your paper in Commander Fleming's presence and he said you worked with him. This is most fortunate,' Fox said.

I cast a quick glance at Fleming, trying to read the situation. What was he up to? Just then an admiral walked into the room.

'Ah, Admiral Philips,' said Major General Simpson. 'Now we can begin.'

'Yes, we have been discussing the invasion of France.' The major general met each of our glances in turn. 'I do not have to say how secret this is.'

We all nodded, and I swallowed, looking at the map of the northern French coastline. It was one of mine.

There was a knock at the door and Bartlett, one of my old lecturers, came in.

'Apologies. The trains were delayed.' He nodded in my direction after the introductions took place again.

'Gentlemen and Miss Tremayne, Calais presents us with the easiest access to France.' The admiral ran his finger across the channel. 'But, as we know, this is the most heavily fortified part of the coast and the build-up is continuing.'

'Dr Tremayne,' said Fleming. 'She has been working with a team who have been crossing to the northern coast of Brittany, so can provide us with up-to-date information from them,' said Fleming.

All eyes turned to me, and I kept a neutral expression because I didn't know why Fleming had brought me into this meeting. Until I understood the reason I was here, it would be best to keep my own counsel.

The meeting went on with all of us looking at this map, debating the pros and the cons of various points.

'Is Brittany an option as it is less defended?' asked the admiral.

'It's too isolated, the sea state with the Atlantic rolling in is difficult on a good day and transport to the rest of France from there is not good.' I paused and pointed to Normandy. 'Normandy is a better choice with suitable harbours, and it's not as well defended as Calais.'

'As has been previously discussed, the beaches could work,' said Professor Fox.

'But you will have to contend with the bocage.' I pointed to the map. 'Just inland.'

'Bocage?' asked the major general.

'The landscape is a mix of woodland and pastures surrounded by sunken lanes and hedgerows.'

'Hedgerows.' The major general waved his hand. 'No need to worry about them.'

'They're not simply a bit of shrubbery but built of stones, large stones,' I said.

'Not a problem for a tank,' the major general said.

The bocage was a problem but I continued as they were listening.

'These beaches themselves—' all eyes were on me when I looked up from the map '—you will need to discover how degraded they are. This will have as much impact as the tides. The sand itself will be an issue for your machinery. It may have been altered by bombing.'

'How does bombing affect the sand?' asked the admiral.

'The heat can change its structure. Think of glass.' I stepped back from the table and waited for someone to say something, but no one spoke.

'When?' I asked.

All of them turned to me.

'That is undecided and, of course, it's on a need-to-know basis,' said the admiral.

'Well, when you go is almost as important as where.' I looked him directly in the eyes.

Silence. They must have considered this, but no one spoke.

'Not only do you have the sea state to factor in, but also the phases of the moon, sailing distance from other harbours and the tides are a serious consideration. All that and more without even considering the strength of German forces.'

'True,' the admiral said, pointing back to the map. 'Places are being readied for troops and scouting has begun for practice beaches.'

'Then you know which beaches you are considering.' I couldn't help myself.

'Yes, Miss Tremayne,' the admiral said.

But it was clear, despite the discussion we'd had, they weren't going to share that information. Calais made sense for the ease of transporting troops, but it was not where I would invade.

An hour later I left the room with Professor Fox, who I guessed to be about forty.

'It's early days. But we will need your input, proper input,' Fox said.

I pressed my lips together.

'They will call you back to this project,' he said. 'They will listen.'

I shrugged. 'If you say so.'

'Thank you for your help, Dr Tremayne.' He held out his hand.

I shook it then headed down the hall, longing for the simplicity of Cornwall and working with a team who knew what their objectives were even if they couldn't achieve them and were forced to do others' work.

25

4 June 1942

The eleven thirty evening train from Paddington was crowded and the journey endless. It was now almost noon and I'd managed something akin to sleep, but as I walked out of the station at Penzance, I didn't feel rested at all. The whole journey down I thought about the meeting on Monday. Invasion. It was the only way, but it wouldn't and couldn't happen this year; favourable conditions had passed. Also, by the time plans would be finalised, it would be winter. Next spring or summer was possible, but would everything be ready? The level of organisation required would be astounding.

Commander Holdsworth, who had had a meeting in Newlyn, was leaning against the car as I walked out of the station. St Michael's Mount basked like a lizard on a rock in the June sunshine. Like London, the weather was fine, but the sea breeze kept the temperatures comfortable.

'Welcome back,' he said, straightening.

'It's good to be here.' I smiled. The sky was clear and the air fresh. I took a few deep gulps and climbed into the passenger seat. We drove off, following the coast road to the fishing harbour a few miles away. On a day like today, it would be easy to forget we were at war, but then the defences on the beach and the minesweepers in the harbour destroyed the illusion of a peacetime summer's day.

The commander parked the car and said, 'I'll be an hour.'

I nodded and watched him head to the harbour master's to obtain his pass. Walking along the old cottages, which housed the Belgian and the French refugees, I noted a group of French women cleaning their cottages, and I knew Maman was made of the same resilient stock. These women had made these derelict cottages shine.

'*Bonjour, madame*,' a woman said.

'*Bonjour, madame*,' I replied then turned to the harbour. The tide was coming in and the air reeked of mud and fish. In the distance I heard children playing. Life was going on but, in this moment, I didn't feel a part of it. I walked above or below but not in it. Things moved past me without touching me. It was the barrier I had placed around myself so that I wouldn't feel the pain nor the love. That was the trade-off for my career. Now glimpses of the disturbed dream from last night flashed in my mind. It was of being below the surface of the water, not swimming, not breathing, not living. I woke gasping and reaching out, but there was nothing to hold on to.

I bent to smell a rose blooming on a garden wall. Sweet and spicy at the same time. There were moments of joy like this, and I must hold them. Entirely cutting myself off from life benefited no one, especially me.

Commander Holdsworth was not back when I reached the vehicle. I leaned against it, enjoying the heat of the afternoon sun. Closing my eyes, I listened to the sounds of the men speaking on the harbour wall. Flemish mixed with Breton and French and a rich Cornish accent. They were all joking together, and I smiled.

'That's better,' said Jake.

I opened my eyes. 'Where did you come from?'

'I came by boat.' He pointed to the *Mutin*. Pierre stood on the quayside, talking to some of the fishermen.

'All of you?' I glanced around.

'No, half of us. The commander apologises for his delay and will be an hour more.' He smiled. There is a rumour there's ice cream to be had here.'

'Really?' I asked, unsure how there could be ice cream with sugar rationed. I hadn't had any in years but a trip to Jelberts had always been a part of every summertime visit to Newlyn throughout my childhood. Bittersweet memories filled my thoughts. A vivid image of Oli with cream dripping down his chin as he'd eaten his so quickly. He had savoured every moment I knew and that I had to hold onto.

Despite my disbelief that there would be ice cream, I walked along the Strand to the ice cream parlour with Jake, and it appeared we were in luck. We found a table and took a seat.

'They only have one flavour?' Jake turned to me in dismay.

'Yes, the best.' I grinned.

'If you say so,' he said but his scepticism was obvious.

'You'll see.'

We ordered.

'How was London?' he asked.

'Fine,' I said, looking away, knowing I might have changed the course of this team's war.

'When I was growing up, fine as an answer was banned because it said nothing.'

I laughed. 'Work was interesting and seeing friends good.'

'That's not much better as far as telling me anything,' he said.

'True.' I shrugged and the ice cream arrived. I tasted a small bit on my spoon, and the richness of the cream covered my tastebuds with a burst of sweetness and the tang of vanilla. It was as good as I remembered, maybe even better.

Jake watched me. 'I can tell it's good by your face.'

'It is.' Was it Jake's company that made it richer, or simply the long absence from the joy of ice cream?

He tried it.

'I agree it is,' he said. 'Verging on the divine.'

'Phew,' I replied. 'Something not dismissed by the Americans.'

'Ouch.' He smiled. 'But I will not be side-tracked about your trip to London.'

I leaned back, looking at him. 'Well, I wrote to my brother's girlfriend.' I put my spoon down. I so wanted to make contact with her but maybe I never would. That was her right. 'And heard nothing back.'

'You weren't in London long,' he said. 'A reply could be waiting for you.'

'True but I'm impatient,' I said and moved the ice cream around allowing it to soften a bit more. 'I wanted to speak with someone who loved him.'

'Did you try and talk to the men in his squadron?' he asked.

'I should have.' I took another small taste of ice cream. Then I stopped rationing myself and took a full spoonful and let the cool cream and sugar melt into my mouth. I tried another and Jake's eyes never seemed to leave me even when he was eating.

'Do I look odd?'

'No,' he said. 'Why do you ask?'

'Well, you haven't stopped staring.' I stared back.

'Apologies.' He looked down.

'As long as I don't have ice cream on my nose or something.' I wiped it just in case.

'You don't.' He paused. 'You are simply beautiful and a joy to watch.'

I blushed, I had no control over it. My nearly empty bowl of ice cream held my attention until my face returned to a normal colour.

'I've embarrassed you and I'm sorry,' he said. 'I shouldn't have been honest.'

'Hmmm . . . that sounds worse.'

He laughed. 'It does. Let's say you're good company and leave it at that.'

'I do believe, Lieutenant Russell,' I paused, 'you are, as they say, rattled.'

He looked down at his bowl and then up, through long fair eyelashes.

'That would be correct. It's been a while since I've been with a bold, clever and beautiful woman.'

'You said you'd taught at Wellesley,' I said. 'You would have been subject to classrooms full of them.'

'True.' He put his spoon down. 'But none were you.'

I looked at him and his smile. He was flirting with me. Something inside flipped and it wasn't the ice cream. I could handle the Flemings of this world and the Georges, but what did I do with an impossibly handsome American? Maman broke into my thoughts, chiding me to accept the compliment graciously. It wasn't a proposal of marriage or even a suggestion of anything else. Enjoy the attention, she would say.

'Thank you,' I said. 'I think.'

'You're welcome.' He paid, and together in silence we walked back to the car. I cast a glance in his direction, knowing my mother would like Jake. Strange thought in these stranger times but she would. My steps faltered as I remembered, she'd met him already.

The commander waved as he strode towards the vehicle. 'Coming with us, Nipper, or taking the *Mutin*?'

'*Mutin*, sir.' He bowed his head and left.

A letter was waiting at Ridifarne when we arrived back. My hand shook as I noted the return address. Before I could read it, Mary was eager for news of London and the commander had apprised me of the current plan for the team. The new operation was to begin shortly where they would be bringing supplies and hiding them, ready for the resistance. They had been testing a waterproof option of leaving containers submerged next to buoys, and, in two nights' time, they were to make their first run in the borrowed MGB. I could see the motor gun boat off Helford Point as I walked onto the terrace.

Brooks Richards came to my side. 'She will make a few things possible during the short nights with her speed.'

'How many knots?' I asked.

'Supposedly close to forty but I would imagine only in ideal conditions, which rarely exist,' he said.

'I'd love to be on her when she does,' I said, enjoying the boat's lines.

'Don't see why you can't come out with us,' Brooks Richards said. 'We're not landing so it's not too risky.'

'Really?' I couldn't keep the excitement from my voice.

'Yes, I'll ask the commander.'

Mary walked towards us.

'I've made tea if you are interested, Francis,' she said and she turned to me. 'I'm dying to hear about London.'

'Shall I bring you a cup?' he asked me.

'Yes, thank you.' I turned to Mary. 'London hasn't changed. Still going full tilt despite everything.'

'I do need to find an excuse to go, although I have come to love it here,' she said. 'Especially on days like today.'

'My father always claimed June was the best month in Cornwall, but I might argue for September,' I said.

'Both.' She laughed.

Brooks Richards returned with a tray. It had cake on it.

'Mrs Newton has been creating magic with the strawberries,' said Mary.

'It looks and smells wonderful.' I took the proffered slice.

'Now that there are some Americans about, Lieutenant Russell has wrangled some key ingredients out of them like sugar while he was away this past weekend,' Mary said. 'In Mrs Newton's hands, it can go a long way.'

I broke a bit off and the smell of butter hit me. That must have been acquired from the Americans as well. The cake melted in my mouth. It tasted of the past, of goodness and I could have cried. But then emotions were close to the surface, and I had to accept that, even if I didn't want to. I touched the letter in my pocket. It would not be an easy read. I excused myself and disappeared into the garden and made my way on to the beach. The tide was on its way back in and for a while I sat watching a large rock slowly be consumed by the water. Once covered, I opened the letter.

Dear Dr Tremayne,

Thank you for your letter. You have been on my mind as well. Oliver spoke so fondly of you that in many ways I feel I know you and should have addressed the letter Dear Merry.

Like me, I know that merry is the one thing you are not at the moment. I am still in shock, but my work keeps me moving and stops me from dwelling too long. Oliver is firmly in my heart. I never knew I could love someone so completely. My parents were not a good example, but Oliver spoke of the great love between yours. As I write this, I know you are also missing your mother and you didn't mention her in your letter, so I assume you have no further news.

I'm due on shift so must sign off. I too would like to meet you when it can be arranged. Until then stay safe and well.

With best regards,
Caroline

I held the letter to my chest. So much feeling said with so few words. She had been perfect for my gregarious brother. I trailed my finger through the sand, writing his name. I mustn't fall into despair. So many were in far worse situations than I was. I had a job I loved, I had a home, and I played a role, however small, in trying to end this war. These are things I must hold on to. I looked down at the sand where I had drawn the letter J. Jake was an interesting distraction and maybe that might not be a bad thing.

26

We reached the Scillies by ten in the morning. This had not been the plan, but the MGB had been called back to Dartmouth without explanation. Now we were here two weeks later than scheduled, thanks to the engine on the refitted sardine boat playing up on our first departure a week ago. We'd lost the no moon period but planned to go ahead anyway.

On this blisteringly hot day, with the tide on the way out, we began painting the boat in her French colours. Daniel Lomenech, of the SIS, joined us and instructed us in our task.

I'd heard tales of this man, his bravery, his handsomeness and the trail of broken hearts from Paris to London to Plymouth, not to mention here on the Isles of Scilly. Women had appeared on the rocks to watch the undertaking and he went off to distract them. His boat, *Le Dinan*, was in Falmouth for repairs which is where we had picked him up.

'He's a good one even though he works for them,' Tom Long muttered as he covered the dull military grey hull in a bright-blue paint.

'Aren't we all on the same side?' I paused mid-stroke.

'Sometimes you wouldn't know it.' Tom laughed.

The sun beat down on us and I was cooking, despite being

dressed in shorts, a men's shirt, and with my hair up and under a hat. Jake had laughed when he saw the get-up. 'You can try all you want but you don't look like a man or a boy.'

I resisted sticking my tongue out at him, which I hadn't done since I was eight, and continued to paint. I wasn't trying to look like a boy, but I had wanted to blend in a bit. Now that most of the men had stripped their shirts off, this was impossible as was concentration. A shirtless Jake was very distracting. Thankfully the damp sand under my bare feet cooled my thoughts as well as my body, and I could look forward to a swim once we were finished. This would make everything better.

Long handed me a tin filled with metal filings as soon as the new colours were on her.

'What is this for?' I asked.

'We're giving her a reverse facelift.' He chuckled.

I shook my head and watched as he threw a handful of the metal filings at the boat. There was no order to it. He chucked them anywhere and I began to follow suit. Tom looked over his shoulder and nodded.

'Why?' I asked.

'When the paint dries, we knock them off and rough it up so that it doesn't look new,' he explained.

Grinning I dispersed my ration of filings with greater gusto. That job done, I went below deck and changed into my swimming costume. It had been hard work and a swim was needed. On deck I stopped, stunned to see the commander standing on the outcrop of rocks and talking on a telephone. I hadn't noticed it when I scrambled down the rough-hewn steps of Braiden Rock earlier. It was well hidden.

Long saw me staring and said, 'That goes direct to London.'

'Really?' I asked.

Long shrugged then walked off to join a group of men heading to the pub. The commander placed the handset down, his face solemn, as he spoke with Jake. The sunlight gleamed off Jake's bare chest.

Turning away, I waded out into the waters of New Grimsby Sound between Tresco and Bryher. The cold hug of the sea helped to cool my thoughts of Jake and wash the sweat from my skin. Strong strokes took me out to the middle of the channel, and I forgot the war and what would be happening tonight.

For this instant I was on holiday even if that holiday was just an hour. The sky was deep blue, and the sea clear enough for me to see the fish swimming and crabs scuttling across the seabed. I flipped onto my back and closed my eyes, loving the feel of the water billowing out my hair and playing with it.

Every so often I would turn my head to the side to locate the shore and Cromwell's Castle, then suddenly Jake was beside me.

'Checking on you,' he said.

'I'm fin . . . good,' I said.

He laughed. 'Pleased to hear that.'

I dropped my legs down to tread water and look at him. His fair hair was sleek against his head and his eyes were bluer than the sea and, in this moment, I might be infatuated with him. No, I was.

'What are you thinking?' he asked.

There was no way I would tell him. Evasion was best. 'Why?'

'The look that crossed your face,' he said then smiled and my skin tingled, which had nothing to do with the sea.

'Good or bad?' My glance followed the line of the hill behind his head to the ruins of King Charles's Castle set high above Cromwell's. Anything so I wasn't looking at Jake.

'Interesting,' he said.

'How so?' I asked, twisting around to look at the small rocky Hangman's Island to my left. As a child Oli was convinced men were hanged there but I knew the name must have come from *An Men*, which was Cornish for rock.

'Just interesting.' He smiled slowly and, despite the cold water, I flushed.

All I wanted to do was to kiss him, so I swam away from him towards a nearby beach on Bryher. The sun was high, but it was three in the afternoon. There were hours of daylight ahead with nothing to do until the tide would be high enough to set sail.

Reaching the shallows, I waded in on the lookout for anything that would injure me. This beach, Kitchen Porth, wasn't as gloriously sandy as some others on the island. As a family we had sailed these beautiful waters around the Scillies most summers through my childhood and Bryher was one of my favourites.

A glance over my shoulder confirmed what I'd hoped. Jake had followed me through the gap in the dunes past the house that served as a pub for this small island. All was quiet and I saw not a soul as I found the old path lining the fields at the base of the gorse-covered hill of Shipman Head Down.

Here, protected from the light breeze, the air was hot and the ground beneath my feet dry. I carefully picked my way along to avoid the brambles, nettles, and the animal droppings. Some early bell heather was already flowering. My bare feet were not hardened as they had been in the shoeless summers of my youth. Reaching the rock outcrop, that had fascinated me as a child, I waited for Jake to catch up.

'That's impressive,' he said.

'Isn't it?' I touched the stone that was poised above my head. 'Somewhere I have a photograph of my father acting like he's trying to hold it up.'

He laughed. 'You know the island well.'

'Not well,' I said. 'But we would often sail here and anchor in New Grimsby Sound.'

'Is it always so deserted?' he asked, looking around.

'Never many people but today it appears there isn't another soul.' Single file we continued across to the west side where the view opened up and the sandy crescent appeared.

'Stunning,' he said.

'Popplestones is and we have it to ourselves.' I cut through the marram grass in the dunes then down onto the sand to the water's edge.

'You knew this was here?' he asked.

'I did,' I said and went knee deep into the sea then dived in, hearing the matching splash behind me. I swam further out until only my toes could reach the sandy ocean bed. I stopped and waited, knowing exactly what I wanted and that was to get Jake Russell out of my system. There was only one way to do that.

'Why did you bring me over here?' His chest and shoulders were well clear of the water while I was neck deep. Water beaded on his beautifully smooth skin. I looked at him and smiled.

'You haven't said a word,' he said. If he hadn't figured out what I wanted, I would need to show him.

I tiptoed towards him, leaving very little cold water between us. 'I brought you here because I couldn't do this—' I placed my hands on his bare shoulders and floated up to kiss his salty mouth '—without the others watching.' I dropped my hands as his hands lightly encircled my waist, holding me close but not too close.

'I see and that was all?' he asked.

'Yes,' I said although I wanted more than one kiss.

'Seems an awfully long walk for one kiss,' he said. 'Was this your head's directive?'

I nodded, unable to remove my glance from his mouth.

'I've found at times like this the head doesn't think properly,' he said. 'For a walk across a whole island a man has earned more than one kiss.'

'Hmm,' I said. 'I suppose one is a bit stingy.'

'Ah, the British use of understatement.' He pulled me so close my legs rested against his. 'I would think we need to kiss again, at minimum, four more times.'

'Four, an interesting choice,' I said as I placed my hands on his shoulders again. His skin was warm from the sun and the water divinely cool.

'Yes,' he said. 'More than three and less than, say, a hundred.'

'A hundred.' I opened my eyes wide.

'It's one way to keep warm in the sea.' He brought me closer still and his mouth met mine. I lost count of the kisses, and I couldn't feel the sea, only him. And I tasted him, salt, peppermint and desire like I had never known. His hands remained at my waist, holding me safely above the surface but the last thing I wanted in this moment was safety. He wasn't an Oxford undergraduate. Or a blundering seventeen-year-old. He was desire itself, and I knew he wasn't immune, even in the cold water.

A seal popped up a little too close for comfort and we pulled apart. But Jake took my hand in his as we walked into the shallows.

'That was unexpected,' he said, sitting on the sand and keeping me with him.

'Me or the seal?' I studied his expression.

'Both.' He pushed a strand of hair off my face. 'Not saying kissing you wasn't what I wanted from the moment I saw you on the sidewalk in London.'

I laughed. 'Me, Merry the mapper.'

'Maps were not the first thing that came to mind on seeing you.' He glanced down at our interlaced fingers.

'Good.' I stood, waiting.

'Where are we going?' he asked.

'Unless you fancy the team noticing us missing, we have to

swim back to the boat.' I began to walk off the beach. He laughed, jumped to his feet and took my hand in his. When the path narrowed, he let go and I wanted to kiss him but it was too risky. Already I could see the boat in her new colours. These men were a team, and I was part of it. We were breaking an unwritten rule, I was certain. I'd never been a rule breaker before but even being on this trip was breaking rules. I was changing how I operated entirely.

27

No one said anything about our earlier absence, which was almost worse than if they had. I was the object of a few strange looks upon our return and I didn't know what had or hadn't been said to Jake. It felt awkward but those stolen moments were worth it except they hadn't scratched my itch but rather intensified it.

We'd all had a gorgeous dinner of lobster and now it was ten past eleven. The sky was clear and still oddly bright as we left. Our cover, a Beaufighter from St Eval airbase, appeared once we cleared New Grimsby Sound on the high tide and the engines were brought to full. Tonight, I couldn't be more excited as the bow cut through the water, making light of the mild swell. These men had made this trip a hundred times, but I had done it at the pace of a sailing boat with our only threat being a large steamer heading into the channel.

Soon we would be crossing a known German convoy route. Excitement and fear played a tennis match in my stomach, making it a bit queasy when it shouldn't be. Sea sickness had never been a problem, but I had never done something so risky or felt so alive in a way I hadn't since the news of Oliver's death reached me. I wasn't sitting at home. This was actively taking on Hitler, not drawing maps for others to do so. But still I kept a chart in my head, marking each known location from the Bishop Rock lighthouse to Ushant and the buoy. The air cover left us as we entered the German zone. I was sad to see it leave. It had felt like a guardian angel on the journey thus far.

I was restless and I wanted to say it wasn't because of Jake that my senses were heightened but I couldn't lie to myself. Tonight's lobster had tasted as no other lobster had. Everything was sharper, funnier and better. I needed to be careful. This was solely a dalliance. He was American and would leave and I would return to Oxford. It was something to distract us both from the reality of now. Wartime relationships were risky, but so was everything, especially being in a boat dressed to look like a French fishing boat that was carrying supplies to France.

Before I saw Jake, I sensed him at my side.

'Nervous?' he asked.

'Excited,' I said.

'Really?' He sent me a quizzical look.

I shook my head. I couldn't explain the fizz inside me. It was the mix of him, the unknown and the thrill of the adventure. Not that I was really a part of this operation, more an observer but I was here.

He smiled. 'I suppose I was too on my first operation.'

Brooks Richards walked up to us and said, 'There's cocoa on offer.'

'I'll pass.' Cocoa didn't appeal.

'No, thanks,' said Jake as he disappeared.

'Feeling OK?' asked Brooks Richards.

'Fine.' I was allowed this word with others.

'Good,' he said. 'All's well so far and no sign of the engine trouble we had last week, and the sea state is not bad.'

I nodded, looking at the swell.

'If we keep up this pace, we will be there in good time,' he said. 'And back to the Scillies by dawn.'

I nodded, saying a silent prayer that this would be true. I went down to check the charts, passing Pierre on the way. He nodded in my direction. The charts meant little to him but the smell, the sound and the feel were his tools.

Below deck, the aroma of the cocoa was a bit sickly; however I was soon lost in calculations. If fifteen knots were kept up, this would be a simple operation and a great way to pass on supplies and retrieve information, providing that the local resistance could make it out of the estuaries and reach the buoys. It all depended on how much threat the Germans saw along this treacherous coast.

Back on deck, I noted cloud cover had been building as we travelled each nautical mile towards Ushant. The engines slowed and Pierre stood by the bow. We remained silent and the engines kept low. If the calculations were correct, then we should be on the buoy any moment.

'There it is,' Pierre called out. We slowed further and circled around it. The youngest seaman, Jean Piron, was over the side and onto the buoy in minutes. It didn't take long to attach the waterproof container holding guns and munitions for the local resistance. I was mesmerised by the phosphorescence when Jean's foot trailed in the sea. Memories of childhood were crystallised in the joy of the light. But too much of it here would attract unwanted attention. Once Jean was back on board, we set off at full speed.

I sat on the deck, looking up at the dark sky, feeling slightly let down, having been so close to Brittany. I wrapped my arms about myself.

'Are you OK?' Jake asked, sitting down beside me.

I nodded. 'Thinking of my mother.'

'I see,' he said.

And from the tone of his voice, I felt as if he did. It would have been easy for him to slip his arm around my shoulders, and I had to hold myself straight and not lean into him. Did he feel the same?

A persistent rain began, and the swell was increasing. 'This wasn't forecast,' the commander said as he walked past. 'Let's hope it's only a passing squall.'

He gave instructions for a reduction in speed and instantly the angry energy of the rain eased, hitting my face with less force.

'Do you want to go below?' Jake asked.

'No, I'd rather be on deck while I can,' I said. In bad weather I would prefer to take the helm; I gained some sort of strange comfort from a sense I was in charge and not at the mercy of the boiling sea about us.

The squall passed as quickly as it arrived, and the stars reappeared. I was soaked through but remained on deck. I couldn't explain it, but I needed to see the water. We were making good progress and still should reach the Scillies by dawn. All was as it should be.

Jake walked up to me with a dry blanket. 'Don't need you catching a cold.'

I laughed and shook my head, accepting the blanket and settling it across my shoulders. He sorted it out where it had twisted on my back. His hand grazed my neck. My breath caught and our eyes met. He felt the connection too. Maybe I was foolish to play with this desire, but I needed to feel alive, and he must too.

So much had been taken from me lately that surely a few moments of happiness, however fleeting, were rightfully mine. But that sounded more like my heart than my head. I knew which one to follow. My head said speak to him, and if he feels as you do, then seize the day and you can enter this affair and enjoy it. But if he does not then step back. After all, we are both free of commitments. That wasn't entirely true. I was committed to my career as if I'd taken a vow.

The commander came up to the deck and said, 'That squall proved we can never predict what an operation will bring.' He looked up to the sky and said, 'Hopefully it will be a clear run from here to the Scillies.'

The thought of being caught in the middle of the channel in daylight hours didn't bear thinking about. The commander moved on to speak to Brooks Richards.

'What did you think of your first operation?' Jake stood close beside me but not touching, despite the rock of the boat.

'Good,' I said. 'I think.' There was a sense of letdown too. It wasn't a real mission.

'Why "think"?' he asked.

'So close to land and not landing.' I pushed a strand of hair off my face.

'A sudden urge to go join the resistance?' he asked.

I grabbed the rail as the boat suddenly dipped. 'It has crossed my mind before.'

He widened his stance as the boat rolled some more. 'I can understand that.'

'Well, it's what you did,' I said.

'In a way it is.' He smiled.

Shivers began and Jake threw his arm about my shoulders. 'Maybe you should go below and warm up. There might even be a change of clothes you could find.'

With my teeth chattering hard, I didn't try to speak but went in search of warmth. Pierre handed me a pile of dry clothing, and, in an empty cabin, I peeled off the wet items and did my best to tighten the rope I'd found for a belt. There was nothing I could do about the size of the shirt but the old canvas smock I pulled over it hid it.

Out in the galley, I was handed a hot cup of coffee and I could smell rum.

'It will put some colour back in your cheeks,' the cook said.

I nodded and blew on the surface, watching the steam rise and swirl. It was mid-June and I was cold. Something wasn't right. Not sure what it was but I sensed it as I took a sip. In the coffee there was far too much rum. I carefully put it down and it was too quiet. The engines had stopped.

'On it,' the chief stoker said on his way down to the engines. I looked about. No one was panicking but it was three in the morning and the sun would be rising in less than two hours. I went on deck. The sea state was reasonably quiet as the boat moved with the current out into the channel and away from Cornwall.

'This is why we are testing her,' Brooks Richards said as he went down to see how things were progressing with the engines. One came to life, and we began to move against the current or more accurately keep time with it.

'This is a bit of a setback,' the coxswain said. 'At this rate we won't make the Scillies before noon.'

'Could we get cover from St Eval?' I asked, looking at the sky. The air felt heavy. A storm was looming despite the quiet seas.

'Good question,' Jake said.

'Not sure is the answer.' Brooks Richards scanned the sky. 'The commander hasn't radioed until we know what the problem is.'

He too went below, leaving me with Pierre, Jake and the skipper on deck.

'Are you worried?' Jake asked.

'Should I be?'

'Well, this has happened before,' he said. 'And we made it.'

I swallowed. If we didn't make it, there would be no big loss from my point of view but there were others who had children, wives, sisters, brothers, mothers, fathers. I pushed the thought aside. One engine worked. We didn't look like a military boat but a fishing one, albeit in a very odd location.

The noise increased and for a moment we surged forward then total silence again.

'Sails,' Jake said, heading to find the commander. I looked up at the riggings. I knew what was about to happen. There wasn't much wind but with one engine and a sail we would move faster. Without instruction, we all set to work.

Occasionally Jake tightened the riggings and Pierre listened to the sea while I sank onto the deck, waiting. The sound of the sea, the hum of the engine and the flap of the sail lulled me to sleep.

I woke to the sound of an aeroplane engine and the dawn.

'Stay down,' Jake shouted.

The men on deck set about looking like French fishermen well out of the fishing grounds. Guns began firing and, before I knew it, Jake had thrown his body over mine as the commander shouted orders. Below, I heard the engines strain and groan, as Jake's weight pressed me to the deck. I held my breath, listening, and then I heard a cry, the sound of another aircraft and felt Jake's ragged breathing.

The commander shouted orders, but I couldn't make them out, only the sound of the engines along with the sound of pain. Jake rolled off me and I ran over to Jean who'd been hit. Brooks Richards and Tom Long were doing their best to stem the blood. Jean Piron looked at me and I knew. Lifting his head on to my lap, I took his hand in mine and stroked his brow as he asked for his mother and begged me to tell her he loved her. I promised and I promised again as the sun rose high and the Bishop Rock lighthouse came into view. I prayed for him, but I knew only one thing as his life slipped away: we had to win this war. Young men were dying; people were dying in Europe from lack of food and as collateral damage. Life was so fleeting, and this young seaman hadn't even known love except that of his mother.

28

22 June 1942

Silence, and yet I heard the sound of the engines in my ears. I'd been off the boat for days. None of us spoke. I wrote words to his mother but they wouldn't help her pain, her loss. The commander did the same. Jean was eighteen. None of us had the heart for much, going through actions automatically. The birds were already up, waiting for the dawn, and any idea of sleep for me had evaporated. I slipped out of the kitchen door into the cool and damp morning. The scenery was lost in greys representing what was inside me and the colour of the young man's eyes. Jean knew what was happening and he didn't fight it, but we had done everything in our power, which was not enough. By the time we had reached the safety of New Grimsby Sound, he had gone.

On the beach, I sat and picked up handfuls of sand, letting it slip through my fingers, tickling, reminding me I was alive. Jake was alive too and thoughts of him filled me. We were still here, still living, still breathing and still feeling. If you love, you have more to lose. But as I settled on that thought, I heard my mother say if you don't love then you have already lost. I looked up, expecting to see her standing on the beach in front of me, but she, in a way, was gone too, as were Oli and my father.

I glanced down the beach and Jake was walking towards me.

What of him? Had kissing him been a test? If it was, then we both passed. The taste of him, the feel of him, had broken through the numbness of grief for Oliver. Could it do that again? The images of Jean dying while I held him, unable to do anything to help, wouldn't leave me. Would Jake be a distraction? My body whispered desire to me and for once I didn't push it away. I wanted to bring it closer, I wanted to feel and to be alive.

He sat beside me. 'You sleepless too?'

'Yes.' I reached for his hand and laced my fingers through his.

'Are you OK?' he asked.

I turned to him about to lie but said, 'No.'

'Same.' He played with my fingers. 'I've lost comrades before. Flying. It happens but God, Jean was so young, so full of promise.'

I brought his hand to my mouth and kissed it. 'Sorry.'

'Me too.' He let go of my hand and wrapped his arm about me and pulled me close. He was warm and felt like a haven in the storm.

In front of us, a fish jumped high from the surface of the water. Something was chasing it and it continued across the river to safety, I hoped. Rays of the sunrise brought colour and activity to the scene around us. Fishing boat engines rumbled, and we watched in silence as they headed out to the bay.

I stood, taking his hand, and I led him to my canoe. Together we put it into the water and paddled out to mid-river to watch the rising sun bringing colour and definition to the landscape. Once it was above the horizon, I pointed behind us and we headed to Frenchman's. I wanted him. More than ever, I was aware how little time we had.

In silence we paddled, disturbing the wading birds. The water was flooding into the creek, and we made it to the quay. Once on land, I turned to him and kissed him. So different than days ago. Gone was the playfulness and in its place passion, and a hunger to know one another. It was so fierce I would explode if I didn't satisfy it. We raced through the woods to my cottage, flinging the door open. We were barely into the room, and I had pulled his shirt off. Mine followed his to the floor. Somehow without taking my mouth from his, we made it up the stairs and fell onto the bed. I pulled at his trousers, and he undid them and then mine.

'Are you sure?' he asked.

'Yes,' I whispered.

The feel of his skin against mine was almost too much to bear. Everything was too much, and I needed him. I'd never felt this much desire. His fingers brought me to orgasm, and once he was in me, I came a second time before he withdrew, climaxing on my stomach. We both lay panting, fingers interlocked. For those few moments nothing existed but the two of us and I wanted it all over again. I didn't want to think. I wanted to feel. I rolled to my side and ran my free hand across his abdomen.

'God, Merry, do you want to kill me?' His laugh was low and deep.

My fingers trailed lower. 'What a way to die.'

Our eyes met and he kissed me, his desire rising again. He was as hungry for connection as I was.

*

Jake rose from the bed, and I stared at his beauty.

'I know you've seen a naked man before.' He leaned down and kissed me.

'True, but not you,' I said.

He laughed and pulled on his trousers. 'We had better head back before we are missed.'

'Fine.' I sat, dropping the sheet.

He sent me a look. 'Don't make this harder than it is.'

I looked down as he struggled with his fly and laughed.

'You may find it funny but . . . '

I leaned forward and adjusted his trousers.

'That really doesn't help,' he said.

I rose and found my knickers.

'Does that?' I asked, once half of me was clothed.

'A bit.' He ran a finger across my breasts before taking my hand. We went downstairs and retrieved the rest of our clothes.

'What now?' he asked.

I turned to him. I knew what he was asking but didn't know the answer. 'The tide should be in so we can head back to Ridifarne.'

'That's not what I meant.' He leaned against the door frame, and all I wanted to do was take him straight back upstairs.

'I know.' I put my shoes on.

'And?' he asked.

I rose to my feet. 'It's what we both wanted and needed.'

'Not arguing that point,' he said.

'Then let's not think any further.' I tiptoed and kissed his cheek.

He frowned. 'Is this your head or your heart speaking?'

'Heart hadn't come into it,' I said. 'My head made the decision.'

'Interesting head.' He stroked my cheek.

'And yours?' I asked.

'Don't think thinking came into it at all.' A slow smile spread across his mouth.

I grinned. 'Good. I feel alive and that, more than anything else, is what I needed.'

He played with a strand of my hair. 'Like the old Irish wakes.'

'What?'

'They used to head into the fields and make love after the wake as a way of giving death the shove . . .' his voice trailed away. 'It's a good custom.'

'I can't imagine the church approves.'

'Not at all,' he said. 'Been banned, I'm sure.'

I scanned the room, seeing my mother's painting. There was a smile in her eyes I hadn't noticed before. I glanced again to check if it was still there when I closed the cottage door and it was.

Following Jake down the path to the canoe, I enjoyed the way he moved. For such a tall man, he walked silently and with grace. The movement of his shoulders caused ripples of desire in me. I had been entirely wanton and wanted to be again and again. But what was going through his mind, he hadn't said.

At the quay he turned. 'Merry, the others . . . '

I nodded. 'Don't worry.'

'But . . . ' he said.

'Seriously, it's fine.'

'How fine?' he asked.

'We're both grieving and have expressed our desire to live and . . . '

'To love,' he said.

'Love doesn't have a place in war,' I said. 'My brother's fiancée was right: why risk it when there's a good chance that we won't see the other side.'

He stilled. 'I can't argue with that.'

'Good. Let's enjoy this . . . now,' I said. 'Tomorrow may not happen.' I climbed into the front of the canoe and Jake, using his long legs, pushed us off then climbed in. The breeze came from the north, bringing a chill. I shivered but once we reached the main river, the morning sun was high, and it warmed me through.

At Pedn Billy Boathouse, the men were sorting equipment. I dropped Jake off with them, continuing the last bit of the journey on my own before securing the boat and making my way back to the house. It was strangely silent. Every other time I'd walked in it was pink gins or talk of boats or riggings. But right now, it was quiet, yet I didn't sense that the house was empty.

Jean's death had hit us all and the rest of the team had worked with him longer.

Upstairs, I turned on the hot water for the bath then went to collect my things. What had I learned so far, working with this team? They faced death calmly, didn't panic unless they heard a dog barking, and loved each other in a bond that was so tight. But what would Jake and I do? It could rupture their trust. I wasn't here to destroy the team but that could easily happen. In fact by confirming Fleming's suspicions I may have already.

29

2 July 1942

I sat in the dining room with a chart unrolled in front of me. It had been two weeks since my fateful trip to French coastal waters and ten days since I'd been with Jake. My emotions, ones I'd forgotten I had, had run riot. We had not had a moment alone. But rather than taming my desire, it whetted it.

During this week, I'd turned all my frustrated energy into the charts. I mapped all the accessible and suitable beaches for lardering, as they call this new series of operations. The buoys they were going to use as a mail system were clearly marked and I was looking at the logistics of both beaches and buoys. In the past they had been able to store collapsible canoes near a church but that was scuppered when a farmer had discovered them as a regiment of Germans were passing. That had foiled their best landing location. Now they needed to find new strategies.

The commander had taken the train to Plymouth yesterday so no doubt there would be new orders on his return. Part of me wondered if this trip was initiated by Fleming. Rather than dwell on that, I focused on the beaches with the best access, those least impacted by the bashing rollers coming from the

Atlantic, and those most affected by the violent swings of the tide. The agents coming out to these points had to be considered as well. How far were they from the nearest house, town, road? Did we know if the beach was mined? So many factors to consider.

'What are you doing?' Jake leaned on the door.

'Obvious, I would have thought.' I tapped my index finger on the chart. 'Studying this.'

'Surely you know it by now.'

I looked from him to my work as he walked closer. His tan was darker, making his eyes bluer. They had been on a training exercise on the north side of Cornwall to do more practice landings in the boats with the pounding surf.

He pointed to the chart. 'What does this tell you?'

'Maps tell stories.'

'Is that so?'

I nodded. 'They tell stories about who made them.'

'That makes sense,' he said.

'It tells me what they were thinking and . . . ' I stopped because he was standing very close.

'And?' he asked.

I listened to his breathing and mine caught. The back of his hand brushed mine as he touched the map.

'It tells how it was used,' I managed to say.

'And you, why do you make maps?' he asked, leaning closer still, his breath tickling my neck.

'To make sense of my world,' I said and stood.

'Is there any sense in it?' he asked, watching me.

I met his glance. 'Sometimes strange things make sense.'

'Where is the map showing me and you?'

He was so close. I could lean forward and press my mouth against his.

'What story does our map tell?' he asked.

'I . . . ' I held his hand for a moment. 'I haven't drawn it yet.'

'There you are, Nipper. We need a hand on the beach.' Brooks Richards smiled. 'Sorry to interrupt.'

'Not a problem,' I lied; it was.

'Looking forward to dinner and dancing at the Ferry Boat tonight. Are you coming, Merry?' Brooks Richards asked, and I nodded. Since that fateful trip, I was no longer Dr Tremayne to the officers. I was Merry but who was I to Jake Russell? I wasn't sure. Maps answer questions and I wasn't sure what was the correct one to ask. But any map of us would involve an ocean and that never made for happy endings.

*

Hours later I was dressing for dinner before heading to the Ferry Boat. Rumour had it that Vivien Leigh and Laurence Olivier were in residence. The king's cousin had been here last week. It was all Lady Seaton could talk about when I had seen her on the bus to Falmouth the other day when I went with Mary to obtain supplies.

The small mirror above the sink didn't reveal too much but the deep crimson of my lipstick. It was almost gone and I wasn't sure when or where I would find another.

The weather had turned wet this afternoon, and I'd been sent several tasks from Fleming that kept me closeted in the dining room, poring over maps of northern France all afternoon and likely for the next few days.

I dabbed a little perfume on my wrists and neck. I wanted to look beautiful tonight. This was my heart speaking and not my head. So I shoved my vanity to the rear of my thoughts, grabbed my gloves and wrap, then went downstairs to join the others. They were all gathered in the sitting room; my pink gin was waiting on a side table. Never had two women had such a wonderful collection of companions.

Over the past weeks, I'd learned of Brooks Richards' love of sailing and of a Wren stationed in Falmouth. Edward Smith had his three kids and wife in Scotland. There was also the shy Thomas Johnson, the navigator. I'd spent a great deal of time with him, going over the maps, and then there was Pierre, who divided his time between the officers and the ranks. Jake stood head and shoulders above them, literally. I risked a glance at him while he was in conversation with Mary. In dinner jacket, he was almost as devastating as he was naked and with that thought I blushed and hid it in the guise of drinking my gin.

'Can't take your eyes from him,' Baker said, offering me a cigarette.

I took it and waited for the light.

'I'm not the only one,' I whispered.

He laughed bitterly and said, 'Very true but my heart won't be broken.'

I frowned.

'While you were in London, he was on leave, and I believe meeting one of his ladies, who works for the Americans.'

I drew on my cigarette, letting the nicotine hit. Was that jealousy or fair warning or both? Glancing at Jake, I didn't let doubt creep in. And if I was one of many that didn't matter either. I was scratching an itch and so was he.

'Take care, Merry. You're far too lovely to have your heart broken.' Baker knocked back the rest of his gin and went to make another.

Out on the terrace the rain had cleared and I saw British troops on Tremayne Quay. I knew that, like Ridifarne, the big house had been requisitioned. On an evening like this, the war felt far away and yet we were here and that was evidence enough. The world was upside down and my inner compass was the same. It had taken a knock and it was not finding a single bearing except to point to Jake.

'You look stunning,' Jake whispered.

I turned and smiled. 'You look pretty good yourself.'

'God knows what my father would think of me in a monkey suit, cavorting with the cream of the English gentry.' He laughed drily.

'War makes funny bed fellows,' I said.

'Indeed,' he said, his voice low.

'Shall we head off?' the commander asked, as he led Mary past us and into the garden. Jake held out his arm and I took it.

'Trust the American to steal the lady,' said Edwards as he lit a cigarette.

'Damn Yanks . . . what is it, they say . . . overpaid and over here.' Brooks Richards' smile softened his words.

'Hmmm,' said Jake, looking over his shoulder. 'Maybe I should join up with them again and be well fed and well paid.'

Brooks Richards slapped him lightly on the back. 'Don't even think of it, Nipper. We need you where you are.'

'The view is pretty good,' he said, looking at me. 'I think I'll stay put.'

'Knew you had some intelligence,' said Baker.

We reached the beach, and the tide was still way out with the bar fully exposed. Children raced along it, chasing a ball including the Newton boys, Peter and John. I'd been helping them with their maths and Latin much to the relief of their mother.

Arriving at the inn, glamorous people stood outside with their drinks as we walked past. I spied Vivien Leigh, and she was more beautiful than I had ever seen her on the screen. Laurence Olivier wasn't by her side but no doubt he was here too.

During dinner, I was seated between Pierre and Edwards, but

my glance continually sought out Jake talking to Mary and Baker. I tried not to be obvious about it. Was there a way we could escape together? To distract myself, I listened to Vivien Leigh, who was seated at the table next to us.

'I had tea in Manaccan in the most charming garden and orchard,' she said.

'Did you take the ferry over?' her companion asked.

'Yes, it was all an adventure,' she said. 'I wanted to see the famous fig tree growing in the wall of the church.'

The waiter arrived and cleared the plates, ending my eaves-dropping, then the commander asked me to dance. That was when I spotted Laurence Olivier. He was as beautiful as his wife. Together they were almost blinding.

'I wonder where they are staying?' I mused as I caught a glimpse of them together by the door.

He frowned. 'I don't think here.'

'Possibly with someone nearby,' I said.

'There are a few big houses still in use,' he replied.

As the song finished, Brooks Richards cut in and before long it was close to midnight, and I hadn't had a dance with Jake. It was if he was avoiding me. Yet I knew that wasn't true for his glance met mine so many times throughout the evening and each time a smile stole across his face. But instead of dancing as would be normal, it stood out because we hadn't. He had with Mary and almost every other woman in the room including Vivien Leigh. Of course, I was jealous. It would be lying to say I wasn't.

As the last song was announced, Jake was at my elbow. 'Dance?'

'Thought you'd never ask,' I said.

He laughed and pulled me a little closer as the music softened to 'Be Careful, It's My Heart'. Jake murmured the words in my ear as we slid around the dance floor. Heart vs head. I wanted to throttle him, but I loved the sound of his voice even if it was teasing me.

'What was she like?' I asked to distract him.

'Who?' He feigned innocence.

I resisted stepping on his toes and said, 'Vivien.'

'Charming,' he said. 'Maybe I should have saved the last dance for her.'

I tapped his arm. 'Beast.'

'Yes, it was a bit like the fairytale, *The Beauty and the Beast*,' he said.

I laughed.

'That's better. Were you jealous?' he asked, twirling me about.

'Yes,' I said.

'Good.' He grinned.

'Why good?' I asked.

'Don't want to be taken for granted,' he said. 'After all, it's my heart.'

'As if I would.' I kept my voice low. 'This is all very frustrating.'

'Exactly,' he said, as we moved about the floor. 'I can hold you in my arms but that is all and that is not enough.'

'I'm pleased you feel the same,' I said. 'I'd wondered.'

'Doubt me?' He put a hand on his heart as he spun me again. 'Yes.'

'You shouldn't.' He pulled me closer than the dance called for, but it wasn't enough.

'Meet me tonight,' I said as the music ended and I leaned closer. 'On the beach when everyone is asleep.'

He nodded and we joined the others who were beginning to gather outside. The night was still warm, and the sky filled with stars. No moon lit the short walk back to the house, but by the time we reached the path, my eyes had adjusted to the darkness.

'Want a nightcap?' Brooks Richards asked.

'Not for me.' I forced a yawn and climbed the stairs, hoping that everyone would decline the offer as I had, but I knew that wouldn't be the case. It could be a long wait but it would be worth it.

*

It was two-thirty when I crept out of the house and down to the beach. I had nodded off a few times, but it was the sound of silence that had woken me. Scanning the beach, I didn't see Jake, so I walked to the water's edge debating what I should do. Going back to bed was a tempting thought but the air was fresh and, if nothing else, the night sky was beautiful. The Milky Way stretched above me while the water gently lapped at the sand.

'You should be careful; you never know who you will find on the beach at this hour.' He reached for my hand.

I turned into his arms. 'I didn't see you.'

'I was near the wall so that I wasn't spied by anyone else lacking in sleep.'

'Good thinking.' I leaned towards him, and he smelled of the night air and soap.

'But,' he said, pulling me closer, 'you are here looking at the stars.'

'And thinking of you.'

'Well, that's OK then.' He laughed. 'It's very awkward, this keeping secrets.'

'You do it every day,' I said. The moon had risen, and his face was covered in shadow and light. 'You are not part of a cartography unit.'

'Hmm, you mean I've been fooled this whole time?' He chuckled.

'You have.' I kissed him lightly.

'What have you hidden from me?' he asked.

'My desire.' I kissed him again.

'Don't think that's true,' he said.

Enough with words, I thought as I wrapped my arms about his neck and pulled his head to mine. We could spar all day long, but we couldn't touch and that was what I wanted most. I wove my fingers through his hair and moved my body closer. All this clothing was not satisfactory.

'This isn't ideal.' He slid his hand under my blouse.

'No,' I murmured.

'I gave up necking on the beach when I was eighteen.' He trailed kisses across my cheek.

'That's good to know.' I drew a breath as his hand reached my breast. 'But I'm not sure we have many options.'

'There is the boathouse.' He lifted his head and looked around.

'Yes, but easy for someone to spot us,' I said.

I pulled away and headed to my canoe. There was enough water to get us at least to the quay by the mouth of the creek.

'I am not making love to you in a canoe.' He stopped moving.

'I agree,' I said. 'But we can reach the cottage this way.'

'Won't work. The tide was high at midnight so there won't be enough water to land on the old quay.'

The silence of the river at night with the call of the owls piercing the air could be haunting but with Jake it wasn't.

'Sorry,' I said.

'It's not your fault.' He placed a hand on my arm.

'I'm not sure what to do,' I said.

'About us or this moment?' he asked.

'Both,' I said, knowing one was easier to sort. Why had I thought a wartime affair would be easy?

'It can't be solved tonight.' He kissed me. 'I suggest you head back into the house and I'll follow in ten minutes or so.'

'Yes.' But I didn't want to go. I longed to stay here wrapped in his arms.

'You're not moving,' he said, kissing the top of my head.

'I know.' I stepped back.

'Go to bed, Merry.' He kissed me one last time and I left him on the beach. This was not the night I had hoped for.

30

With the replacement part for the problematic engine collected from Newlyn, Jake and I had the afternoon to ourselves with a picnic plus the advice from Mary to enjoy the July day. Although it crossed my mind that this was Mary trying to matchmake, I wasn't going to complain. We stopped near Godolphin Hill and together we trekked up to the top. The breeze was stronger and the air cooler, but we found a group of boulders and set up there.

'Alone at last.' He opened a bottle of beer and handed it to me. I leaned against the warm stone and watched him. He slipped his sunglasses off as the clouds arrived.

I picked up a quarter of a cheese and pickle sandwich. 'Tell me about your life before you came over.'

'Boring.' He took a sip of beer.

'To you maybe but not to me.' I ran a finger across his hand.

'You go first.' He handed me another quarter of a sandwich.

I laughed. 'Oxford.'

'That's all?' He raised an eyebrow.

'Well, not entirely true. Oxford and Cornwall.' I picked up his sunglasses and put them on. They slid down my nose and I peered over them. 'Why did you become a journalist?' I leaned forward, watching the expressions cross his face.

'I could write, and it was easier than novels.' One corner of his mouth lifted into a half smile that I couldn't resist.

Leaning forward, I kissed him then said, 'Ah, the great American novel.'

'Wasn't going to be written by me.' He kissed me slowly.

'Why not?' I pulled back. He was confident in everything else.

He picked up a strawberry and turned it in his fingers. 'I could never get past chapter four.'

'What happens in chapter four?' I leaned on one arm.

'They kiss or someone dies,' he said.

I laughed. 'Sounds like a great opening.'

'Maybe I began in the wrong place.' He offered the berry to me.

'A kiss is a good start,' I said, taking a bite of it. 'Better than a dead body.'

'Depends on where the story is going.' He pressed his lips against mine. He tasted of beer and sunshine.

'What story did you want to tell?' I asked with his mouth still close to mine.

'One of great love and passion and death, clearly.' He laughed. 'It didn't work but news articles did, and they paid the rent.'

'Teaching?' I asked while I watched a buzzard circle on the thermals as if it hadn't a care in the world.

'Accidental,' he said.

I turned back to Jake. 'Did you crash into the building?'

'In some ways that is an accurate description.' He handed me another berry. 'I was invited by a friend of a friend to give a talk about journalism and next thing I knew it had become a regular feature, which led to me taking a class every September.'

'Enjoyable?' I asked then wiped the strawberry juice from my mouth.

'Yes,' he said. 'They keep me on my toes.'

'I bet they do.' I laughed, imagining a room full of clever women with Jake at the front of it. Each and every one of them would be in love with him.

'And you, do you teach?' he asked.

'Yes, I lecture mostly on field studies and some cartography as well.' Oxford felt further away than a few hundred miles. It might be Jake, it might be the rawness of the landscape or it might be me.

'In which case,' he said, kissing me, 'we both tell stories.'

'We do.' I pointed to a boulder in the distance. 'This landscape around us tells the story of a very industrial past.'

'Mining?' he asked.

'Yes, but also quarrying too and look at those hedges.' I leaned towards him and directed his gaze away from me and to the fields spreading out at the base of the hill.

'I find it hard to look at fields when you are beside me,' he said. 'And there is the sea.'

'I won't give you a hard time about the sea.' I ran my thumb across his bottom lip. 'It's so clear today you can almost see the Scillies.'

'I'd rather look at you.' He nibbled my thumb.

I made a face of distaste.

'Seriously.' He placed a kiss on each fingertip then moved to my wrist. I closed my eyes trying to summon the distance I needed.

'There is nothing serious about us,' I said, knowing we should have had this conversation right at the very beginning but not wanting to tarnish the now.

He watched me, not giving his thoughts away. Overhead, the drone of an engine caught our attention. I hoped it was one of ours as we were a bit exposed but the boulders might shield us from view.

The plane dipped a wing and Jake waved. 'That's the plane that normally escorts us.'

'Do you feel you have had the support that you needed for

your operations?' My breath eased now that we weren't speaking about us.

He laughed. 'That's a leading question.'

'Well, I know about the rivalry,' I said.

'Fleming.' He closed his eyes for a moment. Opening them, he said, 'He could have asked me directly.' He shook his head slowly. 'Commander Holdsworth has barely been able to contain himself with the frustration. Having said that, we have achieved some things, but we could have done so much more. We want to truly disrupt, making everything harder for them.'

'But surely getting agents to and from does that.' I touched his hand.

'Yes, but with the right boats we could do more.' He threaded his fingers through mine. 'Enough of that. Tell me about growing up here.'

'Idyllic,' I said.

'That goes without saying,' he said. 'But your life is so different to mine.'

I studied him with my gaze resting on his full mouth. 'You've seen my home. I was a farm girl taught at home by a tutor then I went to Oxford at seventeen, which was a big change but I immersed myself in academic life.'

'Loves?' He raised an eyebrow.

I laughed. 'A few. One serious but we had different dreams in the end.'

'That sounds painful,' he said.

'It was at the time, but it was a lucky escape for both of us. Neither one would have been happy.'

'Why?' he asked.

'He wanted a wife,' I said. 'And I wanted a life.'

'Ouch.' He trailed his fingers along my cheek. 'They don't mix?'

'The head of the school of geography is married to the most

brilliant geographer, but she has had to give it all up for the children and the kitchen.' I shook my head. 'She still writes textbooks
but it's not her name on them.'

'That's wrong,' he said.

His sincerity showed but I imagined when he married, he too
would want a traditional arrangement.

'It doesn't have to be that way.'

I frowned. 'I've never seen it any other way except for my
parents.'

'Well, maybe because it is a women's college,' he said. 'But
I know several married women on the faculty who have both
a career and a family.'

'I don't want to say I don't believe you,' I said, taking a deep
breath, 'but I'm afraid I don't.'

'A doubting Thomas.'

'Or in this case a doubting Thomasina,' I said, closing my eyes
for a moment, enjoying Jake and the warmth of the sun and the
effects of the beer. Opening them, I found him looking at me.
I knew I had to say it clearly but that didn't make it easy. 'Jake.'

'Why don't I like the sound of that?' he asked.

'I simply want to make sure you know,' I said then pointed
first at him then at me. 'This is a for-now thing.'

He raised an eyebrow.

'I don't want you to have the wrong idea,' I went on while
I could be truthful.

'And what would that be?' he asked, keeping eye contact.

'Well, that *us* as a couple is anything lasting,' I said. 'It's meant
to be enjoyed for the moment.'

'You are simply using me,' he said with a smile. 'For my body.'

'If you wish to look at it that way.' I hit him lightly on the
stomach. 'We don't know what's ahead. And like Caroline and
Oli, it's best to keep things light so when you return to Boston and

I return to Oxford this will be a pleasant memory in a difficult war.'

'Are you telling me not to fall in love with you?' he asked, stroking my cheek.

'Yes, I am,' I said with my voice not as steady as I would have liked.

His fingers slid down my neck, making it very hard to think.

'And you're not to fall in love with me,' he said.

'Correct.' I nodded.

'You are one interesting woman,' he said before he kissed me.

I lay on the blanket, staring into his eyes. 'I hope that is *good* interesting.'

'You can be very sure I am happy to be with you . . . however you want it, and as long as you want it.' He rolled on top of me, and I knew how much he wanted me.

31

17 July 1942

It was late afternoon and I was heading to Kestle for the weekend to check on things. Jake and the team were out training and I wanted to leave a note in hopes he might be able to join me at some point. He'd been away for a few days and had been very quiet on his return. John Baker's words about a woman in every port crossed my mind. I didn't believe them as I walked across the hall and went into the room Jake shared with Brooks Richards.

All was neat and tidy and I couldn't tell which of the beds they slept in. Both had books on the bedside tables. One was all biographies and the other contained short story collections by O. Henry and Guy de Maupassant. A notebook was under those. I was almost certain which books were Jake's, but I didn't want to leave a note on Brooks Richards' bed, so I opened the notebook. The handwriting was distinctive and different from English cursive. Had his mother taught him to write? It was neat and I tried to picture a small sandy-haired boy working hard at his penmanship. I smiled at the thought then I read the words. Descriptions of the harbourside, boat activity, hedges, stations, and movement of people. I flipped further. Rationing. Blackouts. Bomb sites.

I sank on to the bed. This was wrong, even dangerous. This

could fall into the wrong hands. I stopped there. I stood, straightened the bed then I put the book back where I found it. The note I had written remained in my pocket.

With each step out of the room I told myself that Jake wasn't a spy, couldn't be a spy. But the truth was anyone could be. He had an easy manner and was clever. I needed to talk to Fleming. Picking up my bag, I went downstairs, and let Mrs Newton know that I was heading across the river if I was needed.

I couldn't reach Kestle fast enough. Until I spoke to Fleming, Jake was the last person I needed to see. It was now five o'clock, and I hoped to catch Fleming in the office or maybe at his club. Making good time across the river, I headed not to Frenchman's but through the village as that was the quickest route, so long as I wasn't stopped by someone who knew me. This would be the hardest part.

Tying the canoe up at the slipway by the Shipwrights, I waved to the publican's wife and walked straight into Tom Long, who steadied me.

'Where you off to in such a rush?' Long asked.

'Home to Kestle,' I said, ready to go on my way.

'Have a drink with us,' he said.

'Thanks but no,' I said. 'Things to do.'

'We missed you on the firing range today,' he said.

'Next time,' I said and went a bit further up the lane.

'Merry.' Jake's voice was clear.

I drew a deep breath and secured a neutral expression on my face.

'Are you joining us?' Jake asked.

'Off home,' I said.

He frowned but didn't say any more.

'It's your round, Lieutenant,' Tom Long called as he entered the pub.

'I'll be there in a minute.' Jake took a step towards me. 'All OK?'

'Yes, just fine.' I smiled and walked away, praying that he didn't follow. He had to join the men. Without looking back, I picked up my pace out of the village and up to the house.

Inside I went straight to the study and rang Fleming. In the end I was put through to Harling.

'Merry, this is a lovely surprise,' he said.

'Haven't much time. Where's Fleming?' I asked. Jake had kept my mother's whereabouts from me. He'd been oddly silent on his return and had not mentioned where he had been. In fact, he had evaded the answer when I'd asked. It was strange behaviour.

'Fleming will be back in a few days. Can I help?' Harling asked.

'Sadly no. Can you leave him a message to call me?'

'Will do,' he said. 'Take care.'

Placing the phone down, my hand shook. Was I letting my involvement, my feelings, cloud my judgement? What had happened to me? Never before would I have drawn a conclusion without evidence, but that notebook was evidence. I stood and took one last look about the room before heading to the sitting room to pour myself a whisky. Who could I speak to? The commander was not an option as he would not entertain any suspicions of his team. There was no one else but Fleming that I could trust with this information. I would have to wait and act as if I knew nothing.

'Could you pour another?' Jake asked and I froze. I hadn't heard him come in. I must have left the door ajar. He was very good at approaching unheard but that, my heart said, didn't mean he was a spy. However, my head said otherwise. We rarely receive what we want, and I didn't want this right now.

Taking a deep breath as I poured his whisky, I turned to

him with a smile that I didn't feel. How should I handle this? Minutes ago, I called Fleming to declare him a traitor and now I was about to exchange pleasantries.

He took the glass. 'Thanks.'

I walked to the window. He was sun-touched and dishevelled, and it wasn't good for clear thinking. The view of the farmyard was far better. There things made sense and had an order to them. My feelings didn't and my body was a complete traitor.

'I grew up in a house of women so, although a man, I know enough to realise something is wrong and in fact more than wrong.' He walked to my side.

I didn't say anything.

'I also know from my sisters not to push too far,' he said. 'So I will stop even though I suspect I have done something.'

I bit my lip. Done something. Spying.

He was too damned attractive and now too damned astute. There were so many things I could say but the right words were proving hard to find.

'Shall we see what's in the kitchen and make some dinner?' I asked.

He took a step back. 'Yes.'

I dashed to the kitchen, hoping for space but he was with me all the way. He put his glass down on the table and looked in the basket, full of vegetables.

'Shall I go ask the land girls if they have anything spare?' he asked.

'I'll do it.' I put my glass on the other side of the table from his and fled out the door, hoping that distance would clear my head. Jake Russell was proving too good to be true. And that was another reason I must end this dalliance.

'Hello,' I called as I tapped on the open cottage door.

'Oh, Dr Tremayne.' One of the girls wiped her hands on the apron she was wearing. On the side were five mackerel, still whole. Their bright eyes staring at the ceiling.

'I'm so sorry to hear about your brother.' She put down the knife.

'Thank you,' I said. 'I was wondering if you might have any spare food?'

She looked down and laughed. 'There are so many of them I don't know what to do.'

'May I have one or two?' I asked.

Her look of relief was almost comical.

'Take three. It's only Maisie and me,' she said, placing them onto a plate and handing them to me.

'Thank you,' I said, leaving her to her task. On the short walk back, I stopped to collect some dill and parsley. I hadn't once thought of Jake while I was fully occupied with charts and things but now he was filling more and more of my thoughts. It was clear that I had too much time on my hands. The time had come to return to London.

Jake took the plate from my hands when I entered. 'How were you thinking of cooking them?'

'Fresh mackerel needs little,' I said.

'True.' He paused. 'Do you trust me to cook it?'

I swallowed. The question seemed to be asking me so much more than how to cook the fish. Did I trust him? No, shouted my head.

'You're the son of a fisherman so the fish should be in capable hands,' I said.

He looked me in the eyes. 'Not only the fish.'

I turned from him. I couldn't do this, but I had to.

'This affair, it shouldn't be happening,' I said. 'You know this as much I do.'

'Merry . . .'

'It was reckless and selfish of me to start this.' I raised my hand to stop him from speaking. 'We come from different worlds and will return to them some day. What we've had has been fun, but it is only something that could exist in this time and space, this point on the map.' I took a deep breath. 'Soon we will be at different points and a different story will be told.'

'You can plot your story,' he said quietly.

'As you've tried, and you've abandoned your novels at chapter four; maybe we need to finish this one here and keep it a very short story,' I said, hating myself for every word but they were the right ones.

'I would prefer a novella,' he said.

'Haven't read one,' I lied.

'There can always be a happy ending to a story.'

'How so?' I asked.

He put the plate down and walked towards me. I fought the urge to both flee and to rush into his embrace.

'You can choose to say *the end* when the lovers are in each other's arms like this,' he said.

'Can you?' I asked.

'Yes, or you can take them up the stairs,' he whispered in my ear before he lifted me into his arms and did just that.

*

Near midnight we sat together in candlelight, drinking the second bottle of wine. I couldn't continue to play this game. He could be betraying everything I had worked for and I had to find the strength to end it. Tonight served to remind me that, as good as it felt to be with Jake, it made no sense. There was no way to plot our way forward together. It didn't take a map or a chart to see it with clear vision. Sadly, my vision was easily clouded by my passion for him.

'Jake,' I said, looking not at him but at the red wine in my glass. I couldn't continue with this knowing what I know now.

'Don't say it,' he said, taking my hand in his.

'It has to be said.' I pulled my hand back. 'I am an Oxford academic and as a woman that means that there is no place for this.' I pointed at us both.

'I don't accept that,' he said.

'Well, I live in, and at the women's colleges there is only single accommodation.' I laughed bitterly. 'Think of it as a nunnery without the religion.'

'You'd make a terrible nun,' he said, taking my hand back and kissing each finger, sending threads of desire through me.

'And thankfully I'm not one but the life I have chosen, the career, is incompatible with us even before we add in that you are American, and I'm English.'

'Two people,' he said. 'Divided by an ocean.'

'And differing desires.'

'Are they that different, I wonder?' He sipped his wine.

'They are and I think before either of us falls further into this affair that has nothing but the end in front of it—' I drew a breath '—we need to do it now.' It would make exposing him to Fleming easier if the affair was finished.

I'd finally said it. It was over even though we had made love a short while ago. It was better to end it this way before it all became more tangled, public and difficult.

'I don't agree,' he said, before he turned my hand over and kissed the inside of my wrist.

'Don't try and distract me.' I pulled my hand away.

'Would I do that?' he asked, trying to look innocent but there was too much desire in his eyes for that.

'Look, Jake.' I closed my eyes, hating myself and hating the wine that confused my feelings and the words. He was a spy and that jeopardised everything.

'Merry, how I could have thought you a spy when you can't hide your emotions is the question I ask myself.'

'What?' My heart stopped.

'You were secretive, wandering off in the canoe alone and once to Gweek,' he said.

I gasped. So, I hadn't been imagining things.

'And I knew you weren't being honest about your reasons for being here,' he said.

I rose to my feet, putting my glass down. 'This makes things so much easier to say, it has been fun but it's over.'

'Merry, I'm sorry I've offended you.' He stood.

'You haven't.' I forced a smile and walked away not sure what to think. It was most important that I didn't allow myself to feel, to feel anything at all. But then I turned to him and held out my hand. It had to end but not this way. I had to go on until I spoke to Fleming. It was best to keep your enemies close.

PART FOUR

December 25, 1941

Christmas Greetings

Happy Christmas, as the English say. I haven't discovered what they have against 'Merry' but I'm getting used to saying happy instead. This will be my first Christmas away from home and as a Canadian. There are things that are familiar that will be missing like choosing the tree, snow and an abundance of food. But I will be celebrating all the things that Christmas is truly about – love, family, and friends. We all know that Christmas doesn't require a turkey or a goose. Nor are presents necessary. Peace on earth is everyone's dearest wish but, as the war rages on, it won't be true this year. I have left the skies and now

serve on the seas. A change of perspective is good for the soul or, as they say, a change is as good as a rest.

Here in England no church bells will ring out to call people to services but carols will be sung, nativity pageants will be held and in these congregations I will be pleased to find American GIs. Some of the hymns may have the same words but different tunes, yet the feelings expressed may never be more heartfelt.

This year, Christmas won't be white; it will be most likely wet. I met a GI from Kansas on a train. He was all of eighteen and looked far too young to be so far from home. He'd never left Kansas before and I asked him what he expected his first Christmas away from home to be like. He looked me in the eyes and said, 'Holy as it should be.' I agreed and asked this young man what he thought of the country he'd been in for two weeks. 'People are nice enough, but the beer is warm and it never stops raining.' That made me laugh. I've become used to the beer and don't notice the weather unless it stops me from doing something. I have learned to appreciate the sun when it does shine.

May you be blessed this Christmas with love and let's all pray that by next Christmas there will be peace on earth.

Jake Russell
England

32

30 July 1942

Maurice Cohen arrived with his radio case and an even smaller suitcase in the dying days of July. He was to be dropped off on a beach in Brittany in two weeks if all conditions were right. We knew very little about him as we picked him up from the train station at Falmouth docks. If what Jake had told me about the operations he had done with the SIS were true, we shouldn't know anything about this man and shouldn't engage with him. But it had been made clear that he needed further preparation for landing, so he had been sent to us.

He was paler than a person had a right to be as well as being short and far slighter than I was. I found it hard to imagine this man had been through rigorous training, was a radio operator, nearly captured, escaped over the mountains into Spain and now wanted to return.

He peered at me from behind his round glasses and smiled.

'They didn't tell me my welcome committee would be so beautiful,' Mr Cohen said.

I smiled. 'I'm not sure if you're talking about me or Lieutenant Russell.' I shook his hand.

'You, of course,' he said. His grip was firm, and the eyes danced. 'Hello, Lieutenant.' He looked him up and down before saying,

'I take it you are the rowing instructor and in two weeks I'll look like you.'

'Certainly,' Jake said with a smile.

'Ah, an American,' said Mr Cohen.

'From Maine,' Jake clarified.

Mr Cohen nodded and said, 'From Belgium, in case you wondered.'

'I had,' said Jake, putting the two bags into the boot. 'Your accent was puzzling.'

'Many influences,' Mr Cohen said and scanned the harbour filled with military boats then climbed into the vehicle.

'Do you know anything about Cornwall?' I asked, turning to him in the back seat.

'It has much mineral wealth and—' he paused to look about '—beautiful scenery.'

'All true and a strange food called a Cornish pasty,' Jake added.

'I have heard of these,' said Mr Cohen.

I smiled. 'We will make sure that you have one.'

'Thank you,' he said. 'I hear you have many excellent gardens around.'

'We do,' I said. 'The Victorians became quite competitive with some of these big houses.'

He nodded as we drove past the gates to several of them. Finally, we turned down the lane behind the house. It always struck me how different it looked from this side. The main door appeared grand due to its height and the carved granite but, once through it, the house welcomes you. Appearances could be so deceptive; I glanced at Jake. I hadn't heard from Fleming so I continued to play along but each day it was harder and harder.

As we entered Ridifarne, Mary greeted us, her smile welcoming. Mr Cohen beamed as Mrs Newton's boys raced through the house, stopping briefly to say hello before they barrelled out of the sitting room and into the garden.

'Sorry about that,' Mary said. 'Shall I show you to your room or would you prefer to have lunch first?'

'My room please,' he said.

Brooks Richards and Jake had moved on board *Mutin* with the crew to give Mr Cohen a room of his own. It was a relief. There was no chance of bumping into each other, no reasons to slip up on my resolve like I had that night, and every other opportunity that came my way. I was spineless in the face of desire.

Now I stood alone with Jake in the hallway and he took my hand and lifted it to his lips.

'We need to talk,' he said.

Mary coughed and we looked up the stairs. She stood on the half-landing waiting. 'It's a beautiful afternoon, shall we have lunch outside?' she asked.

'I'll let Mrs Newton know,' I said and fled to the kitchen, wondering how long she'd been there. This was not good. The fewer people who knew, the better. I would try and ring Fleming again today.

To avoid direct questioning from Mary, I collected the plates and the cutlery and brought them out to the terrace. The sun beat down and the river below could not look more beautiful. The commander came up through the garden.

'I thought you'd be back about now,' he said.

Mary, Jake and our new guest came out to the terrace.

'Such beauty.' Mr Cohen stared at the river.

'It is rather special,' I said.

Mr Cohen turned from the view towards me. 'I gather that you are from here, Dr Tremayne.'

I pointed to the south side. 'There's a farm inland from there and that was where I was born.'

'So, Mr Cohen, do you swim?' the commander asked, wiping his brow. The temperature had climbed and a swim sounded ideal.

'Call me Mo, please,' he said. 'And definitely not.'

'Row?' asked Jake.

'No.' Mr Cohen smiled and held up his hands.

The Newton boys, John, a leggy ten, and Peter, a stocky eight, raced from the beach coming to an abrupt stop.

'What a glorious place to be a child,' Mr Cohen said, beaming.

'Boys, come and properly meet our new guest,' Mary said, and the boys immediately came to the table.

'Hello,' they said in unison. John held his hands cupped. I didn't think Mr Cohen would be too pleased to meet their pet, but it was inevitable as the little white mouse crawled up John's shirt and walked across his shoulder. Mary slapped her hand across her mouth.

'What have we here?' asked the commander.

'Albi, sir,' said John.

'And he is?' asked the commander. The smile on his face contradicted his solemn tone.

'Our pet mouse,' said John.

Albi surveyed the table. Mr Cohen held out a hand and the mouse raced down John's arm and straight to Mr Cohen's, who stroked its head. Mary closed her eyes. I laughed, I couldn't hold it back.

'It is a very fine mouse.' He handed Albi back to John. 'But I don't think Mrs Holdsworth likes him at the luncheon table.'

'Off you go,' the commander said and the boys raced around the house to the kitchen door.

'They are fine boys,' Mr Cohen said, taking a seat beside me.

Mary passed the tray of sandwiches around, and said, 'Yes, they are. Merry has been trying to teach them geography, maths and Latin.'

'It's the holidays and their focus has diminished since school broke for the summer,' I said, offering Mr Cohen some tea.

He nodded. 'This is good, they will grow to have strong bodies from the environment and strong minds from the input.' He smiled at me. 'You taught at Oxford?'

'Yes,' I said.

'My wife taught at the university in Warsaw,' he said. 'Before you ask, she was taken away and I do not know any more.'

We all looked down at our hands. Stories similar to this were being heard more frequently.

'This is why we fight or, in my case, I convey information.' He glanced up. 'I am not made for the adventures or the battles like you.' His glance fell on Jake and the commander. 'But we all do what we can. Like Dr Tremayne using her skills, understanding the land and the sea and their use. This is important now and it will be important when all of this ends.'

Mrs Newton arrived with a fresh pot of tea and cleared the empty plates.

'Very true,' the commander said, rising to his feet. 'The men are taking some target practice this afternoon; would you like to join them?'

'Yes, although I hope never to have to fire a gun in defence.' He took a breath. 'It is a necessary skill.'

The commander and Mr Cohen went off together.

'Not joining them, Jake?' Mary asked as she began collecting cups and saucers.

'I'm the best shot they have already,' he said and kept a straight face.

'Ah. Modest as always,' I said, rising to my feet. 'Baker might disagree.'

'Not modest, truthful.' He winked at me, and he set off into the kitchen while I gathered the remaining items onto a tray. I stopped to stare out to the river and thought of Mr Cohen and his wife.

'Are you still with us?' Jake asked on his return.

'How do you live with the not knowing like Mr Cohen's?'

'You just do.' He placed a hand over mine.

I thought about my mother all the time. However, she chose to go. Mr Cohen's type of not knowing was far worse.

*

Finally the house was deserted by three and I placed a call to Fleming. I couldn't keep waiting to hear from him because each day the situation became more awkward. After what felt like forever, I was put through to Fleming.

'Dear God, Merry, what's happening?' Fleming asked.

'Russell,' I said.

'What about the Nipper?' he asked. 'Has he proposed?'

I rolled my eyes. I would not respond to that but clearly our affair was not so secret.

'I think he's a spy,' I said.

A blast of laughter came down the phone line.

'Seriously. He has a notebook and in it are lists of things that shouldn't be noted like harbours, blackouts, even landing beaches on Brittany.'

'He's not a spy,' he explained. 'He's a reporter.'

'He can't be a reporter and working on a secret team,' I stressed.

'And that is where you would be wrong,' Fleming said.

'How?' I asked for I couldn't see any way this would work.

'Since July nineteen forty, when I asked him to turn his journalistic skill to bringing the American public on side. He has been writing with the government's approval ever since,' he said. 'Nipper felt so passionately about the war. I knew that with his gift for words he could make Britain human and real to the American public. It was what he did in all his reports. The man can pull tears out of a stone and that is what he's doing.'

I picked up a pencil and rolled it between my fingers. 'Are you certain?'

'Yes.' He laughed. 'Nipper is the real deal and that's why he is still doing his dispatches even though he's working in secret operations. The man is that good.'

'Oh,' was all I could say. 'But why record the landing beaches?'

'Not sure but leave it with me.'

'Hmmm.' I had no choice.

'Read his work,' he said. 'I'll send them to you.'

'Thank you,' I said.

'What did you think of your journey across the channel?' he asked.

I huffed. Nothing was a secret. 'Eye opening.'

'Good. Learned enough?' he asked.

'No,' I said feeling mutinous for reasons I couldn't pinpoint.

'Will that always be your answer?' he asked.

I laughed and said, 'Yes.'

'Thought so. They can't have you forever. Make the most of it,' he said. 'You know what's ahead.'

I took a deep breath and said, 'I do.' The line cut out and I placed the handset down. Had I jumped to the wrong conclusion? I put my head in my hands and closed my eyes. It wasn't like me to jump into judgements without weighing up the facts. I hadn't even tried to look for other reasons.

Opening my eyes, it was clear the affair with Jake was impacting my ability to come to intelligent conclusions, and this was dangerous. Not only for me but for others. I had to continue to play along until I heard back from Fleming and I didn't like it one little bit.

33

11 August 1942

Sitting out by the water feature in the garden, I opened the envelope, puzzled by what Fleming would be sending me. Two newspaper cuttings fell out along with a brief note.

> *Merry,*
> *Almost forgot I promised to send these to you. Nipper was*
> *a real asset in bringing the United States public on side.*
> *Remember this, even if you don't care for the style.*
>
> *Fleming*

I picked up the first and read it.

Looking up from the article, I knew exactly what Fleming was talking about regarding the style. It was a bit chatty and didn't carry the weight of proper reporting to my mind.

'It is a beautiful day,' Mr Cohen said, coming to sit beside me.

'It is.' I smiled and picked up the other newspaper cutting.

'Is it good news?' he asked.

I handed him the one I had read. 'Some of Jake's newspaper work.'

He looked from me to the cutting. 'You are not impressed?'

'Well, the style is a little . . . ' I trailed off, not being able to find the right word.

He tapped at the other one in my hand. 'Is that one as unsophisticated too? Jake Russell does not strike me in that way.'

I smiled. 'No, he is not unsophisticated but his writing is.' I opened the other cutting and quickly scanned it.

'Ah,' he said, handing the article back to me and taking the other. 'This is propaganda and helpful.'

I knew so little about America other than the shape of it. Like many of my fellow countrymen my knowledge was gained from the books I had read as a child and the movies I'd seen. This did not create a full picture.

'The Americans are a bit earnest and full of themselves, but they are not as world-weary as we are.' He handed the cutting back to me. 'Their energy is so very needed in this battle.'

'This is true,' I agreed. The Americans involvement had invigorated the fight.

'Now, I recall what I came to find you for,' he said. 'Mary was looking for you.'

'Thank you,' I said.

'He is a good man,' Mr Cohen said.

I pressed my lips together but did not answer. The jury was out on whether Jake was good or bad, but he had no place in my life going forward.

*

'This hedge, here, covered in grass and wildflowers and topped with trees, is the same as the hedges we saw at Godolphin Hill?' Jake asked, pointing to the one lining the field we were walking through with Mr Cohen.

'The basic structure is the same,' I said. 'It is designed to withstand the weather bashing in off the channel. You'll see similar structures all the way up to Scotland and down into France. These hedges are very practical.' I pointed to the hillside. 'See those narrow strips.'

Jake nodded.

'Those are medieval fields,' I said. 'And the more rounded ones are a legacy from the earlier settlements.'

'What did you do your thesis on, Dr Tremayne?' Mr Cohen asked coming up beside us.

'The north coast of France,' I said. 'Please call me Merry.'

'If you will call me Mo,' he replied.

I nodded but he didn't look like a Mo, more a Maurice. I peered over the hedge to Jake while waiting for Mo to go ahead of me, as his fitness worried me.

'I love how the trees are bent, showing the prevailing wind.' Mo paused to catch his breath.

'Those winds have shaped the trees and me,' I said, following behind.

Jake laughed. 'Don't notice you stooping in one direction.'

'Thankfully not,' I said and stopped to enjoy the view of Falmouth Bay. Whether from the sea or the land, it never ceased to fill my heart. And today there wasn't a cloud in the sky. In the past few days, we had discovered that Mo was a hopeless shot, his ability to row was abysmal, and he capsized the boat every time he tried to get into it. He had returned to Ridifarne dejected last night, and I suggested a day away from the water might help. Jake and I, tasked with showing him the local beauty spots, had walked inland to Mawnan Smith and then out to Mawnan Church before taking him along the coast for a stretch.

This would aid his fitness, which might help his hopeless rowing. I paused to point out the remains of the forts on the opposite headland. Jake was a way out in front of us.

'How long have the two of you been in love?' Mo asked.

I stopped walking. 'We're not in love.'

He sent me a look. 'You may think you are not, but all the signs say it is so.'

'The signs are wrong.' I shook my head.

'If you say, but I have been watching these past weeks and, although all the men are solicitous of you, there is a difference with the lieutenant.'

'We are not in love,' I said. In the distance I watched Jake's athletic stride with a heart full of longing but not love.

'Do you not want to be in love?' he asked, peering at me over his glasses as we began walking again.

'I don't.' I pressed my lips together.

'Days ago, I wouldn't have believed it, but alas you are a fool,' he said then gulped some air as we moved up the incline. 'Very few are blessed with it, and it should be cherished and not dismissed.' He picked up his pace and caught up with Jake, leaving me behind.

Why was it wrong to choose not to be in love? Surely it was the most logical thing in a world at war. When or if the war ended, I had a career to look forward to and I would be in a stronger position having been involved in this war work. That future at Oxford was worth not risking it for something so fickle as love.

They were laughing when I reached them, and I dearly hoped that he hadn't had the same discussion with Jake. But I couldn't tell, which didn't help my mood at all. My vision was anything but clear these days and it didn't help that I hadn't heard any more from Fleming. Trying to keep up different pretences was wearing thin. In public, Jake and I had no relationship other than as team members, and in private we were lovers – all while I was left scrutinising his every action to see if it would give him away.

*

The boys were sitting at the dining room table with Mo who was working on their maths. He taught them it in such a way that they didn't mind that they were doing schoolwork during the holidays. Or it could have been the maze he had constructed for Albi. That too was part of their learning. Albi worked out the exit more quickly if there was food involved. Mrs Newton said they were the same. Sadly, Mo's rowing abilities were not improved whether he had cake or a beer on offer at the end. Jake was in despair. Mo was not coordinated enough to row and wasn't a good passenger on a boat. He was seasick on an easterly swell on the Helford. His time here had passed with little progress. The commander had spoken with London suggesting they should send another man to go to France, but they had refused. He was told to keep working with Mo and so we did.

From the doorway, I watched them. He looked up and smiled. I planned to take him out in my canoe to see if it could be a success of some sort. Anything at this point as the team were worried about landing him. The weather forecast was not ideal in Brittany although we were bathed in sunshine here. Storms were moving across the Atlantic ahead of September and they created surf that would challenge Jake, let alone a small serious man with a lovely smile and no fitness at all.

'Is it time, Merry?' Mo asked.

'It is,' I said.

'Excuse me, boys,' Mo said, as he rose to his feet. 'Dr Tremayne feels she will succeed where others have failed, or I have failed others.'

'You can do it, Mr Cohen. I know you can,' said John.

'I promise you I will try my hardest, young man.' He removed his glasses and gave them a polish with his handkerchief.

We walked down to the beach in silence until we reached my canoe.

'Are you ready?' I asked.

'No, but I am here.' He patted my arm.

I laughed and pushed the boat into the river. The water was flat, the air was still and the sun warm. Conditions couldn't be better. 'You climb in first.'

'Where do I sit?' He looked from me to the boat.

'You don't.' I held the end of the boat. 'You kneel.'

'You mean, I pray,' he said.

'If you need to, certainly.'

His knuckles went white, gripping the side of the boat. He put one foot in and then the other, almost falling onto his knees in the front of the boat.

'Well done,' I said, using my brightest teacher voice as I waded in. 'Now kneel there and I'm going to push the canoe out a bit. You don't need to do anything.'

Once I was in and the canoe stable, I looked over my shoulder. My biggest worry was capsizing with a non-swimmer aboard. Jake and Tom Long were playing safety boat from a distance.

A few paddle strokes brought us out to the middle, and I let the current carry us upriver a little way. Most of the work that Jake had done with him had been trying to land on Pengarrock beach. I hoped that paddling away from the bay and enjoying the beauty and the peace might ease Mo's fears. He was a man who risked death every day while in France operating a radio and didn't worry about it, but the water troubled him.

He looked over his shoulder at me and the boat rocked. He lost whatever he was about to say and clung to the sides.

When the boat was smoothly moving through the water again, he said without turning to me, 'What's down there?'

'That's Frenchman's Creek and at the head is my cottage. Do you want to see it?' I asked.

'Yes,' he said.

'There's a paddle at your feet. Why don't you try paddling?' I suggested. 'One stroke each side.'

We were in the creek now and I hoped he felt more at ease.

His first stroke was fine, but the switching sides nearly tipped us over.

'Try paddling on the right only and I'll paddle on the left.' It took a moment and some balancing strokes on my part but we made it to Withan Quay without overturning.

'You have a cottage in this wilderness?' he asked.

'I do,' I said. 'Further down where the creek is nothing more than a stream, the cottage is among the trees.'

'Spooky or enchanting?' he asked.

'The latter, I think.' I laughed. 'Do you want to get out and stretch your legs before we go back?'

He lifted himself off his calves and the boat rocked. 'No.'

'As you wish,' I said, and pushed off the quay while he tried using the paddle on both sides until we reached the mouth of the creek. There the current wished to push us further upriver, but our goal was to head back to the beach in front of Ridifarne. With the force required to fight the tide, Mo unbalanced us and went rigid. I paused until the boat had stilled.

'If you would paddle on the left side for ten strokes, please,' I said.

That was enough to point us in the right direction and for him to see he was doing a good job. I kept close to the southern bank to avoid the pressure of the incoming tide. Jake wasn't far away with Tom Long, pretending they were fishing. I don't think that Mo saw them until after he was safely back on the beach.

'Thank you, Merry,' he said. 'That has shown me that being on a boat does not have to be traumatic.'

'Boats are essential,' I said.

'That I will not deny but water,' he said and waved his hand out, 'big water and I do not get on. A bathtub is sufficient.'

The boys raced up to us, kicking a ball. He joined them for a moment.

'Do you have children?' I'd been longing to ask this since the first time I'd seen him with the boys.

'We were never blessed,' he said softly. 'This caused us great sadness, but now I think that God blessed us.'

I reached for his hand and gave it a squeeze.

'Do you want children?' he asked.

I was about to say no but paused. 'I thought my brother would have children and I would have nieces and nephews, but he was shot down in May.'

'I am sorry about your brother.' He took my hand this time.

'Thank you.'

'Merry, you are young and are very good with John and Peter.' He kicked the ball back to the boys.

'I like children,' I said. 'But I will not marry.'

'Ah, I see,' Mo said. 'This is why you will not admit you love the American.'

'You have the wrong picture.' I shook my head. 'We enjoy each other's company and in this world things disappear.'

'They do. Both you and I know that, but I can assure you that having known love makes everything worthwhile, even the loss.' He paused. 'When my wife lost her mother, there was a twelfth-century poem that brought her comfort. It is something like this, if I have translated correctly.

'Tis a fearful thing,
To love
What death can touch.
To love, to hope, to dream,

And oh, to lose.
A thing for fools, this,
Love,
But a holy thing,
To love what death can touch.
For your life has lived in me;
Your laugh once lifted me;
Your word was a gift to me;
To remember this brings painful joy.
'Tis a human thing, love,
A holy thing,
To love
What death can touch

He drew a deep breath. 'This poem brings me comfort now.'

John took Mo's hand and gave him Albi from out of his pocket. I thought about his words, but he was gone before I could say more.

Jake and Tom Long appeared on the beach.

'Mo has to go down as the most awkward person in the world,' Long said. 'He knows more ways of falling out of a boat or turning one over than I thought possible.' He shook his head then walked up to the house.

'You are looking very thoughtful and not merry despite your success in the canoe,' Jake said.

'It was something Mo said.' I watched Mo who held both boys by the hand and I could just make out the mouse on his shoulder.

'He's a very thoughtful man,' Jake said.

'He is,' I said. 'Are you going to teach him to swim? I do think that is half the problem.'

'Really? He only has a short distance to go so why does swimming come into it?' Jake frowned.

'He hasn't said but it was the way he froze when the canoe rocked.' I grabbed the boat and began to drag it up the beach.

'You rocked the canoe?' Jake took the other end.

'He did and that disturbed him,' I said.

Jake sighed then said, 'I'll give it a go.'

Mo and the boys disappeared further along the beach.

Jake put his end down and said, 'You know I think he loves that mouse more than the boys do.'

'They love him.' I lowered my end of the canoe and tied the painter line around a tree trunk at the top of the beach.

He tucked a strand of my hair behind my ear. 'I think you do too.'

'No, he's a risky one to love,' I said. 'His odds of survival are slim.'

He dropped his hand. 'So, you won't love him.'

I opened my mouth to speak.

'You are stingy with love,' he said, taking a step back.

'I prefer careful.'

'The more you love the more love you have,' he said and walked off to catch up with Mo and the boys.

'The more you love the more you lose,' I said to no one then picked up a stone, skimming it across the water. But it only jumped once before it sank.

*

After three days of wind and rain, the weather had turned fine. We had breakfasted in the garden and I walked to the dining room to tackle the photographs in from St Eval airbase. The telephone rang and I detoured.

'Hello,' I said, distracted, watching the boys try to convince Mo into giving swimming a go.

'Merry, Fleming here. You were way off the mark as I suspected regarding Nipper.'

'Are you certain?'

'Yes, without a doubt.'

I wanted to ask how but knew better.

'How is the training going for our Belgian?'

I sighed. 'Slower than a snail's pace.'

'Keep at it. He's brilliant at what he does.' Fleming paused. 'I must run to a meeting but waste no more time or energy regarding Nipper.' The phone clicked.

Waste no more time and energy regarding Nipper. Easier said than done. I walked back into the dining room and pulled a photograph towards me but couldn't focus, hearing squeals of joy outside.

Mary walked into the room, beaming. 'They've done it and convinced Mo to have a go at swimming and I've just found Mo some trunks.'

'That's excellent news.' I grinned.

'Shall we try and watch discreetly?' she asked.

I stood, pushing the photographs away. 'Yes.' I was exhausted from the days of watching and assessing everything Jake did. Now that was to stop.

While Mo changed, Mary and I went to the beach and hid behind some shrubbery because the man was bashful, and we didn't want to make his embarrassment worse. Before long, Mo, Jake and the boys appeared. Mo looked more lost than ever in swimming trunks that were a bit too big. They had deposited the mouse above the high water. Albi was safe in an old box with air holes.

John held onto one of Mo's hands while Peter held the other and they led Mo out until his knees were covered. Mary grabbed my hand in her excitement. Jake walked backwards in front of the trio. With the difference in height, the water hadn't yet reached Jake's knees and I had to stop myself from looking at him. He had been very distant with me last night and we hadn't danced while at the Ferry Boat. This morning he'd smiled, but it wasn't like his ones of the past. It was the polite one he sent to all and sundry.

Fleming's words came back to me. Oh God, Fleming had spoken to Jake. I crumpled against the rocks behind me. Mary sent me a look then pointed.

Mo had reached just above his knees. Both boys were still holding his hands and shouting encouragement, but they had all stopped moving.

'Is everything all right between you and Jake?' Mary whispered.

I turned to her.

'Don't think I haven't seen.' The light in her eyes danced.

'But . . . ' I said.

'We all know,' she said. 'And last night and this morning it was obvious that something has happened.'

My shoulders fell and it felt like I'd been hit in the stomach.

'Mary, I don't know what to say.'

'Frankly, we're all delighted,' she said. 'It is so good to see something blossoming in front of us, despite this wretched war.'

I shook my head. 'It's not like that.'

'I know it must be hard to think of the future when everything is so uncertain,' she said, 'but I'd say Jake is a keeper.'

I frowned. 'I'm not looking for one.'

Mary laughed. 'I wasn't either, but I found one and they are rare.'

I looked to the river. Mo had made it as far as the hem of his swimming trunks and wasn't budging.

'Jake is a distraction from the war and from loss, nothing more,' I said.

'That's what you think,' she said. 'But you'd be surprised how they find their way under your skin until you feel like you can't breathe when they are not near.'

I shook my head. 'There is no place in my life for love.'

'There is always a place for love.' She put her hand on my arm.

'No, because if there's love then I lose everything.' I swallowed a sob.

'You gain everything,' she said.

I turned away from her and watched Mo leave the water. He reached the box and lifted out the little mouse, stroking its head and soothing it. The boys rushed up to his side cajoling him, but he remained focused on the mouse. Jake stood thigh deep in the river with his chest gleaming in the sunlight.

'Jake is wonderful,' I said and I meant it. 'It's been fun, and it had reminded me that it's good to be alive. But we aren't meant for the long haul.'

'That's how you see it?' she asked.

I nodded.

'Have you told him this?' she asked.

I paused. 'I've tried.'

Mary looked out at him. 'He's unlike the others, you know.'

'How so?' I asked.

'He thinks and sees the world in a distinct manner. He reminds me of Gerry a bit but is different still. He's not as traditional.'

Jake walked out of the water and stood next to the boys and Mr Cohen. The mouse was now on Jake's wet hand. It sat peering at the other three. God knows what it thought. Mo looked up from the mouse and right to the spot where Mary and I were concealed. Our glances met and he smiled.

'We've been seen,' I said, accepting the change I'd felt in Jake was because he knew what I thought of him and what I had found.

'Goodness.' Mary leaned further back into the undergrowth.

'It's a bit late for that.' I came out from the shrubbery to walk down to the beach. I would have to do the same with Jake. Things were uncomfortable enough as it was and it was all my fault.

'Is the mouse going for a swim?' I asked.

'Mice can swim,' said John. 'He fell into the bathtub two days ago.'

'He didn't like it,' said Peter. 'He scratched me as he crawled up my arm.'

The mouse watched us all carefully. He looked calm but I should imagine he wasn't, with five people staring at him.

'How was the water?' I asked Mo.

'Cold,' said Mo. 'Very cold.' He smiled and began to walk from the beach.

'It's great once you're in,' said John.

'That's the problem,' said Mo, 'the getting in.'

I walked with him, and he said, 'It's a bit like you and love.'

'Not you as well.' I shook my head.

'Ah, the good Mrs Holdsworth.'

I nodded.

'Lieutenant Russell was not himself this morning.' Mo picked up his towel and glasses from the wall.

'Is that why you didn't swim?' I asked.

'No, I didn't swim because I was once thrown in a river and nearly drowned.' He cleaned his glasses and put them on.

'Why didn't you say?' I shuddered. We could have done things differently.

'Because you are all doing this because you care,' he said. 'Kindness is to be treasured.'

I couldn't argue with that. I looked over my shoulder at Jake playing in the water with the boys.

'Have you broken with Lieutenant Russell?' he asked.

I sighed. 'We weren't together.'

He raised an eyebrow. 'If you say so.'

'I do.' I bowed my head. 'If you'll excuse me, I have some maps to go through.'

'Indeed. Check the one of your heart,' he whispered.

I went into the dining room and shut the door like a petulant child. I could not be more cross with myself. I would find a moment to speak to Jake to end what should never have started.

34

10 September 1942

———————

On the moonless nights in August, Mo had not been ready, nor had the weather on the French coast been suitable for a drop. Now it was the tenth of September, and we were gathered on Bar Beach at almost midnight. The boys had been allowed to stay up to say goodbye. They were under the strict instructions that they were not to mention this to a soul. Peter held the box with the mouse out to Mo who stood with his suitcase and radio briefcase.

'Take him with you. He'll keep you company and help you to remember us,' said John.

I swallowed.

'He is your pet,' Mo said.

'He likes you more,' said Peter. 'And you can teach him more tricks and then bring him back to us when you return.'

I prepared myself for him to refuse.

'Thank you.' Mo's voice hitched as he spoke. 'Your heart's full gift is truly appreciated, and I will love him. Thank you.' He handed the suitcase to Jake and held the box as if it contained the most precious thing in the world.

The boys rushed back to their mother's side, and I stepped forward and put my hand on Mo's sleeve. He leaned forward and kissed my cheeks three times.

'Merry, thank you for all you have done for me. I will think of your Cornish hedges and all the promise you hold inside you.' He smiled and whispered, 'Love is worth the risk.'

'Stay safe,' I managed to say.

'Ah, that is not what I need to do. I need to be brave,' he said, then handed the mouse box to Jake and climbed into the dinghy. He didn't stumble and he didn't cling to the side of the boat as they set off. He looked back at me and waved. He was being brave, and I must do the same thing. When the team returned from the trip, I would find a moment alone with Jake. This team had no further need of me and nor did Jake as he had made clear by his distance. It was time to move on.

Mary stood beside me as we watched them board the MGB that had come down from Dartmouth. The engines growled deeply, and they motored out of the river at speed. Mary's face paled once they were out of sight. She had never been on an operation with them and yet I knew she had been on every single one in her heart and in her mind.

'Shall we have a whisky then try and find some sleep,' she said.

I nodded but I doubted either one of us would sleep tonight. This was their first operation since we lost young Jean. I knew very well what they faced although they were in a more reliable and faster boat this time. As we climbed the stairs to the house, my heart travelled across the channel and that was a very strange feeling. I already knew what it was like to love what death touched and I didn't want to experience more.

*

The boat was not back in the morning. No word had arrived. There was absolutely nothing that could be done. To distract Mary, we took the ferry to Helford then walked on to Kestle.

Matthew waved from the field. The hay had been cut at the start of the month and now they were harvesting swedes.

'What a different perspective from this side of the river,' Mary said as she kept twisting around to look in all directions.

'We are much more isolated here,' I said.

'I can see that,' she said. 'It's the ferry that makes the distance short.'

We followed the lane and on through the woods. Above us the first signs of autumn were beginning to appear and browned leaves of the sycamores crunched under our feet on our way to Kestle.

'What a perfectly charming farm.' Mary looked about the yard and then back to the house. 'I find old houses intriguing.'

I nodded and, as we entered the house, I found Mrs Nance.

'Oh, Miss Merry,' Mrs Nance said. 'I wasn't expecting you.'

'Mrs Nance, I'd like you to meet Mrs Mary Holdsworth. Her husband heads up the cartography unit.'

Mrs Nance smiled. 'There's been some post and one for your mother in a foreign hand,' she said, picking the letters off the table. 'Nothing is right. Your poor father gone, your mother . . . missing and now poor Master Oliver taken too soon.'

I took her hand in mine and she welled up. Shaking her head, she left and went into the garden.

'Oh dear,' said Mary, looking after her.

'She loved Oli like he was hers,' I said, as I studied the envelope with the foreign hand as Mrs Nance put it. It wasn't an overseas postmark but a London one. However, it had been posted months ago on the first of April. Where had it been? I turned it over in my hands.

'Shall I investigate the kitchen and make us a cup of tea while you decide whether to open the letter or not?' she asked.

'Yes, thank you.' I put that envelope down and looked at the others. Another was addressed to my mother and myself. It was from Oliver's squadron leader and the rest were bills that I would forward on to the solicitor. I didn't know where we stood with Oliver's death and my mother not being here. I might need to be made administrator of the farm. No matter what, the bills needed paying.

I walked into the kitchen with the post. Mary had made herself at home and tea was waiting for me.

'There's a letter here from Oliver's commanding officer,' I said, sinking into a chair. 'I don't know if I have the strength to read it.'

'Then put it aside for the moment.' She walked around to me and gave my shoulder a gentle squeeze. 'The time will come when you will be ready.'

'It seems strange to see both mine and my mother's name on the envelope,' I said.

'That's hard.' She placed a cup of tea in front of me. 'What about the other one?'

I shrugged. 'Don't know what to do?'

'If she were sitting here now, what would she say?' she asked. 'Was she protective of her privacy?'

I shook my head. 'No, very open, very un-English.'

'Well, there is your answer then,' Mary said.

I flipped it over in my hands, picked up a kitchen knife and opened it. A single folded sheet was contained in it.

It was in French. And the signature on the bottom shocked me.

'Well?' she asked.

'It's from de Gaulle,' I said. 'He thanks her for her help with the refugees, and his family looks forward to meeting with her in Plymouth.'

'He's an interesting man,' Mary said. 'His wife is charming.'

'You know them?'

'The team were involved in trying to get his family out of France,' she said. 'In the end, they made it onto a commercial ship at Brest and landed in Falmouth.' She put a cup and saucer in front of me. 'Does the letter say anything else?'

I slid it across the table to her. 'It's all very polite and truthfully it doesn't say a damn thing.'

Mary looked up from the page. 'Was your mother working for the Free French?'

'I think so.' This letter was the final piece of the puzzle.

'Ah, you have tea,' Mrs Nance said as she came through the kitchen door, fully composed again.

'Mrs Nance, did my mother make a trip in mid-April to Plymouth?'

She put her basket full of swedes down on the table. The fact we hadn't given Mr Cohen a pasty crossed my mind when I saw the potatoes and onions resting under the swedes.

'No,' she said. 'But she did go to London to see you.'

I was about to say she hadn't when I smiled. Maman had been making plans to head to France.

'I expect you've had so much on your mind with all the map drawing you've been doing that you forgot.'

'Yes, that's true.' I took a sip of my tea.

Mary shot me a look.

I stood and cleared our cups. 'We must be off if we want to be back across the river before evening.' I picked up the post.

'I'll keep looking after things here, don't worry,' Mrs Nance said. 'I know Matthew would like a word with you, but I suspect it can wait if you don't catch him on your way into Helford.'

'Thank you, Mrs Nance,' I said, leading Mary out into the garden. Once out of the farmyard, I looked for Matthew but didn't see him, only golden fields and lazy flies. It was warm until we reached the cover of the beech trees.

Mary's glance searched the river and bay once we'd reached the point. She was incredibly brave.

'This has happened before,' she said.

'How did you cope?' I asked.

'I don't,' she said, wiping her brow. 'But I suppose I do. I can do nothing but pray so I do a fair bit of it at times like now. I know they are fine; they must be fine. If something happens then I shall be lucky if I hear. I know this so instead I am hopeful, always hopeful.' She forced an over bright smile and continued, 'Usually, it's the weather has turned, or they have not been met, or as what happened when you were on board, the engine plays up.'

Putting the sign up for the ferry, I tried to pray but my mind jumped from God to my mother to Jake, to the whole team and especially to poor Mo having to brave his fear of the water and the unknown.

The sky was the faded blue of a late summer afternoon. The river was flat, and a few swallows darted above, feasting on the abundance of insects. It could not be more perfect except the team wasn't home.

Nora Reynolds, the manager of the Ferry Boat, rowed the ferry with John and Peter on board.

'Mum sent us to keep us out of the house,' John said.

'We were under her feet.' Peter grinned.

'I suppose you were.' Mary climbed in first and she sent me a look. The boys were filled with so much energy and left chaos in their wake, given half a chance.

'Have you caught any fish today?' I asked.

'No, just a toad.' Peter stuck his hand in his pocket.

'I don't need to see it.' Mary closed her eyes.

'Where's Jock?' I asked Nora.

'Off to the dentist,' she said.

John rubbed his jaw.

Every time I looked up, I caught Mary staring out to the bay, but there was not a boat to be seen. We landed on the beach and the cook was signalling for Nora. Her glance went to the two women stood on the Helford side, waiting.

'I'll take the boat and collect them for you,' I said.

'Thank you.' She dashed off and I took the oars.

'Can we come too?' Peter asked.

'Don't see why not,' I said. It would give Nellie a few more minutes of peace. She would be as worried as Mary.

'I'll see you back at the house.' Mary smiled.

'I won't be long,' I said as Mary pushed us out. I began to row while the boys chatted about getting a new mouse and I listened to their plans of training it as Mo had with the maze and the bread.

Suddenly the sound of a plane above broke through the boys' chatter. I didn't react until I realised the engine noise was not one I knew. A German plane swooped low over the river, and they had begun firing.

'Get down,' I shouted to the boys, recalling all too clearly what had happened to Jean Piron. We couldn't be their intended target and yet when they passed us, they fired on us and swooped around to do it again. I pulled harder on those oars than I ever had. I don't think I drew a breath until we reached the bank, and the woman pulled the boys out of the boat into the cover of the low trees. I scrambled behind them, trying not to think about the searing pain in my arm.

'Miss, you've been hit,' said John, staring.

Mrs Jenkins took her scarf off to staunch the wound with it while Mrs Hoskine was on the lookout and came running back. 'They've flown out over the bay. We best take her to Winfrey then go to the pub and call the doctor.'

'The boys?' I asked.

'Already securing the boat,' she said.

'I'm fine,' I said as Mrs Hoskine bustled me into the workshop and onto a bench.

'Good God,' said Richard Winfrey, who stopped to wash his hands. 'Go and get some boiled water and clean cloths.'

He took the scarf away and sucked in air. 'Looks worse than it is, I reckon. Lots of blood.'

I closed my eyes and leaned against the wall. Mrs Hoskine returned with a basin of water and a pile of clean rags. Winfrey began to clean the wound. I opened my eyes briefly to see the water in the basin glow red. Grinding my teeth, I tried to think of anything but my arm. My mother and Jake vied for attention. I heard Mo's softly spoken words: 'Be brave, not safe but brave.'

Mrs Jenkins and Dr Rickard arrived at the same time. He was in the village tending to poor Mrs Williams.

'Feel like you're back in the trenches, Winfrey?' Dr Rickard asked.

Winfrey nodded.

'Good job cleaning it,' Dr Rickard said, prodding my arm. I sank my teeth into my lip and looked the other way.

'It's clean and it went through, catching nothing vital, so you're lucky, Merry,' he said.

I nodded.

'I will make a few stitches and you must keep it clean above all else,' he said, smearing it with iodine.

Again, I nodded, for the ability to speak had drained out of me. In fact, all my bones seem to have melted and I was in danger of sliding off the bench. With my eyes closed I thought of blue skies and clear water and Jake swimming with me.

'I'll bring her to Ridifarne in my automobile,' Dr Rickard said. 'She's lost a fair bit of blood and will be very weak from it. The boys can come too.'

I opened my eyes briefly. My arm was bandaged, and Mrs Hoskine was stroking my brow.

'Up you get, Merry. You may feel a bit light headed.' He walked me along the path to his car. Both my arm and my head throbbed as he settled me on the back seat and the boys scrambled in beside.

'You'll need fluids and rest.'

'We'll take care of her,' John said.

'I'm sure you will,' the doctor said, smiling in the rear-view mirror at me, and I tried to do the same, but it didn't work. Keeping my eyes open was an effort beyond me and I must have slept as we wove through the lanes to Ridifarne.

The news had already reached Mary. She and Mrs Newton were standing like a welcoming committee when we pulled up to the front door.

'I leave her in your capable hands, Mrs Holdsworth,' he said. 'I'll call to check in a few days. If she begins to run a fever let me know.'

'I will,' Mary said and led me into the house and straight up to my room. 'Mrs Newton is bringing tea and I think maybe a brandy to help you sleep.'

I nodded, not wanting anything but sleep. My arm throbbed marginally more than my head. But I duly drank both the tea and the brandy and let Mary cut off my blouse and help me into my nightgown, which she altered by cutting the straps and tying them together.

'Rest,' she said as she closed the door.

I stared at the ceiling, willing my brain to shut down but instead it circled and circled, and nothing made sense.

35

18 September 1942

It was three days later that I was conscious of life again but a further five before I could stay awake for more than ten minutes at a time. The doctor had been and gone and finally the infection had diminished. Mary had told me the men were back, all safe, and they'd landed Mo with his radio, dry and intact. But the poor mouse had drowned when Mo, after safely getting from the MGB into the dinghy, had stood, turned and waved goodbye to those on the boat. He went overboard, nearly upending them all. Already the boys were working hard to find a new mouse to train and send to him.

A breeze touched with the smell of fallen leaves blew through the window. Oxford came to mind. Some days my life and work there seemed as distant as Mt Everest but, when I closed my eyes, all my plans for my future were right there. Life in the college and work in the department. Of course, nothing was certain. I needed to clear the decks for a return to London once I'd fully healed. Mo's determination to be brave had refocused me. I knew what was important. Winning the war and returning to academia. Maps would continue to be vital. And the map in my head showed me how far away Boston and Oxford were. There would be other women out there for Jake and one who could be a wife and mother. I wouldn't and couldn't deny him that.

There was a tap on the door. I pushed myself with my good arm to sitting before I said, 'Come in.' I knew it wasn't Mary or Mrs Newton because they would have entered after knocking. Jake stood there with a hand full of hydrangeas and a vase.

I raised an eyebrow and adjusted my nightgown. It was defensive and foolish since he had kissed every part of me.

'Hi,' he said, walking to the sink and filling the vase before arranging the flowers and placing them on my bedside table. The shortest stem was in the middle and the whole thing looked set to fall over.

'I don't think you'd make it as a florist,' I said.

'No? I thought they looked good.' He grinned and my stomach tightened. I worked to keep my focus.

'The flowers are beautiful and the colour stunning, but the arrangement needs work.' I laughed. 'But thank you.'

He frowned. 'That's gratitude for you.'

'They're beautiful.' I paused, looking at the intensified colours on the petals. Now was a time of change. That back-to-school feeling. I cleared my throat.

He sat on the bottom of the bed, making it feel very small.

'Why am I suddenly worried?' he asked, holding out my copy of *Gaudy Night*. 'I hope you don't mind but I borrowed this.'

I took my much read copy, not sure what to make of him reading it.

'You are quite like Vane in many ways.'

I bristled.

'And there's Wimsey,' he said.

I closed my eyes for a moment. I was not going to discuss Wimsey with him. Nor was I going to be side-tracked. I took a breath. 'We need to talk about us and ending it.'

'I knew you had a fever,' he said. 'But I didn't think you were hallucinating; well, not at least on my watch.'

'What, you were looking after me?' I opened my eyes wide in horror. God knows what I was like, what I said or if I drooled.

'To give Mary some rest,' he said.

'Oh, thank you.'

He smiled.

'But that doesn't mean we can continue this affair,' I said.

'I'm lost.' He held his hands out.

'Us,' I said. 'It isn't something that has a future and I think it needs to end.'

He scratched his head. 'Still lost.'

I shook my head and sighed. 'Do I need to draw you a map?'

'Maybe.' He leaned back.

'You belong in Boston,' I said. 'And I belong in Oxford.'

He tilted his head to the side. 'Eventually.'

'I like to be prepared and to know where I'm going,' I said, trying to sit more upright to feel more in control of this conversation.

'And I like to explore.' He ran a hand through his hair.

'That's as good a reason as any to walk away while we're still friends.'

'This is what your head is saying,' he said.

I sighed. 'Yes, it's best if we end our affair.'

'So you said.' His hand found my foot under the blanket and for the first time in a week I felt another part of my anatomy other than my aching arm.

I cleared my throat and refocused my thoughts as his hand reached my ankle. 'It is distracting us both from what we need to do.'

'And what is that?' His hand had reached my calf.

'Win the war,' I said slowly, and with great emphasis.

'Agreed and specifically how?' he asked.

It was hard to think with his hand circling my knee. 'Me to provide information about the landscape through maps and the sea through charts and you . . . '

'Yes, and me, the spy?' His hand slipped above my knee and his eyes danced.

I took a deep breath. 'Sorry about that.'

'Forgiven,' he said. 'Fair is fair. I thought you were and you thought I was.'

Even with his long reach he couldn't move his hand higher without shifting on the bed. Even so the light touch of his hand had me thinking of only one thing.

'And?' he asked with a wicked grin.

'You move people and things into France.' I swallowed.

'I do and I've even blown a few things up,' he said.

I frowned.

'You forgot my career as a pilot.'

'I had,' I said, knowing I'd forget my name if his hand continued higher. I pulled my legs to my chest, creating space between us. 'But we need to be realistic and end this now.'

'Why?' he asked. 'It makes no sense. You said this was for now and not to worry about the later. I'm happy with that. We have today. Carpe diem.'

I hated it when my own old argument was presented to me. I had to be strong.

'Thank you for the flowers, Lieutenant Russell,' I said, knowing if he stayed any longer, I might relent.

'Is that it?' he asked.

I nodded and continued to look at the wall, anything but him. After a moment, I heard him leave and then I closed my eyes. It was done and my insides were twisted. Although it was the right thing at this moment, part of me was broken.

I sat staring at the wall for ages. I had to do something. It was time to get dressed and to engage with the world again. I had lost a week. Today was the eighteenth of September, and I knew nothing. But I sensed an atmosphere change in the house.

There was only one way to discover what was happening and that was to leave this room. I stood with care and pulled out a blouse and a skirt. Dressing was trickier than I imagined, and Mary found me in the process of trying.

'Let me help,' she said, shutting the door behind her.

Once my bra was secured, she helped me slip the sleeve of my blouse over my injured arm and then over the other. As the bullet wound was above my elbow, bending it hurt and pulled on the stitches. The doctor would come tomorrow to see if they could be removed.

'Glad to see you want to get dressed but are you sure you are up to it?' she asked, doing my buttons up.

'I thought I was but it is so exhausting,' I said. 'But I feel it is time to leave my room.'

'I had hoped Jake would have lifted your spirits, but he came downstairs with a dark cloud above him and didn't speak on his way through to the garden. Last seen he was rowing down river.'

Lucky him to have that exercise for release, whereas I needed help getting dressed. Distraction was needed.

'How are the boys? Have they recovered from the experience?' I asked.

'Recovered, ha, they have lived on retelling your exciting exploits.' Mary helped me with my skirt button and stepped back to look. She picked up my hairbrush and smoothed out the tangles. My hair could use a good wash, but it would wait until after the doctor had been. As she pulled the brush through, I recalled my mother doing the same thing.

'There, that's better.' Mary secured my hair in a low ponytail. 'Ready to face the world or at least see the sunshine?'

'I'm as ready as I'll ever be,' I said.

'September so far has been the most beautiful of months, far lovelier than August.' She took my good arm and we walked slowly down the corridor to the stairs. At the bottom was Jake, damp from a swim after his row, by the looks of it. He waited for us to come down and smiled at Mary but looked down when he met my gaze. Mary led me straight through the sitting room and out onto the terrace. I blinked with the bright sunshine, but its warmth was good. Slowly my blood flowed to my extremities.

'I'll get us some tea and there was a package that arrived for you,' she said. 'From Commander Fleming.'

It was not like him to send presents, but I was intrigued.

Mary came back with the package and left again. I untied the string and pulled the paper away from the box. Inside there was a note, written in haste from the look of it.

Merry,
Met Oliver's girlfriend Caroline Moore at her request. She has been trying to reach you. His friends had given her his personal effects, knowing how he felt about her. She wasn't comfortable with this and wanted to speak with you. I explained your situation and we met. Charming girl.

The contents of this box were a compromise. I knew you would want her to have it all, but she wouldn't.

In haste,
Fleming

I dug in and pulled out Oliver's small camera. I remembered when he received it for his twenty-first birthday. Even at twenty-one he'd been annoying taking pictures of all of us for the week we were away. Now those pictures were all I had. Next in the box I found the sunglasses like the ones Jake wore. I slipped them on, and the green tint was soothing until Jake appeared carrying the tea tray. He placed it on the table.

'I like the glasses,' he said. 'They suit you.'

I made a face and took them off.

He poured a cup of tea and added a drop of milk. Handing it to me he said, 'Peace offering.'

I raised an eyebrow.

'Too soon for a truce?' He sat beside me.

'A man who lives in Boston is asking for a truce over tea?'

'Fair point.' He lifted a side plate with a piece of cake. 'Is this better?'

'Somewhat,' I said.

'A romantic dinner for two?' He put his hand beside mine on the table so that our little fingers were side by side.

'Thought we agreed,' I said and looked around to make sure we were alone even though it was clear everyone knew. 'The affair is over.'

'Had we agreed?' He picked up his tea and stood. 'Or had you decided?'

I nodded as my mouth was full of cake. The first of the garden's apples sweetened it.

'I'm not so sure.' He smiled.

'Did you become undecided on your journey on the river?' I glanced behind me. It would be a while before I'd be pulling an oar.

'Rowing always helps to put things into perspective for me,' he said.

Mary came out.

'Isn't that cake divine?' she said. 'It tastes of autumn and all the good things.' She poured herself a cup of tea and sat beside me. 'I've heard from Gerry. He'll be in London for another few days.'

'When did he go?' I asked. His absence explained the difference in atmosphere in the house.

'Three days ago,' she said.

Mary and Jake shared a look and a twinge of guilt turned my stomach. Of course, I hadn't been honest on my full reasons for being here, which Jake knew. Change was in the air.

'Was it a lovely present?' Mary asked.

I looked at the box. I'd rather have my brother, but I couldn't say that.

John and Peter wandered onto the terrace. 'Oh, are you finished with that box?' John asked.

Their mother was hot on their tails. 'Where are your manners, boys? You haven't said hello to Dr Tremayne nor asked how she was feeling.' She gently tapped both boys on their shoulders.

'Sorry, miss,' they said in unison.

'You look good,' John added.

I laughed and handed them the box.

'Thank you, miss. It's for the new mouse for Mr Cohen.' They raced off, clutching the box with their mother following behind.

'It's good to see you smile.' Mary rose to her feet. 'Being in the sunshine has done you the world of good, but don't try and go anywhere without someone with you.' She smiled at Jake and walked back into the house.

Peter came dashing back. 'This was in the bottom of the box, miss.' He handed me a letter.

I turned it over and stilled when I saw the writing. Oli's writing was unmistakable.

'Shall I leave you alone with this?' Jake asked, topping up my teacup.

'I don't know,' I said.

He studied me.

'This is from my brother and these things have taken a very indirect route to me via his girlfriend and Commander Fleming.'

Jake stood and placed a hand on my shoulder, giving it a squeeze before he walked to the far side of the terrace.

I opened the envelope. There were two sheets of paper.

15 May 1942

Dearest Merry,

I'm jealous that you're in Cornwall and wish I could be with you. I hope to have some leave and come down. I feel it's wrong that you've had to deal with Maman's disappearance, but I know you will have done everything that can be done.

We lost Freddie Simpson yesterday. This one really rocked me. Don't know why him over the others but it did. He was a great chap.

But enough of that. I enclose a picture of me with some of the Yanks who were passing through. It's great to have them on side. Can't tell you how much it has lifted us here. They are a bit loud and maybe a bit brash, but I'm pleased to have them with us. Not that I hadn't met a few in the Eagle Squadrons but suddenly the Yanks are everywhere.

When you're back in London let me know. I'm longing to see you again and of course I need you to meet Caroline. She is my world. I can't tell you how different I feel about everything, absolutely everything.

I won't finish this letter tonight but will finish it in a few days when I have a few more things to add.

I looked up. Jake was by my side in seconds.

'He wrote this the night before he died.' My hand shook as I looked at the second sheet.

Dear Merry,

It wasn't right that Oliver's friends brought me his possessions. They should have been sent to you. Commander Fleming has convinced me that I should keep most of them. I still don't feel I should. He was mine for such a short time and looking back I thought we had grabbed every moment, but we hadn't. We missed times when we could have been more . . . done more, held more. I can't turn back the clock to gain those missed moments again. God, how I wish I could.

In selecting what to send you I have chosen his camera for how he saw the world. It was unique and positive and him. He spoke often of your mother teaching him the technicalities of composition and his own careless attitude to that. He wanted people in his photos, not pretty scenery.

I have also chosen his sunglasses. Oliver said he saw the world more clearly with them. He called them his lucky glasses and they must have been because he didn't have them with him. I hope they will help you to see your future. I keep thinking how difficult this must be for you.

I look forward to meeting you in person soon.

With fondest wishes,
Caroline

I slipped the sunglasses back on and squinted into the distance. Caroline and Oliver had missed moments, but they had had them too.

'Are you OK?' Jake asked.

I nodded and took the glasses off and looked at him. Moments. 'Jake?'

'Why am I worried?' He sent me a sideways glance.

'What do you want to do with this affair of ours?' I asked.

His eyes opened wide. 'Exactly what are you asking me?'

'Well, both of us know that it isn't a permanent thing. Someday you will return to Boston and I to Oxford. Is it still worth having?' I held my breath, waiting for his answer.

'Live in the moment,' he said, and he stepped closer.

'You have echoed the words of Caroline,' I said. 'She wrote of missed moments.'

'I know one thing. I don't want to miss a moment with you.' He picked up my hand. 'Shall we grab the ones we are given?'

'Yes. They may be few but . . . ' I thought of Oliver and Caroline. They had some and they were worth having.

'They will be ours.' He leaned over and kissed me.

'About time,' Brooks Richards said as he walked up to us. He clapped slowly. 'We've been running a bet on when, not if, but when you two would come together.'

I stood, not sure how I felt about our affair being public knowledge but there was little I could do about it now.

36

25 September 1942

On this late September day it was warm and I perched in my canoe. Behind me, Jake paddled in a leisurely fashion towards Frenchman's. I longed to join in and move us along faster because I needed to see how things were at the farm. I'd tried ringing several times but never managed to catch either Matthew Skewes or Mrs Nance and now my concern was growing.

We were a few days past the autumnal equinox and the trees were turning. The white feathers of a herring gull on an overhanging branch dipping into the creek contrasted sharply with the greens and browns on the foliage behind it. I let my good arm trail in the water. Lazy bugs flew low over the surface. They were lethargic and I was not. Each day I was stronger and itching to do something, but Mary was a stern nurse and even Fleming wouldn't hear of me coming to London. I was trapped by kindness.

We reached the quay and I jumped out, not waiting for Jake. I was halfway to the house when he caught up with me. He didn't speak but fell into step beside me.

The farmyard was deserted, not even the chickens were about. Had something happened? I raced to the house. The door was locked and it never was. I dashed around to the kitchen door.

That too was locked. I went to the glass house, unearthed the spare key, and let us into the kitchen.

There were signs of life. My shoulders relaxed a bit and I rubbed my arm, trying to figure out what was wrong. I left the kitchen and headed to the study where I found more post was piled up. Why hadn't Mrs Nance sent it over? Something wasn't right. A quick flick through revealed no further correspondence from de Gaulle but more bills.

'Hello?' Matthew's voice echoed in the hall.

I walked out to see him with a shotgun in his hand.

'What on earth?' I asked.

'Ah, Miss Merry. It's you.' He lowered the gun.

'Yes, what's going on?' I asked.

'Didn't Mrs Nance telephone?' He shuffled from one foot to the other.

I shook my head.

'Well, she went to the cottage and found people there.' He looked at Jake. 'She was all upset but I couldn't say anything . . . like you know, loose lips and . . . '

'Where is she?' I asked.

'She's spooked. She stopped coming, and the girls have been looking after the place. Mrs Nance doesn't feel safe. These people were . . . foreign.' His glance kept straying to Jake. 'But I thought Mrs Nance had called you.'

I shook my head. 'She hasn't.'

'She's gone to her sister in St Agnes,' he said.

'Are the girls managing?' I asked.

'Yes, they're a good lot,' he said. 'What are you going to do?'

I took a deep breath. 'As long as you are coping on the farm and the girls are helping then nothing will change.'

'Thank you,' he said, the colour returning to his face. 'I'll send the girls to you, shall I?'

'Yes, please.' There was much to do. Jake followed Matthew through the kitchen, and I went back to the study. It would make sense to move the girls into the house if they didn't mind. I would feel better with it being used.

The sound of Jake's voice chatting to the land girls drifted into the study. A small part of me was jealous but how could I be when I wasn't offering him all of me. The more time we spent together the more I realised that I longed for the one thing I couldn't have. Out of the window the fields were yellowed and that sense of time slipping away filled me. Closing the study door, I went and joined them in the kitchen. It was time to sort out the farm. I didn't know how much longer I would be so close to look after things.

*

The light was golden as it slanted across the fields. We had missed the tide but, after a quick chat with the solicitor, I had things for the farm in hand. For the time being the girls would look after the house for me and I was grateful. They would move in over the weekend. Now Jake and I were on our way to the cottage.

The afternoon light didn't filter too far down through the trees as we walked to the creek, but it was hitting the cottage when we arrived. Even if I hadn't had evidence from Mrs Nance's actions, it was clear the cottage had been used again. My map and my mother's paper had been moved and the fireplace had been swept clean of all ash, yet a light musty scent lingered. I opened a window. What was going to happen to the farm? None of it fit with my life as an academic.

'Penny for them?' Jake asked.

I shook my head. 'Nothing.'

'You're not a good liar.'

I sighed and he stepped closer, wrapping me in his arms. I rested my head against his chest, and I listened to his heartbeat. It was a good heart.

'Is there anything aside from collecting the painting you need to do here?' he asked.

I kissed him. We hadn't had any time alone in a while.

'That's better,' he whispered.

'It is.' I pulled away and walked up the stairs with Jake close behind.

'Let me get that for you.' He took the painting off the wall. 'Ready?'

I nodded, and, with a lump in my throat, I followed Jake downstairs.

'Shall we see what we can make for dinner?' He held the painting and a can of SPAM.

'A good plan.' Taking my hand, he led me out of the cottage. I took a deep breath. The smell of decaying leaves was sweet on the air. I recalled past times collecting damsons towards the mouth of the creek. They would be ripe. I picked up the old bucket by the door and we walked along the creek. It was such a different place when the smallest trickle of water meandered its length. Rooks shouted at our presence in their domain and across the creek I saw my canoe resting on the mud. There wouldn't be enough water until well after midnight. We would spend the night at Kestle. Different this time from the first. We weren't lovers then and that time was so full of sadness. My heart ached for Oli especially here where we had spent so much time. But as we collected the fruit, I knew moments of happiness too. Those were the ones to hold tight to and to make them last.

Jake took over in the kitchen again, stewing the damsons for pudding and creating another omelette-type creation from borrowed eggs and the SPAM. I raided the wine cellar and found another good claret.

With curtains drawn, I lit the chandelier and we ate in the dining room at one end of the table. The memories of happy meals wrapped themselves around me or maybe that was the wine.

After dinner, Jake selected some music to play on the gramophone and we danced until my arm had had enough. Taking a candle, I led him upstairs to my room. I hadn't had the pleasure of him in a while.

'Are you sure?' he asked as I unbuttoned his shirt.

'Yes, I am collecting moments,' I said.

'Collecting moments . . . that sounds like a head thing rather than a heart.'

I paused. 'Actually, it's a bit of both.'

'I'll take that as an improvement.'

I kissed his chest and murmured, 'You would.' Then I undid his belt and a low groan escaped from somewhere deep inside him. We fell onto the bed and I lost myself in the moment. Something told me there were few of these left.

*

The sun streamed in where the blackout covering had slipped. I could see the sky, blue and cloudless. The air was sharp and cool. Jake was asleep beside me. I could still taste him, and my body still felt heavy from the passion we had shared. Watching the rise and fall of his chest, I tried to imprint the memory of his touch, the feel of his strength, the weight of his body in my mind. I wanted to map the geography of him and us and this moment. It couldn't and wouldn't last. That was the way of things. There was no future for us, so it was now. Everything was now. I had never been so complete as I'd been with Jake.

From the conversations I'd caught snippets of over the past few days, I knew things were about to change. Like the swallows preparing to leave the river the team was too. Nothing had been said, but it was all in the action. They had made three trips to Brittany and few more were planned for when some new men arrived. But things were different. Operations were directed out of Dartmouth and the crews were collected at the mouth of the river.

'What are you looking at?' he asked, with a slow smile spreading across his mouth.

'You.' I ran a finger down his chest.

'Why?' he asked.

'I'm mapping you.' I traced my finger along his collar bone and up to his chin.

'Are you trying to find something in particular?' he asked.

'Your heart,' I said.

'You have that already,' he said. 'Do you remember when I saved the last dance for you?'

I nodded, recalling my frustration that that had been the sole dance that evening.

'The song was "Be Careful, It's My Heart".' He took my hand and brought it down to his chest. 'It's yours and it beats for you.'

I leaned forward and kissed where my hand had been. Then I rested my ear there and heard the steady drub. My hand, palm down, felt the contours of his torso until I came to his hips. He gasped as my fingers found his arousal and I traced that as well before I climbed on top and pleasured myself against him.

'I can't take much more.' He reached for a johnny when I rolled off him, and soon he was inside me. I came first and he followed. We didn't say a thing until the sounds of the rooster crowing broke the silence.

PART FIVE

Springtime

Springtime in England stops my heart with its beauty. After the endless rains of winter, spring arrives with clear skies, bright greens and flowers so vividly coloured that they almost blind me. It's the merry month of May and everything is bursting to life despite the war. April rains have brought May flowers and they bloom in the hedges along the roads. Woodland floors are carpeted with bluebells as far as the eye can see. It's those moments of being in nature that restore the soul.

When the sun shines, the waters of the South-west of England look more like the Riviera and I will confess to losing a bit of my heart to Cornwall. Unlike the flat tracts of land while I was flying, I find myself surrounded by valleys, rivers and a rocky coastline reminiscent of parts of Maine. That must be why it pulls on my emotions so much. Having spoken to others finding themselves here, I've discovered we each cling to the things that remind us of home and what we are fighting for. The pilot from Newfoundland finds himself drawn to England's coastline and filling his lungs with the tang of sea air. The twenty-year-old from Florida finds he is attracted to the palm trees he's seen in the south-west.

What these glimpses of home

in a foreign land do is to firm our resolve as each day away becomes another. And what of the poor people here who are putting up with this influx of Americans, all bright-eyed and bumbling through their landscape, driving on the wrong side of the road? Thus far they have been welcoming to these strangers. Dances have been held in village halls and in the pubs they tolerate our loud disapproval of the beer. What unites us all is the desire to defeat the enemy. So the earnest and eager new faces of the US service men are taken at face value. Meanwhile the young men, many of whom have never left home, are seeing how big the world is and how small at the same time. The farmer still tills the land, the butcher sells the meat, the chemist dispenses the drugs, the nurses tend the sick. These things are universal and we are united in ordinariness of life and our desire to end evil.

Jake Russell
England

37

The journey north to Dartmouth in *Mutin* was a gift on the bright November day. The wind had made it a quick journey. No one spoke of the changes ahead and I could almost pretend that nothing had altered and we were just out training. But the atmosphere here on the boat and back in Helford was livelier and excitement bubbled in everyone except Mary, Nellie Newton and me. Mary carried the news that her husband was off to another front with great dignity. I didn't know what to feel.

Despite understanding that this was all for the best and that they would be more useful doing what they had been trained to do, I hated seeing the team divided. Over half the men would go with the commander to the Mediterranean and the rest would remain on the Helford, continuing the operations and the training. What I didn't know was who was going where, and therein lay my concerns. Tonight's dinner with the SIS team might provide that information but it might not. I had no idea what to expect of this evening or why I had been included.

After a tepid bath in the hotel, I was dressed and waiting in the lobby for Jake to collect me. I'd been with this operational unit for six months, learning something new every day. Their rhythms and routines were second nature to me now. Each man no longer had just a name but they were friends. I knew of their girlfriends, their families and, for some, their hopes and dreams. Men in the services were used to this bonding but it was new to me.

And then there was Jake. He figured so largely in my days and in my nights when we could. Aside from George, I had never allowed a man to fill my life in such a way. Unlike my relationship with George – which had assumed a normal course, thinking that it would go on for a lifetime – this relationship had an end date. I simply didn't know what that date was. Once it occurred, I would retreat into the world of books again and let Lord Peter Wimsey be the only love in my life. I laughed. Wimsey and Jake could not be more different but there was something of Wimsey in my American. I couldn't put my finger on it though. Maybe it was the womanising. Even his dispatches referenced it. But it could be simply the excuse to cover his disappearances, or was that wishful thinking on my part?

I looked up to find Jake walking into the hotel. It was odd to see him in naval uniform as I had that first time.

He grinned when he saw me. I looked him up and down. 'The uniform suits you.'

'Do I look English?' he asked, as he brushed down the front of the jacket.

I laughed. 'Not possible.'

'Why not?' He peered over my head into the mirror.

'It's hard to put into words but you simply don't,' I said.

He shrugged and helped me with my coat. I added a scarf to cover my hair. Although it wasn't raining the air was heavy with moisture.

Outside I slid my arm through his, and we walked through the mist. It took a few minutes for my eyes to adjust to the darkness. Commander Holdsworth and Brooks Richards met us en route to the home of Commander and Mrs Davis where we were due for dinner.

'Merry, I think you can help the men remaining make the transition more easily,' the commander said, as we walked along together.

'Really?' I asked, turning to him. His features were lost in the fog and darkness.

'Yes, I've had a promise from Fleming that you'll be here until the new year before he steals you away.' He paused and dropped his voice. 'He also mentioned that you were instrumental in this reorganisation.'

'Oh,' I said, glad that my expression wasn't visible in the darkness.

'Don't sound so worried. I believe it's the right thing and so do the men.'

'They know of my involvement?' I couldn't keep the surprise from my voice.

'No, they don't, only myself, and Mary, of course.'

My shoulders dropped. She must hate me. How long had she known? Ahead of the commander and me, Brooks Richards and Jake were in deep conversation. I quickened my pace to join them because I didn't want to think about what Mary must be going through with the commander heading away from her.

'Warington Smyth is a good lot,' added Brooks Richards.

'His father, Herbert, lives at Calamansack,' I added, thinking of the retired naval officer and the property on the north shore of the Helford opposite our farm.

'That's right. His brother, Bevil, has been working for the SOE in Falmouth and he's been with the SIS based here in Dartmouth. He'll be in attendance this evening.'

'Here we are,' Brooks Richards said as he stopped in front of a house with a blacked-out Georgian fan light over the door.

I wiped the accumulated mist off my nose. Such a quick change in weather from the glorious day earlier.

The door opened and we quickly slipped inside, wary of the light coming from the hallway.

A woman smiled, saying, 'Foul night.'

'Yes, very,' I said, pulling the scarf off my hair and handing her my coat.

'Follow me.' She opened the door to a large room dominated by a blazing fire, above which was a huge mirror reflecting all the men in the room. It appeared that Mrs Davis and I would be the only women.

'A dry sherry?' she asked.

'Yes, thank you,' I replied.

The commander introduced me to Lieutenant Commander Steven Mackenzie.

'I've heard a great many things about you, Dr Tremayne, from Commander Fleming,' said Mackenzie.

I cleared my throat. 'All of it good, I hope.'

'That you are fierce, no one reads a chart better and that you have scared most of the men you have trained,' he said.

'Definitely good,' I said with a smile.

'Have you met Commander Davis?' He pulled the gentleman in question over to us.

'Miss Tremayne,' Commander Davis said and studied me intently.

Jake appeared.

'It's Dr Tremayne,' he said, meeting Davis's glance. Jake's hand grazed mine.

'Commander.' I held out my other hand.

He took it, saying, 'Dr Tremayne, I hear you will be staying on at Ridifarne to steady the ship.'

'I doubt that will be required. I believe several of the men are remaining. Pierre is the key,' I said, watching him closely, remembering Jake's comments. Jake was pulled into a conversation with Commander Holdsworth, leaving me alone with Davis.

He nodded. 'He is a bit scruffy.'

'It belies the skill he holds,' I said.

He met my glance, and I didn't flinch.

'Believe me, commander, when you are sailing to the Breton coast in the dark, and in bad weather, the one thing you require is Pierre.'

As I had reported to Fleming, these teams needed to remember we were all fighting Hitler and not each other. No doubt Mackenzie had fed information to Fleming about displeasure from the SIS side. Both had valid points. Now I also worried for the men staying behind. But Warington Smyth would run the operation on the Helford well.

Mrs Davis arrived, took her husband's arm, and announced that dinner was on the table.

I looked across the room. Jake hadn't told me if he was staying or going to the Mediterranean. It would be easy to say that it didn't matter. I told myself this repeatedly, but as I looked across the room at him, I knew I was lying.

*

The fog was so thick we practically felt our way back to the hotel. The wine hadn't helped with clarity, but the evening had calmed my few worries regarding Lieutenant Commander Warington Smyth. He knew the Helford, the conditions they would be working in and the boats. I thought the men would work well with him. He was not a larger-than-life Commander Holdsworth, but his serious personality would get the job done.

'You're very quiet,' Jake said as we reached the hotel.

'Thoughtful,' I replied.

'Should I be worried?' he asked.

I shook my head and tiptoed to kiss him. I wanted to take him by the hand and lead him up to my room, but that wouldn't and couldn't happen. It had to be a chaste kiss on the doorstep.

'God, this is worse than I thought,' he said, pulling me close.

'What is?' I placed my hands on the warmth of his chest.

'Leaving you.' He kissed my hair.

It was clear what he meant but now wasn't the time to address this. He was definitely going with Commander Holdsworth from the snippets of conversation I'd heard from his end of the table.

'I'll see you in the morning.' I stepped away from him.

'That's not . . . '

I put a finger over his mouth. 'I know.'

He kissed my finger and brought my hand to his heart.

'Promise me you won't go on any missions after we've gone.'

Of all the things I expected him to say, this was not it. 'Why?'

'Just promise me.' He brought me close again and kissed my temple.

'Why?' I pushed, knowing what I wanted to hear and yet I couldn't and wouldn't say the words myself. If they were said aloud then it would be harder to walk away and forget.

'Promise me.' He held me closer still.

'I can't.' I placed my palm over his heart, the one he had given me.

'You can,' he said. 'You're not officially part of the team.'

I pulled back, wanting to see his face but in the dark and the fog it was impossible.

'We have treated you as part of us and you are equal to us,' he said. 'But, for me, please do not go on another mission.'

I closed my eyes for a moment, thinking of Jean Piron dying in my arms and of my mother somewhere in France. 'I can't promise that.'

'You can,' he said.

I shook my head. 'What reason? Why?' Under my fingers his heart raced.

He pressed his lips to my temple. 'Just promise,' he whispered.

He wasn't going to say why he asked this no matter how much I pushed. 'I can't, and you know that.'

He kissed me. 'Then stay safe.'

As I breathed in his scent of woodsmoke, wine and chocolate, I heard Mo's words . . . be brave.

The door to the hotel opened and I raced in, not feeling brave at all. For if I was, I would tell him how I felt.

38

10 November 1942

London was bleak. November was never its best month. The fog was thick and cold. No light fell from windows to warm my way this late afternoon. My thoughts lay back in the south-west. I'd left Dartmouth early this morning. Already last night was a lifetime ago when Jake had held me close. He wasn't there this morning when I left. He'd been in meetings. The commander had walked me to the station and had said he would see me on my return. Their days on the Helford were numbered as were mine.

Although it was four o'clock, I couldn't tell from the sky. The Admiralty appeared in the gloom once I was nearly upon it. Fleming was waiting for me inside the entrance. Instead of heading to Room 39, he took my arm and we walked through the fog together.

'Where on earth are we going?' I asked.

'A little tea shop,' he said.

I stopped and stared. 'Tea shops are not your usual haunt. White's, the Savoy or the Ritz or Claridge's.'

'Very true,' he said. 'But sometimes a change in routine is good.'

He led me down an alley, through a side street and to an unimpressive door. Once inside it was warm, bright and filled with a fug of steam. We went to a table at the back of the room by an unlit fireplace.

My head swivelled. 'This is most unexpected.'

'Good,' Fleming said, and he pulled out his cigarette case and he lit one for me. 'I would hate to be predictable.'

I laughed. 'Surely never that.'

He smiled then ordered tea for two.

'I thought you'd be parched after a crowded train journey,' he said. 'How was last night?'

My thoughts returned to Jake but that was not what he was referring to.

'Interesting,' I said. It had been cordial but with an almost tangible undercurrent of mistrust. It wasn't unexpected but I had hoped it would have been otherwise.

'How so?' he asked then lit his own cigarette.

'Where do I start?' I inhaled deeply. 'Your friend, Mackenzie.'

'What about him?'

'Charming but why haven't I met him before?' I asked.

A smile spread across Fleming's face. 'You would have broken his heart.'

I pursed my mouth. 'He's clever, good-looking, but I wouldn't have given him the time of day.'

'Therein is the reason,' he said. 'And he's now madly in love with Slocum's secretary. They are engaged, I believe.'

I shook my head. 'You are . . . ' I couldn't pinpoint the right word.

'What am I?' he asked.

'Incorrigible, for a start; meddling, to continue,' I said, warming to the topic.

'Add brilliant and I'm content,' he said.

The tea arrived and I poured, noting the tired but determinedly cheerful people around us. What did we have to look forward to with no end in sight for this war and more lives lost every minute. The future, whatever it was to be, felt very far away.

'Now, back to last night and the important things,' he said.

I paused with my teacup midway to my mouth.

'Such a change between the commanders,' I said, 'but I think that is best.'

'Good,' he said.

I shook my head. 'Don't tell me you had a hand in this.'

'I shan't then.' He pushed the plate in my direction. 'I don't think you would have eaten since Dartmouth this morning.'

I bit into a meat spread sandwich. It wasn't good but it would ease the emptiness in my stomach that had less to do with the lack of food and more to do with the realisation that my time with Jake was coming to its natural conclusion.

'Have you heard anything about my mother?' I looked up from the plate.

He waved his hand, and his signet ring caught the light. 'She was alive a month ago.'

'Thank you.' I played with half a sandwich of uncertain filling and glanced across the room. There was a rather appalling oil painting of a half-naked woman that I think was meant to be like the *Toilette of Venus* by François Boucher. Maman's voice was loud and clear in my head. 'A man painting a woman—' she'd raised her hands and rolled them from the wrist as we'd looked at the Michelangelo '—he does not understand the heft of the breast or its reaction to a cool draught, nor the softness of the stomach, or the curve of the thigh and the body's power and strength.' She shook her head. 'No, ma petite, his other brain takes control, his desire takes control even as in this case he prefers men.'

'I've lost you,' Fleming said.

'Sorry.' I smiled at him.

'I have said to them,' he said, 'that they can keep you until mid-January and then you are needed back here.'

'But you've replaced me with Margaret Priestly,' I said.

'I have indeed, and she is a wonder,' he said. 'But you recall that meeting you came to?'

I nodded.

'Well, they want you,' he said. 'And I am involved in other things.'

I remained silent.

'I've agreed that you will join them when you have completed this project,' he said.

'What project have you told them this was?' I asked.

'Ah—' he paused and sent me a wicked grin '—that was Project Merry, making a tougher, smarter, more whole woman.'

I opened my mouth but couldn't find the words to express my outrage. How could he even think that? Such blatant arrogance astounded me.

'How is your arm, by the way?' he asked, changing the subject.

'Fine,' I said. 'But forget that. What do you mean a more whole woman?'

'I shall not answer that and will let you resolve it yourself,' he said. 'And I'd have thought Brooks Richard's more your type or no one at all.'

I sent him a look that would have cowed most men, but he laughed, the pompous bastard.

'Now I'd like you to come into the office the rest of this week to go through some new intelligence,' he said, lighting another cigarette. 'Then you are free to head back to Cornwall to say farewell to your American.'

Clasping my hands together on the table, I wanted to say he was wrong, but he wasn't. Jake was my American and of course Fleming knew about him. It was not only his job but part of his nature. This was why he was good at what he did, even if that varied from day to day.

In the silence between us, I finished the last sandwich as it was clear he wasn't going to have any and I couldn't let it go to waste.

'Your colour has come back,' he said as he paid the bill. 'You do look tired. Don't rush in tomorrow. I have meetings until noon so come in then.'

Weaving through the tables, I was still stunned by his Project Merry, and I shouldn't be. He searched for a taxi in the fog.

'Either get some rest or go dancing,' he said. 'Both would do you the world of good.'

I couldn't respond to that or anything else at present. We walked along in silence until we found a taxi.

'Merry, it's not all bad you know, this falling-in-love business,' he said. 'I've avoided it thus far but, like you, I may well trip up.'

I was about to tell him I wasn't in love with Jake, but he opened the door of the taxi and told the driver the address.

Leaning forward, I said, 'I'm not in love.' He closed the door, and I couldn't see his response but heard his chuckle.

*

Constance wasn't home but there was a hastily scratched note on the kitchen table.

Sorry to miss you, Merry, but am off to Bristol to see Hester. Benedict is away so you'll be in the house alone for a few days. I had so longed to see you but this chance to see Hester was too good to miss.

You had a phone call as I was leaving. Didn't get his name but he said to dress in your finest and meet him at the Savoy in the American Bar for 6. Sounds dishy.

Constance x

It was five now. I hoped there was hot water and that I had something appropriate to wear to go and meet this mystery man. It was probably one of my old colleagues who was in London for a night or two. I sighed, not sure I had the energy, especially as there was no hot water. So a brisk wash with a flannel and cold water had to suffice. My array of evening wear was scant. It was either an ivory satin or a pale-green gown. The ivory called to me, so I swept up my hair then slipped the gown on. The rubies in my mother's cross contrasted beautifully with the soft colour of the gown and the paleness of my skin. But, as I checked myself in the mirror, if felt very odd to be dressing for a meeting with a mystery companion. Whoever it was had charmed Constance, so I wasn't too concerned, and I was curious.

At half past five I'd found my evening wrap and gloves and set out into the gloom. By the time I'd reached Eaton Square it was becoming quite damp, and a taxi pulled up. The door opened and Commander Fleming said, 'Decided on the dancing rather than rest, I see. Where can I drop you?'

'The Savoy please,' I said.

'On my way.' He smiled. 'You look rather beautiful, Merry.'

'Thank you.' I sent him a fierce look.

'Who is the lucky man this evening?' he asked.

'I wish I knew,' I said. 'Constance left a message for me, but she hadn't caught his name.'

'How very intriguing,' he said.

The taxi drove to the entrance on the Strand.

'Have a wonderful evening and don't do anything I wouldn't do,' he said, holding my hand for a moment.

'That leaves many possibilities,' I replied.

'Precisely.' He grinned and closed the door.

I walked into the lobby with a funny feeling in my stomach. This wasn't a good idea. It would be fine if I simply turned around and went back to Constance's. It wouldn't be a problem. People were always missing trains or were delayed. This was madness. I made up my mind, I was leaving.

I felt a hand on my elbow and turned.

'The American Bar is this way,' Jake said.

'What are you doing here?' I asked.

'Meeting you?' He raised an eyebrow. 'Who did you think you were joining?'

'Constance didn't catch your name but liked the sound of you.' I looked up at him, both relieved and excited.

'Did she?' He grinned, leading me up the stairs into the bar. He towered over the maître d' who led us to a table.

'Pink gin?' Jake asked, and I nodded, suddenly feeling homesick for Ridifarne. He gave the order to the waiter then turned to me.

'What are you doing in London?' I put my hands on my lap to keep them from reaching out to him.

'Some leave and a plan to see an old colleague tomorrow,' he said. 'And I'm acting as a messenger as well. I caught the train after you left.'

He looked so handsome and then I noticed a difference. 'You've been promoted, Lieutenant Commander Russell.'

'You don't miss much, Dr Tremayne,' he said.

'I try not to.' I smiled.

The waiter brought our drinks.

'Here's to—'

'You,' I said, interrupting him, suddenly afraid of this evening and anything he might say.

'And you,' he said.

Our glasses touched and our eyes met. His look was so intense that confusion filled me.

Sipping my drink, I was not sure what to say to fill the silence.

Everything that came to mind was either dull or controversial and not what was truly sitting unsaid in the space between us.

He looked across at me then took my hand. I didn't pull it back. My protective instincts were kicking in and that wasn't fair. I must live in the now and experience every moment. *Be brave*, I told myself.

*

Sandwiched on the dance floor in Jake's arms this evening didn't feel real. It was the two of us doing normal things that couples did. Drinks, dinner, dancing. It was one night. One night to make memories, to hold hands, to laugh, to kiss, to be in love. I couldn't believe I'd even thought those words but as I looked up into his eyes it was all I felt, and this was dangerous. Everything about me was in jeopardy while somewhere in the fug of smoke and chatter a band played and a woman sang of love.

Maybe that's all it was: a spell created by the drink, the dancing and the atmosphere. It was designed to make you feel different. But right now, in Jake's arms, slowly moving to the music, I was different. I wasn't Meredith Tremayne, BA (Hons), MA, DPhil (Oxon) but Merry, a woman hungering for the man holding her and longing to keep this moment forever.

The band stopped and Jake whispered, 'Shall we go?'

Taking his hand, we collected my wrap and bag and headed out into the night's thick fog. It held us and kept us from the world. We couldn't locate a taxi and we were lucky to find our way, but we arrived at Constance's, and I let myself in, bringing Jake with me.

Once the door was closed, I found the light switch and shed my wrap.

'Would you like a drink?' I asked, feeling unsure.

'No, I've had enough tonight,' he said.

'Me too,' I said, as we stood looking at each other poised for escape.

'Where is everyone?' he asked.

'Away,' I said.

His smile was slow and meaningful as I took him by the hand and led him up to my room. There he carefully helped me out of my gown and placed it over a chair. I unbuttoned his uniform jacket without the haste I was feeling inside. That joined my gown and soon his shirt and trousers were there. Then he turned his attention to my stockings, which he rolled down each leg so slowly I was mad with desire by the end.

Together on the bed we explored each other as if it was our first time. Every touch of his hand or lips raised the desire in me to a level that was unbearable. The feel of his skin under my fingertips and the curl of his hair on his chest tickling my face nearly broke me.

We took all the time we'd never had in the past. Nothing was rushed and each second savoured until we lay spent on the bed, wrapped in each other's arms.

*

'Morning, sleepy head.' Jake put a cup of tea beside the table.

I pushed my hair off my face and enjoyed the sight of his naked chest. He'd thrown on his trousers, but his feet were bare, and it wouldn't take much to bring him back to the state I was in. I sat up and sipped my tea.

'It's nine, he said, running his hand through his hair. 'What time are you due in the office?'

'Not until twelve.' I smiled.

'I'm meeting my friend at eleven.' He sat on the side of the bed.

I made a face, and he took the cup from my hands and kissed me.

'I thought we could share the bath,' he said.

I grinned.

'Thought you'd approve. I've run it,' he said and tucked my hair behind my ear.

I stepped out of bed and helped him out of his trousers then grabbed my towel and, on the landing, found one in the airing cupboard for him. The cold morning air on my bare skin was as intoxicating as last night's wine and walking through the house without a shred of clothing on was freeing. There was no one here to judge, or to care.

Steam rose from the tub and I dipped a foot in then turned the cold tap on. Jake ran his fingers down my spine, I shivered but not from the cold. His hand moved between my legs, and I held tight to the edge of the bath as he brought me to climax.

Turning, I kissed him and wanted to return the pleasure, but he stopped me. He turned off the cold water and climbed into the bath. Although the tub was big, with him in it, it looked small. He held out a hand and I climbed in, having no choice but to sit on top of him. He lathered the soap and washed my back then moved his hands forward under my arms and caressed my breasts. I could barely contain myself by the time he reached to my stomach. He finished between my legs and I came again. His arousal was obvious but sitting on top of him it was impossible to do anything except move my bottom. This had the desired effect and finally I rose out of the water. I turned, taking the soap I slowly cleaned him from top to bottom and back to the middle. It was moments before he came in my hands. The water around us had cooled but our passion hadn't.

39

Fleming looked up from his desk as I arrived.

'Your night of dancing has done you the world of good,' he said. I blushed.

'A very good evening, I see.' He stood. 'Come and see the new aerial photographs that have come in, and meet Professor Gamble from Harvard.'

We left Room 39 and walked down the corridor to one of the meeting rooms. Photographs covered the table and the walls and a man stood with a notebook in hand.

'Professor Gamble,' Fleming said, 'I'd like you to meet Dr Tremayne.'

The professor put down his notebook and held out a hand. 'Dr Tremayne. My colleague Professor Fox has sung your praises.'

'Professor Gamble,' I said, shaking his hand. He was a well-built man with short, cropped ginger hair and glasses.

He pushed a few photos forward. 'Now please tell me what you make of these new images.'

I studied them.

'The beaches have been degraded and no doubt mined,' I said, looking closely. 'There is evidence of a building being removed and defences being built since the last set of photographs I've seen.' I scanned them again. 'But it's not too much.'

I went to the pictures on the walls. In the area around Calais, the build-up was far greater. 'They've been very busy here.'

'Agreed,' said Professor Gamble.

'Have you had samples of the beaches?' I turned from the photographs.

'No,' he said, putting his hands into his jacket pockets. 'Not approved yet.'

I glanced at the pictures again. 'That will be key.'

Professor Gamble nodded. 'If the grains are too small it will interfere with machinery.'

'Sometimes I think these men have never walked across a beach.' I shook my head. 'For insight they should visit ten different beaches, some with soft fine sand, some with hard compact sand, some with a mix of fine and coarse, and so forth. They should also wear different shoes on each one and test which is better.'

'On some, easy progress, while on others, slow and painful steps,' he said.

The range of photographs on the wall were mostly of the Calais area but towards the end I saw some of the Normandy beaches.

'I shall leave you to it,' Fleming said. 'Stop to see me before you leave, Merry.'

'Of course.' I turned to Professor Gamble. 'What's teaching in an American university like?

He looked up from the map on the table. 'I was about to say much the same as what you've experienced but then Oxford is different.'

I nodded.

'You should come and visit when we've won this damned war.'

'If and when you mean.'

'I take the positive approach.'

'Very American.' I smiled. 'I'd love to visit. What is Boston like?' My time with Jake was soon to end and I longed to have a more complete picture of his world.

'Like most cities in the US but with more charm.' He smiled.

'Charm?'

He wiggled his hands. 'The streets are not all straight and the architecture is mixed.'

'Is it snowy in winter?' I'd seen enough Hollywood movies with glorious winter images to long to experience snow in that way.

'It can be, or simply wet, windy with arctic cold.' He shivered.

'Sounds frightful,' I said.

He laughed. 'The winters can be tough, but they are more than made up for by glorious summers, and falls that are so golden they hurt.'

'Falls?' I asked.

'Autumns,' he clarified.

'Ah, what a lovely descriptive term.'

Together we began noting the differences in the most recent intelligence photographs. The villages near the coast had suffered and the shore itself had been altered by the military machinery, making it more defensible. Around Calais it was heaviest, yet the Normandy coast was still lightly covered at present.

'What do you think this is?' he asked.

I examined the photograph in question. It was military but exactly what I had no idea.

'Best to have someone with army experience look at it,' I said.

He excused himself and went in search of an expert but returned unsuccessful. We sorted photographs, marked maps and made lists of concerns together in near silence.

'It's nearly six,' he said. 'You need to catch Commander Fleming and he may know the person we need.'

'You've figured out there is no one worth knowing that he doesn't know,' I said.

He pushed his glasses to the top of his head. 'Yes, that has become exceedingly clear.'

'I'll be back in tomorrow but then I'm off to Cornwall,' I said as I collected my things.

'Until mid-January,' he replied.

'Yes. See you tomorrow.' I left and walked towards Room 39. I heard Fleming before I saw him with Jake. My heart stopped for a moment, forgetting their friendship.

'Hello,' I said, as I came up to them.

'Merry, this is excellent timing.' Fleming waved to the seat beside Jake. 'We were just discussing you. Were your ears burning?'

'Should they be?' I asked and looked from one man to the other. One urbane and so very English, while the other so handsome and so American.

'It was all good, I assure you.' Fleming glanced at us both.

I cast him a sideways glance, not liking his tone.

'Professor Gamble and I need to speak to an army expert,' I said.

'I'll ask your ex, Garfield.' Fleming rose to his feet. 'He's aide de camp to Field Marshal Dill.'

'Thank you, and you wanted to see me,' I said, feeling awkward to be sitting beside my lover in front of my boss referring to my former fiancé.

'Yes, but it will wait until tomorrow.'

I stood fighting a sense of frustration. 'I'll be off now.'

'See you tomorrow.' Fleming waved and turned back to Jake.

As I made my way out of the building, I didn't know if I would see Jake tonight or not. We hadn't arranged anything, but it had been implied. However, if he was caught up with Fleming then there was a good chance I wouldn't and with that depressing thought I went back to the empty house on Bywater Street.

*

Walking from the station to Manchester College, it felt like I had never left Oxford. The city was unchanged, and it settled around me, reminding me of all I'd wanted and had worked for. These past two weeks, extended from the original plan which was what Fleming had wanted to discuss, had left me exhausted and confused. I hadn't seen Jake again. He had written a quick letter that had arrived on the Friday, the day I was supposed to return to Cornwall.

The general who had been called in to discuss the photographs with us was truly useful and his time limited, so we'd worked all the hours of the days straight through until we had a clear picture of the changes that had been wreaked on the French coast. All I could see when I closed my eyes were legends and the hierarchical organisation of the maps. Applying a military purpose to maps had been happening forever, but it still tripped me up. Each time I drew a new one I had to remind myself of its purpose so that I could lead the reader through the map to the information that they needed quickly. The embarrassment of that day months ago still stung.

Passing the Bodleian, I walked on to Holywell Street and turned onto Mansfield Road. Bicycles whizzed past and gowns flapped. It was all very reassuring, though I couldn't help but think of how I had changed since I had last worked here at the start of the war.

A pregnant woman pushing a pram came towards me. As we neared each other, she smiled widely. 'Merry,' she said.

I blinked, taking a closer look because on first appearance I didn't know her.

'It's Charlotte Timms that was,' she said. 'I married John Park from the history department.'

'Oh, congratulations.' I swallowed. 'Weren't you heading up the team doing the pamphlets on Egypt?'

'Yes, but sadly not anymore,' she said, looking down to the child in the pram.

'No childcare?' I picked up the rattle that the baby had thrown.

'John doesn't want his wife to work outside the home.' Her voice was flat as she spoke.

'And you're fine with this?' The words were out of my mouth before I could stop them. She had been the brightest and the best of my year.

'Well—' she looked down '—I didn't think it would be this way, but it is, so I must make the best of it and I wouldn't give them back.' She ran a hand over her stomach.

I forced a smile. 'Then I am happy for you.' I didn't add appalled, which is how I truly felt.

'Thank you, that means a great deal,' she said. 'Miss Price was quite cruel.'

'She's always been direct,' I said.

'Direct is one thing, but the things she said about me wasting my education and my brain simply for sex and security were harsh.' She shivered. 'John's set to become master of Balliol.'

'That's brilliant news and I'm certain you will make a wonderful master's wife.' But you could have been so much more, I added silently.

'Will you be in Oxford long?' she asked.

'No, a few days at most.' I wanted to be in Cornwall more than anything else. If the commander and his men hadn't left yet I knew it wouldn't be long.

'That's a shame; it would have been wonderful to see more of you.' She moved to stand behind her pram.

'When I'm back.' I smiled.

'Yes, that will be something to look forward to,' she said as she passed me and I continued towards the college.

How could she have thrown everything away? I wouldn't do that. I had worked too hard to reach this point. Looking up at the heavy sky, I took a deep breath. This was where I belonged, and someday I would be back here, continuing my work. It would be wonderful, but it didn't excite me as it once had. No doubt this was because we were still at war and that coloured everything, including every map I now made.

40

28 November 1942

The train slowed as it entered Falmouth and my body ached
with each jolt. I'd spent most of the journey on the night train
standing, and my only thought was that I would see Jake again
soon. I was both excited and dreading it. In one way it would
be easier if they had left already but that was me being afraid
of the goodbye, the finality of it. My days in Oxford had passed
in a blur. But still so clear was the moment when I'd bumped
into Charlotte's husband. I'd had to stop myself from yelling
at him that he could have a wife and not tie her to the kitchen
table. But that just wasn't the way things were done in Oxford.

The train slowed again as we approached the docks. Taking
my suitcase, I stepped onto the platform and I saw Jake waiting. He was unexpected and I had hoped to have more time to
prepare myself to see him again.

'Hi,' he said.

'Morning.' I yawned and we walked together to the car.

He opened the passenger side door for me then took my
bag. His fingers brushed mine and my heart raced. The nearly
three weeks I'd been away felt like a lifetime. November was
almost at a close and the Falmouth docks were crowded with
servicemen. A huge gap of all the unsaid things filled the space

between us. We were awkward with each other; maybe it was only me.

Once we set off, he turned to me and took my hand for a minute. The feel of him stilled my nerves and reminded me that I knew him. He hadn't changed. He was as I had last seen him, but he wasn't. There was a wound-up energy about him.

'It's good you made it back,' he said. 'We're off in two days.'

'Only two?' Forty-eight hours was never going to be enough time even if I was alone with him.

'The weather looks like it will be settled for our departure,' he said.

'So soon.' I looked out on the passing scenery with the bare trees.

He changed gears as we went uphill then he took my hand again. I loved the feel of it, of him and soon that would be gone. There was no marriage or happy ever after in our future. I knew that and so did he.

We crested the hill and Swanpool Beach appeared below. Winter sunlight broke through the dense cloud and the water sparkled silver.

'Do you want to stop and stretch your legs?' he asked as we neared Maenporth Beach.

I nodded, trying not to think of the few moments we had left. The beach was empty except for a few people collecting seaweed. Time alone with Jake would be good before I saw the others. They would watch us to see how we would deal with this change. But we were both old enough not to be stupid about an affair even if our hearts may have tangled a bit.

He parked and came round to my side, taking my hand. The fresh east wind nearly took the scarf from my neck. It was my mother's. What would she say in this moment? For this could be the last minute Jake and I had alone. I didn't know what the exact plans were and what was yet to be done.

Passing the large concrete blocks strewn about the beach to prevent invasion, I noted the man in the pillbox. At this moment it felt as if there was nowhere untouched by war and there was certainly no person free from it.

In the lee of the cliff, we took shelter and Jake placed an arm over my shoulder bringing me close to his side. 'I'd hoped we'd have more time,' he whispered into my ear. A shiver chased down my skin mixing desire with fear.

'In London I thought we'd have another night.'

'I did too but Fleming had other plans,' he said. 'He wanted to meet Mike Moriarty, another reporter.'

'Do you know Joe Gamble from your Harvard days?' I asked.

'No,' he said and kissed my hair. 'I don't want to spend my last private moments with you talking about others. I want to talk about us.'

I moved in front of him so that I could see his face. He took both my hands in his.

'Merry, I didn't mean for this to happen,' he said.

'Our affair has been most inconvenient.'

'That wasn't what I was about to say,' he said. 'Surprising, yes, but inconvenient, no; tricky, yes.'

'Jake, I . . . '

He kissed me and stopped all words and all thoughts. Hunger took over and I moved against him, wanting to have him as close to me as possible. I didn't want clothes in the way, I wanted to feel his skin and to taste him fully again so that I wouldn't forget. If I could, I would imprint him onto my skin as he was in my soul.

A wolf whistle was followed by someone shouting, 'Get a room.'

The moment was lost.

'If everyone wasn't expecting you, we could go to Kestle, but the team awaits.' He pushed a strand of hair from my face. 'Merry, I . . . '

I pressed my finger against his mouth. This leaving would be worse if we said anything about love. The parting was going to be terrible. So, I kissed him with everything in me and let the kiss speak.

When we pulled apart, he studied my face. Afraid of what he might see, I looked out to the water. We would never work so this parting was good. It was doing what would have been harder to do, walking away. With him near I wouldn't have the strength.

He stroked my cheek. 'Merry?'

I turned back to him, and drawing on all my discipline, I said, 'We'd better get back.' I kissed him again to ease the sting of my words, and took his hand in mine and walked to the vehicle.

*

Duffle bags lined the downstairs hallway when we arrived. I turned to Jake, and he nodded. This was worse than I thought. Mary came out of the kitchen, opened her arms, and I walked into them.

'This is hard,' she said, still holding me tight. 'But we are made of stronger stuff and so are they.'

She led me into the kitchen and poured me a strong cup of tea.

I took it and looked around. Mary had packed up things here too. 'You too?'

'Yes, there's no point in me staying on here,' she said. 'I'll be in the way, and they will have me back at my old job at the War Office.'

I nodded.

'Less time to think.' She looked away. 'You and Pierre, Howard Rendle, Tom Long and a few others are the continuity for the operations.'

'I'm only here for a month and a half,' I said.

'Enough time to settle them.' She poured herself some tea. 'You're the right person for the task.'

I stared into my cup. The tea was stewed and dark despite the milk.

Her normal easy smile was forced and her eyes full of unshed tears. 'We can do this.'

I nodded not feeling very strong, but I would be for her. I took her hand in mine and squeezed it.

'Mary,' I said. 'I feel I need to apologise. You know I was sent here by Fleming to assess the situation.'

She nodded. 'You saw they were underused and in a war that is not tenable, and Gerry and the men are more than ready to go.'

'I'm sorry,' I said.

'Don't be. I knew the man I married and I wouldn't change him,' she said. 'I love who he is, and I pray that he stays safe.'

Outside, Jake stood talking with Brooks Richards. It was unbearable that I would never see him again but that was the reality.

'It's hard saying goodbye.' Mary came to stand beside me.

'But it was inevitable,' I said.

Mary looked at me. 'Why inevitable?'

I sighed. 'Different worlds.'

'You can overcome anything if you try.' She placed an arm across my shoulders.

'I'd like to believe you but an ocean and more stand between us.' I forced a smile. 'And that is fine. I have my career.'

'Which is wonderful. But . . . '

'No buts.' I put my cup down. 'It's clear there is a great deal to do.'

Leaving Mary in the kitchen, I headed upstairs, passing the many items in the hallway. Once in my room, I closed the door, leaned against it and prayed for strength. Or maybe I should be following Mo's words to be brave. I could do that; Mary was seeing off her husband and Mrs Newton too. All I'd be doing would be saying farewell to a lover. In the context of this war, it was small.

*

We walked back from the Ferry Boat arm in arm. The rest of the team were far in front. The new men had joined us. They were staying in Pedn Billy, and it had been a riotous farewell dinner. A few of the men were swaying slightly on their feet. But neither Jake nor I had consumed much. Unlike the others, whose excitement was tangible, Jake was quiet. When we reached the beach below the house, he held me back.

'I wanted a few minutes alone with you,' he whispered.

I did too but at the same time I feared time alone with him. The silences between us would leave room for things to be said and I didn't want to fill them with words that couldn't be taken back or ones that couldn't be unheard.

He took my hand in his and we walked along the beach. The waning gibbous moon was bright, and with the clear sky it was cold enough for a frost. But November could do that, and it could feel spring-like on Christmas Day by contrast. We walked down towards the Pedn Billy boathouse. There he put his arm around my shoulders and I snuggled into his warmth.

'I know you don't want to talk about the future,' he said.

I shook my head.

'But I do.'

I turned so I could see his face in the moonlight.

'Jake, we've had now, and it has been wonderful. I have never felt like this with anyone, but tomorrow you head off to face God knows what. We have different lives and different plans.'

'But . . . ' he began.

'No buts. I go back to Oxford and the job I've worked so hard for and you will head back to the States and win another Pulitzer.'

'Merry, I—'

'Hold me.' I wrapped my arms about him. 'No words.' If he didn't say them then this would be easier, and I could keep my own words too.

'I want to hold you forever.' He nuzzled into my hair.

'Hold me now; we have now,' I said, not ever wanting to leave his embrace.

Somewhere a dog barked, and an owl cried overhead. Our time together was at its natural end.

*

The dawn broke bright and crisp and I was empty. Normally a frosty morning lifted my spirits, but as I heard the pipes for the bathroom, I knew it was all change.

I dressed with care and practicality then tiptoed down the stairs, afraid to see anyone. Jake stood in the sitting room, looking out on the river.

'I'll miss this view,' he said, turning, 'but I'll miss you more.'

I went to his side and leaned against him. His fingers slipped between mine and I didn't trust myself to speak. The sky was a pale-blue and the ground frosted white. I needed to freeze hard like the land and become impervious to sun and rain and become unbreakable even with a metal spade. But next to the warmth of Jake, I was soft and malleable.

'Morning,' said the commander. 'Ready for the off, Nipper?'

'Yes, sir,' Jake said, turning from the view, 'but I'm going to hate leaving the Helford.'

'It's been a great training ground,' the commander said. 'But we'll be more effective elsewhere. The new team will act as transportation while we will cause destruction.'

'Boys,' I said, rolling my eyes then walking into the kitchen. Pierre was there, which I should have known from the smell of the coffee. He always made it as my mother did and hopefully still did.

'Hard, this,' he said, handing me a cup.

I nodded then took the coffee outside and down to the Celtic Cross. The water still flowed, but there was ice about the edges and my breath created my own personal fog. Perching on the stone bench, the coldness penetrating the wool of my trousers. It would be good if it would numb me through. I needed to find my inner strength and determination and I would.

The coffee was a thick, dark and slightly bitter reminder of who I was and what I wanted. If I'd wanted love and marriage, I would have stayed with George all those years ago. I would be pushing a pram and not here on this cold November morning, missing my lover before he'd left. It's not as if I could go with them; my role going forward was to help plan the invasion of France.

Thanks to my time here, I had seen first-hand how difficult it was to land even the smallest of boats on unmined beaches while practising with the surf boats. What I would contribute going forward was far more important than what my body wanted, and my heart begged for. My head was more valuable, and it was correct.

I finished my coffee and returned to the house to join the others bringing the bags down to the beach. A stream of dinghies transferred the supplies and the belongings to the *Mutin* and the two other French fishing boats. They were still in their military greys and they would stop at the Scillies to change their colours. And, like the boats, I needed to change back to who I had been before.

Work had stopped briefly for some lunch, but, before we knew it, the light was low and we stood on the beach below the house. The rum was brought out and everyone given a half measure.

In a clear voice, Bonnie Newton began singing 'The Parting Glass'. I was stunned to hear Jake's deep baritone join in.

As I listened to the words, it took all my reserves not to give way to tears. I risked a glance at Mary who was pressing her lips together and holding the commander's hands tight.

So fill to me the parting glass
And drink a health whate'er befall
Then gently rise and softly call
Good night and joy be to you all
Good night and joy be to you all

The last note drifted on the cold air.

'To you all,' the commander said, raising his glass.

We all lifted ours and I turned to Jake. Our glance met, then I downed the rum in one as everyone did. I shook hands and had a laugh with the men as they began to be ferried to the boats. Finally, it was Mary, the commander and Jake and me left on the beach.

What could I say in these last few moments? He took my hands in his.

'I didn't know you could sing so well,' I said.

He laughed. 'Merry, God knows if we'll ever meet again, and you comment on my singing.'

I nodded. 'Stay safe and be brave if you must.'

'I'll miss you.' He bent down and he kissed me. Everything that we hadn't said was there.

I traced his jaw and said, 'Same.'

'Come on, Nipper,' said the commander.

Jake wrapped me in his arms, kissing me hard and fast. Pulling away from him, I put my hand into my pocket and pulled out the heart-shaped serpentine stone. I slipped it into his hand. He looked from the stone and to me.

'My heart,' I said. 'I don't need it.'

He closed his hand around it and held it to his own. 'If we survive this war, meet me again, Merry, and I'll return your heart.'

He joined the commander in the dinghy and I stood watching as it reached the *Mutin*. I finally saw Jake when he was on board. He looked back but didn't wave, nor did I.

The sun was nearly set as they made way out of the Helford under orange-tinted clouds. A freezing haze developed under the clear sky with the first stars appearing. I didn't move until I could see the boat no longer.

*

The walk to Mawnan Church didn't take long. It was ten in the morning and the sky was solid with no break in the cloud. It hung low and sent down mizzle relentlessly. I hadn't slept well last night. It might have been the wine Mary and I drank, but I knew the truth as I walked past the lych-gate and down the path through the woods to the headland. Eventually clearing the trees, I scanned the horizon, such as it was, for there was no distinction between the sea and sky. Everything in me yearned to see that flotilla of boats coming past the Manacles on their way home. It was a foolish wish, and one from a heart full of regret.

I hadn't uttered the words expressing how I truly felt. That would have left me unprotected with no place to go. How could I have believed that I could return to being the old me? That six months of being with someone wouldn't alter me and him. That I could conveniently have an affair then walk away. I was a fool, a giant one. Of course, I loved him even if I had never said it. He had truly taken my heart with him. If he returned to me, I would tell him.

Mizzle mingled with my tears as I stared out on a grey world. The colour and joy had gone with him, thanks to my foolish head. As I walked towards the church, I hungered for him. Images of him trying to coax Mo to swim, venting his frustrations rowing, and walking across the beach towards me, circled in my thoughts. With each step, I longed for something that I tossed away as if it had no worth.

The feel of his hand at the small of my back, the anticipation of being alone with him covered my skin. With each step I remembered what was lost. He was gone.

At the church I stopped and went in to say a prayer. My mother had always been fond of Mawnan Church as it was said that the church was named after a Breton monk, St Maunanus, who'd lived around 520. I liked the church because it was built on an already sacred site. Like the sister headland on the other side of the Helford, there was evidence of early civilisation on this one too. For years the church tower acted as a key marker for vessels navigating Falmouth Bay. I needed a guide, a navigational marker to help me to re-find my way through life. But rather than pray for that, I fell to my knees and prayed for the men making their way south.

'Is that you, Merry?' asked one of the Seaton twins as she walked toward me.

I quickly wiped my eyes and blew my nose.

'Yes.' I squinted and said, 'Adele?'

She laughed. 'Well done, very few ever pick the right one.' She arrived at my side. 'Are you OK?'

I forced a smile. 'Yes, a bit overcome with everything for a moment.'

'I was so sorry to hear about Oliver.'

'Thank you,' I said.

'I'm so pleased I've seen you.' She cleared her throat. 'I'm still planning on applying to university. But my parents and my grandmother don't think I should. They think it is a waste of time, and squandered on women.'

I laughed bitterly. 'Sadly, they are not alone in that.'

'But you don't believe it.' She sat beside me.

'No, but the world has strong views,' I said. 'And there are sacrifices that will be required of you if you choose university and a career.'

'Sacrifices?' she asked.

'A career and a marriage are not a viable combination today,' I said. Adele was younger and maybe the world would be different for her. 'I was told this at the interview stage and surged forward clear-sighted, but I hadn't really thought of the life alone ahead of me. But, as I've seen among old friends, once you are a wife you lose independence, and they think you lose your abilities as well.'

'That's terrible,' she said.

'It is,' I said. 'But I have seen some of the brightest women forced to leave their work, their careers behind.'

'You will never marry?' she asked.

'No, I have chosen my career.' I smiled, knowing it was still the right choice. I had worked so hard for it.

'It's terrible that you can't have both,' Adele said.

'Both is not an option if I want to achieve professorship in the school of geography at Oxford,' I said.

'Thank you for being so honest.' Adele took a deep breath. 'I know this is an odd question, but has it been worth it? Giving up love and marriage?'

I was ten years her senior. Ten years of independence and making my own decisions and being so sure. Yet today when I was uncertain of everything, she asked this question. Honesty was best. 'Yes, it has been worth it, but it hasn't been without pain.'

'Oh,' she said.

'Think about what you really want that degree for,' I said. 'And if it will lead you to your ultimate goal.'

'Thank you, I will.' She stood and said, 'I'll leave you in peace.'

I watched her go and turned back to the stained-glass window above the altar. We all make sacrifices for love – love of a person, love of learning and love of a country. Right now, country was utmost, and everything else second. If we didn't win this war, nothing else mattered. Nothing. Not my academic work, not a permanent role at Oxford, not Jake, not Maman and certainly not my foolish heart.

PART SIX

A Citizen

I'm officially a citizen of the United States again. Those of us who crossed the border and fought in this war in units belonging to other countries before the seventh of December 1941 have been officially pardoned. It's been a long few years of being out in the cold so to speak but I'm glad to be an American again. Although I am forever grateful to the Canadians for taking me on.

Being here in the green and pleasant land of Great Britain feels almost as far away as the beaches of Maine. These days I meet more frequently with my American comrades. I delight in their surprise at the world they see around them. It helps my increasingly jaded soul to see the landscape and people through fresh eyes. As this war has worn on, my view of things has been tarnished but not my opinion of the people. The plain ordinary people, many who are hungry, homeless and without hope, fill my thoughts. There are too many innocent people caught up in man's greed and need for power over other men.

Humans are the same no matter what country they come from or what language they speak. Everyone needs food, water and air to survive. What makes people different is the powers ruling over their lives.

I still believe in the American dream of hard work and reward for labor. But the same rules are not applied equally.

In the distance I can hear bombing but I don't know which side is causing the destruction. I do know that to the people whose homes are being destroyed it matters little, for the results are the same. It is for them that I continue to fight. The sooner this war ends, the better for all, especially those caught in the midst who won't share in the power, no matter which side wins.

Jake Russell
England

41

My mother's self-portrait with me in her arms stared at me from the corner of my little room at Ridifarne. It was Christmas Eve and I had returned from London three days ago after delivering the latest 'mail bag' direct to the prime minister which was followed by a brief catch up with Fleming. I had requested a return to London as it was clear I was not needed here and was more in the way. But he told me to sit it out as planned.

Ridifarne now housed Wrens, including Brooks Richards' fiancée, Helen. Through her, I knew the team had had an uneventful trip south to the Mediterranean, but I told her I didn't want to know anything more. She gave me a hard look but said she understood. I don't think she did but was too polite to say so.

In order not to think, I trained regularly with the men and made suggestions to Lieutenant Commander Warington Smyth on refining the boat he designed to be more effective for the beach landings. Our discussions and my experience would be useful moving forward. With that in mind, I reworked maps, like the ones in front of me now but the fact that it was Christmas Eve kept playing on my mind bringing back memories. Tomorrow there would be no church bells, no stockings, only me on my own. The past was a time of family and faith and now I have none of the former and little of the latter.

Being here at Ridifarne made missing Jake worse. He was everywhere, even in the clanging pipes. The sound brought images of him walking down the hall with a towel wrapped about his hips.

I must not think about him because desire colours my skin and fills me with a restlessness that can't be fixed. It was best to work and forget the holiday. I wasn't in the mood for celebrating. The Wrens who now shared the house with me were all out at the Ferry Boat. The telephone rang and I went to answer it.

'Ridifarne,' I said.

'This is Commander Davis and I'm trying to reach Warington Smyth.'

'He's at Pedn Billy,' I said.

'There's no answer there.'

'Can I take a message?' I asked.

'You must locate him,' Commander Davis said. 'And have him ring me immediately.'

'I will.' I put the phone down and walked up the unmade lane to deliver the message. Why the call hadn't gone through to them I didn't know. But it became clear as I reached the house and singing filled the air.

''Bout time you arrived,' said Rendle, as I entered the sitting room.

I laughed and scanned the room, looking for the commander, and found him by the piano. I made my way to him and quickly apprised him of the situation. He went to the hall and made the telephone call.

The lieutenant commander returned to my side a few moments later and surveyed the room.

'We are making a run to France tonight,' he said.

'It's Christmas Eve,' I stated the obvious as I looked at the slightly drunken men.

'They'll sober up on the crossing and so will I,' he said to me as he entered the room and tapped a glass to draw their attention. 'Right, we're off in a half hour. Ready yourselves.'

He turned to me. 'Could you let the men on *Sunbeam* know?'

'Of course,' I said, glad to be of some use.

The air was cold after the warmth of the house and I shivered as I made my way through the garden, down to the boathouse, then along the beach to my canoe. The moon was rising, and appeared huge on the horizon.

As I approached the new headquarters for the flotilla, Lord Runciman's magnificent sailing yacht *Sunbeam*, I heard singing that was a bit more alcohol-fuelled than the voices in the house. But these men were more in tune, if that was possible.

I tied my canoe on and climbed the rope ladder onto the deck, where I found a man vomiting over the other side of it. This didn't bode well. I didn't disturb him but went below where the fug of smoke and alcohol was potent.

'Dr Tremayne,' said Tom Long. 'Happy Christmas.'

'Happy Christmas,' I replied, scanning until I found the skipper and worked my way through to him. 'You need to be ready in less than a half hour.'

'Tonight?' His mouth remained open, showing his disbelief.

'Afraid so,' I said.

'Merry bloody Christmas.' He put his drink down. 'Sorry for swearing, Dr Tremayne.' He turned to the men and said, 'Right, lads. Glasses down, time to sober up and get ready. We're off in twenty minutes.'

'Can I do anything for you?' I asked.

He shook his head, and I went on deck. The sick man had curled into a ball and was fast asleep. I ran through the lists of things they would require but they didn't need my help. It was best if I left them to it and hoped that they would work off the drink on the crossing.

Warington Smyth was on the beach when I landed my canoe.

'How are they?' he asked.

I wrinkled my nose. 'Very merry.'

He inhaled deeply and said with more confidence than I suspect he had, 'They'll be fine.'

'You'll be one man down,' I said.

'How do you know?' he asked.

'Saw him on the deck,' I said. 'Didn't see his face but he's out cold.'

The lieutenant commander shook his head. 'As long as it isn't the engineer, we'll be fine.' We both looked out to the *Sunbeam* in the moonlight. *MGB 318* was anchored quietly beside her. No doubt this was the reason that Helford was called on rather than Dartmouth to run the mission. The boat had been here for training the past three days. I'd spent the day out with them yesterday, raising, lowering, and storing the surf boats. Tedious but essential practice.

'A truck will be arriving shortly,' he said. 'Can you meet it for me?'

'I'll grab a coat and wait on the beach for it,' I said.

'May I borrow your canoe?' he asked, already pushing it out into the river.

'Of course.' I handed him the paddle and went to the house where I pulled on my father's old gansey jumper, a waxed jacket, boots and a hat and mittens. Instantly I felt better.

Back on the beach, Mrs Newton met me with a thermos and a sandwich. 'I heard the noise.'

'Thank you,' I said.

'Will they be OK?' she asked.

I nodded and said a silent prayer. The lieutenant commander had gone from slightly tipsy to stone-cold sober and I imagined the freezing air and their duty would have the same effect on the rest of them.

She also held a box out to me.

'The mouse for Mr Cohen?' I asked.

'The boys insisted,' she said. 'See you tomorrow and Happy Christmas.'

'Happy Christmas,' I replied, and looked up at the clear sky, thinking of those I loved not with me. Two in heaven, one somewhere on the Mediterranean and the other somewhere in France. I hoped Maman was well. Christmas Eve was her time. There would be the specially selected Yule log of fine oak placed in the spotlessly clean fireplace ready for Christ to descend into the house and to leave a present. We would attend midnight mass, and on our return, we would eat the hearty pork stew that had been cooking all day, filling the house with the most divine scents.

Christmas Eve was special in Brittany because, like on the eve of All Saints', the veil between the living and the dead was believed thin and the dead could walk among the living. The year my mother's father passed away that had seemed truer than ever when a candle had lit itself. After my father died, my mother had left a candle in the same spot, but it did not light itself, so she'd lit it.

When the lorry arrived, I directed them to unload and I watched the various provisions piled on the beach. Soon the officers appeared and, like Warington Smyth, were well on their way to leaving the Christmas festivities behind. Amongst their crew was another American. Thompson was an observer, and an outspoken one at that. He had provided the turkeys for the Christmas lunch tomorrow, along with a few other delicacies that we hadn't seen since before the war, like oranges and bananas. Peter and John were delighted.

I counted the men on the beach.

'Two men down and unfit for service,' Thompson said.

'Who?' I asked.

'Sampson, the navigator, and MacDonald,' he said. 'Now we're waiting for the lieutenant commander to return for a powwow.'

The lorry drove away and several dinghies from *Sunbeam* arrived on the beach. The men began loading them.

Pierre was here so landing in Brittany wasn't a problem. It was the journey there. Warington Smyth came ashore and spoke to his second in command.

'I don't know what they are going to do,' said Thompson who then blew on his hands. The temperature was bitter and would drop further with the clear skies.

Warington Smyth came up to us. 'We will have to abandon the mission.'

'Surely one of you can navigate,' said Thompson, putting his hands into his pockets.

'No one feels competent enough,' said the second in command.

I closed my eyes for a moment, taking a deep breath. I opened them again, saying, 'Then take me. I can do it.'

'We can't do that,' said Warington Smyth.

'Is the mission important?' I asked, already knowing the answer.

'Yes,' he said.

'Then I don't see you have a choice.' I looked Warington Smyth directly in the eyes. If it had been Commander Holdsworth, he wouldn't have hesitated but the man in front of me was not a chance-taker.

'We can't,' he said.

I pulled my shoulders back. 'I am more than qualified.'

'You're not in the Navy.'

I glanced at the American. 'Thompson isn't either. You have precedent.'

'She has a point,' said Thompson.

Tom Long walked up the beach to them. 'We're ready to go, sir.'

Warington Smyth looked from me to the boat and back.

'I assure you I can navigate,' I said. 'I've done it before.'

'As a civilian,' he replied.

'Yes.' There was no point in reeling off my credentials.

Baker joined the group. I was surprised to see him. He had been sent off on a special assignment when the others departed.

'Is there a problem?' Baker asked.

'Lieutenant Baker, what are you doing here?' asked Warington Smyth.

'I was in Falmouth,' Baker said, 'and was told to report immediately.'

'Can you navigate?' the second in command asked.

'Unless you mean through stocks and bonds, no.' He lit a cigarette.

'Then it's Dr Tremayne,' said Thompson. 'Or abort the mission.'

'Exactly what is Dr Tremayne?' asked Baker.

'We have no navigator,' said Warington Smyth.

'She's good,' Baker said.

'How do you know?' Warington Smyth asked.

'I've seen her work with charts, and I would trust her with my life.' He flicked the ash from his cigarette.

Warington Smyth looked from me to the boat and back again. 'No one must know of this.'

'Of course,' I said.

'Is there anything you need to bring with you, Miss Tremayne?' he asked.

'Are all the charts, navigational tables, sunrise and sunset information and tides on the boat?' I asked, running a check list through my mind.

'Yes,' said the second in command.

'Then I'm set.' I still clutched the box with the mouse.

'What on earth is that?' Thompson asked.

'A companion,' I said.

'For you?' Thompson sent me a funny look.

'No, for a wireless operator.' I smiled, thinking of Mo and hoping that he was still alive to take receipt of the mouse.

'Ah, Operation Mouse or a mouse for Mo,' Baker said. 'Excellent.'

The American shrugged. 'And they say Americans are crazy.'

I laughed. 'And you aren't?'

'Oh, we are but we wouldn't be bringing a mouse on board,' Thompson said. 'Nor, come to think of it, be putting a beautiful woman in danger.'

'Don't worry about Merry,' Baker said, putting his cigarette out in the sand. 'She can take care of herself.'

Tom Long came up to me. 'So, you'll be joining us on this cruise, Dr Tremayne.'

'I will.' I handed him the mouse.

'Best we get you on board then,' he said.

I climbed in the dinghy and looked up. The moon was high and bright. I heard Jake's voice. *Promise me you won't go on another mission.*

He might be looking at the moon too wherever he was. There was comfort in that. There was also comfort in the fact that he would never know, no one would, that I was going on an active mission.

The mouse scratched in the box. Be brave. I could do this.

42

By the time we passed the lighthouse at the Lizard, I had obtained my fix, the sky had clouded over and the swell had picked up. The confines in the map room were dire but we were making good progress with the engines at full. Each time a crew member came down to check on me, the smell of stale alcohol mixed with the diesel fumes. I felt a bit queasy and went on deck to clear my head and ease my stomach.

Pierre stood by the bow. Light spray rose every fifth wave and I sensed this was only the beginning.

'Not ideal,' I said.

'*Non*, it is coming in.'

Above the clouds thickened, the wind rose, and the moon was hidden.

Baker joined us and handed me a cigarette. 'Enjoy it now. Before long we will be too close to the shore and the light could be seen.'

Another thing I hadn't considered. We stood in silence. I was lost in thought while Baker scanned the sea and listened. Cigarette finished, I went back down to my calculations and reworked them. We couldn't afford to miss the mark. I also tidied the table. My heart stopped when I found *Mirabelle*'s charts. I tugged at my father's sweater and wrapped my arms around myself.

'I thought this might help,' Warington Smyth said as he handed me a mug of coffee.

I cleared my throat. 'Thank you.'

'The weather is worsening, and we've had to slow,' he said. 'You'll need to recalculate.'

I scratched out fresh calculations.

'It had been arrival at two,' I said. 'But now more like three twenty.'

'That will mean a fast turnaround to get the fifteen airmen onboard.'

'Thankfully Christmas is late sunrise,' I said and sipped the coffee which was hot and bitter. The crumbs from the mince pie the cook had brought up to me I gave to the little mouse. I could hear him moving around in the box. I was not sure that he was enjoying the motion of the boat.

'Funny old way to spend Christmas,' the lieutenant commander said.

'Agreed.' I stood. 'I'd better get the latest bearing because, with this increasing gale, we will be moving off-course.' I glanced at my calculations. We didn't have much leeway with the timing and the tides. The later we were, the harder it would be to get the boats onto the beach, and that was tricky enough when the Atlantic wasn't throwing everything at you.

*

Pierre stood by the bow, listening while the commander watched the horizon for a signal light. From training I knew this was achieved by small balls covered in luminescent paint to signal to others when on the shore, but their glow wouldn't be strong enough from this distance. I only hoped that I'd charted us to the right beach. It was three thirty in the morning. A light rain fell, the sea state was vile, and the wind was blowing straight on to the beach. I didn't know if the ropes, not chains because of the noise they make, would hold the anchors in place. It was so different from the clear crisp night we'd had on the Helford.

'There it is,' said Baker pointing to the briefest of flashes. 'Drop the boats in.'

I stood back and watched as each boat was manned and loaded. I held the box with the mouse. Each boat would need to make a second trip. The first boat went off toward the beach while one of the *MGB*'s engines remained engaged to hold us in position.

The second dinghy with Baker onboard went out and the third waited because we didn't need collisions on the beach or submerged boats. The first boat should be on its way back soon, but the sea state was worsening. The third boat nearly overturned.

The coxswain called up, 'Can I have someone lighter. We're too heavy.'

Warington Smyth looked around the deck and every man left was bigger than those on board.

'I'll go.' I stepped forward.

'You can't,' he said.

'She's good,' the coxswain shouted over the wind.

'I can't risk it,' he called back.

'Do you have any choice?' I asked glancing at the sea state. 'The other boats aren't back, and the fifteen airmen won't all fit in those.'

'Fine.' He looked me directly in the eyes and said, 'If anything goes wrong . . .'

'I know. The government knows nothing.' I swallowed. It was best not to think.

'If something goes wrong tonight,' he said, 'we'll be back tomorrow or the night after.'

I nodded and handed down the mouse who was secured with

a rope. Then I climbed into the dinghy and took the oars. We began the journey to the beach I couldn't see, but I listened to the water and the wind. The surf was big and loud as we neared the shore. Each wave nearly submerged us, and I feared for the survival of this mouse. If it drowned as its predecessor had then I would have to lie to the boys. That was if I didn't drown as well. My feet were covered past my ankles and more water was coming in as each wave hit us. The noise of the surf was deafening.

Near the beach the man to my left jumped out as did the man to the right, pulling the boat in the last stretch so that we didn't overturn. I knew the routine. We hit the sand and worked quickly to get the boat safely up the sand. The other crew gathered around. No airmen. But there had been a signal.

'We wait another fifteen minutes and then we return,' said Baker.

I checked on the mouse. He'd survived. The rain was becoming heavier, not that it mattered; I was wet through already. We'd begun to get the boats ready to return when the airmen appeared. The supplies were quickly unloaded, and the mail was handed over. There were seventeen people to transport, not fifteen. One of our boats would have to make an extra trip.

The first one set out and I couldn't watch as it disappeared in the surge then the second boat left.

'Dr Tremayne, we'll leave you for the last boat as you are the lightest.'

'Fine,' I said, trying to stop my teeth chattering.

One of the airmen left with us took off his coat and covered my shoulders.

'They won't make it back tonight,' said the local man who had led the airmen here. 'The weather is getting worse.'

We waited another half hour and no sign of them.

'Enough,' the local man said. 'It is getting late.'

Baker and I and the remaining airmen piled into the back of his cart and were covered with hay. It was good to be out of the wind and the rain and I nodded off to sleep, clutching the mouse in his box to my chest.

When I woke, we were at a remote farmhouse and were quickly hustled inside. So much felt so familiar from the style of the furniture, the Yule log, the decorations. The woman of the house took me into a bedroom and helped me out of the wet clothing and into something dry.

'*Nedeleg laouen. Trugarez*,' I said, wishing her merry Christmas and thanks.

She looked at me and smiled as she took my wet things. Changed, I joined the men at the table, eating a hearty bean soup with crusty bread. I'm not sure if food had ever tasted so good.

Once I'd helped to clear the plates, she encouraged me to sit by the fire. The airmen were well known here for they had been staying a while.

'Funny old Christmas,' said a fresh-faced airman.

'I've never spent one like this and would prefer not to again.' I laughed drily.

'Surprised to see they are using women as crew,' said one. 'Risky.'

'We only use the best,' said Baker, winking at me.

'I've had some practice,' I said then dropped some crusts of bread into the box.

'A mouse?' asked the man who had brought us here.

'He's a gift for a radio operator.' I smiled at him. 'Can you find a way for this mouse to reach Mo?'

'I will try,' he said. 'It was sad when the other mouse drowned.'

'A drowned mouse?' asked the rude airman.

There were four sharp knocks on the door. The men jumped quietly to their feet. I was handed my clothes, which had been drying by the fire and I followed the airmen into the cellar and was directed into a corner behind shelves of preserves.

Above, voices were raised and Germans shouted at each other. I couldn't make out the words, but I didn't need the translation. They were looking for us. I pressed against the wall, still clutching the damp clothes. They would have been a giveaway.

Feet above stomped and light came through cracks in the floorboards and pierced the darkness. A draught blew across my cheek, and I shivered. I must always have an exit, Maman had said. But from the basement there was none that I could see. And I definitely needed a physical exit. Words would be no good.

Voices went silent above then I heard furniture shifting. The hatch we had climbed down opened. I prepared myself to die for that was preferable to what would happen, and in that moment, I saw that I knew too much. What was I going to do? I would have to run, escape somehow? The only exit would be a gun. I didn't have one but Baker did.

A cold hand covered my mouth, and I was pulled through a small door and pushed along a dark tunnel. I heard feet ahead and the steady sound of those behind me. The space narrowed and I bent low, still clutching the clothing. Finally, the tunnel came to an end, and I climbed up the ladder. No one spoke but I saw the airmen and Baker.

We walked into the woods for an hour until we came to a lane and an old truck arrived. We climbed on the back and travelled for miles in the dark without anyone speaking. Eventually we arrived at an old barn. Once inside the young airmen I'd been chatting to said, 'That was close.'

'Too damn close,' a woman said in barely accented English.

I swung around. I knew that voice. My mother stood with a rifle in her hand, dressed head to toe in black, her thick hair all grey.

I slapped my hand across my mouth.

'Are you all right?' the airman asked.

'Yes,' I squeaked.

Maman turned and paled. 'Meredith, ma petite.'

'Maman,' I said.

I closed the distance between us and, despite the rifle pressing into both of us, I hugged her until my arms had no strength left and then I wept. I cried for her, I cried for me, and I cried for Oli. She gently wiped my tears away, pulling me towards the back of the barn.

'Ma petite, you should not be here,' she whispered.

'No, I shouldn't be,' I said. I knew something of the proposed invasion plans. It was early and things might change but it was all inside me. If I was captured, it would be a disaster. My mother didn't know this. She was speaking from her knowledge of the life she was living.

'But to see you again,' she said. 'What a Christmas gift.'

'Oh, Maman, there is so much.' I looked down at my hands still clutching my father's old gansey. I held it out to her.

A sad smile crossed her face.

'How did you know that you loved him?' I asked.

'It was a gamble. I didn't know then if my career would end, but I knew that life without him was unthinkable.' She studied me and she stroked my cheek. 'You have found love.'

I swallowed.

'And you have sent it away.' She shook her head slowly. 'You are so afraid of losing what you have gained in your thirst for knowledge.' She laughed. 'Always you would do this. But open your heart, risk all and you will not lose but win. It will be different, but it will be wonderful.'

'I sent him away,' I said.

'Find him,' she said. 'Tell him. If it is right it will happen.'

'Five minutes, Odette,' said the small man who had been with us on the beach.

Odette. It suited her.

'Maman,' I said, 'I don't want to tell you, but I must.'

'Oliver,' she said.

I nodded. She clutched my hand.

'He was brave and beautiful. He served well but the fight is not over, ma petite,' she said. 'Only when it is, will we have time to grieve. But Oliver lived. He lived big and bold and this, this will hold me.'

She pulled me into her arms. I rested my head on her shoulder and she stroked my hair as she had done when I was a child. 'Come, we must get you safe to your beach and back to England.'

She squeezed my hand and led me out to a different truck and covered us with more hay. I had no idea where we were when we were bumbled into another barn.

'Get some rest while you can,' Maman said. 'It will be a long day but hopefully the Germans will be celebrating Christmas.'

'*Nedeleg laouen*,' I said.

'Happy Christmas.' She threw a blanket over me then kissed my head.

'Are you going to kiss us all?' asked an airman with the thick Scottish burr.

She laughed. 'I'm old enough to be your mother.'

'All the better for it,' he said.

She chuckled and I closed my eyes. Here was my beautiful artistic mother, slinging sassy comments back and forth with men my brother's age. She had reinvented herself and, as I took one last look at her before sleep claimed me, I saw she was relishing it.

*

It was midnight when we climbed into the truck with full stomachs and sufficient sleep. This time we weren't hidden under hay but sitting visible. My mother's shoulder rested against mine while we travelled together. Never had we sat shoulder to shoulder like this on a cold Christmas Day, but we had on many a beach, boat and car, laughing, talking, listening. Now was the time to say anything that hadn't been said. We might not have another chance.

She took my hand in hers. I studied it. No longer were there the tell-tale bits of paint under her nails. The hand, so like my own, still had the power to convey love and safety. And yet in her other hand she clutched a rifle as if this was something she had done every day.

We reached the beach and stayed hidden in the dunes, waiting. There was no guarantee the MGB would make it back. After a blow like that, it took days for the sea state to settle, but if they weren't fighting the wind, they could be here by one in the morning.

We had buried my English clothes earlier except the gansey. Neither my mother nor I could do that. I was dressed in the clothes of a Breton housewife and Maman had laughed. Now, hidden in the dunes sharing a cigarette, a thousand questions waited to be asked but only one mattered.

'Why?' I asked.

She tilted her head as she used to when she would study her subjects.

'When I heard de Gaulle's call to all Frenchmen, and I met the refugees, I knew I had to do something. While your father was alive, I was powerless, but he knew my frustration.' She laughed. 'He knew what I wanted to do and had finally agreed to let me go.'

'He knew,' I said, shocked.

'Our love was born in war,' she said. 'And he knew how much my country and my adopted country meant to me.'

'But why didn't you say?' I asked.

She took a long drag on the cigarette and slowly exhaled. 'Because leaving you was hard enough without seeing your pain. The loss of your father hurt you and I have no doubt you have not begun to deal with Oliver's death, but you and I . . . '

'We are alike,' I said.

'Yes, and no. I see the world in colour and light, and you see it in shapes and numbers.' She smiled. 'You have your father's logic and for that I am glad.'

'But . . . '

'You need to learn to use your heart more,' she said. 'It is as much a guide as your head.'

I leaned forward and her cross fell out from the blouse. She touched it. 'I'm glad you found it. This is what I wanted.'

I went to release the catch, but her hand stopped mine. 'No, it is yours.'

I tried again.

'Let it rest over your heart to remind you,' she said, 'of what is important.'

I dropped my hand. Maman ran her finger over the cross.

'May God protect you,' she said.

There was a noise, then someone singing in German. Maman raised her gun and placed a finger on her lips. Through the grasses the moonlight picked out the buttons on his uniform like baubles on a Christmas tree and then I saw the gun in his hand. We didn't move. He came closer still, singing. We were in the middle of nowhere. Why was he here and not out celebrating?

'*Wer ist da?*' he asked.

Maman looked at me. His question *who is there* was clear.

'*Wer ist da? Zeige dich!*' he said.

I scanned the distance, hearing his command to show ourselves. The cover of the grasses made it hard to see despite the brightness of the moonlight. Hopefully he would move on. He raised his gun and swung around, firing a shot to the right of us. The airmen were to the left of us.

We bent low, but he walked in our direction, pointing the gun. Maman raised hers. He was within her range.

'*Zeige dich!*' he came closer and Maman raised her gun a little higher. She wasn't aiming for the knee, but the heart. I prayed he would pass out for it was clear he was drunk, but he kept walking closer. '*Ich sehe Sie.*'

And then he was there right in front of us, his gun pointed directly at me. He fired and so did Maman. He dropped to the sand and Maman fell back into my arms. The others came out from cover.

The small local man came running. 'Thank God he was alone.'

'We need to bury him,' said Baker.

'Check his pockets first,' Maman coughed.

'Why?' I asked.

'Because he could be carrying plans,' the little man said, rifling through them. 'Nothing but a photograph of a child and . . . this map.' He handed the picture into Maman's hands as I used Papa's gansey to stem the flow of blood from her shoulder.

'There's the signal,' said Baker. 'Quickly, everyone.'

They shifted the soldier and roughly buried him in the grasses. One of the airmen said a quick prayer for his soul.

The dinghy came into view and an airman came and helped me to get Maman to her feet.

'You're coming with us,' I said.

She shook her head. 'Don't fuss, ma petite.'

'But you must come,' I pleaded.

'They will take me to a doctor here.' She looked up at the moon and the paleness of her skin frightened me.

'But . . . '

'No buts.' She lifted her hand.

'I . . . '

She interrupted and said, 'I love you too, but you do not need me; France does.'

She held the gansey to her shoulder. Her face was so pale, and her comrade held her upright.

The first dinghy reached the beach and the airmen climbed in.

'Come on, Dr Tremayne,' the coxswain said, putting a hand on my shoulder.

'You can't stay, ma petite,' she said. 'You know that.'

'But you can come home,' I said.

'No, this is home again.' She touched my face. 'Home is where the heart is. You know that. Your first map.' She collapsed onto the sand.

'Maman, I don't . . . '

'Want to leave me nor I you,' she said.

I helped her to her feet with her comrade.

'Miss Tremayne.' An airman stood at my side.

The man handed me the map from the soldier. Baker took her other side.

'Go, ma petite,' she said. 'If I survive, I will find you. If I don't . . . ' she touched my heart and the cross ' . . . I will be with you.'

I kissed her cheek and ran to the boat.

'But Baker?' I asked as the coxswain rowed us away. No one answered me as I watched them struggle up the beach, praying that I would see her again.

43

A freezing fog obscured everything, and the daylight barely breached it. The Helford River felt more than two hundred and eighty miles away as I stood outside Fleming's new office. I'd arrived back yesterday and would begin my new position tomorrow. Had I learned all I wanted to? No, but I certainly had a greater understanding of what information needed to be conveyed and in what order it needed to be presented.

The door opened and Fleming ushered me in. I glanced around the two desks and both were empty. Fleming waved to the chair in front of the larger of the two.

'What on earth were you thinking?' He paced the room.

I didn't answer.

'If you had been captured . . . ' He stopped and placed his hands on his desk. 'That was, bar one, the most successful of the flotilla's operations but could have easily gone down as the cause for our defeat.'

I looked down at my hands. He was right, completely correct. That fact had haunted me since my return. None of the men involved had any idea though. They were not to blame; I was.

He drew a breath. 'Say something, damn it.'

I raised my glance to meet his. 'I was wrong to go on the operation.'

'That's not what I wanted to hear.' He sank into his chair.

'I could say that the operation wouldn't have gone ahead or if it had they would have missed the beach,' I said, drawing a breath. 'Or because of the delay we never would have found that piece of intelligence.' The map found on the officer showed the plans for new defences being built along the Normandy coast.

He tapped the table. 'Yes, that is the only saving grace in the whole fiasco.'

'Twelve airmen returned and five agents in total,' I said, recalling the relief on their faces of the ones that travelled back with me as we sat in silence on the deck of the boat grateful to be heading back to the Helford.

'Those facts are all that will be recorded.' He picked up a pen and sat down.

'Yes.' The only people who knew I was on the mission were sworn to secrecy as we all had signed the Official Secrets Act.

'Not that you acted as navigator,' Fleming said. 'And crew on a dinghy.'

'Good.' I risked a small smile.

He stared at me. 'Not really,' he said. 'You deserve a medal for stepping in well out of your depth, but no one must know.'

I nodded.

'I've spoken with Warington Smyth and the men involved as well as the airmen.' He rose to his feet again. 'You did not go on this mission.'

'I did not,' I said. 'I spent it in bed with a chill and surfaced on Boxing Day to eat the leftovers.'

'Good.' He pulled a sheet of paper closer.

'My mother?' I swallowed.

He met my glance.

'Did she . . . is she . . . ' I paused.

'She is alive.'

I breathed again. 'Baker?'

'In position as a new agent,' he said.

I looked at him. 'The mouse?'

'Of all the things I've seen in this war, this is the strangest,' he said. 'But the mouse made it, thanks to Baker.'

My hand went to my neck. I breathed deeply until I had control of my emotions. Where before I held back tears, trying to be brave, I heard Maman's voice again: 'Ma petite, tears are the words you cannot yet speak. Let them flow.' But here and now was not the time to do that.

'I'm handing you over completely to the team headed by General Pine and Professor Gamble,' he said. 'From here on your life will be very restricted, and certainly, no more jaunts to France.'

'Fine.' Work was what was important. I would not have Oli, Jean, or any of the many others die in vain. My dreams were haunted by the officer that Maman had killed. It was shoot or be shot, yet, in my sleepless hours, I saw the photo of the little boy who looked so like his father. No one wins in war.

'May I continue to meet Mary Holdsworth?' I asked.

'Yes,' he said. 'She is sound, but no romance.'

I laughed bitterly.

He looked up saying, 'Unless of course it's with me.'

'No worries on that account,' I said.

'Thought not,' he said. 'But had to try my luck.'

'Always,' I said, smiling, then set off to join my new team.

*

In Waterloo station I watched the ebb and flow of people. Caroline should be here in a few minutes if her train was on time. I'd waited for this moment for so long and now I was strangely afraid of it. Above, the clock showed it was five to six. Caroline had been to visit her parents and was on her way back to St Thomas'. Oliver had never said what she looked like but I scanned the many faces more to pass the time than to try and pick her out.

'Merry?' a woman asked.

I spun around and there in front of me was a petite red-haired woman. Her brown eyes sparkled, and it was clear immediately why Oli had fallen for her.

I opened my arms and we hugged, neither of us wanting to let go. Eventually we stepped apart.

'I am so happy to meet you,' I said.

'I feel as if I know you.' Caroline slipped her arm through mine. 'Shall we find a place for a cup of tea? I'm on duty at eight.'

We made our way to a small tearoom not far from the station. Once we had ordered, I found I was at a loss for words.

She dug in her handbag and slid a box across the table. 'This was in Oliver's things. Fleming said I should keep it.'

I recognised the box. It was my mother's engagement ring.

'I refused it when Oliver proposed.' She took a deep breath.

I placed my hand on hers.

'I thought it was the right thing to wait.' She looked up at me.

'I don't think there is a correct way to behave in . . . war.' I slid the box back to her. 'He would want you to have it.' And I knew Maman would too.

'But it's a family heirloom,' she said.

'Oliver was our hope for the family continuing,' I said.

'But you . . .'

'No, I made my choice a long time ago,' I said, and Jake's smile came to mind. 'So, please take the ring and wear it. He would want that.'

She shook her head. 'It doesn't feel right.'

'You loved him,' I said, and her expression told me she did. 'Then it is right.' I smiled at her. 'He would want you to have it. Fleming was correct.'

Caroline made a face but then opened the box and slipped the delicate ruby and diamond ring onto her right hand. 'Only he could put it on the other,' she said.

The tea arrived and she asked, 'Are you heading back to Cornwall?'

'Not for the foreseeable future,' I said. 'My work is all up here now.' I thought of the team I'd met today.

'Hopefully we can meet more frequently.' She poured the tea. 'Oliver was so proud of all you've achieved. He said you had the finest brain and weren't afraid of using it.'

I laughed.

'He also mentioned all you had given up, acquiring your degrees.' She added milk to her tea and passed it to me. 'Matron is a bit like that.'

'Oh, goodness, I have this picture of a dragon,' I said.

'Not at all,' she said. 'She is a determined beautiful woman. Nursing is her calling.'

'That sounds much better,' I said. 'How old is she?'

'Forty,' Caroline answered.

The tea was weak but warm and I sipped it, seeing my future.

'I love nursing, but I also want a family.' She glanced quickly at me.

'Good,' I said. 'I would hate to think you felt you couldn't love someone else.'

'Thank you,' she said.

I picked up her hand. The ruby caught the light like the ones in the cross about my neck. 'Oli would want you to find happiness. I know this.'

'I wish I could be like you and matron,' she said.

'Why?' I asked.

'It would be wonderful to have my career be as fulfilling as love.'

I swallowed. 'It's not for everyone.'

She glanced at her watch. 'I must dash.' She stood and dug in her purse.

'I'll take care of the bill,' I said.

'Are you sure?'

'Yes, I am.' I stood and gave her a hug. 'Let's meet again soon.'

'Yes, please.' She raced out the door.

I sat back down and poured the remainder of the tea into my cup and watched the leaves swirl and settle to the bottom. I couldn't read them because everything was too murky.

PART SEVEN

44

25 February 1944

Life had developed a rhythm of work, sleep, work and occasionally eat. I smoked like a fiend, had developed a fondness for gin that might be bordering on the unhealthy, and had found there was solace in work. I'd arrived home an hour ago and made tea. I'd taken it out into the garden where the daffodils bloomed, making my heart ache for Cornwall and the past. Each day I thought of my mother and promised her when this wretched war was over, I would find Jake and tell him how I felt. I'd half written letters and burned them. I needed to do it in person. I'd changed and he might have as well. Most importantly, his feelings for me might have altered with the absence. Therefore, I needed to speak to him.

Mary, despite me telling her not to, kept me up to date with what little she knew. My time working with the flotilla seemed decades ago instead of years. I met regularly with Fleming, and Harling too, when he was back in London. He had escaped the Citadel and was back in active service. On rare nights out, I'd seen Muriel sometimes with Fleming and sometimes not. Margaret Priestly kept me up to date with the volatility of that relationship. Not that I was one to judge these things but they loved each other in their own way.

Entering the kitchen, I considered cooking, but it was too much effort. Toast would suffice. The telephone rang and I debated answering it. No one except Fleming and Gamble called me. I lifted the handset.

'Chelsea five-six-five,' I answered, thinking it could be Constance's cousin Lady Alice. She might be in London with her husband who was a member of parliament.

'Merry?' Mary's clipped tones asked.

'Yes.' I smiled.

'Are you alone?' she asked.

There was only one reason she would ask that question. 'Yes.'

'I'll come over,' she said.

My heart stopped as the reason sunk in. 'Jake?'

'He's missing, presumed dead.'

The wall took my weight as I slumped against it.

'Merry, are you there?' she asked.

'Yes,' I said.

'I'm coming over,' she insisted.

'No. I'm fine,' I lied. 'Where? Do you know?'

'Italy, I believe,' she said. 'Gerry's devastated.'

I wasn't sure what to say or ask.

'You shouldn't be alone,' she said.

'No,' I said. 'I'm good at being alone, it's my natural state.' I glanced about the hallway expecting everything to be misplaced and broken but the black and white floor tiles were exactly placed as they should be, in rigid order.

Alone.

No Jake in my future. I sucked in air forcing myself to breath. 'Don't worry, Mary, I'll see you next week as planned.'

I put the phone down and went to the kitchen. Lighting another cigarette, I poured cold tea into my cup. The tea was tasteless, and the cigarette didn't do what it needed to do. I was numb.

The words that Mo had recited came to me.

A thing for fools, this,
Love,
But a holy thing,
To love what death can touch.
For your life has lived in me;
Your laugh once lifted me;
Your word was a gift to me . . .

I couldn't recall the rest. Too many times I have loved what death can touch.

Announced by a blast of cold air, Constance arrived. I was always grateful for her unquestioning company. But in this moment my grief knew no bounds and I turned from her.

Constance took one look at me, went straight to the sitting room and came back with the cognac bottle and two glasses. She poured us both a large measure. She raised her glass and knocked it back in one. I was still sucking in air and couldn't stop the sobs that had begun shaking my body. Constance filled a smaller measure into her glass and set about the kitchen making toast.

She placed it in front of me. 'Try.'

I nodded.

'When did you last eat?' she asked as she lifted my wrist, which was so thin, the skin transparent. 'I've been holding back commenting. I know the stress you are under even though we never say a word. I can only put two and two together and come up with five.'

I frowned.

'Mr Lloyd at number two told me of the man who stayed back in nineteen forty-two.'

I snuffled.

'For a while you bloomed while you were with this unmappable man,' she said. 'Now you are all work.'

After blowing my nose, I tried a corner of toast.

'I know we all are,' she continued.

'He's dead,' I managed to say.

'Oh, Merry.' She came around the table and wrapped me in her arms.

'He's dead,' I repeated, trying to make myself believe it. 'And I didn't tell him how I felt.'

'Don't you think he knew?' she asked, rubbing my back. 'I could tell by your happiness that you were in love. Regret is the hardest thing,' she said. 'Especially regret over love.'

I raised the glass and knocked back the contents.

'I'll run the bath for you,' she said. 'And you need to try and sleep. These sixteen-hour days are taking their toll on you.'

I couldn't argue. I consisted of eighty per cent coffee, ten per cent nicotine and the rest wasn't worth talking about. But the former two had kept me going in front of generals, admirals and a prime minister. I'd fought for the beach samples, checked beach gradients, and I had drawn and redrawn and drawn again the beaches of Normandy until I could see nothing else. I was Merry the mapper and that was reason enough to keep going. It had to be.

*

Each day was like the one before. It was easy to forget who I was in the many calculations. We worked day and night and that suited me. How I was feeling didn't really matter. Death seemed to be everywhere. The once happy house was gloomy with Constance missing Hester and me mourning.

I rubbed my fists into my eyes. They ached. Looking up, Commander Fleming stood in front of me.

'I thought you should see this. It's Nipper's final article. Holdsworth found it and sent it to the newspaper.' He handed me a copy of the *Washington Post*. 'Page five.'

February 1, 1944

I've been writing these dispatches for a while now. Sending you my thoughts on what I see and some of the men I've spoken to. All of us have a dream of the perfect place that we go to in our minds when we need a break from the reality of now.

Like most Americans, I thought mine was of the cottage with the white picket fence located just off of Main Street with the country store and the white church steeple in view. The Russians have their dacha, the Spanish have their villas. And for many of my British comrades it's a pint of warm ale in a country pub. Everyone has their ideal.

Of late, I've found myself thinking about a place surrounded by ancient stone hedges holding wildflowers and wildlife. As this war wears on and I've been away from those picket fences of my childhood, I find I long for grass greener than I'd ever seen, cliffs like those home in Maine, and a little cottage by a creek. It has a stone hedge with towering ash, beech and wild cherry trees. That is where my heart now lies. It is where I dream about as the bombs hit, colleagues die, and we spend another year immersed in this war.

I left the United States in May 1940. It's almost four years now and, in that time, I've learned what fear is. I've learned what resilience is and I've learned what kindness is. Sadly I've also seen what discrimination is because I've seen it through other people's eyes. I've watched my own countrymen think less of their coloured comrades. I've been witness to women denied the life they want because women can't have both a career and a family. I've been privileged to know a Jewish man who faced his fears to fight this war, to make a difference so that others wouldn't see their families taken from them.

I am not the same man I was. Like many I have loved and lost. I have tried and failed. I am weary. But we must not stop until the wrongs are made right and we are all safe and we don't have to be brave.

Jake Russell
Italy

I lifted my eyes to Fleming.

He put a hand on my shoulder. 'I thought you should see it.'

I couldn't speak so I nodded.

'I'm sorry, Merry,' he said. 'Nipper's death has hit us all but you loved him.'

'You always said love was messy.' I blew my nose. 'I don't suppose you've heard anything?'

'I spoke with Holdsworth but he had no further details of how it happened,' he said.

I handed the paper back to him.

'Keep it,' he said. 'Can I take you to dinner?'

I looked at the work in front of me. There was so much to do.

'You need to eat even if you come back here after,' he said.

I blew my nose again and collected my handbag. I needed to eat so that I could think clearly. That was all that mattered.

*

February had become March. Magnolia trees bloomed in the parks. They were joyful on the darkest days and mine felt dark, but I had a purpose. That kept me going. A discreet cough alerted me to the young sub-lieutenant standing in front of me. His clear bright eyes were familiar. I'd met him previously when I joined Fleming for drinks in January. The young man had been fresh from Eton, top scholar in Latin and Greek, and fluent in other languages. By rights he should be at Oxford or Cambridge but as this war marched on, the young were taking the place of those lost, and my heart broke with it.

On that night he had regaled us with his last trip to Cornwall. He had been on the branch line to Helston and the train had teemed with US troops. At Praze-an-Beeble Station, the station guard had called out, 'Praze, Praze, Praze.' The black American GI sitting beside the young man had leaned out the window and replied, 'Amen.' The young sub-lieutenant had explained to the GI that the village was called Praze-an-Beeble. They had laughed together until they had reached Helston.

'Excuse me, Dr Tremayne,' he said.

'Yes.' I smiled recalling his name: Tom Martin.

'I'm trying to locate Commander Fleming.' I paused. 'Dr Priestly said to check with you if I hadn't located him.'

'He was here an hour ago,' I said, 'but he didn't mention where he was heading.'

His shoulders dropped. 'Thank you.'

'Can I help in any way?' I asked.

His serious face paled. 'It's his girlfriend.'

'Muriel?' I asked.

'I'm afraid she's dead,' he said, looking down. 'She was found with her dog staying loyally by her side. The rest of the building was fine but masonry fell on her and they need Commander Fleming to identify her.'

I covered my mouth with my hand, thinking of the vibrant woman. This was awful.

'Have you tried his club?' I asked.

'I have,' he said. 'And Dr Priestly has rung several possible locations.'

Professor Gamble walked in with a cup of tea.

'Have you seen Commander Fleming, sir?' asked Sub-Lieutenant Martin.

'He left the building with a blonde-haired woman about twenty minutes ago,' said Professor Gamble.

'It might be a long shot,' I said, collecting my coat and hat, 'but he may be in another unlikely spot. I won't be long.' I led the sub-lieutenant out of the Admiralty.

'Where are we going?' he asked as we both battled the March wind.

'He once took me to a small tearoom, and it came to mind when the professor mentioned a blonde-haired woman.'

The young man sent me a look, but I knew my old boss well. I'd met the blonde woman in question at a dinner dance when we had all expected Muriel to be his date. The tearoom was where no one would think of looking for him.

We turned a corner and, like the previous time, the windows were obscured with steam. The bell rang as I pushed the door open and there at the back table sat Fleming with the woman in question. Sub-lieutenant Martin squared his shoulders, ready to interrupt.

I put a hand on his arm, saying, 'I'll get him for you.'

I knew how hard it was to hear these words and to this day I was still grateful that it was Mary who broke the news to me. She understood. I could do this for Fleming.

As I approached the table Fleming looked up and his eyes flashed. 'This is a surprise.'

'Excuse the intrusion,' I said, sending a smile to the woman who wasn't responding in kind. 'You're needed urgently.'

Fleming rose without question, put some coins on the table and excused himself. I followed him out of the door and watched the colour drain from his face as the sub-lieutenant spoke to him. I had wanted to tell him myself but maybe this was for the best. He glanced at me.

'Ian, I'm so sorry,' I touched his arm. 'Would you like me to come with you?'

He closed his eyes for a moment then met my glance.

'Thank you, Merry,' he said, 'but no.'

He hailed a taxi and disappeared. My heart made the journey with him even if I wasn't there at his side. I understood the need to be alone to try and come to grips with the enormity of the loss. It created a gaping hole in your life. Each day I navigated the crater of grief where Jake should be with care trying not to think and only to work.

'Thank you for . . . ' The young man's words trailed away.

'It's what you do for a friend,' I said. Light rain had begun to fall and I turned the collar of my coat up as we walked briskly through the rain. This war had to end.

45

5 June 1944

The moment was here. All the hours, elevations, gradations, photographs, logistics were complete. The maps were drawn and printed. Endless hours thinking about slopes and beach materials were for this moment. I wasn't sure I wanted to think about sand ever again. Now I stood at the back of the room, trying not to draw attention to myself. This was certainly a case of don't speak unless spoken to. Weather reports varied wildly, and the window for invasion was so tight. Three possible days and we'd passed one already. Time, tide, moon and weather would mean success or failure and it had to succeed.

Beside me, and as quiet, was Professor Gamble. We were here to answer any questions as they arose. I prayed there were none. The rest of the team, the best geographers, hydrographers, climatologists and engineers from Britain, the United States and Canada were on call.

So many factors had come into play in choosing this time. It needed to be low tide with three miles' visibility for naval gun support, air cover and bombing. A full moon needed for night-time actions. Calm seas which we didn't have. All these things circled in my mind. So many things we could know, but the weather forecast was only reliable two days ahead and weather moved in on the fourth. Now it was the fifth and the sea state was not good.

General Eisenhower studied the charts and looked at the latest forecast. The great map, my map, on the wall showed both sides of the channel and where the men were based. Already the 29th Division of the US Army had left the Helford and the Fal. Right now, as these leaders debated, those troops were on a rolling sea and no doubt their stomachs were roiling in conditions that were far from ideal.

The first opportunity had passed. A storm had raged through and now they had to decide. If they didn't go tomorrow, the sixth, it would be another month before the tides would be favourable again. It was essential the tides were low enough to see the submerged defences. Without that visibility, the casualties would be too high. But they needed the water too to bring the equipment in. So many factors to consider and it was my map that they were studying. I prayed we had asked the right questions and it told the story of success.

The decision was made. They would go tomorrow, the sixth. Gamble and I left the room both elated and exhausted, feeling our job was done, but in many ways our work was only beginning. More information would arrive, and maps would need immediate updating. The army would struggle getting through the Norman bocage. I'd tried as best I could to explain this to the American officers in the run-up, but it wasn't until one of their own, Captain Webster, explained it to them did they understand or seem to.

As the hours wore on, I slept in short bursts on a chair and then worked for hours updating the maps with the incoming intelligence from aerial photographs and reports filed. The loss of life was heart-breaking but the invasion worked. Normandy was not the expected location, thanks to all the hard work sending out false information.

Days later, I cried with relief when the operation seemed to succeed. There was hope at last. Maybe the tide had finally turned in our favour.

46

8 May 1945

Outside, bells were ringing and the noise of the joy penetrated even to the basement of the Admiralty. It was a Tuesday and Victory in Europe Day and I was alone, packing up my desk. I was no longer needed and after all this time I would be returning to Oxford. It was a strange thought especially after the intense months bringing us to this point.

The war in Europe was won. The maps covering the walls showed our success but not the cost. The nameless men and women who had given their lives for this day ran through my mind, like the litanies I'd heard in the Breton churches as a child, the names of those I knew: Blessed be Oli . . . the fearless; blessed be Benedict . . . the healer; blessed be Jean Piron . . . the young; blessed be Muriel . . . the beautiful; and blessed be Jake, the kind. Those litanies in church had gone on for hours and if I added the others whose names I did not know, like the German with the photo of his son, I would never finish the task at hand.

I walked to the map. Oli had died somewhere over the channel, and Jake somewhere in Italy. It was not a map I would make. It was not a story I wanted to tell. They were all in my heart.

I picked up my bag and climbed the stairs. Tomorrow I would

leave London and head to Cornwall to resolve the farm then on to Oxford to lecture and continue my research. Life would find a rhythm again.

'Merry,' Fleming called.

'What on earth are you doing here when there is the biggest party ever happening out on the streets?' I asked, walking towards him.

'A bit like you, I imagine.' He took my arm. 'Counting and remembering the lost.'

I closed my eyes for a moment. I was done with tears, but emotions still lived too close under my skin.

'A drink?'

'That would be good,' I said as we walked to the main doors together.

'Where would you like to go?' he asked.

Looking at the conga line working its way down the street, I said, 'Wherever we can find one.'

'I like your thinking.' He held out his arms and we followed the conga line out onto Horse Guards and ended up in the Ritz. Fleming knew half the people and I saw a few familiar faces. It wasn't long before I was slightly drunk and in need of air. I waved farewell to Fleming, collected my things and walked into my ex-fiancé George with a pretty petite woman. It was strange to see him with another woman. Turning, I looked for an exit but there was none. Besides, sometimes you had to stand your ground and face your past.

'Merry, so glad I bumped into you,' he said, turning to his date. 'Excuse me for a minute. Merry is an old friend.'

I smiled at his turn of phrase.

'I'll head into the bar,' she said, casting me a hands-off-my-man glance. It was all I could do in my tipsy state to refrain from saying I didn't want him. But he had proved a good ally in work these past few years, always finding exactly who we needed when we needed army input.

'I just wanted to say well done, Merry.'

'Why?' I asked, trying to read his features.

'Well, it's a damn good thing you threw me over and chose your career.' He paused. 'Your maps.'

I was surprised as my name was nowhere on them.

'Most people don't know but I could tell your work and I overheard Fleming talking with Dill.'

'Really?'

'Shame you'll never receive the recognition you deserve but that's the way of the world.' He laughed. 'But if you'd married me you wouldn't have been free to do what you did.'

He was drunk too.

'I think I should say thanks.'

He planted a wet kiss on my cheek and said, 'Still bloody beautiful.' He went to join his date and I emerged into a London filled with light, grateful too that I hadn't married George but for different reasons than his.

Streetlamps shone and windows glowed golden. I worked my way through the crowds on Piccadilly and past the couples making love with abandon. Life went on and I wouldn't let jealousy eat away at my joy that we'd won. Hitler was defeated.

By the time I reached Constance's, I had turned down a few dances, a half a dozen drinks and my head was ringing. I fell through the front door, expecting to find no one home, but Constance was. Her face was blotchy and her eyes red.

Hester was due home in two days and Constance had been full of excitement. This change surprised me. I sat next to her on the sofa and took her hand in mine. I couldn't imagine what news she had heard on this day of celebrations that could trigger this. Her expression when she looked at me was so sad.

'Do you want to tell me?' I took her hand in mine.

She shook her head. 'I don't know what to do.'

'Can I help?' I asked.

'No.' She pulled her hand from mind and stood. 'I've brought this on myself.' She paced the room. 'Hester will never forgive me.' Her hand found her stomach when she stopped in front of the window.

'She loves you.' I stood and walked to her.

'She won't when she discovers I've betrayed her,' she said.

I frowned. They were two of the most intelligent and loving people I knew, and I couldn't think of anything Constance could do bar leaving Hester that would shake Hester's love.

'Have you fallen for someone else?'

She turned to me with her hands still stroking her stomach. 'I'm pregnant.'

That was the last thing I expected. 'How?'

She opened her eyes wide and gave me a look.

'I know how,' I said. 'But who and how?'

She paced the length of the room again.

'Does the father know?' I asked.

'No,' she said. 'He's dead.'

Then I knew. It was easy to see. 'Benedict?'

She nodded. 'One night, after we'd been nearly hit by a V-2, we came back here and drank. Drank way too much and it happened,' she said. 'I was stupid but didn't really consider that pregnancy was an issue. I'm forty-four.' She sat down. 'The awful thing is . . . part of me is thrilled. I've always wanted a child.'

I joined her on the sofa, taking her hands in mine. 'Hester will forgive you.'

'I don't think she will.' Constance blew her nose. 'It's not as if everyone won't know soon.'

'I can't argue with that,' I said. 'But most people don't know you are a couple.'

434

'We can't show our love,' she said.

'What will you do?' I asked, thinking about her return to Oxford.

'I will keep the child,' she said, stroking her stomach. 'I will lose everything, but the only thing that matters is Hester.'

'Your family?' I asked.

'I imagine my brother will be fine,' she said. 'His wife less so. My cousin Alice will be wonderful. In fact, I may go to her in Cornwall.'

'Hester will surprise you,' I said. 'You weren't having an affair. She is a mature person who will see you made a mistake.'

She tucked her hankie back into her pocket. 'I can pray you are right.'

'I know I am,' I said. 'Can I make you something to eat?' I rose, waiting for her answer.

'Yes,' she said. 'And thank you.'

'Thank you for what?' I stood and held out my hand to her.

She took it and stood, looking tired. 'For not judging.'

I gave her a hug. 'There is nothing to judge. You are human and as humans we sometimes make mistakes.' This I knew too well.

*

Constance and I walked back to the house after a long stroll, not talking except when spoken to by the many revellers still celebrating on the bright clear morning. It was now past two and we were both tired and hungry.

'What do you plan to do now?' Constance asked as we entered the house.

'Back to Oxford,' I said, taking off my hat.

'I shall have to resign my position,' Constance said with a sigh. 'But it will be worth it.' She ran her hand across her stomach.

435

'I wrote to the head of the department last week,' I said, putting the soup on the stove to warm.

'They'll bite your hand off and be thrilled to have you back.' Constance sat down, allowing me to fuss over her.

With the bread under the grill, I laid the table, thinking about work. I would miss being part of something that was so much bigger than anything I would ever work on again. Sadly no one would know what I'd been a part of because the work had been so secret, as George had kindly pointed out.

'I'll miss the dreaming spires, but I have so longed to be a mother that I can't quite believe that it's real.' She smiled sadly. 'God knows at my age it's a miracle.'

'I am so happy for you,' I said. 'The funny thing is I never knew this about you.'

Constance laughed bitterly. 'Some dreams are best kept to oneself, especially when they are verging on the fantastical.'

That I understood. Some hopes and dreams were so secret we didn't even acknowledge them to ourselves. But, unlike Constance, mine would stay secret. I didn't need to share these private thoughts, and with luck they would fade from my consciousness.

'Hello?' Hester called from the front hall.

Constance's glance met mine. Hester wasn't due back until tomorrow. Constance stood and I gave her hand a squeeze then watched her walk through to Hester.

I took the soup off the stove, laid another place and went into the small garden. My heart was so full of love for both of them and I believed if anyone could make this situation work, they could, despite the huge changes it would mean for them both.

To distract myself, I set to weeding the vegetable patch and collecting some potatoes to bulk out the soup to feed three. I didn't want to think about my plans going forward but forced myself to do it. Since 1939 I had had one goal: to do all within my abilities to help win the war. Although it still raged in Asia it was won here and I was no longer required. Would I find the return to Oxford anywhere near as stimulating? I needed to refocus and locate my excitement of the past.

'It's safe to come in,' Hester said, standing at the door to the kitchen, and she smiled at me. Taking the basket of potatoes with me, I walked up to her, studying her face. Tears pooled in her eyes.

'Are you OK?' I asked.

She opened her arms and hugged me. 'A little bit broken, to be honest, but I love Constance more than life itself.'

I stepped back. Her smile was genuine, and I breathed a sigh of relief.

'I always wanted to have children and gave up that idea so many years ago,' she said, then blew her nose. 'God knows what my mother will say or anyone else for that matter, but Constance and I will make it work.'

'I know you will.' I hugged Hester again and saw Constance standing by the table.

'This child will be so loved and so blessed to have you both,' I said.

Constance walked to us and took Hester's hand in hers. 'I'm forgiven and so grateful to be loved by this woman.'

'Now, shall we all have something to eat?' said Hester, walking to the stove. 'We have so much to catch up on.'

'We do,' I said, relieved that my faith in love was justified. When love worked, it was a glorious thing.

47

On the train to Oxford, I opened my map to my life ahead. By the time we'd reached Didcot, I'd plotted the next few years until I would hopefully be tenured, my planned travels and the papers I would write. It would be strange to be teaching again but I was looking forward to it. This was the way ahead, leaving the war behind. Looking out at the passing countryside, things appeared unchanged, but everything had. Women had taken on roles that previously had been restricted and society had evened out somewhat. There was still a long way to go but hope filled me. I would not have nephews and nieces to look forward to, but Constance and Hester had asked if I would be godmother to their child and I had accepted readily.

The train came into Oxford station, and I couldn't help recalling my first visit at sixteen. Excitement abounded, and some of that remained in my thirty-year-old self. I'd achieved a great deal and there was still so much ahead of me. With a spring in my step, I walked to my old college. My appointment with the head of geography was in an hour, which would give me time to stop by my rooms.

The sun beat down as I made my way to Somerville College. At the gate I slowed, taking a deep breath of the roses still in bloom. The porter emerged with a welcome grin. 'Dr Tremayne, how lovely to have you back.'

'It's good to be here,' I said.

He nodded and handed me my keys. 'Rooms ready and waiting.'

'Thank you.' I smiled at him then glanced at my watch. I would need to be quick.

'If you wish, I can bring your bags up for you,' he said. 'You don't want to be late.'

I nodded, left them with him and strolled to the school of Geography. I arrived with five minutes to spare. I hadn't seen the head of the school since 1940. Our paths had never crossed in our war work. We would have a lot to catch up on.

'He won't be a minute, Dr Tremayne. Would you like a tea?' his secretary asked.

'No, thank you.' I smiled, not envying her job of soothing nerves and calming disgruntled lecturers and students. But I was neither and I planned on celebrating my return with my old tutor later this evening.

The door to the office opened.

'Ah, Dr Tremayne, do come in,' he said.

I walked in, and he waved to the seat in front of his desk. Something wasn't right but I couldn't pinpoint it. This was a done deal, a formality welcoming me back onto the faculty.

Professor Timpson sat then leaned forward, resting his forearms on his large desk. I perched with my hands clasped and ankles crossed. The dean looked at me across the large book-covered desk.

'We are pleased you have decided to return but I won't beat about the bush,' he said. 'I'm sorry to inform you, your former role of demonstrator is the only position available.'

'I was a lecturer in thirty-nine,' I said almost sputtering in my surprise.

'You were indeed,' he said.

'Who is taking my position?' I kept my voice even and reasonable. This was a mistake that could be resolved once I understood the problem.

'I have filled it with a man returning from the war.' He tented his fingers and wouldn't look me in the eye.

Running through all the possible candidates, I could think of none. I had worked with the most senior geographers in my role in Operation Overlord and all had returned to their previous positions.

'And his qualifications are equal to mine?' I asked.

The dean looked up briefly. 'He is better qualified.'

'How so?' I asked.

'It is not for me to explain the decisions that I have made,' he said.

'You seem to forget that women also worked to win the war,' I said.

'There is nothing you can say on this matter.' He laughed. 'You left a good job at the ISTD drawing maps to become Commander Fleming's secretary. You should be grateful we are welcoming you back and you can work your way to lecturer again.'

I blinked, trying to absorb his words. Oxford. That had been my driving goal. Did I now want it no matter the terms?

'Your college is happy for you to remain in your rooms.' He stood. 'The first department meeting is tomorrow. You can act as secretary.'

Bile rose in my throat and I bit back my reply. He didn't deserve one. It wouldn't change anything, and it was clear that no one would acknowledge the work that women had done; that would upset the system. There was only one answer.

'Thank you very much for your offer of demonstrator but I will take my skills elsewhere,' I said, rising to my feet.

'Nowhere is like Oxford.'

I laughed. 'And we can be grateful for that.'

I strode out of his office and into the bright sunshine. I had no idea what I was going to do. It had never crossed my mind that I wouldn't have a place at Oxford. Without thinking, I found myself heading to the rooms of my old tutor, Miss Price. I waved to the porter and climbed the staircase.

'Merry, I thought you'd come.' She ushered me in and closed the door behind us.

'You know what they've done?' I asked.

'I fought it,' she said. 'The man only has a BA.'

'I suspected as much.' I settled into the comfort of her sofa.

'But he's a veteran and has a family.' She poured me a large sherry.

I ground my teeth. 'So, all my war work doesn't count.'

She handed me the glass. 'Not in their eyes.'

'But to demote me,' I said.

'I know, but you can show your worth.' She poured one for herself and sat opposite. 'It wouldn't take long to show them all.'

'No, I refused,' I said. 'I'd rather go farm in Cornwall than be nothing more than a glorified secretary.' I took a large swig of the amber liquid.

'Merry, you must continue,' she said, putting her glass down. 'Your mind is a valuable thing.'

'Clearly not.' I knocked back the rest of the sherry and rose to my feet.

'I am truly sorry,' she said.

'Thank you,' I said. 'I will clear out of my rooms and be gone by tomorrow.'

She held her hand to her heart. 'I feel this is the wrong decision.'

'I don't. It is the only right one,' I said. My steps were light as I set off to clear my rooms.

Hester came into the kitchen with the post. I was making a list of universities to contact. It had been a month since I walked away from Oxford and things didn't look good. Constance had said my room would always be available here and if I sold Kestle I would have enough money to live for a while. I hadn't yet decided to sell but it seemed the most realistic thing to do as managing a farm was something that I had never wanted or planned to do.

'Here's your post, including one from America,' Hester said, handing it to me. The letter was postmarked Boston, and my heart did a little flutter. *Jake*. But a letter couldn't be written from the grave so most likely it would be Joe Gamble.

Cambridge, Massachusetts

Dear Merry,
I hope this letter finds you well and that your return to academic life wasn't too much of a shock. I must confess that planning lectures doesn't have the same adrenalin rush that planning the invasion had.

Life back home feels unchanged. It's good to be with my family. They have grown so much during my sojourn in London.

I know you are committed to your life in Oxford, but I'm afraid I mentioned you to an old colleague who heads the geography department at a women's college in Western Massachusetts. Mount Holyoke College was founded in 1837 and has produced our first female cabinet member Harriet Perkins and many other fine scholars, including my wife. They need a new professor for the geography and

*geology department, and I thought with your drive and keen
mind you would be the perfect candidate. Patrick Wendell
will be in London the second week of July and staying
at the Over-Seas Club in Park Place. Even if you are not
interested in the position, do meet him. Patrick is a breath
of fresh air and is so keen on women's higher education he
verges on fanatical.*

Wishing you all the best.

Yours sincerely,
Joe

I dropped the letter on the table and Constance came up to me.

'Are you all right?' Hester asked as she joined us. Both sets of eyes studied me and I handed them the letter.

'This is marvellous,' said Constance. 'Of course we'll miss you.' She gave my shoulders a squeeze. 'And I've always wanted to visit Boston.'

'I don't have the job,' I said.

'They'll snap you up in a minute, and America, how exciting,' Hester added.

'A new start, and all those lovely eager brains to train,' Constance said. 'You'd love that.'

'Of course, you won't be around to look after the giant.' Hester stroked Constance's rather large stomach. They had both come up from Cornwall to see a consultant. The appointment was tomorrow.

'And it is the second week of July so you had better call the club this minute,' Hester said, pushing me out of the kitchen and into the hallway.

'I suppose there is no time like the present.' I picked up the handset and asked the operator for the Over-Seas Club. After it connected I asked, 'May I leave a message for Professor Wendell please?'

'He walked in the door this minute. Would you like to speak with him?' the receptionist asked.

I drew a breath. 'Yes.'

'Hello, Wendell, here,' a man said.

'Hello, Professor Wendell, this is Dr Meredith Tremayne. Professor Gamble said to contact you,' I said.

'I am delighted you rang,' he said. 'When can we meet? Today?'

A glance at the long case clock said it was five. 'I could be with you by six.'

'Wonderful,' he said. 'See you then.'

Both Constance and Hester were standing by the kitchen door, listening.

'Wear the blue dress,' Hester said.

'Why that one?' I asked.

She laughed. 'It's my favourite and it brings out your eyes.'

I made a face. 'He's not interviewing me for my looks.'

'It never hurts,' Constance said as she nudged me up the stairs.

I laughed as I dashed up to my room. I didn't have time to dither. The blue dress it was. I wasn't sure about moving to America, but I could use a new start.

*

My meeting with the charming Professor Wendell had gone well and he offered me the position on the spot. I liked him immediately and I said I would give him a response by the end of the week. It was a big decision and he understood that.

He had apologised that he had a dinner engagement so I left him in the lounge. At the front desk, the receptionist came out to me.

'Dr Tremayne, I've just taken a call for you. You are to go straight to the Savoy's American Bar as your mother will meet you there.'

I stood still, unable to move. 'My mother?'

'Yes, the woman speaking was very clear. I was just on my way into the lounge to inform you.' She smiled.

'Thank you,' I said, not believing that this could be true. But it must be. I'd had no news of my mother in over a year. Fleming had only been able to discover that her network had been betrayed. Each day I had hoped she could be alive. What had she said? 'If I am alive I will find you and if I'm not I am with you.'

The walk to the Savoy passed in a blur. I could not recall one detail. My mouth was dry as I entered the hotel and took the familiar journey to the bar.

Maman sat at a table in the corner. There was elegance in her pose. She put on glasses to scan the menu. I walked towards her, and she looked up. She smiled and the past years disappeared from her face.

'Ma petite,' she said as she stood, and I walked into her arms. 'You received the message. Constance said you were at an interview.'

I nodded, unable to speak, too much emotion, too close to the surface. Maman was real and alive and in front of me.

'I was about to order. What would you like to drink?' She waved her hand and I noticed she was wearing a gold band on her wedding finger. It was not the one my father gave her.

'A pink gin,' I said, picking up her hand in mine.

'You miss nothing,' she said, smiling.

'Who? When?' I was stunned.

'Don't look so shocked,' she said.

'But I am,' I said.

She laughed. 'I am not the same woman who crossed the

channel, and I don't think you are the same woman you were before either.' She placed a finger under my chin. 'You've changed and so have I.'

'You have married,' I said, trying to take it in.

'Yes, I'm on honeymoon,' she said.

The waiter arrived and I held back the many questions until we had ordered.

'You will meet him shortly, but I wanted some time alone with you,' Maman said.

'Will you live in Kestle?' I asked.

'*Non*, that is no longer my home,' she said. 'I will return to France with Antoine. We were in the resistance together and I found there was still love in my heart.' Her eyes danced.

'So what will become of Kestle?' I asked.

'It is yours, ma petite,' she said.

Our drinks arrived.

'Are you heading back to Oxford?' she asked.

I blinked. I was thinking of her and her marriage yet she had moved past it as if it didn't need to be discussed.

'I have left Oxford,' I said.

'What will you do?' she asked. 'That was all you wanted.'

I laughed bitterly. 'I suppose, like for you, things change but, in this case, they didn't want me.'

'*Non*?'

'Well, not the woman I am now,' I said. 'They wanted me to take a lower role because a veteran coming back with a lesser degree needed the position.'

'I see,' she said. 'You are brave to walk away.' She twisted the glass in her hands. 'So, you will become a farmer like your father.'

'No,' I said.

'What do you want?' she asked. 'You have always been so passionate about your study and teaching others.'

'True.' I looked at her. 'I've been offered a position at a women's college in the United States.'

She opened her eyes wide. 'This sounds good, very good.'

'It's an unknown,' I said.

'Our lives are unknown. It will become only what we make from it with the chances we are given,' she said. 'Ma petite, nothing has a guarantee. When I fell in love with your father, I didn't know I would lose him when we should still have years in front of us. You are now thirty and still young. Follow your passion, be open, and, above all, live and love.'

I drew a deep breath. I could see she was right.

'What of the man that you loved?' she asked.

I swallowed and shook my head.

'Oh, Merry, this is hard.' She took my hands in hers. 'I cannot tell you what to do, but like me I think you deserve a new start.' She squeezed my hands. 'It is not easy to be brave.'

She looked up and smiled.

'Here is Antoine.' From the look on her face, I was a bit envious and this was wrong. I should be thrilled that my mother was in love and had found something good in the awfulness of war.

I stood, angry with myself. Just because I had lost love, I shouldn't be bitter that my mother had found it again.

'Ah, Elise was correct when she said how beautiful you were,' he said, taking my hand in his. 'I want you to know that I am honoured that your mother has accepted me. I am the most fortunate man alive.'

His brown eyes smiled when he looked at my mother and her expression matched his. He waved the waiter over and ordered a bottle of champagne.

'We must toast to love and life,' he said. 'I am grateful for both.'

48

1 September 1945

The day was unbelievably hot as I unpacked. Despite crossing the Atlantic and a few days in New York City, I still couldn't believe I was here in South Hadley, Massachusetts, and in a shared house with several other female faculty members. The fall term, as it was called, began in four days.

I hung one of my mother's paintings of Frenchman's Creek on the wall by my bed. Although South Hadley was rural, with farms all around, the land here was different from Cornwall. Out of my third-floor window I could see the foothills leading to the Holyoke Range. Yesterday, I'd been shown the Connecticut river and the boathouse. Professor Wendell had been delighted to hear of my experience of rowing when we'd chatted. I paused to look out of the window again; before long this view wouldn't feel so alien.

There was a knock on the door and I opened it to find Patricia O'Leary from the room next door. She was the college archivist.

'Thought you might need some tea,' said Patricia, handing me a tall glass with ice and lemon. Her round freckled face held bright hazel eyes that spoke of a fierce intelligence. She was reputed to be an unbeatable golfer and in her spare hours was never far from the college's course, I'd been told.

'Tea?' I asked, taking it from her.

She grinned. 'Iced tea is ideal for this weather. It's set to hit ninety again today.'

There was not a breath of wind to cool us either. The smaller windows flanking the large picture window were wide open.

'But we need to enjoy it while we have it.' She leaned against the large desk I'd been allocated.

'How quickly does it change?'

'If we're lucky the Indian summer lingers until the end of the month and possibly into October. Then the days can be still warm but the night-time temperature turns cold.'

'Take a seat,' I said, trying the tea, which was pleasantly cold and slightly sweet. 'This is good.'

'Don't sound so surprised. We drink it by the gallon all summer long, but it's just the first of many things you'll become accustomed to.'

I took a deep breath. 'I can tell I have a steep learning curve in front of me.'

'Culturally, yes,' Patricia said. 'I still recall how everything struck me as different on my trip to England in thirty-five.'

'I can imagine, because, right now, I feel like a toddler finding my way.'

'That will pass quickly.'

'Is this building, Dickinson House, named after the poet?' I cleared a spot to sit on my bed.

She shook her head. 'That's what everyone thinks but it was named after another alum, Emma, who became a missionary. Before then it was called Faculty House.'

'Practical.' I scanned the room which was so different to my rooms at Oxford but I wouldn't let my thoughts linger on the past.

'I'll let you finish in peace, and later when the temperature drops a bit I'll give you another tour of the campus. And we've been invited to dinner at the Wendells' this evening.'

'Oh.' I looked about in panic at my clothing still thrown across my bed.

'It's a barbecue and everyone will be casually dressed.'

'Phew.' I had bought some new dresses in New York that I thought would be appropriate for teaching. It would feel odd not lecturing in a gown. But again I must let go of the past and focus on my future here.

*

I woke to the sound of the bells ringing. It was seven and they had just kept going. Today I had a seminar with my geography seniors and a large lecture to the freshmen. I was still trying to understand the concept of liberal arts. The students were required to take courses in all the areas to balance their education. So many of my freshman year students had no intention of studying geography further than this one introductory course, but I was informed by several of my colleagues they might decide to if only to listen to my accent. A fellow Englishman in the history department increased the number of students majoring in history simply to listen to him, I was told. I found this deeply amusing.

A knock on my door interrupted my thoughts and I opened it, yawning.

'Morning,' said a bright-eyed Patricia. 'Those bells you hear mean it's Mountain Day.'

'What?' I pushed my hair back from my face.

'It's one of the oldest college traditions. Classes are cancelled and the students climb Mount Holyoke, eat ice cream and appreciate the great outdoors.'

'What do we do?' I asked.

'As it's your first one, I'd say we climb Mount Holyoke, which, as you know, gives the college its name.' She was already dressed in shorts and stout boots.

'OK. Shall I meet you in the dining room?' I yawned again.

'Yes, dress in layers as it's cool right now but by the time we reach the summit you'll be boiling.' Patricia grinned and shut the door behind her.

*

At the base of the mountain, I found the crew team I coached. Patricia and I joined them on the trek up to the summit. Around my neck hung Oliver's camera and I wore his sunglasses. I'd sent photographs to Maman at the start of the term to try and give her a feel for what my life was like here. She and Antoine had helped me prepare for the move and make the arrangements to let the farm and my cottage out. We'd also agreed to sell the property at the mouth of the creek to pay the death duties. It had all happened in a whirlwind of activity to accomplish everything so I could be here for the start of the term.

It had been a tearful farewell as they then went back to Paris where Antoine, a doctor, was working. Watching them together, I had seen how much in love they were and how their shared experience fighting for the resistance had bonded them. It saddened me that we were so far away but they planned to come to visit at the end of the summer term.

Patricia grabbed my camera at the summit and insisted on taking a photo of me with the eight women and the cox of my crew. We posed beside the sign which read

MOUNT HOLYOKE SUMMIT
ELEVATION 942 FEET

'Well done, Professor Tremayne,' said the cox of the crew. 'You've made it.'

Thanks to the daily training with them, I was fit. The climb, although taxing, had been worth it for the view. Below, the Connecticut River snaked its way through the valley, and to the west the foothills of the Berkshires were clearly visible. Mount Holyoke itself was a volcanic traprock composed of basalt. I'd heard from my colleagues in the department that the mountain was the westernmost peak of the Holyoke range and part of the Metacomet Ridge. This ridge spanned a hundred miles and created a unique ecosystem with rare species found only here. I would need to explore further but Patricia was urging me back down and the crew joined us.

As she had mentioned, layers were essential and by the time we were back on the campus it was a gloriously warm day. The leaves on the trees were jewel bright and I knew I would never tire of this beauty around me.

'You've earned your ice cream,' said Patricia, and she led me to one of the dormitory dining rooms. 'What flavour would you like?'

The array on offer was astounding. I recalled Jake's dismay at only one choice at Jelberts in forty-two. I hadn't had any since that day.

'What flavour would you like?' Patricia asked.

'Vanilla, please.'

'A bit boring but as you wish.' She made a face at me.

I watched as the scoop was placed in a cone made of biscuit. I held it in my hand, not sure I was ready for this.

'It won't bite.' Patricia had chosen maple walnut, which I was certain would be lovely as I had been introduced to the delights of maple syrup on pancakes. Every day I encountered something new, and I loved it.

I licked the cone and it was delicious if bittersweet. I never discovered what flavour Jake would have preferred if he'd had a choice. I found myself thinking of him most days, and in my head I wrote dispatches to him about my new life here. Looking around now, I saw the students dressed casually in shorts, embracing the outdoor life. The unofficial uniform of most days were skirts with blouses and a string of pearls about their necks. They were polite, incredibly curious and kept me on my toes in the classroom.

*

As I walked past the grave of the college's founder, Mary Lyon, on the way to the library, the trees were bare. I'd experienced my first Thanksgiving, been to several football games at nearby Amherst College, and the scenery was no longer alien; I had found my feet, only tripping up on the occasional difference. This morning I'd received a letter from Constance with a picture of the christening of the twin girls, Jeanette and Sophia. Mary Holdsworth had stood in for me at the service. Constance's cousin Lady Alice was the other godmother, and her husband Sir Arthur Carew and Constance's brother, the Duke of Exeter, were the godfathers.

I had sent over a package with maple syrup and silver Tiffany bracelets for the girls. Rather than being the hands-on godmother as I planned, I would have to love them from a distance. I was not certain when I would make the journey again. There was so much for me to discover here, like Maine where Jake was from and Boston too.

I walked through the cold crisp air to the library to meet Patricia in her office. The seasons were sharper here, the temperature swings more dramatic. Snow was expected this week but it was December. At the moment the sky was blue with not a cloud in sight.

In the library, the familiar smell of books surrounded me. I waved to Patricia who was engaged with a group of students. The day's newspapers were spread out on the entrance table. I scanned the headlines and turned to the second page to read more about war debts and reparations when my heart stopped. *Jake Russell*. The by-line read Jake Russell. He was dead. He'd died in Italy in February forty-four. It wasn't an unusual name but how many of them wrote for the *Associated Press*?

I couldn't breathe. Jake was alive. I needed more information. But, more than anything, I needed to see him. He must hate me if he hadn't been in touch, but I had promised myself that, if he lived, I would tell him the truth. It had been almost three years to the day since I last saw him.

'Merry, you look like you've seen a ghost.' Patricia came up to me. 'Sorry about the delay. Let's head to my office.' She peered at me.

As we walked up the stairs she asked me, 'Are you OK?'

She unlocked her office.

'I'm not sure, to be honest.' I sank in a chair.

Patricia opened her bottom drawer and pulled out a bottle of whisky. 'It's just gone five and we need to put some colour back in your cheeks.' She poured us both a healthy measure.

I took a large gulp. Jake was alive.

'Now that you've had a sip, can you tell me about the ghost?'

'A man I thought dead is alive.'

Patricia knocked back the rest of her drink. 'Not just any man, I can tell.'

'No, one I had loved but had been told he died in February forty-four in Italy.'

'How do you know he's alive?' she asked, cradling her glass.

'His article is on page two of the *Boston Globe*.'

Patricia leaned forward. 'Who is he?'

'Jake Russell.'

'*The* Jake Russell?' she asked.

I nodded. I didn't think of him as *the* Jake Russell but *my* Jake. Not that I had any right to. He'd clearly changed his mind about returning my heart to me.

'I remember an article he wrote a month ago.' She took a deep breath. 'He'd been badly wounded and, thanks to some Italians, he survived but he was still not fully recovered by VE Day.'

That was seven months ago. Dear God, what had happened to him? 'Did he say what the injury was?'

'No. He didn't but apparently it's a full recovery if he's working. What will you do?'

'I don't know.' I looked into the glass, hoping to see answers but saw nothing except a blurry section of the patterned carpet on the floor.

'Go and see him. You have nothing to lose.'

I had already lost my heart. 'True, but how do I find him?'

'He writes for the *Associated Press*.'

I nodded and looked above Patricia's head. Her diploma from Wellesley was framed on the wall behind her. 'Do you still have contacts at Wellesley?'

She nodded.

'In the English department?' I asked, wondering if Jake had found someone else.

'Yes, I keep in touch with one of my professors.' She opened a desk drawer and pulled out a battered address book then wrote down a name and number on a sheet of paper. 'But I am confused, why Wellesley?'

'He used to teach a journalism course there. He might still.'

'I see. When will you go?' She handed me the diary on her desk.

'Term finishes on the fourteenth. I could go then.'

'Yes, but you'll miss him if you leave it until then. Wellesley finishes then too.'

'I don't have any classes on the twelfth, thirteenth and fourteenth. Do you think I could leave early?'

'In the circumstances, I don't see why not with a little planning. Do you want to borrow my car?'

'Don't you need it?' I asked.

'I won't, I'm staying with an old friend in Northampton.' Patricia looked at me intently. 'You'll be OK driving on the correct side of the road?'

I laughed. 'Time will tell.'

'At least I know you can read a map.' She poured us both another whisky. 'Now tell me all about you and Jake Russell.'

49

12 December 1945

Two maps lay on the passenger seat as I set off. One of the college campus marked with an X where I hoped I would find Jake. Fear fluttered along with snow flurries during the eighty-mile journey from South Hadley to Wellesley. I didn't know what I would say to Jake, but I needed to see him. If nothing else to say I was sorry. I wasn't going to burst out with the news I loved him. I still didn't see how we could work, but, in my heart, I wanted to find a way.

Snow blindness was an issue as the journey wore on. The windscreen wipers struggled at times to stay ahead of the snow and I followed snowploughs most of the way. Instead of arriving at the campus three hours ago as planned, I was late thanks to the terrible driving conditions. Jake's lecture had finished two hours earlier and, to be honest, I was no longer sure why I was here as I climbed out of the car. He hadn't come to find me and he could have.

Five inches of snow covered the ground and uncertainty held me to the spot. I could climb back in the car, find a hotel and tomorrow explore Boston putting thoughts of Jake out of my mind. I took a deep breath and opened my eyes wide. The world appeared beautiful and the twilight felt magical with the snowflakes illuminated in the light streaming out of the college buildings. Two students clutching their books made their way across the academic quad.

'Excuse me,' I said, smiling. 'Where's the Founder's building?' I held out the map in my hands.

'You're English,' one of them said. 'I love your accent.'

I smiled and nodded.

'It's that building over there.' She pointed to the one they had just left.

'Thank you,' I said.

'You're welcome,' they said in unison.

The falling snow swirled and eddied at my feet. I'd come this far; I could at least introduce myself to Patricia's professor. She was on the second floor of the building. Jake's lecture was finished so I wouldn't find him but maybe she could give me a telephone number or an address.

The rate of snowfall was increasing, and visibility was dropping. On the path a figure walked towards me, but I couldn't make out any details except that the person was tall. As we were about to pass each other, I slipped, bumped into the man and dropped my map.

The man bent and picked up the map. He held it out to me. My heart stopped. I couldn't move but finally I found my voice. 'Jake?'

'Merry?' He shook his head like he couldn't believe I was real.

'Yes.' My mouth went dry.

'I'm normally off campus by now. How did you find me?' he asked, still holding the map.

I pointed to the X. 'But you're here not there.'

'Why are you here?' he whispered.

There were a thousand things I could say but I would start as I meant to go on, with the truth. 'You.'

'Me?' Snowflakes were caught on his eyelashes. 'You were lucky to find me.'

'I'm glad I did,' I said.

'I am too,' he said. 'When did you arrive?'

'Just now,' I said.

He smiled and despite the cold I warmed. 'To the US, I meant?'

'September,' I said, studying every detail of him. There was a scar on his forehead and his crow's feet were more marked.

'Why?' He glanced from the map to my face.

'I'm teaching at Mount Holyoke,' I said.

'You've moved?' he said. 'Left Oxford?'

'Yes.' I smiled.

'Why?' He tilted his head in that endearing way I loved.

'I needed a new start.' I couldn't stop staring at him. How did I ever think I could walk away?

'I can't believe you're real,' he said. His free hand reached towards my cheek but stopped.

'I thought you were dead until I saw your article in the *Globe*.'

He wiped the snow from his eyes and then from the map. 'That was my last one for them.'

'Your final one?' I stepped a bit closer.

'Yes, my first novel is published in January,' he said. 'And I'm finishing the next.'

I grinned and resisted throwing my arms about him. 'You did it. You made it past chapter four.'

'I did.' He laughed. 'It seems learning about maps taught me a bit about plotting and stories.'

'I'm pleased.' I too had to brush the snow from my eyes. 'I still can't believe you're alive.'

'I wouldn't be except for some wonderful Italians,' he said.

I touched his arm. 'I'm so grateful.'

'But why are you here?' he asked, taking my hand in his.

'You as I said and . . .' I swallowed, thinking of Mo. Be brave. Love was worth the risk. 'Because on the day you left, three years ago, I didn't say what I should have, and I swore that if you made it through the war then I would tell you.'

'And what was that?' he asked.

I could do this.

'I love you.'

He stepped closer. 'I knew that.'

'You did?'

He dug in his pocket and pulled out the heart-shaped stone. 'You gave me your heart.'

'You still have it. I can't believe it.' I touched it and looked up at him. 'But why didn't you let me know you were alive?'

'I wanted to and almost did,' he said. 'But I love you, and I wasn't going to be the reason you lost your career, I couldn't ask you to choose.'

I punched his arm.

'What was that for?' he asked.

'For dying, for not helping me to see the truth.' I moved nearer.

He rubbed his arm. 'You've been training?'

'As a matter of fact, yes,' I said. 'With the crew team.'

'Now you're telling stories with maps, cracking ice on the Connecticut River and looking more beautiful than ever.' He pushed the snowflakes from my cheeks. 'So, what story does the map from me to you tell?' He folded the map of the campus and gave it back to me.

'It isn't finished yet,' I said. 'But it's much closer than before.' I slipped the map into my pocket.

He leaned down and kissed me. *Home*, my heart said, and I settled closer in his arms.

A student in the distance whistled.

'Not good for the lecturers to be seen kissing in public,' he whispered against my mouth.

'True. Bad form. Is there some place we could go?' I asked, moving a respectable distance away.

'My place.' His voice was low, and I shivered but not from the cold.

'Is it far? I have a car,' I said.

'We can walk, I can hold your hand and you can tell me everything.' He threaded his fingers through mine and I leaned my head against his shoulder.

'Sounds wonderful.'

'Then I could cook dinner for you,' he said.

'I'd like that.' I smiled slowly. 'And then what?'

Christmas lights gleamed through the windows of the houses along the street and the world could not look more beautiful.

'Let's draw that bit of the map later,' he said as we crossed the street.

'I'd love nothing more.' I turned and kissed him. The map to my future wasn't fully plotted but there was no longer an ocean in the way of my happiness. Jake Russell was finally in my arms.

Acknowledgements

First and foremost, I want to thank my readers. I'm honoured and humbled that you have read and enjoyed my stories, for I have loved creating them. Thank you for spending time with my characters. Each message sent to me means the world.

Most of the time, writing a book is a lonely old business, with me and the characters and the world in my head. It's easy to forget that, although writing a book is a solo experience, making a book shine is the work of many. I normally mention my husband, Chris, at the end of the acknowledgements but this time I wanted to say what a huge help he is as the first reader, the research sidekick, and, sometimes, the one who delves deeper and deeper until things like train timetables are sent to me so that the small details are correct. He keeps me company on many plot walks, puts up with my sulks when the writing isn't going well and acts as my personal cheerleader. He believes in me, and loves me, even when I don't believe in myself. Every day I am grateful he is in my life.

My children Dom, Andrew and Sasha have listened, read snippets and provided moral support. Namely they remind me, when I declare I can't write, that I can. I am blessed with their love and support.

The inner circle of my writing life is filled with Brigid Coady and Deborah Harkness. They brainstorm, cajole, read and counsel. Deborah has spoken to the right librarians in the correct departments so that I spent my time researching geography wisely. They both encouraged me to follow the path of Merry, even when it meant deleting 90,000 words. I needed their strength to do it.

Two early readers, John Jackson and Gwen Hammond, provided much needed 'reader' feedback as opposed to writer feedback. I am grateful for them both. And I'm thankful for the many times I have walked Gwen's beautiful dogs on my plot walks.

My editor Kate Mills has trusted me and provided me with the time and space to find this story. She has cast her skilled eyes over this story more times than it is wise to admit. But she wanted Merry's story to be the best it could be. Alison Bonomi has been right there with her, coaxing the best out of me, while Luigi Bonomi championed my writing and provided wise words when needed.

The whole team at HQ especially – the design team, sales, marketing, public relations, support – makes it a joy to be one of their authors. As a dyslexic writer, I am indebted to the eagle eyes of Rachael Nazarko, the copy editor Donna Hillyer and the proofreader Mary Chamberlain.

Merry's story was a road of discovery, and there was so much research along the way. I have always wanted to tell the story of the secret flotillas that operated out of the Helford River but it was Merry who gave me the means.

My research began first with Wilf Long and Brenda Steer. Their father Tom Long was one of the brave men who were part of the Helford operations. They shared not only the stories of their father that they remember but also his voice in the form of a cassette recording of him telling his story. They also spoke of their grandfather Wilfred Skinner, who was the gamekeeper at Bosahan (which is called Pengarrock in the book).

Further local people who shared their knowledge are Rob Hewett, Chris Hosken, Jane Benney and Chris Broad, each of them adding layers with their personal stories and photographs. Huge thanks to Kathy and Dave Stefeford with their help on Bryher information.

Looking from Helford River Sailing Club on the south side of the river, both Ridifarne and Pedn Billy are clearly visible. Thanks to Cornish Holiday Cottages, I met with the current owners of Ridifarne, Mike and Joan McLeod. They welcomed me into their home and shared what they knew of the history of the secret flotillas and the SOE.

The Imperial War Museum has been a wonderful resource. To be able to listen to recordings of Commander Holdsworth and others has helped to colour in my imagination as has the cine film of the Dartmouth operations.

Finally a special thanks to John Baker who won the auction in aid of Dementia Research to have a character named after him. John and I had several conversations regarding who he was to be. I told him I could name the 'hero' after him but that didn't work for John because the hero was straight; whoever held his name had to be gay. So therefore Lieutenant John Baker in the story bears some of John's characteristics, and I hope he enjoys seeing a fictionalised version of himself on the page.

Author's Note

Where possible I have used the real names of the men and women to honour them in some small way for the brave roles they played in the Second World War. Everything else about them is from my imagination with the exception of a few phrases taken from Tom Long's handwritten account of his time with the flotilla.

Reggie Cannicott
Commander Davis
Commander Ian Fleming
Pierre Guillet
Lt Robert Harling
Commander Holdsworth
Mary Holdsworth
Lt Daniel Lomenech
Tom Long
Lt Commander Steven Mackenzie
John Louis 'Bonnie' and Ellen 'Nellie' Newton and their sons
    Peter and John
Lt Commander Nigel Warington Smyth (took over from
    Commander Holdsworth)
Lt Commander Bevil Warington Smyth

Vice-Admiral Godfrey

Lt Commander Shawcross

Lt Commander Montagu

Commander Drake

Commander Slocum

Jean Piron

Richard Winfrey

Muriel Wright

Margaret Priestly

Howard Rendle

Nora Reynolds Butler

Lt Commander Francis Brooks Richards and Hazel Williams (married in 1941 and honeymooned in the Pedn Billy Boathouse)

Wilfred Skinner

As none of them are still with us, I've relied on books and a few audio recordings made by these people to try and capture their deeds. I've moved dates of various missions to work for the story. Jean Piron was killed by enemy fire on a mission in June 1941. *Mutin* was renamed *Jean Piron* for a while in his honour. The Christmas operation was held in 1943. The surf boat was developed by Lt Commander Nigel Warington Smyth in 1943 and 1944 when extensive small boat trials and training took place on Praa Sands.

At some point during 1942, Ian Fleming was promoted from Lieutenant Commander to Commander. For the sake of simplicity, I stuck to Commander. He was a friend of Commander Holdsworth and did place Bonnie Newton on the Helford. He and Harling visited the Inter Services Topographical Department in Oxford. Harling liaised between the two and Margaret Priestly was their bluestocking who kept them organised. In several of the biographies of Fleming that I read, Muriel Wright's death shook him badly.

From almost my first visit to the Helford River in 1989, I had heard of the war-time activity that had taken place here. I had planned to write about the SOE when I'd researched *A Cornish Stranger*, but a different story emerged. In *The Returning Tide* I wrote about the 29th Division of the US Army departing for D-Day from the river. Finally in *The Secret Shore* I found a way to shed light on these secret flotillas. Thanks to the kindness of Wilfred Long and his sister Brenda Steer, I listened to their father's words and the story came alive. Sadly I wasn't able to find enough evidence to include their father's story of Churchill coming to Ridifarne.

Rt Hon Walter Runcimen's yacht *Sunbeam* wasn't on the Helford until June 1943 but it was unclear where the crew were housed once *Mutin* moved to the Mediterranean.

The United States was neutral at the start of the Second World War and it was prohibited for US citizens to join the armed services of foreign nations. However, many Americans surrendered their citizenship in order to fight, including the men who became the Eagle Squadrons. I knew about these squadrons because John 'Jack' Fielding, the father of a dear friend Janet Buck, was one of these men. These squadrons were integrated back into what was then United States Army Air Forces on 29 September 1942. A blanket pardon to all US citizens who had joined armed services for foreign nations was issued by Congress in 1944.

Since 1958, almost every summer there is a sailing race from the Helford River Sailing Club to L'Aber Wrac'h in Brittany as a tribute to these flotillas and the close links between the communities. The sailing club itself began after the war in 1948 from Pedn Billy Boathouse and was moved to a permanent home on the south side of the river in 1970.

One thing that compelled me to write Merry's story was just how much women did in the war, playing vital roles with no acknowledgement at all. The story of the map girls working in the Ordnance Survey Department, in meteorology, intelligence, and in the Inter Services Topographical Department, has almost been lost. A few historians are now unearthing the work that they did. In many early histories, there is no mention of them, as if they hadn't been there at all. In Tom Long's words Mary Holdsworth was one of these women not acknowledged. 'She had given up a very good well-paid job so she could assist her husband . . . How a woman who was so patriotic, honest and efficient and such a big asset to us was never rewarded by our government or France has always been a mystery to me.' Merry, for me, was a way of trying to acknowledge their work and their worth. Also a little of what they faced when, post-war, they lost their positions to the returning servicemen.

The keen-eyed among you, who have read my previous books, will have recognised Lady Constance Neville and Hester from *The River Between Us,* along with Constance's cousin Lady Alice Carew. Lady Seaton and her twin granddaughters Adele and Amelia are from *The Returning Tide.* And the young sub-lieutenant Tom Martin is in *The Path to the Sea* and *The Cornish House.*

Finally, the story of Mo and the mouse needs to be addressed. They did exist. Tom Long tells the story of trying to train Mo, a Jewish radio operator, to be better on boats. They knew he had evaded capture before, escaping by way of Spain. The Newton boys gave Mo the mouse for company. The mouse drowned when Mo, on the surf boat ready to land, stood to wave farewell to the men he'd been working with. He and the mouse went overboard nearly capsizing the dinghy. He survived, the mouse did not. A second mouse was sent to him. From what Tom said,